PRAISE FOR T. KINGFISHER

"Dive in...if you are looking to be charmed and delighted."

— Locus

"...[A] knack for creating colorful, instantly memorable characters, and inhuman creatures capable of inspiring awe and wonder."

— NPR Books

"The writing. It is superb. T. Kingfisher, where have you been all my life?"

— The Book Smugglers

PALADIN'S GRACE

PALADIN'S GRACE

T. KINGFISHER

Paladin's Grace

Production Copyright © 2020 Argyll Productions

This is a work of fiction. All characters are fictional and anybody who says differently is itching for a fight.

Copyright © 2020 by T. Kingfisher

http://www.tkingfisher.com

Published by Argyll Productions

Dallas, Texas

www.argyllproductions.com

ISBN 978-1-61450-521-1

First Edition Hardcover April 2020

For Kevin

CHAPTER 1

Stephen's god died a little after noon on the longest day of the year.

The Saint of Steel had not been a major deity, but neither had He been entirely obscure. He had four temples, staffed with priests and paladins, and the bishop of His church sat on the council in Archon's Glory beside the elders of the other local churches—the Forge God and the Four-Faced God and the Temple of the White Rat. His paladins, Stephen among them, rode out when the Saint's duty demanded swords and men to wield them, and rode back to the temple nursing their wounds, only to ride out again when they had healed.

It had never occurred to Stephen or any of the others that a god could die. Such things happened in mythology, not in real life.

He had just come back from a long, grim journey, hunting demons. It was not the Saint of Steel's primary function, but the Dreaming God's paladins had asked for assistance, so Stephen and three of his brothers had gone out with them. Demon hunting was ugly work, mostly involving possessed livestock, and while the Dreaming God's chosen were skilled at exorcism, a two thousand-pound bull inhabited by a furious demon was not something anyone wanted to tackle alone. The Saint's paladins were killing machines, first to last, and the god did not seem to mind loaning His chosen to the Dreaming God when demons were what needed killing.

They were riding over the ridge on the road to the temple when Stephen felt his god die. His first thought was that his heart had stopped. It was as if someone had punched a mailed fist into his gut, reached up under his ribs and torn everything out. It did not feel like a wound, it felt as if he'd been *cored*.

He collapsed forward over his horse's neck. Distantly, he heard the sound of a body hitting the ground, and the shout as one of the Dreaming God's paladins saw what was happening. And then he heard the sound of his brother Istvhan praying, harsh and rapid, and it was such a strange thing, that prayer, because Stephen knew instinctively that no one was listening.

"What is happening?" he said, gasping into his horse's neck. "Where is the Saint? What...?"

The world spun around him. He could feel the black tide rising, crawling up from the ground, the tide that whispered of battle and bloodshed, but there was no sheen of golden light over it to sanctify it and make it holy.

He was dragged off his horse and looked up, baffled, into the face of one of the demon hunters. *Jorge,* he thought vaguely. A handsome man, at least when he wasn't coated in road grime and still stained with the blood of demon cattle. Strong enough that he could hold Stephen upright, even in full armor. Strong enough that killing him would be difficult, and he must be killed, surely, he was the enemy.

"Stephen!" snapped the other man, shaking him. Stephen tried to focus his eyes. It seemed very difficult. The black tide lapped around his vision. He reached for his sword.

"Stephen, what's *wrong*?" the enemy said. *Was he the enemy? He must be, he was here and the god was dead* and the tide was closing over Stephen's head. "What is happening to your people?"

"It's the Saint," said Stephen, as blackness closed over him. He drew his sword. Somewhere, not too far distant, he heard a man scream. "The Saint is dead."

CHAPTER 2

Three years later

Stephen stared at the ceiling of his room and thought, as he did every morning, about simply not getting out of bed. He could stay here until the end of the world, looking at the plaster ceiling and the long, dark wooden beams, while the square of light from the window crawled down the wall and across the floor and faded away to nothing.

As he did every morning, he prodded the space in his soul where there had once been glory. There was only silence. There would never be anything there again. And then, as he also did every morning, he swung his legs over the side of the bed and got up. Grace was lost to him but he still had duty, and duty would carry him forward.

The Temple of the White Rat was quiet at this hour, or as quiet as it ever got. In an hour or two, it would be a beehive of activity, filled with clerks and clerics moving back and forth, hundreds of people solving small, practical problems and occasionally even the large intractable ones. The Rat's priests fixed things that could be fixed, and when things were broken past all mending, they helped people pick up the pieces.

There was no mending seven paladins whose god had died, and who had shattered themselves to further pieces in the carnage that followed. Still, the Rat had taken them in, broken as they were. Both the Dreaming God and Forge God had offered, but the Rat priests had been the ones who ushered them inside, still bloody from the wounds they had taken and inflicted in return.

Even now, Stephen did not know if he should be grateful for that kindness. He did not think that he could bear to stand beside the paladins of living gods and be eaten alive with envy for what they had. *But at least in the house of those warrior gods, there would have been someone able to stop us.* The White Rat claimed no paladins. He was served by law clerks and healers and diplomats, not by steel. Stephen often felt as if he was a dog in a hen yard, a protector who might turn feral and the gods knew how much damage he might cause before he was brought down.

The Rat's servants were not fools. They had seen the damage the Saint of Steel's chosen wreaked in the aftermath of the god's death, and they had faced it, unflinching. The temple set aside a wing for the broken paladins and asked nothing in return. As soon as they could rise from their beds, one by one, the remaining paladins had asked to be allowed to serve.

Stephen pushed open the door to the dining hall. There was strong tea and biscuits for those who wanted it. A dozen other early risers were hunched over their mugs, some of them already going over the day's work, a few simply sitting with their hands around the mugs, staring blearily at nothing. On the far wall, a mural of the White Rat gazed down benevolently, holding a book in one paw and a balance in the other.

Stephen took a mug of tea and a biscuit, and sat down at a bench. Istvhan came in a few moments later to join him. He had always been the biggest of the paladins, a great bear of a man with shoulders like an ox. People tended to assume that he must be stupid because of his size. This was a very dangerous thing to think.

"We are both still alive this morning," said Istvhan, as he had said nearly every morning for three years.

Stephen grunted, as he had also done nearly every morning for three years.

There had been a time when that was not so certain. They had lost many of their brothers and sisters early, some to suicide, more who had simply not woken up from their stupor after losing the god. A few to darker things. For a time, they had thought they might lose others, but the final seven survivors had rallied. The care that the Rat priests had shown, tending to those who would never wake, was part of the reason that the broken paladins had asked to serve. A debt was owed. The dead could not pay it, so the living must pay it for them.

It would have been difficult to explain to anyone other than Istvhan how that debt had kept Stephen alive. He could not give up while he owed others so much. Even if the Rat denied any such debt, until the ledgers had balanced, Stephen could not allow himself to stop moving.

These were depressing thoughts. He was grateful when Istvhan looked over at his plate and said, "What in the name of the little household gods is *that?*"

"An abomination," said Stephen. "I believe the cook called it gravy."

"Gravy is not that color."

"I did not say the cook was correct."

"Can we burn them at the stake?"

"We're not those kind of paladins. Anyway, it tastes okay if you close your eyes and pretend you're eating literally anything else."

Istvhan groaned and went to endure trial-by-gravy himself.

After breakfast, Stephen and Istvhan went back to the paladin's wing together. The schedule was posted on a chalkboard at the head of the corridor. His fellow paladin read it, then clapped him on the shoulder. "Off to look menacing in court," he said cheerfully. "You?"

"Walking one of the healers through a rough neighborhood."

"Ah, lucky you. I do not mind scowling for hours, but my feet don't care for the standing. And it's hard to look menacing if they bring me a stool."

Stephen snorted. "Still with the one trial?"

"Sadly. I could break the man and be done with it, but these so-practical Rats say that would look bad." He shrugged.

The trial in question was of a man who had become obsessed with one of the Rat's servants, following her and sending her unwanted gifts, until finally obsession had tipped over into something much darker. The Temple would undoubtedly win their case but it was a grim, wearying job, and Istvhan's part in it was to make sure that no one physically intimidated the woman while justice was done.

A great deal of the work that the paladins did for the Rat was along those lines. *Stand here and look scary. Walk here and glower at anyone who might be tempted to bother the healer in their work. Guard the bishop, not because we expect trouble, but because it needs to be known that the bishop is not without defenses.* It was a far cry from their old duties, but not, in truth, an unpleasant one. Although if the enemy did not kill him, it was possible that his charges would.

"These Rats are going to turn my hair white," Stephen said. "This healer's never had an escort before. He works in Weaver's Nest and I am told he said he didn't think he needed one."

"Is Weaver's Nest the slum where that fellow is chopping off people's heads and dumping their bodies by the river?"

"One and the same." Stephen rubbed his face. "How did they live this long without us?"

"No idea," said Istvhan cheerfully. "But on the bright side, no one's stabbed me in months."

"Me neither."

They both made a sign to avert the evil eye, then laughed. Stephen gave Istvhan a friendly shove and went to sword practice.

The Rat called no fighting men, so the Temple had never had a formal training ground. A small salle had been built in the city's heyday for visiting paladins from other faiths and guards that might travel in a bishop's entourage, but that had been long ago. The salle had filled up with dust and cobwebs and broken furniture that no one could bring themselves to throw away. The labor of cleaning it out had sweated the last of the illness from the seven broken paladins. Stephen remembered that the first spark of enthusiasm he had felt, after the god had died, was when he stood in the doorway of the salle and thought, *We can fix this.* It was the first positive emotion he had felt in a long time.

He touched his lips out of habit as he passed the tiny shrine in the door. It was probably the last shrine of the Saint of Steel left on earth. Someone—a Rat servant—lit a candle in it every morning. There had originally been five candles. Stephen had removed four of them and left the single one remaining so that it was no longer a shrine to the living, but to the dead. The unknown maintainer of the shrine had only lit a single candle the next day. With such tiny, unspoken gestures, the broken paladins and the servants of the Rat had negotiated the way forward between them.

Stephen hung his sword on the wall, took down a practice blade, and set to work.

Forehand, backhand, parry, thrust. There was no chance, in such bloodless work, of the battle tide rising. It was repetitive, often tedious, but it was as close to meditation as he could manage these days. The sword required focus and concentration, a narrowing of the world to the next motion and the next instant, no farther ahead, no farther behind. When he practiced the sword, for a brief time he was not broken.

He had found, in the first year, that he could no longer pray. The silence where the Saint had been was too final. Prayer only reminded him of his emptiness.

Prayer reminded him of what he had become, however briefly, when the god had died. The sword, though, the sword was still good.

After practice, he joined the others in the washrooms, sluicing the sweat and grime off his body. For creatures who sometimes lived in sewage, rats were fastidious about grooming, and the Rat's servants were no exception. This, at least, Stephen could admit was an improvement over the temples of the Saint of Steel. The god had cared a great deal about battle, but not so much about washing up afterward. Hair still damp, he emerged from the baths, looked up at the sun and realized it was time to go and meet the healer.

CHAPTER 3

The healer in question was a middle-aged man with a creeping bald spot across his skull, and long-fingered, delicate hands. Stephen had not met him before, and extended his hand. "Stephen."

"Brother Francis." He looked Stephen up and down with sharp, kind eyes. "The Saint of Steel?"

Well, it was obvious enough what god he had served. Stephen still wore the cloak with the god's insignia on it—the stylized sword, the gold flames, the hand holding the blade and pouring golden blood down the length. All the broken paladins did. The Temple not only mended them, they replaced the cloaks once a year with new ones, the symbol already embroidered onto the back. The Rat had accepted their offer of service, but did not require them to forget who they had been.

Stephen had not forgotten. Neither, apparently, had anyone else. "It is, yes."

"You're one of the berserker paladins."

"I was, yes." Stephen gazed over the healer's head. "If you are concerned that I am dangerous, you may ask the Bishop to assign a different guard."

"You're a large man with a sword," said the healer, surprising him. "Of course you're dangerous. I believe that's the *point.*"

Stephen felt his lips twitch. "You have me there, Brother."

"I still think it's all foolishness," grumbled Brother Francis. "I've never had a problem in Weaver's Nest. They're good people, they're just poor and desperate."

"Three severed heads were found in the river in a *month*."

"Yes, but they *know* me." Brother Francis waved his hands, as if to indicate that severed heads were either inconsequential or one of the normal hazards of the job, Stephen wasn't quite sure which.

I believe I can actually feel the individual hairs turning white on my scalp. "Nevertheless, the Bishop feels that it would be wise to take precautions. Shall we go, Brother?"

"Yes, yes."

A heavy satchel of remedies lay at his feet. Stephen picked it up automatically and the other man smiled.

"Well, if you don't mind doing the heavy lifting. I'm not quite as young as I was."

"You have essential skills," said Stephen. "I am merely the muscle today."

The healer grinned. "Six stops," he said. "And unless things go very much better than I fear, I will send you home at the last one. That's going to be a watch through the night, until the fever breaks or..." He didn't finish the sentence, but he didn't need to. Stephen was familiar with the fevers that took men after wounds, and knew how they could go.

They set out through the city together from the Rat's temple, the little round healer and the broad-shouldered knight. The route took them past narrow buildings set on narrow streets, little better than alleys. Two or three steps above slums, but the specter of poverty hung over the area. Everyone knew how easy it would be to slip. Stephen had grown up in a building like that himself. He knew all about the slip.

The healer was a talker, but he did not expect Stephen to do more than grunt occasionally, which was oddly restful in its way.

It was nearly noon when they reached the first house. Stephen took up a guard post outside the front door while the healer went inside. He leaned his back against the worn brickwork. Because it was only a poor neighborhood, not a bad one, people looked at him directly, at least at first. When their faces changed and they hurried away, he could not be sure if it was because of the insignia on his cloak or because he was, as Brother Francis said, a large man with a sword. A group of children in an alley across the way were jumping rope. They looked at him too, but in the disdainful way of children for strange adults, not fearfully. Stephen strained his ears to catch the rhyme they were using.

Mister Brass
  Didn't pay his tax
  Headsman gave him forty whacks
  Two, four
  Six, eight
  How many whacks did it take?
  One...two...three...four...

On *take*, the tempo increased dramatically and the child in the center, face deadly earnest, began jumping as fast as she could, determined to outlive the unfortunate Mister Brass. Stephen smiled. He remembered that one from his youth. The best he'd ever managed was thirty-three whacks.

Funny how I can remember that, but I can't remember half of last week. Getting old, I guess. He wasn't even forty, but some days he felt positively ancient.

The healer bustled out again, closing up his satchel. "Next!" he said cheerfully, and he and Stephen went to the next stop, while the little girl was still trying to out-jump the headsman.

Stephen stood guard outside until the third call, where the healer called him in. "Brother Francis!" said his patient, aghast, struggling to sit up. "You can't—a caller—and me looking such a sight—!"

"Miss Abernathy," said the healer, pushing her gently back down, "you're beautiful no matter how you look."

Not the most coherent sentiment, but he means well. Stephen bowed. "You look magnificent, madam," he said. "I should apologize to you for coming in armed, in all my dust."

Miss Abernathy, who was at least eighty, blushed.

"Forgive me," murmured the healer, after they left. "There's not a great deal with her that I can fix, but she's bored and lonely on top of her aches." He grinned up at Stephen. "Having a handsome young fellow to look at for a few minutes was better than any medicine I could mix up."

"Young? I'm thirty-seven."

"And I'm sixty-one, so I don't want to hear it, child."

Stephen abandoned that line of argument. "And she isn't bothered by...?" He flicked the cloak with his hand.

The healer did not pretend not to understand, which was another reason Stephen liked him. "She's forgotten what happened, if she ever knew."

"Ah, well." Stephen eyed the steps to the next building. "Would you like me to go to this visit as well? Perhaps lift some heavy objects and flex a few times?"

Brother Francis considered this. "Wellll...one never knows about an individual's tastes, but I don't think Mister Coates would enjoy that on *quite* the same level."

Stephen snorted. The healer grinned at him.

This one lasted quite awhile, and there were no children jumping rope to distract him. Stephen opened his pack and pulled out his needles and a thick ball of yarn. Knitting socks was not a particularly glamorous hobby, but it filled the same mental need as the sword—careful work that held his attention and hopefully did not allow his mind to wander too far afield. Plus at the end, you got socks out of it, and no one appreciated good socks like a soldier.

His current project was faded red. Well, pink. The dye hadn't taken properly and washed out almost at once. The merchant sold him the whole lot for a quarter of what it was worth and Stephen had been making dusty pink socks for over a month. His fellow paladins had groaned when they saw the color, but they all wore the socks anyway. Archenhold was cold in winter and proper footwear was important. You never knew when you were going to get called upon to do a forced march somewhere.

Not that the Rat does many forced marches. I'm not sure where we'd even go. To deliver a set of law clerks to an urgent trial, perhaps.

The healer came out again. Stephen put the needles away.

They proceeded this way, through neighborhoods getting progressively worse and stops getting progressively longer. Brother Francis came out of one stop with his face grim and pinched.

"Problem?"

"A growth," said the healer. "Looks like a cauliflower, in the breast and under the ribs. There's nothing anyone can do, but make her comfortable." He sighed. "Well, nothing that any of us can do. A true healer, perhaps, with a god's gift on them, might be able to give her ease, but we have only medicines and our two hands."

Stephen bowed his head. "Making her comfortable is not so small a thing."

"I know," said Brother Francis, sighing. "It feels like a small thing, in the face of..." He gestured aimlessly. Stephen nodded.

They fell into step together, though Stephen had to slow his stride so that the healer could keep up. Francis glanced up at him. "May I ask you a question about your order? I do not wish to give offense."

Stephen braced himself internally. *Now it comes.* At least the healer had asked him, not one of the others. *Better me or Istvhan than Galen, or god forbid, Wren.* "If you wish."

"Why do you still wear the cloak?"

It was not the question that Stephen had expected. *What happened?* or perhaps, *Why did it happen?*

What did you do, when the god died?

Were you one of the ones at Hallowbind?

"The cloak?" He looked down at it as if he had never seen it before.

Brother Francis made an impatient gesture. "The cloak with the saint's symbol on it. If the god is no longer alive, why continue to wear a symbol that so many fear?"

Stephen was silent for a moment. A rivulet of brown water gurgled past them. There were no drains here, and he could smell nightsoil and decay.

"It is good that they fear it," he said finally. "It is a warning."

Brother Francis raised his eyebrows. "A warning?"

"That we are still dangerous."

The healer tilted his head back to look Stephen in the eye. "You'll forgive me, youngster, but you don't seem particularly dangerous to me. Large man with a sword not withstanding."

The bishop had said something similar to Stephen, three days after his god had died. "Are you still dangerous?"

"I will always be dangerous, your holiness," he had answered. Even weak as a kitten and shackled to the bed by leather restraints, it had seemed the truth to him.

She smiled. She was an older woman and the bones of her face were handsome rather than beautiful, and she was not a fool. "Are you a danger to me?"

"Not right now."

"If one of your fellows is lost to the rage, will you stop them from harming the innocent?"

"Yes," he said, without hesitation. "As long as I draw breath."

"Then I think we had best keep you here." And she turned to the acolyte with her, and ordered him unbound.

He shook his head, as much to clear the memory as to disagree with Brother Francis. "If they see the cloak, they know that the battle tide might take me without warning. And if it happens, they will know to get out of the way."

"Can it still take you? Without the god?"

"Yes." That came out very curt, and Stephen regretted it at once. The healer was putting his safety in Stephen's hands, he deserved to know what manner of bodyguard he had acquired. It was simply that he wanted explanations, and Stephen was so very tired of explaining. "It is not the same, but it is still possible."

It is all darkness and fumbling and rage. It is a black tide lapping over my head, where once the god poured golden fire over my nerves and turned me into the holiest of killers.

It had happened twice in three years. The first time, Istvhan had picked him up by the throat and held him until he blacked out. The second time, Galen had snapped while they sparred and then Stephen had snapped trying to hold him back, and they had battered each other insensible in the training salle. He'd broken Galen's arm. Galen had smashed half his ribs. No one else had been hurt, but it had been too close, too damned close. It had been over a year since the tide had risen for any of them. If the paladins were not precisely healing, at least the scars had grown thick. Sometimes Stephen thought they might yet live through this, as broken and battered as they were.

"I am sorry," said Brother Francis. "I do not mean to prod old wounds. Is there a sign that I should watch for? Some way that I might bring you out of it?"

He thinks it's like a fit or a seizure, thought Stephen wearily. *He has no notion of the truth. But he is trying.* "It's unlikely. If we stumble over the fellow cutting off heads, perhaps, or are set upon by a dozen men. If it should happen, I suggest that you run. And if you can, bring back another paladin from the temple."

"And they'll know how to stop it?"

"Yes," said Stephen.

"Nothing you can teach me, though."

Stephen looked at the small, round man and stifled a rueful smile. "I'm afraid not."

You do not seem the type, my friend, to leap on my back and strangle me until I black out, or to bash me over the head, or simply to cut me down where I stand. Better you leave it to my brothers and sisters.

That was the debt owed, and the promise. He would watch the other six. They would watch him in return. And the moment any of them fell to the blackness, they would turn on each other and try to stop the tide.

CHAPTER 4

At the next stop, the healer went up a rickety flight of steps, then another. Stephen almost insisted on going with him. This neighborhood was definitely teetering on the edge of very bad indeed. Buildings leaned together over the narrow streets and trash clogged the gutters. Some of the buildings had collapsed and were now roofed over with tarps and blankets. No one looked at him here, but probably because he was large and armed, not because anybody knew or cared about the Saint of Steel and His paladins' crimes. They had far more pressing concerns. Slum-weavers had built a colony in the eaves of the houses, and the evening air was full of the little dark gray birds coming to their hanging nests to roost. It was the birds that had given the Weaver's Nest slum its name. Possibly there was a loom somewhere in the neighborhood, but Stephen wouldn't count on it.

Ironically, had it not been for the severed head issue, he was probably safer because he was with Brother Francis than Brother Francis was because he was with Stephen. The White Rat's servants were sacrosanct, even in such questionable places. You did not touch the Rat's people, because you might need them to stitch you up later, or spring you from prison, or make sure that your elderly mother didn't starve once you'd been hanged. There was little honor among thieves, but there was a great deal of practicality.

It is a safe bet that whoever is out there chopping people's heads off is not terribly concerned about long term consequences to the community, though.

A gnole scurried by, staying close to the wall. The small, badger-like creatures had moved into Archenhold a decade or so ago, and they proved so adaptable and such inoffensive neighbors that hardly anyone could remember a time when the gnoles hadn't been living in warrens in the poorer parts of the city, engaging in street cleaning and odd-jobs. Stephen nodded to the gnole and it nodded back, striped face flashing in the gloom.

Brother Francis came back out a few moments later. "Yes, as I thought," he said, his voice low even though there was no way that anyone inside the house could have heard him. "I will be here until sometime tomorrow. Please tell them at the Temple."

"Is there anything I can do to help?" asked Stephen.

Brother Francis shook his head. "If we could fight sickness with swords, even I might take up the blade." He sighed. "No, the fact is, paladin, that we healers like to believe that we make a difference, but when it comes to illness, the patient will usually live or die regardless of what we do. If we are lucky, we do not make it any worse. But it is a comfort to the families to know that we are there. So I will sit with this poor woman and bear witness to her fight, however it ends."

Stephen bowed to the healer. "Promise me one thing before I go, Brother."

"Eh?"

"You will not leave until daylight. Even if she loses her fight tonight."

The healer pursed his lips. "I do not wish to be a burden to the family in their grief."

"There is a man going around chopping off people's heads."

"But I *know* these people. They all recognize me."

Stephen almost said, "Will they recognize you without a head?" but clamped down on it. Instead, he said, "Promise me, Brother, or I will stand here until dawn." He did not scream, *You daft man, this person won't care you're a healer!* but he suspected the effort cost him a few more white hairs. Was *no one* suitably worried about the severed head situation?

The way people are treating this, you'd think decapitation was just a natural event that happens sometimes, as if people's heads tumble off like leaves in autumn.

"Oh, very well." The healer threw his hands in the air. "If it will make you happy."

"Ecstatic," said Stephen gravely.

"Hmmph!"

He turned to go, when Brother Francis called after him: "Do you pray?"

Stephen blinked at him. His first mad thought was that the man was trying to proselytize, which was frankly absurd. The Rat sent lawyers and healers to a crisis, not missionaries.

"Not much, any longer," he admitted. "Not since..."

The healer nodded. "Of course," he said. "I should have thought. Well, if you find yourself so moved, pray for this woman. And for me, that I do nothing to make her suffering worse."

Now there is a prayer that I can get behind, thought Stephen, as he walked away. *Oh gods, if any of you are listening, please grant that we don't make things worse.*

Stephen made his way back through the side streets. No one bothered him. Once he'd crossed out from under the slum-weaver nests, things improved. This particular one wasn't a dangerous neighborhood, at least if you were large and male and had shoulders like a warhorse. Seedy, maybe. The Scarlet District, where licensed prostitution occurred, kept hired guards, both to protect their workers and to keep unlicensed prostitution from happening nearby. He was just outside that band of protection, but not so far outside that it became truly dangerous.

His boots clicked on the cobbles in an even beat. Left right left right...*Mister Brass didn't pay his tax*...left right left right...*two four six eight, how many whacks did it take?*

One two three four fivesixseveneight—wait, what?

Running footsteps broke the pattern. He looked up, startled.

There are many kinds of running footsteps, of course—panicked flight, hot pursuit, and many shades in between. The hunter always sounds different than the hunted, because the hunted is looking over their shoulder while they run. These were hunted footsteps. Stephen turned, seeing a dark shadow in the mouth of the alley, and then the shadow was rushing toward him. He grabbed for his sword, cursing the inattention that left him vulnerable—and the shadow threw itself...herself?...into his arms.

"Hide me!"

CHAPTER 5

Stephen said, "Um, what?"

This was not particularly suave, but he had not held a woman in his arms for a number of years. In the reflected lamplight, he caught a glimpse of large gray-green eyes and dark, fog-frizzed hair.

"I'm so sorry. Hide me!" she hissed into his ear, then ducked her head down and tried to angle him so that he was between her and the mouth of the alley.

His god might be dead but chivalry still lived. Stephen grabbed her to hold her upright and looked around for pursuit.

Was someone about to cut her head off? True, he was a bit far afield of Weaver's Nest, but it wasn't as if the sort of people who chopped off other people's heads obeyed strict neighborhood boundaries. Bare moments later, he heard more footsteps. Not a headlong flight this time, but the heavy tread of booted feet. Two of them. He peered through the rising fog and saw indigo at the end of the alley.

Only one religious order--Stephen balked at calling them holy-- wore that shade of indigo. The Servants of the Hanged Mother, a goddess so unpleasant that even the priests of the Four-Faced God couldn't find much nice to say about her. Given that the Four-Faced God treated even locusts and maggots with reverence, this was saying something. He hesitated to say that they weren't murderers, but it was doubtful that they had anything to do with the severed head situation.

"Keep your head down," he muttered, and moved so that she was up against the wall of the alley and his cloak covered both of them. The scent of sage and lavender rose from her hair.

He felt a pang of guilt for what he was about to do, but it was a vast improvement over anything the Motherhood was likely to do to her.

"Hey! You there!" called one of the Motherhood men. "Have you seen a woman go by here?"

Stephen turned his head and gave the man a slow, hopefully lascivious smile. "I'm seeing one right now!" he called back, and bucked his hips a few times, pressing her farther against the wall. "I'm very sorry, ma'am," he said under his breath.

The Motherhood men wore twin expressions of disgust. One actually stepped back.

"Try Carmine Street," Stephen suggested. "There's more girls down that way. You can get your own. This one's taken." And, very quietly, "*Extremely* sorry, ma'am."

And once they've left, this young lady will want to put a knife in my good bits and frankly, I should probably let her.

The young lady in question let out a sudden moan, loud enough to make him jump, and shouted, "Oh, *yes!*"

Oh Saint, she isn't.

She was. In fact, she was trying to climb him like a tree. Stephen had to brace himself against the wall and grab for her leg, which she was trying to wrap around his waist. To his mild horror, she let out another cry of feigned ecstasy.

"Please," he whispered. "My ears!"

"Sorry," she whispered back. "Yes! *Yes!*"

The Motherhood priests were still staring at them. Suspicion? Voyeurism? Stephen had no idea.

"Oh, is that how you like it, then? Like that?" He watched the pair out of the corner of his eye and whispered, "I am so *incredibly* sorry about this."

"You're doing great. I hope. *Yes!*"

His unexpected partner in this deception was not a particularly tall woman, but she was solidly built, with ample breasts and a back-side to match. Stephen was in a unique position to observe this without being able to appreciate it in the slightest.

The only saving grace of the situation was that, despite the fact that he had a moaning woman in his arms, Stephen had not been less aroused in recent memory. The angle of her leg around his waist meant that she had missed the aforementioned good bits and was grinding against his swordbelt, which had caused the padding he wore under his chainmail to ride up. A narrow band of skin over his hip was now caught between the leather swordbelt and the mail links, with her full weight upon it. It was not a good sensation. Also, the Motherhood burned people at the stake when they thought they could get away with it. This sort of thing focused the mind remarkably.

He felt the Motherhood men's eyes traveling over him. The young woman was moving enthusiastically against him, but she was, well, frankly she was very bad at it. She was pumping her legs like a child on a rope swing. He clamped his teeth on a groan as the chain links embedded themselves deeper into his skin.

I am going to have a truly unique bruise when this is over...assuming the metal doesn't just tear the skin right off...

The Motherhood men stepped closer. Stephen slid his hand up the back of the woman's neck and pressed her face down against his shoulder. His hip screamed at him. Saint's blood, he'd had sword wounds that hurt less.

In fairness, the swords were usually sharp.

The two Motherhood priests turned on their heels and stalked away in disgust. "Heretic," one said, just loud enough for Stephen to hear.

He couldn't quite make out what the other one said in response, but he caught the words *saint* and *steel* and *dead*.

For a moment the rage touched him, the black tide lapping at his feet. *Heretic.*

He could turn and advance on them. He would not draw the sword until he was upon them. You did not waste the power of the draw if you did not need to. Not hearing the sound of steel unsheathed, they would be a half-heartbeat slow in turning, and that was all the time he would need. The one on the left first, the taller of the two, who moved like a man who might have a hidden dagger. Then the one on the right, while the first was still falling. The black tide would roll over him and it would be tinged with red and...and...

...and there would be no god to draw him back from the tide. And there was an innocent in his arms.

The priests vanished at the end of the alley. Stephen heard their booted feet on the cobblestones as they walked away. He and the woman stood in silence. Well, *he* stood in silence. She clung to him, half-supported by the brick wall of the building behind her and by his arm around her waist. He managed to shift just enough that the mail was no longer in danger of actually ripping his skin off, and that was as much as he could hope for. She looked up at him, wearing a rueful expression. Her eyes really were quite large, even when they weren't wide with fear. There were lines at the corners of her mouth that made him think she frowned more often than she smiled. Her quirked lips softened those lines, but only a little.

"Are they gone?" she asked softly.

He looked both ways, then nodded and set her down. His hip cried out in relief.

"Thank you," she said, as he adjusted the hauberk and tried, discreetly, to see if he was bleeding. "I'm so sorry!"

"My profound apologies for the liberties, ma'am."

"Don't be absurd. I was the one taking liberties with you. You saved my life." She peered around him, checking the mouth of the alley. "Ugh, I hate those Motherhood thugs."

"We all do," he said wearily. "May I offer you escort to wherever you are going?"

She frowned up at him. "Are you really a paladin? You've got the cloak, but I wasn't sure..." She trailed off.

"I was," he said. "Now that my god is dead, I am a paladin of...no one in particular."

And now she knows exactly what I am. He braced himself for her to flinch and step back as if he might run mad at any moment. But instead her face cleared and she reached out and took his elbow.

Either she is extremely sheltered or she banged her head while she was attempting to climb me like a tree. Either way, chivalry demanded that he come to her assistance.

He just wasn't used to people looking at him as if he wasn't a pariah. *Other than the Rat's servants, of course, and that may simply be because they would work with any number of pariahs if it would solve problems.*

"My shop is in the Glover's Quarter," she said. "If you could just see me past the Scarlet District, though..."

It was Stephen's turn to frown. The Glover's Quarter was an expensive and fashionable district in Archen's Glory, at least twenty blocks from the street in which they stood. "You're quite a long way from home," he said.

She heaved a sigh. "I was going to the graveyard," she said. "I needed startleflower, and it usually only grows in areas that are burned over, but of course you never get that in the city, but then I was near the Rose Street Cemetery, and I saw some. Because they scythe the areas around the edges, where they haven't put any bodies yet, right?"

Stephen had only a vague idea what she was talking about, but nodded anyway.

"Well, they do it a few times a year, and that takes down the tall grass, so it has some of the same effect. You get it sometimes in sheep meadows, too, if they haven't got very many sheep."

This was more than Stephen had ever contemplated the growth habits of plants in graveyards. "All right," he said. "So you were picking flowers in the graveyard?"

"After hours," she said. "Err...I mean, I wasn't stealing, it's not like startleflower is worth anything. And I wouldn't touch flowers on a grave." Her wide eyes grew alarmed. "Errr...You're not going to turn me in, are you?"

"You are clearly a hardened criminal, madam," said Stephen, trying not to laugh. "But I think I can let you go with a stern warning."

She glared at him, then broke into a grin. It was a broad grin, showing a crooked front tooth, and it made her very briefly beautiful.

"So why did you need this startleflower?" asked Stephen, trying to move past that unexpected moment.

"I'm a perfumer," she said. "Startleflower doesn't smell like very much, you'd think it was a very weak floral, but it brings out the notes in sandalwood much better than anything else I've found." She paused. "Ah, don't tell anyone that, will you? I mean, it's not like it's a trade secret, except it sort of is, and it's hard enough to find startle-flower as it is."

"Your secret is safe with me."

"Well, if you can't trust a paladin..." She flashed that crooked grin again, and Stephen's heart lurched in response.

What the devil is wrong with me?

Istvhan would clap him on the shoulder and tell him that it had been too many years since he had a woman. Istvhan had a somewhat earthy approach to life. And there was nothing remotely seductive in the woman's manner.

Other than the bit where she had her legs wrapped around you and her arms around your neck. He hadn't felt the least twinge while she was doing that, though. Of course, the throbbing bruise on his hip hadn't helped.

"Anyway," the perfumer continued, "I was coming out of the graveyard and pretty much fell into the Motherhood fellows' laps. They'd seen me through the fence and were just waiting. They accused me of scavenging mandragora from graves. Which is stupid, because who in their right mind wants to smell like mandragora?"

She looked up at him as if expecting an answer to this and Stephen had to admit ignorance. "I'm afraid I don't have any idea what it smells like."

"Oh! Bitter and rather herbal. The leaves smell like tobacco, so you could maybe use it as a base note but extracting the scent's a terrible business, you can get enough under your nails to kill you just cleaning the equipment, and at that point, why not just use tobacco?"

"Indeed," said Stephen, with what he hoped was appropriate gravity.

She shook her head, her downturned mouth turning down even farther. "I tried telling them that, but...well...you can guess how well *that* went over."

Stephen could indeed guess. The servants of the Hanged Mother were not noted for their sense of humor, or for the ability to admit a mistake. If the Archon had not looked with such favor upon the Motherhood, no one would have tolerated their presence in the city for very long.

"When I got my chance, I took off running. I thought I could hide in some trash or something, but dammit, this area is relentlessly clean." She scowled as they walked. "And then I saw you and thought that we must be near the Scarlet District—um, I'm not implying anything—"

Stephen's lips twitched.

"—and I thought maybe you'd help me. And here we are."

"You weren't wrong. We're only two streets over from the Scarlet District. That's why it's so clean; the Scarlet Guild pays for street cleaners," said Stephen. "Says it cuts down on unlicensed prostitutes trying to work the district edges."

The woman loosened her grasp of his arm and leaned away from him.

"I don't use their services," said Stephen, not sure if he should be offended or amused. *Prostitution bothers her, but not the possibility that I'll suddenly go into a berserk rage?* "I serve at the Temple of the Rat, who brokers deals like this. I was acting as a guard for a Temple clerk when they laid out the grid and determined who would pay for each street. There had been an arrangement before, but with the gnoles taking over most of the street level cleaning, it all needed to be re-negotiated."

"*Ohhh.*" She gave him another crooked smile. "Sorry. I should have known...I mean, a paladin wouldn't..."

"Well, there's no reason a paladin wouldn't," said Stephen, honesty compelling him. "Just not this one."

Her smile grew. "You must think I'm ridiculous, granted what I was doing to you earlier."

"I would not presume," he said. "Someday I may even get the hearing back in my right ear."

She laughed, then sobered abruptly. "I fear I've had to learn how to make the noises for...that sort of thing."

Had to learn. Interesting. Was she an actress? A prostitute? No, the woman who had thrown herself at him with such profound lack of skill was definitely not a prostitute.

Stephen had no idea how you complimented a woman on her ability to imitate someone in the throes of passion without sounding like an unrepentant lecher. He took refuge in directions. "If you don't mind going the long way around the Scarlet District, we'll come out closer to the Glover's Quarter. But cutting through the District can be...ah...awkward." Which was putting it mildly. The very *best* assumption that anyone would make was that his charge was a lady of negotiable virtue and he was a hired bodyguard.

"That's fine," she said immediately. "After all, we need to protect the hearing in your *other* ear."

Stephen burst out laughing, as much from a sense of difficult waters navigated as from the joke. It was such an unexpected sensation that it surprised him.

Has it really been that long since I laughed? Have I become so sour?

He had lived through things that would sober a man, certainly. Still...

I used to have a sense of humor. I remember it quite vividly. Istvhan and I would snipe at each other for hours.

Perhaps he had simply taken to keeping his humor behind his eyes, as if laughing aloud would be disrespectful to the dead.

And it does not take divine insight to know that is a great foolishness.

He laughed again, several times, on the walk past the Scarlet

District. The perfumer had a dry sense of humor and whenever he laughed, she would break into that crooked, charming grin.

"This should be close enough," she said at last, as they emerged from an alley onto a larger street. Unlike the ones controlled by the Scarlet Guild, trash had piled up around the edges.

Stephen's eyebrows drew together. "Are you certain?"

"I *have* lived here for several years," she said, unthreading her arm from his.

"It is no trouble to walk you the rest of the way." He tried for his best winning smile. *I used to know how to smile at women.* "I hate to leave a rescue only halfway finished."

It was the wrong thing to say. Her gray-green eyes chilled. "I am afraid that I do not require further rescue, but thank you."

"I apologize, madam." He shook his head, feeling his smile turn rueful. "I just put my foot in it, didn't I?"

A long pause. Then she either took pity on him, or the awkwardness of the situation bothered her as well. "It's not you," she said, rubbing the back of her neck. "If I go in at this hour with a man, the woman who lives over the shop next door will begin shouting about sins of the flesh at me."

"Completely understandable." Should he bring up the severed heads? No, they were a good ways off from Weaver's Nest now, with the Scarlet Quarter between them, and the streets to the Glover's Quarter were all well-lit and well patrolled by guards. Best to let her go her way and not become one more problem that she was trying to get away from. "I will wish you a pleasant night, then."

She studied him for just a little longer than necessary, then her eyes softened. "Thank you, paladin."

Stephen watched her cross the street and vanish around a corner. He had turned away from the mouth of the alley and started toward the temple before it occurred to him that she had never told him her name.

CHAPTER 6

Grace could not get the paladin out of her head. It was ridiculous. It had been a week. She'd seen the man for less than thirty minutes. She didn't even know his name. Granted, in that thirty minutes, they'd been quite physically close, but that wasn't the same as knowing anything about him. She'd taken a risk grabbing onto him, but she'd seen the paladin's cloak as she approached, so it was less risky than it might have been. There was the chance, of course, that he could have stolen the cloak and been impersonating a paladin, but that happened less often than one might think. It was held to be extremely bad luck. You had to contend with both an angry temple and an angry god, and neither of those were conducive to a long life.

Her gamble had paid off. He'd treated her with absolute propriety, even while she was mashing her breasts against his chest and doing her best impression of a prostitute.

Well, she hadn't really been worried. Paladins, whatever their many, many flaws, stopped when you said, "Stop." Their gods tended to get very irate otherwise.

Which gives them points over some people I've known.

A puff of steam from the flask in front of her brought her back to the present. Dammit, she'd nearly let the water boil instead of simmering. It was only rosemary, which didn't require careful handling, but there were oils that would have been ruined by such carelessness.

She'd been far too careless. Leaving the graveyard without even thinking to look where she was going? Forget the Hanged Motherhood. A runaway carriage could have done her in. *I was extremely lucky, even if I did have to count on a paladin to rescue me.*

She hated being rescued. Admittedly, he probably hadn't meant anything by it. If you were a paladin, that was something of a professional hazard, wasn't it? Saving people?

Grace slapped the table, making the glassware jump. God's teeth, why was she still thinking about him? She had orders to fill and she was probably never going to see the man again. Oh, in passing, perhaps—Archon's Glory wasn't enormous, not like nearby Anuket City—but she certainly wasn't going to be in a situation to talk to him again, let alone to wrap her arms around his neck and smell the scent of his skin...

"Bloody hell," she said out loud.

She liked the way he'd smelled. That was the problem, certainly. She always did respond better to smells than to looks. He'd been handsome enough, in an unremarkable way, but it wasn't like she could even remember what color his eyes had been—

Blue.

"Bloody, bloody hell!"

He smelled clean and warm, with notes of leather and metal and, for whatever reason, gingerbread. You didn't expect men to smell like gingerbread. It might have been whatever soap he was using, but Grace didn't think so. She'd have bet money on the type of soap he was using, which smelled vaguely of lemon balm and was bought in bulk by the military, the college, and most of the temples. It was inexpensive, it got the job done, and it definitely did not smell anything like gingerbread.

Could it have been something in the armor? His armor had smelled faintly of frankincense and even more faintly of lanolin, but that was because of the oil they used on metal. Everybody in armor smelled something like that. You could tell how much money someone was willing to spend by exactly how much they smelled of sheep. In Anuket City, Grace had been able to estimate the rank of military officers by what scent had been added to the oil. Everyone used clove oil and chalk on their weapons, but only the highest ranks could afford clove oil for their armor as well. As you moved down the ranks, the oils got cheaper and stronger. Rank and file got nothing but lanolin, and in a wet season they smelled like a flock of sheep. Frankincense was mostly reserved for holy orders.

Grace couldn't think of anything that would make oiled metal smell like gingerbread, but the gods knew she didn't know every single smell in the world.

She wondered if she could blend a mixture that would be masculine, but with gingerbread notes. *No, don't be ridiculous. I could blend it, I just couldn't sell it to any of these accursed nobles. Manly, so far as they're concerned, is sandalwood and tobacco. Leather if you're lucky. Amber sometimes. But definitely sandalwood.*

Grace was really quite sick of sandalwood. She'd tried to move the fashion toward cedar, but they used cedar to keep away moths in this city, so everyone had entirely the wrong associations with it, which was a damn shame. Cedar was one of her favorites. But no, she was still stuck mixing a signature scent for nearly two dozen noblemen, each of whom wanted something distinctive! Unique! And which also smelled like sandalwood!

She stared at the flask in front of her, now reduced to a proper simmer. She had only needed a small amount, not enough to break out the big copper distiller, and a good thing too, since apparently she couldn't even be trusted to heat a simple solution at the moment.

He'd offered her his arm and she had taken it, almost involuntarily, because that was what you did. And then, when she might have pulled back, she didn't want to. He'd been wearing a chain vest with a tabard over it. She'd heard the soft sound of the links. But his sleeves were leather, plain and serviceable, and she could feel the hard muscle underneath when she slid her arm through his.

Leather, metal, gingerbread. Soap. Warm skin. It had been a good scent. And there was just no way to reproduce it. You couldn't distill skin.

Well, maybe you could, but the authorities would frown on it. Certainly you wouldn't get a scent you wanted to wear. I don't think perfume that smells like burnt meat is going to catch on any time soon...hmm, well, okay, maybe you could do it with a cold-fat technique, the way you do with the florals that you can't heat... Annnnnd now I'm thinking about how to make perfume out of human flesh. Yep, that's completely normal behavior. Nothing odd going on here.

Grace put her hands to her cheeks. Her face felt hot. Granted, it was fairly warm in her workshop right now, and she did have a flame going to steam the oils. It was a large room, but workbenches against every wall and tangles of glassware made it feel smaller. Stacks of books teetered on the edges of the tables, and Grace had a bad habit of writing notes to herself in grease pencil on the walls.

The front room, where Grace spoke to clients, was spare and uncluttered, holding only three tall cabinets that in turn held dozens of tiny, elegant jars. Marguerite said that it was important to present clients with an illusion. It made them much more likely to part with their money.

Why did he smell like gingerbread? Maybe he'd been baking. Baking was a totally normal activity that normal people did. Unlike, say, mooning around for days thinking about how a total stranger smelled and how to duplicate it.

She lowered the heat and looked around the cluttered workshop. At last her eyes settled on her most prized possession, an ancient leather-bound journal written by a man who didn't know if he wanted to be an alchemist, a cosmetologist, or an herbalist. The perfumer who had taken her as an apprentice when she was nine had given it to her...well, not *given*, exactly. *Threw at my head while shouting, "Useless! As useless as you are!" but who's quibbling?* He'd never been able to make any sense of the thing, but Grace had kept trying, deciphering the crabbed handwriting and the absurd alchemical notation by candlelight, until she could unlock the secrets within its pages.

Which were all, let's face it, fairly divorced from reality. The author had been more concerned with making things fit into his notion of divine spheres of influence and concocting scents based on the beauty of their alchemical formulas than actually making anything that smelled good.

When her articles of apprenticeship had been purchased, the book and the clothes on her back were the only things that Grace had taken with her. Her master had not even allowed her to take her own journals, claiming that she was trying to steal his secrets. She'd had to work backward from memory to recreate her own scents, and it had taken months.

The book, though...she still felt a great affection for the book. Even if these days, she used it more for divination than inspiration.

She closed her eyes, flipped pages blindly, and stabbed her finger down. "All right, book, let's see what you think about the paladin."

She opened her eyes and found her finger resting on the line "... *the black milk of the virgin beyond the grave, simmered in a dung heape under a magnetic fielde for 33 1/3 dayes will turn to a homunculus, red in colour, which may be fed on...*"

"Well, that was helpful," she told the book.

The door to the shop clattered open. "Appointments only today!" Grace called over her shoulder, slamming the book closed.

"Yes, I know!"

Grace moved the flask off the heat, relieved. "Oh, it's you. How goes?"

Her landlady and dearest friend swept into the room. Not that she had much choice—

Marguerite wore an enormous plumed hat, the sort that swept into the room whether the wearer wanted to or not. Grace gaped at it.

"What in the name of all the saints is on your *head?*"

"It's the latest fashion," said Marguerite, pulling it off her head. The motion released a smell of hair oil and a dusty, powdery feather smell. Her hair had been flattened down and rumpled by the hat and she tried helplessly to fluff it with her fingers. "Simply *everyone* who is *anyone* at court has them."

"It looks like you stuck an entire dead egret on your head."

"Two egrets," said Marguerite. "On some of the more expensive hats, they've stuffed the actual bird and have them wearing little jeweled collars. It's quite awful."

Grace shook her head, horrified and amused. Marguerite's hair was rich blue-black, which made the bits of egret down stuck to it stand out even more. Her clothes were exceedingly fashionable and immaculately tailored, a rich wine-red that brought out the tawni-ness of her skin and turned her natural plumpness into the sort of curves that caused men to walk into walls.

Grace envied her the ability to carry off clothes like that. She would have been so ill-at-ease in a similar outfit that she would have tried to take it off within fifteen minutes, convinced that everyone was staring at her with horror, or worse, with pity. Marguerite claimed that it was all a matter of attitude. "Get the attitude right, and every-thing else follows," she always said.

Marguerite had plenty of attitude. She was, in fact, a spy for Anuket City, the neighboring city-state. Grace knew this because Marguerite informed her up front when they discussed the terms of her lease.

"Why are you telling me this?" Grace had asked, boggling at her.

"Because you are a perfumer," Marguerite had replied. "The most close-lipped profession on earth."

Grace had opened her mouth, shut it again, thought of the man who trained her, who had also frequently threatened to cut out her tongue so that she could not tell his secrets to his rivals. "Fair," she said finally.

Marguerite had smiled like a cat with a bowl full of cream.

So far as Grace could tell, being a spy mostly involved talking to servants a great deal and buying drinks for sad young men in the Archon's employ. Marguerite took her rent in perfumes, which she turned around and sold to the nobility and the upper levels of Archenhold's government. The situation suited Grace just fine, particularly since many of Marguerite's informants continued to buy perfumes long after Marguerite had extracted as much information as possible from their servants.

"The Squire wants more of his special scent," said Marguerite, as if to emphasize this chain of thought.

"There's a batch already mixed," said Grace wearily. "It's just sandalwood with a dash of orris and myrrh. He could get it made up on half the street corners in the district."

"Yes, and he could send a boy to pick it up, too, but he wants the excuse to look at me meaningfully and press my hand to his clammy bosom and tell me how sad his lodge has been since I left it."

"You stayed there for a week during hunting season. A year ago."

"And it was dreadful," said Marguerite, with a theatrical shudder. "All those idiots in fancy outfits racing about on over-bred horses, while the hunt master tried not to scream. I felt for the man, I really did. And he was absolutely the best informant in the place, too. Knew every single visitor to the lodge, how they treated their horses, and who had mounts too expensive for them to afford. Give me one like him in every house, and I could retire a rich woman."

"You'll never retire," said Grace, sliding the Squire's bottle of perfume into a padded box. "You enjoy judging people too much."

Marguerite grinned at her. "Well, there's that. Anything exciting happen while I was away?"

Grace gnawed on her lower lip. "Yes. No. Well..."

"Now I'm interested." Her friend grabbed a stool and perched on it.

"What do you know about the Saint of Steel?" asked Grace.

Marguerite's eyebrows went up. "The god that died, wasn't it? That was...hmm, must have been three, four years ago now. Were you here yet?"

Grace shook her head. "It was just before I got here from Anuket," she said. "I remember hearing about it, and that's probably why I recognized the cloak at all. But I didn't pay very much attention at the time, what with..." She spread her hands. There was a man's name on her tongue, but she didn't particularly want to spit it out.

Marguerite knew the name as well as she did. "Yes, certainly. You had a lot more to worry about. Let me think. There was quite a kerfluffle at the time among the temples, because nobody knew you could kill a god—or that they'd stay dead, anyway. Not just mythological dead. The Hanged Mother killed herself, but she didn't cease to exist."

The Hanged Mother again. Grace shook her head, disgusted. The indigo-cloaked Servants of the Motherhood were a nuisance to more than just innocent perfumers lurking in graveyards.

Marguerite continued, tapping her fingers on the edge of the stool. "Anyway, nobody knows why the Saint died, so everyone in holy orders was panicking because if the god had been *killed,* what if one of them was next? But it hasn't happened again, so everybody relaxed after awhile. If it was a murder, the killer got away with it."

"What happened to the pala...people who served the Saint?" asked Grace.

There was no chance that Marguerite hadn't caught that slip, but her friend let it pass. "Well, it wasn't good. A lot of them ran mad, attacking people, killing themselves. The worst was the temple near Anuket. The high priest went completely berserk and burned the whole place down. From what I heard, he was screaming about making a pyre fit for the god. There were some other incidents, but that was the worst one. It was a mess, though, and a lot of people died." She drew her knees up onto the chair, heedless of the wrinkles in her court dress. "With any temple, of course, you get the genuinely god-touched and then the ones who are working as support staff. The god-touched ones had the worst of it. The priests mostly died or went mad. Even if they lived through the initial shock, there were a lot of suicides after. Hard to keep going when you've lost your god, I guess."

Grace licked her lips. There was no point in trying to be subtle, Marguerite would get the story out of her in short order. Still... "What about the paladins?"

"The paladins?" Her friend tipped her head back and gave Grace an amused look down the sides of her nose. "Holy berserkers. Very death-or-glory, come back with your shield or on it types, as I recall. The god also supposedly made them very hard to kill, and also kept them from hurting the innocent, which is the main problem with your usual berserkers. When the god died, though, they all ran mad for a bit, until somebody bashed them over the head or stabbed them or whatever. Why, what about them?"

Grace felt herself blushing. "Well, clearly they didn't *all* die."

"You are making me very curious," said Marguerite. "No, they didn't all die. A great many did, I'm afraid, though I don't know the exact numbers. The survivors mostly went to the Temple of the Rat, I believe." She shrugged. "Worked out well enough, since the Rat doesn't call fighting men of His own, and now they don't have to hire out. And I'm not sure what other god would have taken them."

"Hard for them, though," said Grace. She thought of the paladin in his grey cloak, the amused lilt to his deep voice. It was impossible to imagine him running berserk and killing anyone. "Having to live on some other god's charity."

Marguerite shrugged. "Even gods have poor relations, I suppose. Now tell me why you're so interested in the late Saint of Steel and His paladins."

Grace coughed. "Well, I was out looking for startleflower…"

CHAPTER 7

Marguerite was an excellent listener, which was probably why she made such a good spy. Just by listening to a story, she could make you feel fascinating and clever and funny. Even when she was listening as a friend rather than as an operative in the pay of Anuket City's spymasters, she provided a rapt audience. She groaned in the appropriate places, exclaimed over the nefariousness of the Motherhood, and burst out laughing when Grace described throwing herself into the paladin's arms and pretending to moan.

"Very quick thinking, my dear," she said. "Very quick. You know, if you ever desire to brew up more than fragrances—"

"No, no. Your job involves talking to too many people."

"So was he good-looking?" asked Marguerite, leaning forward. "Tall? I know he had to have muscles on top of muscles, all the sword-swingers do."

"Uh..." Grace tried to remember. She could call up the memory of his scent with ease, but his face was another matter. "He smelled like gingerbread?"

Marguerite put her face down on the table, shoulders shaking. "Of course you'd remember that," she said, voice only slightly muffled.

"He had blue eyes," said Grace, nettled. "And...uh...hair?"

Marguerite's shoulders shook harder. "Glad to know he wasn't completely bald," she gasped.

"*Dark* hair. And..." Grace floundered. *And he was wearing leather gloves, not gauntlets, and his fingers were on the back of my neck when he was trying to hide my face and the leather was warm and I think he was being very careful not to hurt me because when he pushed me against the wall, I didn't get so much as a scratch and that's hard to do when you're pinning someone against brick and pretending to screw their brains out. And when he laughed, it sounded like he was surprised, as if he hadn't laughed often. And I'd like to hear him laugh again.*

None of this sounded like anything she could say out loud, not even to Marguerite.

I'm being ridiculous anyway. He probably thinks I'm a helpless fool.

"Well, he was taller than me," she said finally. "And had all his teeth."

"You're not giving me a lot to work with here," said Marguerite. "But there simply can't be that many paladins of the Saint of Steel left in the city, I suppose. Dark hair and blue eyes ought to narrow it down a bit."

"What?"

"To find him again," said Marguerite, blinking at her, a cat who had no idea where the cream had gone, none at all.

"Why do I want to find him again?"

Her friend grinned. "Well, I could say it's because this is the first man you've expressed even the faintest interest in, as long as I've known you."

"He is not!" Grace protested, and then had to stop and think about it. "Wait, is he?"

"Yep." Marguerite poked her in the collarbone with one elegantly manicured finger. "I pay attention to these things. And when you talk about him, your voice goes all wistful."

"I have never been wistful in my *life*." Grace had no idea what being wistful entailed, but she was pretty sure that you had to be younger and thinner and possibly have consumption.

"But the *main* reason," said Marguerite, "the *important* reason?"

Grace folded her arms and waited.

"Because he smells like gingerbread. *Obviously.*"

"We are both still alive this morning."

Stephen looked up from his mug of tea as Istvhan settled down at the bench across from him.

"No thanks to this tea," Stephen grumbled. "I think they've run out of herbs and are throwing in hay instead."

Istvhan took a sip and grimaced. "Gah. You're not wrong." He stared into the mug. "Do you remember when we were on campaign southwest of here? South of the Dowager's city?"

Stephen groaned. "Vividly. We ran out of tea and Marley—you remember him?—whipped up something from roasted chicory and kept swearing it was just as good." He slugged some of the hay-flavored tea. "It wasn't."

"And we all had the runs," said Istvhan. "So the chicory didn't stay in us long enough to change our minds."

"I'd forgotten that bit." Stephen rubbed his forehead. "Oh Saint, we did, didn't we? When we came to after the fighting...after the tide faded..." He waved his free hand. "I had to throw out that pair of trews. There was no saving them."

"They never warn you that you won't stop to take a shit when the battle tide is on you," said Istvhan. "Some of the old berserkers used to fight naked, if you believe the stories. I never believed it until after that campaign."

"Would have made clean-up a lot easier."

"Did we win that one?"

"Somebody must have. Might have been us." Stephen shrugged.

The two men ate the rest of breakfast—fried oatcakes, dense but dripping with butter—in companionable silence.

"You're in a good mood lately," said Istvhan, licking the last crumbs off his fingers.

"What?"

"You," said Istvhan. "A good mood. Not stoically miserable. Perhaps even *cheerful*, although I hesitate to go quite that far." He narrowed his eyes over the tea. "Why is that?"

Stephen opened his mouth to deny any such thing, then stopped.

Truth was, he *had* been in a good mood. He had woken up the last few days and instead of thinking about not getting out of bed, he had thought about the girl in the alley. The perfume-maker, who had cried out like a woman in the throes of passion and flopped like an injured fish.

The perfume-maker who had made him laugh.

It was not that Stephen had any intense desire to seek her out, he was simply glad that she existed. His world of late had narrowed down to the Temple of the White Rat and his paladin brothers. Now it seemed that it had grown a little larger again.

He did hope that she wouldn't go hunting through graveyards for herbs again, though.

"You've met a woman," rumbled Istvhan, who could not actually read minds but occasionally did a startlingly good impression.

"No! Err...yes. But not like that."

Istvhan leaned his elbow on the table, propped his bearded chin in one hand, and gave Stephen his full attention.

Stephen sighed. "When I was coming back from escorting the healer, I ran into a woman who was...ah....fleeing from some Mother-hood goons."

"Oh, *them*." Istvhan didn't spit, but presumably only because the cook would yell at him for spitting on the floor.

"She more or less jumped into my arms," said Stephen.

He tried to explain how it had happened, while the other paladin's eyebrows climbed higher and higher. When he finished, Istvhan's fist landed on the table with a thump.

"You're telling me that a beautiful woman jumped into your arms and began moaning in your ear, you rescued her from the enemy, and you didn't even get her *name*?"

"I didn't say she was beautiful."

"All women are beautiful," said Istvhan, dismissing this. "It is the job of their lovers to make them feel that way if they do not already."

"I'm not her lover!"

"And you won't be, if you continue to be so craven-hearted. You never used to have this problem."

"I can't! You know I can't."

Saint's teeth, even if he hadn't been prone to berserker fits, there was nothing about Stephen that would set a maiden's heart alight. He was solid, reliable, and worried about people getting turned into severed heads or standing around with wet feet. Bards did not compose wistful ballads about men like him.

Istvhan's brow furrowed in sudden concern. "Brother," he said, setting a hand on Stephen's shoulder. His voice dropped to a grave whisper. "Do you mean you can't get it up?"

"*No*, I do *not* mean—Saint's balls, Istvhan, everything works fine!"

"Oh thank the gods. Well, then."

"We spoke for fifteen minutes! Twenty if you count the bit where we were hoping the Motherhood didn't try to stab us both."

"Really, man, are you waiting for the gods to send you a signed invitation? For it seems that they have dropped a rock on your head from a great height and still you do not see it!"

"It wasn't like that!" protested Stephen. "And it doesn't mean anything! She might be married with six kids! She might not even *like* men!" He hadn't gotten that impression, but one never knew.

"Six kids is workable. A live husband...mm, well, why was he letting her chase through graveyards in the dark without assistance? Clearly unfit for such a woman." Istvhan nodded to himself. "We will have him killed."

"We're paladins, Istvhan. We don't have people killed unless they're evil."

"To leave such a woman in the clutches of the Motherhood? And her with six kids at home to care for? Bah! Clearly an evil man."

Stephen put his forehead down on the table and moaned softly.

"We shall make inquiries," said Istvhan. "There cannot be that many perfume-makers in the city."

CHAPTER 8

"Grace, darling, you haven't heard a word I've said."

"I'm sure it's fine," said Grace automatically, staring down at the workbench in front of her. Marguerite had been talking at her for the last five minutes and none of it had registered. She had far more important concerns.

"But what do you *think?*"

"I think my supplier's cheating me. Look at this!"

"It's a blank piece of paper?"

"Yes! Now look at this!" She thrust another strip of paper at her friend.

"Uh..." Marguerite took the strip and scrutinized it thoroughly. "There's a spot on it."

"Exactly! And it's greasy!" Grace shoved her hands into her hair and clutched at her head.

"You will have to explain this to me," said Marguerite. "I'm just a simple government informant."

"It's essential oil," said Grace. "Grey balsam. When it evaporates, if it's pure, it shouldn't leave any residue. But if they're diluting it with some cheaper oil, it leaves the grease spot." She narrowed her eyes. "Two years I've been buying this man's oils, and he thinks I won't notice that he's started cheating me."

"Yes, but will you actually say anything about it?"

Grace scowled. She hated confrontations. They made her feel dizzy and sick and like she must absolutely be at fault. "I'll tell him that there was something greasy in the last batch and that the formulation must have changed, and I thought he'd of course want to know. That ought to shame him into giving me the decent stuff again." *I hope.*

"If he doesn't, let me know."

Grace stifled a sigh. She didn't really want Marguerite rescuing her either. It was less objectionable than having a paladin do it, but... "I'll manage."

Still, she had to admit that Marguerite's words warmed her heart. Having men want to rescue you was worlds different than simply having a female friend who had your back. If she needed a body buried, the only question Marguerite would ask was, "How deep?"

The workshop door creaked as it opened, and a narrow, striped head poked through at ankle height.

"Tab!" said Marguerite happily, dropping the greasy paper. Grace grabbed it as it fell.

The civette bounded through the doorway and leaped up Marguerite's legs. She caught him and settled him in the crook of her arm, where he rolled over on his back and looked extremely smug.

"Aww, who's my handsome stripey boy?"

"Your handsome stripey boy is in disgrace," said Grace, sweeping up the rest of the paper strips and throwing them away. "He dug a hole in my bolster pillow and tore out the stuffing, then climbed inside. I went to lie down and my pillow started moving. It took twenty years off my life."

"Well, he probably didn't expect you to lay on him, either." Marguerite scratched the weasel-cat under the chin. Tab stretched his paws and dangled his head upside down over her arm to give her better access to the itchy spots.

"There were feathers *everywhere.*"

"Tab, were you a naughty stripey boy?"

Grace shook her head. The civette was one of the few things she'd brought with her in her flight from Anuket City. She didn't regret it—Phillip would have starved the little beast out of negligence, if he didn't kill him in a rage—but she did wish he had slightly less of an attraction to pillows.

"So will you do it?" Marguerite asked, looking up from the content civette.

"Do what?"

Her friend heaved a sigh. "You really didn't hear a word I said, did you? I need you to make a gift for the Archon's guest."

"Guest," said Grace blankly.

"The Crown Prince of Charlock is coming for a state visit. It's a big deal. They're looking for a trading partner and the Archon is trying to convince them that Archenhold would be a better choice than Anuket City. So there will be a formal presentation of gifts to the Crown Prince from the city's artisans. I need you to make something elegant to give the Prince."

"You don't want them to trade with Anuket?" said Grace, puzzled. Anuket City was, after all, the power that Marguerite was ostensibly working for. *Although in practice, I suspect that Marguerite works mostly for Marguerite...*

"Don't care in the slightest," said Marguerite, waving a hand. "Having you—and thus me, as your representative—in the Archon's good graces is far more useful to me than some merchants in Anuket City improving their profit margin by a percentage or two." She grinned. "Besides, if Archenhold becomes more powerful, I become more essential to Anuket's spymasters. A woman has to look out for her own interests sometimes. Isn't that right, Tab?"

Tab snored.

"See, I wish I could fall asleep like that."

"Well, it's daylight," said Grace. Civettes were mostly nocturnal, although Tab usually found plenty of mice to entertain him during the night. "So you need me to make something special for this Prince?" She already had something in mind, something masculine but with warm, spicy notes and no goddamn sandalwood. Something like gingerbread, say...

"And come with me to present it," said Marguerite, clearing a spot on a side table and setting the unconscious Tab down on it. The civette rolled up into a tight ball, tail over his nose, without ever waking up.

Grace paused. "What?"

"It'll be fine," said Marguerite. "You'll be the eccentric genius. I'll do all the talking. You just look brilliant and distracted."

"Are you talking about a formal audience?"

Marguerite draped an arm over her shoulders. "Oh, something like that. Don't worry. It's a couple hours of standing around the reception being bored silly. Nothing will go wrong."

~

"An honor guard?" said Stephen. "Really?"

Bishop Beartongue gave him a wry look. *"You're* complaining? At least you just get to wear armor and stand around looking militant. I have to actually *talk* to people."

Stephen shook his head, amused. He wasn't at all bothered to be in the honor guard, but teasing the bishop kept him entertained. "All right, but why the three of us? Istvhan here looks less like an honor guard than a bandit and—"

Istvhan elbowed him in the ribs. "I'll have you know that some of my favorite aunts were bandits!"

"Were?"

"Well, they're mostly dead. Now my favorite *cousins* are bandits."

Beartongue rolled her eyes. A tall woman with iron-gray hair and iron-gray eyes, she was one of the highest-ranked of the Rat's servants. Stephen had long suspected that she was the one who had ordered that the paladins of the Saint of Steel be taken to the temple.

Unlike many high-ranked priests he'd known, she also had a sense of humor.

"If you must know, it's because the three of you have beards," she said.

Istvhan raised his eyebrows. Stephen raised his hand involuntarily to his jaw and the narrow line of growth there. So did Shane, the third member of their party. "Beards?"

"Beards," said the bishop, sighing. "Charlock's prince is in one of those old warrior traditions. You know the kind, Istvhan, your homeland's lousy with them."

Istvhan nodded. "The sacred order of this and that and that thing over there. Usually wolves. Or bears. Sometimes blood."

"Blood?" said Stephen.

"Look, you can only have so many Sacred Order of the Wolfs in one region or it gets embarrassing. So then you have to be the Sacred Order of the Blood Moon, which still sounds impressive and you can keep all the wolf paraphernalia around and don't have to get new sword hilts and standards and whatnot."

Stephen rubbed his face, not sure if Istvhan was serious or not.

"Hmm, yes. If we ever have to rebrand the Temple, I'll argue for calling ourselves the Sacred Order of the White Mouse," said Bishop Beartongue. "It will save us a fortune in statuary."

"See? This woman understands."

"Beards, though?" said Shane. Shane was serious even for a paladin, which Stephen had to admit was a high bar.

"Right. Warrior tradition, very manly. They all have beards. Which we wouldn't care about very much, except that their mythology has it that facial hair makes you trustworthy—no, don't ask me why, I don't know, it's mythology, it doesn't have to make sense. The translation of their great evil is 'the beardless devil.' None of which is particularly relevant here, except that they have a knee jerk reaction that men without beards are suspicious. And since it is my job to get us all through this reception for the prince of Charlock without causing a diplomatic incident and without allowing those bast—ahem, my esteemed colleagues from the Hanged Motherhood —to worm their way even further into the Archon's graces, you three get to be the honor guards."

"Well, we can certainly stand in one place and look...ah...beard-ed." said Stephen.

"That's all I ask. And keep your ears open." The bishop raised an eyebrow at Istvhan. "And you, see if any of their guards want to talk to you. Not about anything important, just keep your ears open."

"Why me?" asked Istvhan, as the three paladins fell automatically into a wedge behind the bishop.

"Because people like you," she said over her shoulder.

"I *am* very likable."

Stephen rolled his eyes. So did Beartongue.

When the time came to leave for the reception, the paladins all piled into a carriage and then out again in front of the Archon's palace. It was less opulent than many state buildings, probably because Archons could be deposed relatively easily, so they did not invest a lot of personal wealth in furnishings. The effect was elegant and understated, if largely by accident.

The current Archon was a lean, ascetic man with brooding, deep-set eyes. Stephen had only ever seen him at public events, but did not trust him. *Spend enough time with priests and you learn to recognize the sort that enjoy mortifying other people's flesh and telling them it's for their own good.*

He was also entirely too fond of the Hanged Motherhood and their brutal goddess. *Speak of the devils.* There were six guards in dark indigo in the courtyard, and two priests in intense blue and violet robes.

"Six," said Istvhan under his breath. "Are they expecting an attack in the middle of the reception?"

"If so, they chose poorly. Look at number five there." Stephen jerked his chin almost imperceptibly at the fifth guard in line.

"Sweating like a hog in a butcher shop," said Istvhan.

"No beard, either."

"I don't think he's old enough to grow one."

The unlucky Motherhood guard was almost a head shorter than his cohorts and kept plucking at the opening of his tabard as if he couldn't get enough air. He looked over at the three paladins and turned a bit green.

"Form up," murmured Istvhan, and the three fell into their protective wedge around the bishop. Shane and Stephen matched their stride together like carriage horses, purely to spite the Mother-hood guards. Istvhan's laugh was so soft it might have been mistaken for a breath.

Two four six eight...how many whacks did it take? One two three four...

They swept past the Motherhood and made their entrance to the reception. The receiving hall had dozens of archways flanking a broad central area. It vaguely reminded Stephen of the cloister walk at a convent, but those present were anything but secluded.

Nor are most of them celibate, I would imagine. There was an aston-ishing amount of flesh on display, and not just on the women. The Crown Prince's guards wore harnesses instead of breastplates and many of the male courtiers—at least those with the figure for it—had adopted a kind of ornamental version.

Better them than me. I was probably in my twenties the last time I could have dressed like that. Stephen, like all the Saint's paladins, was in fighting form, but that meant that he was powerful, not sculpted like bronze statuary. He suspected some of those guards had been chosen as much for their ability to fill out a harness as for their sword skills.

The Archon stood at the far end with his guest. People gathered in the shadows of the archways, talking and laughing and watching carefully. The walk up the central hall seemed to take forever. Stephen flicked his eyes over the assembled group, watching for enemies. Not that anyone was going to attack the Bishop of the White Rat in full view of Archenhold's elite, but old habits died hard.

Let me see...if it comes from the left, Istvhan will take care of the bishop, I will charge the attacker, Shane will drop back to protect the bishop's retreat. If the attack is from the right, same again, but Shane will charge the attacker. Hmm, there's an ice sculpture over on the right. Very difficult to attack if you have to duck under an ice swan. I suppose you could try to use the ice swan as an improvised weapon...

The Crown Prince was a handsome man, with a tightly trimmed beard and a raptor's fierce gaze. He wore ceremonial armor, but he wore it easily. Stephen studied the designs and noted that the embossing was all low and angled away from the body. *Nothing to guide a sword somewhere vital. Probably a few pounds heavier than ideal, but he can fight in it if things go ill.*

The Bishop was announced. The Archon greeted her with courtesy but no deference.

"You have many gods here," said the Crown Prince.

He was probably speaking to the Archon, but Bishop Beartongue inclined her head as if he was speaking to her. "It is our strength, your highness," she said.

The Crown Prince's eyebrows went up and he nodded to her, less agreement than acknowledgement.

The Bishop turned and took a place near the front of the assembly. Stephen found himself only a dozen paces or so from the Crown Prince.

The Hanged Motherhood priests came in next. They'd shed their extremely young guard, or maybe he was off being sick somewhere in a corner. Little as Stephen liked the Motherhood, he could muster a pang of sympathy for a youngster on what was clearly his first guard assignment. It was easier for some men to face battle than the prospect of a royal reception.

The Archon greeted the Motherhood men with far more warmth than he had shown to the bishop. Judging by the way that the Crown Prince turned his head, this was more warmth than he'd shown to any of the other priests, either.

Well, that is hardly any surprise. We knew the Archon favors the Motherhood, or they wouldn't get away with as much as they do. He was still behind Beartongue and could not see her face, but he would have put money that her expression was serene and her eyes were glittering like steel.

The Motherhood men crowded closer than was seemly to the Archon, on the opposite side of the hall. Shane stood still and solemn as a statue. Istvhan traced the embossed pattern on the hilt of his sword with his thumb. Stephen scanned the scene again, looking for possible avenues of attack.

"Istvhan, you ever kill someone with an ice swan?" he whispered.

"I clubbed someone unconscious with a frozen goose once. That's similar?"

The Bishop suffered a mysterious coughing fit.

"No, you had to use the goose as a bludgeon, didn't you? For the swan, I figure you'd snap the head off and try to stab with the neck."

"Hmmm..." Istvhan eyed the ice sculpture speculatively. "It's pretty big. And not well balanced."

"I figure you'd have to go two-handed with it."

"I think I'd grab one of the candelabras instead. Some of those are nice and heavy."

"Far too unwieldy. I could take you apart with the ice swan while you were still trying to get the candelabra off the ground."

"Gentlemen," said Beartongue, "I forbid you to smash the Archon's decor and try to duel with it."

"Yes, your holiness."

"I'll have you both excommunicated."

Stephen coughed. "Technically we're not in your church, your holiness."

"Then I will have you confirmed so that I can excommunicate you *even harder*."

"Yes, your holiness." He and Istvhan traded smug looks. Shane gazed into the distance, perhaps imagining a place where he had suitably serious colleagues.

The next group to be presented to the Crown Prince was the Four-Faced God's priests. The Forge God had already been announced, Stephen guessed, based on the priest in fire-red robes who was quietly decimating the refreshments. The Dreaming God had sent one paladin, but that was more than enough. She was six feet tall and looked like an avenging angel. Even the Archon needed a moment to catch his breath after talking to her.

"It's really not fair," muttered Istvhan. "They all look like that, too."

"Their nuns don't," said the bishop under her breath.

"What do the nuns look like?"

"Like nuns. *You* know."

Istvhan grunted. So did Stephen.

There was a pause in the presentation. "The nobles will be next," said the bishop. "Then the guild leaders and finally the unaffiliated tradesmen. I hope you gentlemen are wearing comfortable boots."

"Your holiness—"

"Don't start."

Stephen felt a strong urge to smile and squelched it. What was coming over him lately? He was supposed to be the steady, reliable one. He was going to be as irreverent as Istvhan if this kept up. "Bishop, we have done forced marches through snow and kept vigil on our knees. I believe we can stand for a few hours without difficulty."

"And we're all wearing Stephen's good socks," said Shane.

Her chuckle was so quiet that he doubted anyone beside the three of them heard her. "Ah, the Rat forgive me. I forget sometimes what paladins are like..."

CHAPTER 9

"I should never have let you talk me into this," muttered Grace, trying to rearrange her breasts in the low-cut bodice. If one went in, the other immediately mutinied and tried to pop out. "This doesn't fit. There is no world where this will fit. I'll flash the Crown Prince and cause an international incident."

"I don't understand," muttered Marguerite, trying to loosen the fabric in the back. "It fits *me.*"

"I'm six inches taller than you."

"Yes, but your boobs aren't."

"My...wait, how does that even—?"

Marguerite muttered even more loudly, did *something*—the sound of ripping fabric filled the room—and then stepped back. "Ha! Now does it fit?"

Grace jammed herself into the bodice. "Um. Yes. Mostly. The corset may be too tight."

"Look, if we adjust the corset we have to take half this stuff off you first."

Grace shuddered at the thought. "I'll manage."

They were in Marguerite's dressing room, in the suite of rooms she kept above the perfume shop. When Grace turned to look in the mirror, her eyes swept over dozens of outfits, some carefully laid out, others on dressmaker dummies and still others stacked in piles. Strangely, it reminded Grace of an armory.

Well, maybe not so strange. These outfits are her weapons, after all. Which I suppose makes me the newly drafted farmer trying to pick up a sword and charge into battle.

"This doesn't look like I'm an eccentric genius," she said, looking in the mirror. The bodice did dramatic things to her chest. "This looks like I'm a prostitute on her first day on the job."

"Don't be ridiculous," said Marguerite. "Prostitutes wear clothing that's much easier to get in and out of. Half my good clothes come from the Scarlet Guild." She picked up a long silver scarf. "Now hold still."

Grace stood like one of the dressmaker dummies while Marguerite wrapped the scarf around her neck in artful falls. The result was superficially modest with unexpected flashes of cleavage. "How does that look?"

"Beautiful. There's no chance it'll stay like that."

"It will once I'm done pinning it."

Half an hour later, no part of Grace's clothes were moving so much as an inch. Glue had been involved in several places. Grace looked in the mirror again and found herself wondering if the paladin would like the way she looked.

Oh, now you're just getting ridiculous. Besides, men like that probably prefer women who can wear armor as well as they can. Come to think of it, I might be more comfortable in armor. At least I wouldn't feel quite so vulnerable.

Marguerite surveyed her work, frowning. "This would be much easier if you were older. One of those tough old ladies with long gray hair who don't take any crap from anyone. I can make one of them look like an eccentric genius with three pins and a hat."

Grace, who was plump and dark haired and only thirty-two, said, "Would you like to come back in a decade or so? I might feel better about this reception then."

"No."

A sudden thought struck her. "Err, there aren't going to be any nobles from Anuket City there, are there?"

"Dozens, probably," said Marguerite. "No, don't panic! Do you think I'd just throw you to the wolves?"

Grace gulped. Phillip had cut quite a swath through the lower ranks of noblewomen in the city. Surely none of them would remember his mousy little wife, not after all these years. But still... "I...um...can I wear a mask?"

"You will not wear a mask," said Marguerite. "Not in the presence of the Archon. But you will carry one of these." She brandished a silk handkerchief in front of Grace. "It shall be soaked in scent and you will hold it in front of your face at all times, save when you are bowing to the Archon. And I shall explain that the great perfumier has far too sensitive a nose and rarely leaves her laboratory, but to do honor to the Archon's guest, she made the pilgrimage. And you will keep your face mostly covered with the handkerchief. Now which scent do you want?"

"I don't want a scent at all," muttered Grace. She went downstairs, accompanied by Marguerite, stretched—gingerly, given the dress and the pins—and pulled down a jar from a high shelf.

"Gah!" said Marguerite, sniffing. "That's strong! Not bad, but...strong."

"Charbeans," said Grace absently. "They'll kill the smell of just about anything. That way if anyone's got a scent worth noticing, my nose will be clear."

She poured a handful of the little beans into a muslin bag and stowed it in the handkerchief. The smell of charbeans was sharp and acidic, like burnt lemon but without sweetness. She kept the jar on hand for when she had smelled too many things and her sinuses began to feel like a jumble of odors.

"Well, you're the eccentric master perfumer," said Marguerite, leading her back upstairs.

"I'm not a master," said Grace. "My articles of apprenticeship—"

"Yes, yes, fine." Marguerite waved her hand. "You were never filed as a master with the guild because your ex-husband is a sniveling little shitweasel."

"Poetic, but accurate."

"Listen to me. No one cares that you're not registered with the guild. No one even knows. Anuket City might as well be a thousand miles away, for all the guilds talk to each other."

Grace gave it up as a lost cause. If anyone asked, she would explain that she was not a master perfumer and Marguerite was getting carried away. Hopefully no one would ask.

"Shoes fine? Not pinching? Good. Now, the final thing..." She pulled open a closet door and drew out a silver cloak that glinted in the light. Metallic threads woven through the fabric glittered like a snowdrift.

"My god," said Grace, laughing. "You want me to wear that? Everyone will notice me!"

"Yes, but they'll see the cloak, not you," said Marguerite. She twirled the cloak around Grace's shoulders and pulled the hood up, pinning it in place. "There. If you were a man, you would have to go bare-headed before the Archon, but you're not, so you will be fashionably shadowed. I'll do most of the talking."

"I'll hold you to that," muttered Grace.

"Now," said Marguerite, cracking her knuckles, "for the paint."

Grace sighed.

It was not as painful as it could have been. All she had to do herself was scrub her teeth down with sage and salt tooth powder. Then she sat still while Marguerite wiped her face down with chervil water and applied powders and colors to her skin.

"Not too much," she said faintly, watching Marguerite wield brushes like a berserker.

"You know as well as I do that looking like you're wearing no makeup takes twice as much work."

Grace snorted, but had to agree.

There was a carriage waiting by the time Marguerite finished her own, much quicker preparations. She looked, if anything, more elaborately attired than Grace, complete with the hat, but she was also much more comfortable in her clothes than Grace would ever be.

The driver handed her up into the carriage. Grace sat down and immediately felt suffocatingly trapped. The interior smelled like wood and leather and the last passenger's cologne: lavender, bergamot, clove, and lemon. It wasn't a bad scent, but it did not combine well with the faint smell of mold that also lingered in the carriage.

She slumped back against the cushions. What if someone she knew was there? Not Phillip, of course. There was no world where Phillip would be there. The gods weren't so cruel. But someone who knew him, who remembered *her*...

"I found your paladin," Marguerite said abruptly.

"What?!" Grace sat bolt upright. She—no, she definitely should not feel so excited, this was very silly, he was a paladin, he might be sworn to celibacy for all she knew, that was a thing some of them did and even if he wasn't, he'd only walked her home, it's not like he'd done anything to make her think he had the *slightest* bit of interest—

"Well, not quite found. But narrowed down the list, anyway. Fortunately for you, there's only seven of the Saint of Steel's paladins in the city. Two of them are women, and I suspect even you would have noticed *that*. Of the remaining five, one's blond and one shaves his head. That leaves us three dark haired paladins, and I'm being very generous and throwing in the one with dark red hair because it was night-time."

"Do any of them have blue eyes?" asked Grace, leaning forward.

"My informant didn't remember."

"Your informant?"

Marguerite shrugged. "Well, the acolyte I asked about it."

"What did you tell them?"

"The truth. One helped a friend of mine and she wanted to thank him, but didn't know his name." She held up three fingers. "Stephen, Istvhan, and Galen. One of those three is your paladin."

"He's not *my* paladin. He just walked me home. And we talked about...err..." *What did we talk about?* Startleflower and street cleaners and Grace couldn't remember half of it. Except she'd laughed a lot. Probably out of relief.

"Paladins of the Saint of Steel aren't sworn to celibacy," said Marguerite, wiggling her eyebrows.

Grace felt herself turning pink and was glad for the relative dimness inside the carriage. "It's not like that." The last thing she needed was to disappoint someone else in bed.

Marguerite took pity on her and changed the subject. "What's the scent in the bottle?"

"You're only *now* asking?" said Grace, amused despite herself. "When you're going to present it to the Archon and the Crown Prince?"

Her friend shrugged. "You're a genius," she said, as if commenting on the weather. "Whatever you made will be genius. I'm not worried."

Grace pinched the bridge of her nose. *Genius. Sure.* She'd spent half the week driving herself mad on the scent, getting it almost right but missing...something. She'd finally stayed up late reading random passages from her baffling alchemist's tome. The magnetic fields of dung heaps could not help her and a sketch of a sheep's eyeball, dissected, wasn't much good. A list of constellations with their respective primary association and scents was marginally more interesting. She wasn't sure if the moon did indeed smell of juniper, but some of the others were interesting.

Tab had been sitting on the desk, batting at her hand with his paws, when she finally read the word "saffron" under the constellation of the lion and thought, *Well, why not?*

It seemed to have worked. She'd added some other things too, trying to get the balance right. It still wasn't perfect, but she was on the right track, and the Crown Prince didn't need to know that she still thought she could do better.

She'd written the prince's recipe down, though, just in case. If, somehow, it found favor, she could make a few months' worth of sales duplicating it for nobility. Best of all, she could get Marguerite to sell it for her.

The carriage halted at the Archon's palace. "Come on," said Marguerite, as the driver opened the door. "Time to impress a prince."

"Oh," said Grace, lifting her handkerchief to conceal her face. "Joy."

CHAPTER 10

Stephen was bored.

They had not gotten a chance to circulate. Technically they could have, but they didn't, because their opposite number wasn't moving either. The Motherhood guards stood behind their priest and the paladins stood behind Beartongue and the priest tried to bait the bishop and the bishop responded with silky pleasantness. None of the paladins were going to leave Beartongue alone for more than a few moments, even given the unlikelihood of a fight breaking out directly in front of the Archon.

He wished that he could break out his knitting, but for some reason, people didn't take you seriously as a warrior when you were knitting. He'd never figured out why. Making socks required four or five double-ended bone needles, and while they weren't very large, you could probably jam one into someone's eye if you really wanted to. Not that he would. He'd have to pull the needle out of the sock to do it, and then he'd be left with the grimly fiddly work of rethreading the stitches. Also, washing blood out of wool was possible, but a pain.

Still, if he had to suddenly pull out his sword and fend off an attack, there was a chance he'd drop the yarn, and since he'd been feeling masochistic and was using two colors for this current set of socks, there was absolutely no chance the yarn wouldn't get tangled and then he'd be trying to murder people while chasing the yarn around. And god forbid the tide rose and he went berserk. You never got the knitting untangled after that; you usually just had to throw it away completely.

He and Istvhan had exhausted the weapon possibilities of everything in the room, from the banners to one of the courtier's hats, which had an entire stuffed egret on it. Even Shane had chimed in on that one. Beartongue eventually told them that if they didn't stop trying to make her laugh in front of the Motherhood priest, she'd throw them in the stockade.

"You don't *have* a stockade," said Stephen.

"You will get to build one so that I can throw you in it!"

"Well, that *does* seem practical."

"That's the Rat's priests for you," said Istvhan. "Always very practical."

"I bet the Motherhood's got a stockade."

"Next time, I am leaving you three at the temple."

Shane made a quiet sound of protest. "Don't lump me in with these two."

"I will excommunicate everyone and *no one* will get to go the circus."

"Oh come on, look at this guy." Stephen jerked his chin toward the group opposite them. "You know he's got a stockade. Probably in his back garden." Beartongue sighed, but didn't argue.

This was a more highly ranked priest than Stephen was used to, the indigo robes nearly black and slashed with violet at the cuffs. He'd forgotten the Motherhood ranks, if he ever knew. What was their leader called? Not a pontiff. High priest? That didn't sound right. Archpriest?

"I am surprised the Archimandrite isn't here," said Beartongue loudly, answering the question for him.

"He is busy attending to heresy in the west," said the violet-cuffed priest.

"Ah, yes." Beartongue sipped her drink. She had ordered Shane to get it, when it became obvious that none of the paladins were planning on moving. Shane had presented it to her as gravely as a man handing over a naked sword, then resumed his position behind her. Stephen thought he'd seen the Crown Prince's lips twitch at that, but it was hard to tell. "So many heretics. And it seems like you find more all the time."

"Heresy is a great concern," said the priest, gazing directly at Beartongue and enunciating each word clearly.

"Subtlety doesn't seem to be," muttered Istvhan. Shane looked inscrutable. Stephen studied the carvings on the opposite pillar until the desire to laugh had passed.

"The Motherhood's concerns are, of course, of great concern to us all," said Beartongue, so blandly that if one didn't know the long and tortured legal history between the two faiths, one might have taken the statement at face value. Someone in the Crown Prince's retinue evidently did know of the history, because Stephen heard a stifled chuckle from within their ranks.

The Motherhood priest was too wily to show that he took offense, but he folded his hands in his sleeves and stopped attempting to make conversation with the bishop. Instead he turned to the Crown Prince. "What do you think of our land, your magnificence?"

The Crown Prince took his time noticing that he had been spoken to. Stephen wondered if he bothered to acknowledge the man because he thought it would please the Archon, or if he had delayed doing so specifically to needle him. Finally, he looked over at the priest. "It is unlike Charlock," he pronounced, in the tone of one who has now said all that needs to be said about the matter.

"In what way?" asked the Motherhood priest. Stephen had to give the man credit for persistence, if nothing else.

The Crown Prince's gaze traveled over the assembly, the courtiers in their ridiculous costumes mimicking his guards, the nobles playing out their own games of rank in the shadows. He looked across the rows of priests, the Forge God's chosen standing next to the demonslayer from the Dreaming God. He looked back to the Motherhood man.

"It is...*damp*."

Stephen did not know if he had ever heard a comment on the weather delivered in more shattering tones. The Archon folded his hands over his cane, expressionless as always. Beartongue had turned slightly toward the prince, and Stephen could see her smile into her drink.

"Yes," said the Motherhood priest. "Yes. Of course. Charlock is very...very dry, is it not?"

The Crown Prince did not see fit to reply. The words hung in the air and became more and more agonizing the longer they went unanswered.

It was a profound relief when the Archon banged his cane on the floor and stated that they were ready for the craftsmen to present their gifts.

"Put away the handkerchief," murmured Marguerite. "We're next. Follow my lead and speak if spoken to. Curtsy when I say 'master perfumer'."

"But I'm not a—"

"From Grace Angelica, master perfumer, a gift of scent," said the tall, thin man who seemed to be announcing everything.

Marguerite stepped forward and Grace followed her like a duckling after its mother. She felt terrifyingly visible.

"Your wisdom," Marguerite said to the Archon, bowing and sweeping the floor with her hat. "Your highness. The master perfumer has compounded a special scent for this momentous occasion, and hopes that your highness will enjoy a small taste of the craftsmanship of our fair city."

How does she say things like that? And make it sound like a thing that normal people would say? Belatedly, Grace remembered that she was supposed to curtsy and did so as deeply as she could. Her knees were shaking and her mouth felt bone dry. *I'm not a master. I'm not.* She wanted to declare it loudly, but her voice was nowhere to be found.

No one ran from the wings to denounce her. The man beside the

Crown Prince moved forward to accept the small glass bottle, but stopped when his ruler raised a hand.

"You let your servant speak for you?" the Crown Prince said.

Oh shit oh shit he's talking to me. Oh shit oh shit what do I say what do I say?

She settled on the exact truth. "She speaks better than I do, sir," croaked Grace. And then "I mean highness. Your highness."

Well, that's it, I've misrepresented myself as a master, caused an international incident, and cost the city a trading partner. I knew it would happen. I'll have to leave the city and change my name. Again. Normal people don't have to keep leaving cities and changing their name. This is a terrible habit.

The Crown Prince stretched out his hand. He had fierce eyes, a brown so light they appeared almost gold. She could smell clove on him. Well, of course. Princes didn't need to worry about how expensive the oil on their armor was. "What is this scent?"

She was on firmer ground here. "The head note is spice, your highness. Ginger and clove. The heart is amber and resin and a touch of saffron." She swallowed. "It makes me think of strength, and, and, and warmth."

Stop talking, she told herself, and for once she listened.

To her horror the prince turned his hand over and extended his wrist in an unmistakable gesture.

Am I supposed to put some on him? Of course I am. It's what I'd do. At least it won't clash with the clove. Oh dear. Grace looked at Marguerite. Marguerite handed her the bottle, giving her a very meaningful look. She was obviously trying to convey something, but Grace had no idea what it might be.

As if in a dream—the sort of dream where she was late for something and would eventually realize she did not have any clothes on—Grace took the bottle, opened the lid with a practiced twist, and tilted it up against her thumb. She brushed her thumb across the Crown Prince's wrist and saw the shine of oil across his skin. Her mind was absolutely blank.

Marguerite took the bottle back.

The Crown Prince lifted his wrist and sniffed it, then smiled at her. "As you say, Master Perfumer," he said.

And then it was over and Marguerite was leading her away and pulling her into the shadows framing the brightly lit hall.

"That was amazing!" whispered Marguerite. "I knew they liked perfume in Charlock but I had no idea he'd actually talk to you! This is wonderful!"

"Is it?" asked Grace numbly.

"You did wonderfully."

"I stammered and I called him 'sir.'"

"Yes, that's fine. Royalty are used to people being nervous. But he liked it. And you were so obviously earnest."

"It was the paladin," said Grace vaguely. "Like gingerbread. Only it had to be warm so I added the amber. And there's some civet in there to bind it all. I didn't tell him about the civet, did I? Oh dear."

"Let me get you something to drink," said Marguerite firmly. "You look like you're about to keel over."

"Can I?"

"No."

"Then a drink would be good."

"Stand right here, smell your handkerchief, and don't go anywhere."

"I think I can promise that."

CHAPTER 11

Stephen saw the perfumer again when she presented her gift to the Crown Prince. He knew her at once, almost before he saw her face. His first thought was to push through the crowd and speak to her, but training took over. One did not interrupt a royal presentation. That would go badly for him and for her. She had a companion with her, all curves and animation, who spoke to the Archon and the Prince and bowed low, sweeping off her plumed hat which was, ironically, the one with the potentially weaponizable stuffed egret. By contrast, the perfumer was a figure of ice, silver cloaked, her hood drawn low as if she did not wish to be recognized.

He held his place and his tongue. He would not presume. *A man... any man, not just a paladin...should know better. And you have no right. She owes you nothing. She may not even wish to speak to you again. That she was pleasant to you while you walked home means nothing. She was afraid and needed your help. She may have been afraid of you as well. Most women would be pleasant to a strange man that they were wary of. It means nothing. And what are you thinking? You can't possibly...even if she was interested, your soul is half scar now. Your god is dead. Have you forgotten?*

No. That, at least, he would never forget.

Istvhan glanced at him. They had known each other long enough that the other man could sense Stephen's sudden tension, even if he did not move. "Problem?"

"From Grace Angelica, master perfumer," announced the herald, "a gift of scent."

Grace. Her name is Grace.

Istvhan grinned broadly, teeth flashing white against his beard. "Ah. Not a problem."

"I walked her home," said Stephen under his breath. "It didn't mean anything."

"It meant something to *you*."

"What does that have to do with anything?"

"Go see if it meant something to her, too!"

"I can't! I'm not...I can't."

"Saint's breath, man, what's come over you?"

"Nothing!"

"You used to have no problem meeting women."

"Things change."

"Just *talk* to her, you blithering idiot."

"I am an *honor guard*."

"For the Rat's sake, go talk to her," growled Bishop Beartongue. "If only so you two stop whispering behind me like a pair of schoolgirls."

Stephen watched the presentation of the gift. The Crown Prince spoke to the perfumer—*to Grace*—and held out his hand. Grace looked terrified. Stephen had a strong urge to go and thrash the Crown Prince, which would have been quite undiplomatic.

He could not quite hear what she was saying. She spoke very quietly, applying the scent to the prince's wrist. The urge to thrash the man deepened, darkened.

He is frightening her. He is touching her, and she is frightened.

If the black tide rose now, he could push forward. Istvhan would stand between him and the bishop, and all he would need to clear was two dozen paces. If he did it quickly, the Prince's honor guards would not see him in time. The Prince himself would fight, but by then the tide would be over his head, and Stephen need only trust to it.

Shane turned his head sharply to look at Stephen. Stephen caught the gesture from the corner of his eye and it snapped his thoughts back. Grace retreated. The Crown Prince lifted his wrist to his nose and said something he couldn't hear.

Then it was over and the small, curvy woman was leading Grace away into the crowd. Stephen tried to track where they went but lost sight of them quickly. *Damn!*

"Well, go on!" whispered Istvhan.

"I can't!"

"I cannot believe that I call a man as dense as you 'brother.'"

"I'm not—"

"I never figured you for a coward, either."

"Dammit, Istvhan—"

"Paladin Stephen," said Bishop Beartongue crisply, "you are relieved of your duties. Go talk to this woman or at least go somewhere Istvhan won't keep whispering at you."

Stephen was too well trained to gape at her, but he felt his eyes go wide. Unlike her previous talk of the stockade, she did *not* sound as if she were joking.

"If I may interject," said Shane, as solemn as ever, "if you are speaking of the lady wearing silver, she is standing over there and I believe she is about to faint."

Stephen bolted.

I will not faint, Grace told herself firmly. *I will stand here and I will breathe and I will not faint. Fainting would cause a scene.*

Causing a scene was somewhere slightly above murder as Things We Do Not Do. Normal people did not cause scenes.

Her corset was much too tight. It hadn't felt that way before, but now that she was actually here and the room was warm and stuffy and other people were taking all the air... She took a deep breath of charbean. The acrid odor steadied her and cleared her head. When she lowered her handkerchief a little, she could taste the scents going by without drowning in them.

Let's see...Sandalwood, of course. Always sandalwood...lavender, berg-amot...someone has a very nice orange blossom and clove, that wasn't cheap.

A well-dressed young man went by wearing more civet than came out of Tab's rear end in a year. Grace shook her head, mostly to herself, and lifted her handkerchief again.

I can do this. I am doing this. Marguerite will come back with water or punch or something and I will drink it and then we will go back to a quiet corner and soon we will be able to leave and I will go home and take off these clothes and see what pillow Tab has destroyed in my absence.

And then she heard a voice behind her and the whole world tilted sideways.

"Oh, my dear, I love those shoes! Wherever did you get them?"

She knew that voice.

Lady Vance, wealthy, wedded, widowed, and fond of married men who would not attempt to trap her in matrimony. Lady Vance, who had been in Anuket City four years ago, who boasted of the special scent that a certain perfume-maker had made just for her.

A hot wave swept over Grace. She felt dizzy and sick. She would have bolted, but her feet were nailed to the floor.

"Really?" said Lady Vance, in response to the owner of the shoes. "Why, how delightfully daring! You were *slumming!* Oh, what fun!"

She isn't talking to me. She isn't talking to me. She hasn't seen me. She doesn't know I'm here. Grace shoved the handkerchief to her face and gasped the acrid odor of charbeans. She was torn between an intense desire to turn around and see where the woman was so that she knew which way to flee, and an equally intense desire to stay absolutely still, like a mouse waiting for the cat to leave.

She looked desperately for Marguerite and saw her over by the refreshment table, clearly trying to extract herself from a conversation, but she was too far away. To get to her, Grace would have to pass directly in front of Lady Vance.

I can do it if her back is turned. I can go quickly. I'm being eccentric, no one will notice. I just have to look and see which way she's facing, and if she's looking at me, I turn back this way, but not too quick, not so she notices, oh gods, gods, if any of you love me, Rat and Lady and Dreaming God, please...

She turned her head as little as she dared and saw Lady Vance's profile move into view.

Oh gods oh gods she only has to glance this way and she'll see me.

Lady Vance laughed at something her companion said and snapped her fan. Her gaze moved over the crowd, passing over Grace with vague curiosity but no recognition, and then she turned back to her companion.

Grace's knees felt weak. She inhaled charbeans. The hot dizzy feeling didn't recede nearly as much as she hoped. In fact, the charbeans seemed to be making it worse, and she had to lower the handkerchief a little and gulp clearer air.

Am I going to faint? I can't. No, I can't faint. If I faint, I'll drop my handkerchief and she'll see me and she'll know. I didn't faint the last time. I won't faint now!

Vance fanned herself and the smell of her perfume drifted past. She was wearing too much. She always wore too much.

Angelica root, Grace thought grimly, *clove, lavender, bergamot, resin, citrus and white musk, damask rose, and dammit, it's the same, it's exactly the same.* She was even wearing it on her skin and it was turning powdery and insipid and it was too much, scents pulled up memories, that was why perfume worked at all...

A long, narrow room with enormous windows. The sales room for the perfume, transformed for an elegant private opening. Patrons moved back and forth, sniffing the testers and drinking wine and being dreadful to one another. Grace hated these events, but Phillip said it was the only way to get the nobility to buy anything, if they could be seen doing it.

"Oh, my dear," said Lady Vance, fluttering her fan at Grace. "You must be Phillip's wife."

"I am," said Grace, dipping her head politely.

"Oh, my! Well, I must beg your pardon—you must forgive me—I have been monopolizing Phillip atrociously." She winked at Grace, a conspiratorial, aren't-we-being-naughty gesture. "I know he says you don't mind, but of course, men haven't the least idea about women, do they?"

Grace forced a smile. "I don't mind," she said. She knew that Phillip enjoyed hobnobbing with the upper crust, and she was more than glad to leave him to it.

"You are so *sweet*." Vance beamed at her. "And he made me this lovely perfume, have you smelled—oh, I'm silly, of course you must have!"

Grace had. Grace had actually made the perfume in question, of course. In small quantities it was pleasant, but too much became cloying.

"He's *such* an amusing lover, too. But of course I needn't tell you that!"

She'd said something else, too. Grace remembered her lips moving, but that hot, dizzy wave had swept over her and closed over her heart.

Such an amusing lover.

Phillip had sworn that he'd never done anything of the sort, that he didn't even like the women he sold to. He'd gotten angry at her for asking. Didn't she trust him?

I know he says you don't mind.

"Oh dear," said Lady Vance, making a moue. "Have I said something wrong?"

"You shouldn't wear that perfume on your skin," said Grace flatly.

"What?"

Grace shook her head. The world was roaring in her ears and she could hardly hear herself talk. "That perfume. It's the essential oils, it's not working on your skin. Some people can't wear them. You're one of them. It's turned powdery, like talc."

Lady Vance gaped at her. "But Phillip made it for *me*," she said, her voice rising.

"Wear it in your hair or in a vial, then. Not on your skin. Your skin doesn't work with it."

She stared at Lady Vance and Vance stared back. Then she saw Phillip coming toward them, over Vance's shoulder, and she turned and walked away. If she had to talk to Phillip, she would burst into tears or rage at him and then they would all know...everyone would know...

Everyone will know already. Lady Vance will tell everyone what a strange little mouse Phillip's wife is.

But none of that mattered, if she could just get away in time, if she could walk through the long room with her head high, to the curtain that concealed the door to the back stairs and then she was through and everything was dark and blessedly cool and the smell was of whitewash and the oil rubbed into the boards. She fell forward and then she was going up the stairs on her hands and knees but that didn't matter because she had gotten away and no one could see her and it was still so very dark...

The memory faded. The panic took longer to recede.

There were arms around her, holding her up. That wasn't part of any memory, was it? Phillip hadn't held her like that in years. Not after the first few months, anyway. Before that...well, the old perfumer certainly hadn't.

No. This was real. And her face was bent down against someone's chest and the darkness was starting to recede. She'd lost her handkerchief somewhere and she was gasping in great breaths of...gingerbread?

She tilted her head back and looked up into deep blue eyes.

"We meet again," said the paladin.

CHAPTER 12

"We meet again," said Stephen, and immediately thought, *Well, that was an incredibly stupid thing to say.*

The perfumer had a puzzled expression, as if she was not quite sure where she was or how she'd gotten there. Probably not surprising, given that she'd looked on the verge of blacking out when he finally reached her.

He'd moved as soon as Shane pointed her out, but he hadn't been able to run. When a man in armor runs in a crowd, people tend to scream and get out of the way. The Bishop would have had words. So he'd had to walk with what felt like agonizing slowness, watching her head slowly slump forward, thinking, *Let me get there in time, let me get there in time, please gods, let me get there in time.*

That slow crawl through the crowd had probably taken a year off his life, but he'd made it before she went over. "Miss Angelica," he said, putting his arm around her shoulders, "it's so good to see you again."

Her breathing was fast and shallow and she didn't lift her head or even acknowledge his presence. Stephen held her upright and steered her toward the back wall, looking for a door or an alcove or something private enough that he could see if she'd been poisoned or drugged or if it was just the heat of so many bodies in one room.

The back wall looked distressingly blank. He stared at it, thinking, *Now what?* and then someone tapped on his shoulder.

The priest of the Forge God was barely over five feet tall, older than Brother Francis, and had biceps like tree trunks. "Go over to the screen," he said, jerking his head to the right. "There's a door behind it, takes you to the privies."

"The Saint bless you," gasped Stephen reflexively, forgetting for an instant that the Saint was no longer around to bless anyone. "I mean—ah—well, the Rat would probably—"

The Forge priest grinned. "Either or. Forge keep you, youngster."

The hallway on the other side of the door was at least ten degrees cooler. Stephen was pleased to see that Grace hadn't collapsed, but she was shuffling along like a sleepwalker.

"Hey," he said. "Are you all right? Miss? Grace?"

She lifted her head and actually seemed to focus on him, and that's when he said the remarkably stupid thing about meeting again.

A little more awareness crept into her eyes. Stephen pushed the hood back from her face. He knew that he should release her and step back, but perhaps not just yet, not until he was certain she would not fall.

"Are you hurt?" he asked. "You seemed to be close to fainting, so I brought you out here. I thought the air would be cooler."

"Cooler," she said. "Yes. It was very hot, wasn't it? And I smelled a scent that I knew, and...and the air was very close." She shuddered, and he fought the urge to close his arms around her more tightly until it passed.

If you were really worried about her being too warm, you wouldn't be draping yourself over her like a comforter made out of meat.

"Do scents often take you like that?" he asked, ignoring himself.

"Sometimes," she admitted. "Scents are very good at calling up memories and not all memories are good ones."

"No, they are not."

Grace was still leaning against him. Her lips were slightly parted and if he bent his head only a little, he could kiss her. For a heartbeat, he actually considered it. Would it be so terrible? Merely brushing his lips across hers, demanding nothing, then stepping back, and—

What in the Saint's name is wrong with you? You're actually thinking of taking advantage of a woman who blacked out a few minutes ago? And you call yourself a paladin?

His body was not feeling chivalrous. His body was suddenly keenly aware of how close she was, of the fact that her breasts were pressed against his chest. She was wearing a corset and her struggle to control her breathing meant that a great deal was going on in that vicinity.

Her hair, freed from the hood, had fallen over his hands in dark waves. It smelled of something clean and familiar, not sweet at all. Cedar? He'd never met a woman who smelled like cedar before. Perhaps it was a perfumer thing. He lifted one hand and pushed her hair aside, away from her cheek.

There was a pulse beating in her throat. He could picture, very clearly, covering her mouth with his, kissing the color back into her lips, then sliding down her jaw and feeling her heart race under her skin.

Stop. Stop. You do not get to have these thoughts. And even if you have them, women like this do not have such thoughts about men like you.

Stephen released her shoulders and stepped back, still keeping his hands on her upper arms in case she was less steady than she seemed. She shook herself and took a step back of her own, rubbing her hands over her forearms.

"Will your...ah...assistant be looking for you?" asked Stephen.

"Marguerite? Yes. Yes, she was going to get me water, but I think someone waylaid her."

"It was the Squire again," said the curvy woman in the enormous hat, emerging from the doorway. Stephen wondered how long she had been standing there, watching the two of them. "His wife is making a pilgrimage and will be gone for simply *months*. A fact he emphasized repeatedly, while winking."

"Poor Marguerite!" said Grace, laughing. She turned away from Stephen, and he let his hands drop to his sides.

"Yes, well. I told him I had taken a terrible aversion to the country. Here, this is the closest they have to water. It's flavored with orange peel and some sort of fruit, but nothing too dangerous, I don't think."

She sipped it, rolled it around on her tongue. "Grape, elderberry, lemon balm..."

"It's almost unsettling when she does that," said Marguerite to Stephen. She looked him up and down, clearly sizing him up, although Stephen felt rather less like a potential conquest and more like a horse on the auction block. "Hmm, you must be her paladin."

That wrung a startled laugh out of him. "We've met before, yes. I was able to walk her home. My name is Stephen."

Marguerite shot Grace a triumphant glance. Stephen wondered if he had been supposed to notice it or not.

"I've heard so much about you," said Marguerite, extending her hand.

"Um...you have?"

"Yes. Absolutely." She elbowed Grace in the side. Grace jumped. It would have taken a very dense individual indeed not to see that there was some kind of communication passing between them, but Stephen did not have the foggiest idea what it might be.

"If you're feeling better," he said, suddenly awkward, "please don't let me detain you here..."

"Better. Yes." Grace took a deep breath, then scowled. "It's this damn corset, I swear. I knew it was too tight."

I absolutely will not offer to loosen it for her. I will not. I am a gentleman. Stephen schooled his face into an expression of polite interest and kept his eyes strictly above her collarbone, while his brain conjured up lascivious images of laces being undone, one by one.

Down.

"Can we leave now? Is the presentation bit done?" asked Grace, a bit plaintively.

"Yes, yes," said Marguerite. "We'll take you home. I'm sorry things got out of hand there for a moment, but you did very well."

She started to turn back to the doorway, and Grace said, "Not that way!"

Marguerite lifted an eyebrow. So did Stephen.

Grace flushed. "I...we can't go that way. There's someone who knows me. Err. From Anuket."

From Anuket City? Is she from the city originally herself? Interesting.

...not that it's any of my business.

Marguerite's other eyebrow shot up. "Who?"

"Lady Vance," said Grace reluctantly.

"Oh, blast," muttered Marguerite. "Of *course* it'd be the biggest gossip this side of Archenhold." She scowled. "I don't spend enough time here, I'm not sure how to get out without going through the crowd here."

Stephen cleared his throat. "If you are looking for a different way out of the building, I believe I've worked out where we are now. This corridor should be shaped somewhat like a horseshoe, and if we follow it around the bend, we will come to the area behind the Archon's dais. There will be guards there, on the entrance that he uses."

"Guards?" said Marguerite, looking skeptical.

Stephen spread his hands. "Well, they can't let people wander in behind the ruler of the city. But guards will also know multiple ways out of the building. If we go up to them and simply ask if they can direct us, I suspect they will be happy to offer direction."

Marguerite gave a short bark of a laugh. "That is so uncomplicated that I would never had even considered it. Lead on, Sir Stephen."

So the paladin's name is Stephen. And he still smells like gingerbread. And I just pretty much fainted on him.

Grace was not sure if she was horribly embarrassed or not. Her first, irrational thought when she'd realized what was happening was that he would somehow know about Lady Vance and Phillip and view her in the same contempt and pity as everyone else. She had to take several deep breaths before she remembered that the memories were all in her head and strangers couldn't read her entire history in her face.

But twice now, you fall into his arms? Once making the worst moaning sounds you could think of and now you collapse on him like a noblewoman having a swoon?

He had to think that she was an irredeemable idiot.

He hadn't acted like it, though. There had even been a moment, as he looked down at her, when she had the wild thought that he might lean in and kiss her.

Which was absurd, of course. He barely knew her. And now that she was looking at him again, she suspected that he was quite good looking, and Grace...well, she was what she was. It was probably just the angle that had made it look as if he were staring at her lips.

Or maybe his hearing's going and it's the only way he can tell what I'm saying, she thought. *Anyway, strange men bound by religious moral codes don't go around kissing women they barely know. I don't think. And dammit, he saved me again while I wandered around like a sleepwalker. This is getting to be a really shitty habit, all this rescuing.*

She'd try not to hold it against him.

He couldn't know. Normal people don't faint when they smell a familiar perfume. He probably thought there was actually something wrong with you. Well, there's a lot wrong with you, but most of it's not physical.

Grace studied the width of his shoulders as he walked in front of them, a guardsman scouting for danger. The white cloak belled out, hiding anything below it, but his shoulders...*Muscles on top of muscles, as Marguerite said. Huh.*

Surely there was no harm in looking, so long as she didn't get her hopes up.

They rounded the curve in the corridor and Grace forgot all about shoulders, hopes, muscles or anything else.

A man lay on the floor in a puddle of blood. His neck was at a grotesque angle, propped up against the wall, but the tabard of the Archon's personal guard was clearly visible. Another man—a boy, really—was slumped against a doorframe set in the wall, staring down at the dead body. He'd wrapped his arms tightly around himself and his eyes were huge.

He looked up at the three of them, focused on Stephen, and said, "I didn't mean to do it!"

CHAPTER 13

Grace half-expected Stephen to draw his sword and charge. It was the sort of thing that swordsmen did, didn't they? It seemed that she was mistaken, because he did nothing of the sort. Instead he spread his hands out at waist height and said, "No one's blaming you, lad."

His voice was gentle and understanding, as if there wasn't a dead body on the floor next to them. Grace stared at the back of his head, astonished. Marguerite's face was absolutely blank.

"I didn't mean to!" said the boy, his voice cracking into a sob.

"I know," said Stephen kindly. "Can you tell me what happened? We'll get this sorted out, never fear."

He took several steps forward as he talked, hands still held out.

"I've made such a mess of it," sobbed the boy. "I was only supposed to knock him out, they told me just to hit him on the head, I didn't have to kill him, I didn't *want* to kill him, nobody was *actually* supposed to get killed!"

"No, of course not," said Stephen. He was beside the body now. The boy slid partway down the wall, as if his knees would no longer hold him, and Stephen crouched down, as if it was perfectly normal to have a conversation over a corpse. "Hitting people in the head is tricky though, isn't it?"

"*Yes.*" The boy stuffed a knuckle in his mouth. His next few words were mumbled and Grace couldn't make them out, but Stephen nodded. He reached out and patted the boy carefully on the shoulder, as if he was soothing a nervous horse.

"Now start at the beginning," said Stephen, still in that gentle, trustworthy voice.

Marguerite made a small, appreciative noise under her breath.

"I was just supposed to knock him out," repeated the boy miserably. "So he wouldn't raise the alarm. Then I'd go through the door and...and..."

"Nobody was supposed to get killed," said Stephen. "So you weren't going to actually attack anyone."

The boy nodded. "I'm not a killer," he said, ignoring the evidence to the contrary at his feet. "The guards would stop me. The guards would..."

His gaze slowly traveled over Stephen and froze, staring at the paladin's chest. Grace tried to remember what had been on Stephen's chest when she'd had her face mashed against it.

Sigil of the Saint of Steel. Of course.

"Shit," breathed the boy. "Shit, shit, shit. You're one of the filthy Rat's heretics. You're...and you saw me...and I killed..."

"Easy—" Stephen began, but the boy wasn't listening. He jumped up, grabbing for something at his side.

Grace's first thought was that he was going for a weapon. Then the boy's hand went to his mouth, and she knew it was something worse.

"Poison!" she tried to shout. It came out as a squeak.

Stephen lunged, grabbing for the younger man, trying to slap him on the back of the head to make him spit it out, but it was too late.

"There," said the boy. "There. Now you can't...can't make me..."

He trailed off, looking confused. His eyebrows drew together and his legs buckled under him. Stephen lowered him gently to the floor. Blood leaked over his lower lip.

"It hurts," the boy said, sounding baffled. "They said it wouldn't hurt."

"Go for help," said Stephen. "I'll stay with him."

Marguerite shook her head. "There's nothing that will help," she said. "I'm sorry."

"What? How do you know?"

"I know."

Grace caught his eye and said quietly, "She knows these things."

"You could slit his throat if you want to do it faster," said Marguerite in a detached voice. "But he was dead the moment he took the poison."

"...hurts..."

Stephen inhaled sharply, then nodded once. "Shh," he said, holding the boy's head against his shoulder. "I'm here. You're not alone."

The young man's death throes took less than five minutes. Whatever he had taken, it was fast and ugly. Grace had to look away as he convulsed, blood and foam running down his chin, and felt ashamed for not being able to watch.

This is terrible. I am terrible. If he's dying, I should be able to...he's human, I should...I should do something.

She knew that watching or not watching wouldn't make a damn bit of difference, and yet it felt like failure. She covered her eyes, feeling useless and broken, but she could not stop her ears, hearing his gasping breath as he died.

His last coherent words were, "I'm sorry, mother."

"It's all right," said Stephen, in that terribly kind voice. He kept his hand across the would-be assassin's forehead, gently wiping the sweaty hair out of his face. "It's all right." It wasn't all right, and would never be, but something in Grace's gut wanted desperately to believe him.

It seemed impossible to her that no one would come to see the commotion, but the crowd noises on the other side of the wall must have drowned out their voices. It seemed equally impossible that no one could *smell* the blood and urine and the harsh, flat scent of poisoned saliva, but Grace had learned long ago that most people could not.

A minute later, Stephen set the dead assassin on the ground and rose to his feet. "Damn," he said softly. "Damn it all to hell."

"You couldn't have saved him," said Marguerite. "They make the poison out of blowfish livers, and put it in a blown glass pill so it cuts the mouth and gets into the blood right away. The minute the poor bastard bit down, it was over."

"You seem to know a great deal about poison, madam," said Stephen, his blue eyes going chill.

Marguerite shrugged.

"What do we do?" said Grace, hurrying to smooth the moment over. The smell of death was in her nostrils now, foul and coppery. "We've got to tell someone—he was going after the Archon, wasn't he?"

"We have to tell someone," Stephen agreed. "But damned if I know who. I recognized him."

"*What?*" said Marguerite and Grace together.

"He was in the Motherhood's guard train earlier. Looked like he was about to be sick. Now we know why."

"Why would the Motherhood want the Archon dead?" asked Grace, baffled.

"No idea. Aaaannnnd...you're going through his pockets. I see."

"An assassin as incompetent as he was is bound to have evidence on him," said Marguerite briskly, checking the corpse with practiced ease. She lifted his hand and frowned at the fingers. His fingertips had gone red-violet, probably from the poison. She relieved him of a signet ring, muttering, then pulled a sheaf of papers out of his vest, flipped through them, and shook her head. "The gods have mercy."

"Evidence?" asked Grace.

"Too much and the wrong kind." She glanced at Stephen. "I'm taking these."

"Are you?"

Marguerite stood up, facing him over the pair of bodies. She started to turn away, holding the papers, and his hand shot out and grabbed her wrist.

"And where do you plan to take those?"

Despite the difference in their heights, Marguerite stared up at him without a trace of fear. "Somewhere safe."

Grace tried to get between them, which was useless because there was a dead body in the way. She grabbed Stephen's arm in both hands, hoping to pull him back, which was equally useless. She might as well have been hauling on a bar of iron.

"Let her *go*," she said, hating how weak and useless her voice sounded.

To her profound astonishment, he obeyed. A flash of embarrassment crossed his face and he dropped his hand.

"I am not your enemy, paladin," said Marguerite.

Stephen's eyes moved over her face, then to Grace. "No," he said finally, still looking at Grace. "No, I don't believe you are. Which makes me wonder who exactly *is*."

"That is what we're going to find out." She shoved the papers into her jacket. "Give us a few minutes to get moving before you raise the alarm. Come to Grace's shop later, we'll talk this out. My intentions, believe it or not, are good."

Stephen inclined his head. "I'll do that."

It occurred to Grace that she was still clutching his forearm, and she released him.

Marguerite put her arm around Grace's shoulders as if she were a chick to be sheltered under a wing. "Come on. We'll have to go out past Vance, I'm afraid."

"Vance?" said Grace. "Oh...right." It seemed like hours had passed since she'd heard the woman's voice. It all seemed so stupid now, with two dead bodies in front of her. What did she care if Phillip had cheated on her? She was alive, wasn't she? And maybe she'd been stupid, but not as stupid as this poor dumb boy who'd killed himself. She wished that she could convince her traitorous memory so easily.

Marguerite led her away. Grace cast one look over her shoulder, and saw the paladin standing there, the dead at his feet, watching them go.

CHAPTER 14

Stephen waited until the women had vanished around the corner and then gave them a dozen more heartbeats to get to the door. It tore at him to let Grace go without him, as fragile as she had seemed, but she had her assistant who clearly knew...well, a great deal more than one would expect about assassins and their poisons.

She didn't seem particularly fragile when she was shouting at you to let her friend go. And what good would having you hovering over her do, anyway?

He grimaced. Perhaps it was simply a desire to save *someone*, since he'd failed so spectacularly with the young man.

He'd used the paladin's voice, the one they all learned. The calm, kind, trustworthy one, the brother's voice, the father's voice, the one that got under people's skins and soothed them until they were willing to listen, and once they were listening, to get them the hell out of the way before the killing started. The Saint of Steel's followers weren't particularly known for it—not like the Dreaming God's paladins, who had honed their voices into weapons that controlled demons—but they could all still do it. People *listened* to that voice. It was as useful a weapon in its way as swords.

It had almost worked, too. But then the youngster had stopped listening, and it had only taken a moment for everything to slip. And then it was only poison and death and dying and now he was standing here with a pair of corpses, about to sound the alarm.

Stephen took a deep breath, squared his shoulders, and hammered on the door.

Two hours later, Stephen was finally released back to Bishop Beartongue. The Motherhood people didn't like it, but they also didn't have any authority to keep him there. It strained even their credibility to claim that Stephen had shoved a poisoned pill into an assassin's mouth and then banged on the door to alert the Archon's guards. Paladins were, by and large, considered above reproach, and as the Hanged Mother took no paladins of her own, it was very difficult for them to argue the point.

One had started down the road about the Saint of Steel's paladins being known for berserker fits and killing rages, but Stephen had looked down his nose and said, "Did I poison him before or after I started frothing at the mouth and gnawing on my shield, do you think?" and the objection faded quickly. He was grateful for that. He had not felt even a trace of the battle tide when confronting that poor, stupid child, but it was very difficult to argue that you were completely in control when any indignation whatsoever made you look the very opposite.

The Archon himself had been coolly grateful. Stephen was careful not to mention that he had seen the young man earlier, in the Motherhood's guards. He had a feeling that he would not have been going back to the Temple of the Rat so easily after dropping that particular tidbit.

"Well," said the bishop, as Stephen fell immediately into the honor guard position, two steps back and to her left. "I tell you to go talk to a girl and you foil an assassination attempt. I'm a little frightened to think what might happen if I told you to go get laid."

Stephen muttered something between clenched teeth.

"Would the city survive, do you think?"

"Gnnnrrrghhh."

"That's '*gnnnrrrghhh, Your Holiness,*' to you."

"Sorry."

"Don't mention it. Did you get to talk to the girl?"

"Yes."

"Well, then the evening wasn't completely wasted."

They cleared the first set of corridors toward the palace courtyard. Bishop Beartongue glanced over her shoulder at him. "I got the official report, of course. How much did you leave out?"

"A lot."

"Then we'll wait until we're in the carriage, shall we?"

"Where are Shane and Istvhan?" asked Stephen, glancing around for the absent paladins. "They shouldn't have left you alone."

"For some odd reason, the Archon got very peculiar about letting other people's guards into his presence. They're in the outer palace."

Well, he could see that. Still... "You shouldn't have come alone."

"Yes, I hear there's assassins about."

"Not very good ones."

"Sometimes that's what you want in an assassin. But we should wait for that talk, too."

They reached the outer palace. Two grim-faced guards waved them through the door. Istvhan and Shane descended upon them immediately, snapping into formation around Beartongue. Istvhan took point, hand on his sword.

"Stand down, Istvhan, there isn't rioting in the halls."

"If there is, we will be prepared," growled Istvhan, looking rather less friendly than usual.

Bishop Beartongue had to reach up to smack him on the back of the head, but she did it anyway. It was a measure of Istvhan's training that he took the blow without breaking stride.

They crowded into the carriage and Stephen watched the palace pulling away through the window. Beartongue leaned forward. "So. Talk."

Stephen delivered as detailed an account of the evening as he could, divided into two parts that he mentally labeled "What I Told The Archon" and "What I Did Not Tell The Archon."

"You're sure it was the same boy?" said Istvhan.

Stephen nodded. "He'd changed out of the Motherhood tabard, but it was him. Believe me, I spent long enough looking at him while..."

He trailed off. Shane gripped his shoulder in silent sympathy.

The bishop sighed and leaned back, looking older than her usual fierce middle-age. "It's a hard world when people are sending children to do their dirty work." She shook her head. "But that's the sort of thing we're here to stop. So. Thoughts, gentlemen?"

"He was never meant to succeed," said Istvhan. "What was it he said—no one was supposed to get killed? A very young assassin might still panic over killing the wrong man, mind you, but not like that."

"Agreed," said the Bishop. "Now. What is the point of a fake assassination attempt?"

"To make the Archon afraid," said Shane.

"Or to cause such a mess that his guest changes his mind about the trade deal," said Istvhan.

Stephen had almost forgotten the Crown Prince. He nodded. "He did not seem like a man who would be patient with weakness."

"No, he didn't, did he?" said the Bishop. "Which, if that's the reason, could point to a motive. Archenhold has been a thorn in Anuket City's side since...well, since the founding. They'd probably be delighted to see the trade deal falter, particularly since Charlock would then come to them."

"They've got a better port anyway," said Istvhan. Anuket City and Archenhold were both set on two tributaries of the same river, which came together and flowed southeastward toward the sea. Anuket City just happened to have the larger tributary, a fact that Archenhold never, ever forgot.

"Yes, but they'll make Charlock pay through the nose for the privilege of using it," said the Bishop. She drummed her fingers on her knee. "Other possibilities?"

"He came in with the Motherhood," said Shane. "To humiliate them?"

"They were certainly not amused," said Istvhan. "Although I suppose it could be because he was caught. Did you tell the Archon that you recognized the lad?"

"And paint a giant indigo target on my back?" said Stephen. "No. The Archon's religious advisor was already trying to cast polite doubts upon my character."

"You're a *paladin*," said Shane.

"Of an order which ran mad not long ago," said Stephen. Both Shane and Istvhan winced, but didn't argue.

They sat in silence for a moment, then Shane offered, "All the Motherhood men seemed jumpy all night."

"Yeah, but they're always jumpy," grumbled Istvhan. "Moreso than usual?"

Shane gave this his full, grave consideration. "I don't know," he said finally. "I think perhaps, but I am remembering it after the fact, and I may be changing it in my head. I do not think my opinion is trustworthy in this."

Which was a very Shane thing to say, thought Stephen. Constant, sincere awareness of his own fallibility made him a good paladin and a good warrior, but it was also frustrating when you were trying to dredge answers up out of a handful of observations and a little certainty would have gone a long way.

"Could it have been one of theirs? But why would the Motherhood want to assassinate the Archon?" asked Istvhan. "Or fail to assassinate the Archon? He practically lives in their hip pocket."

"He'd install their Archimandrite as state spiritual advisor in a heartbeat," said the Bishop. "If he thought the political consequences wouldn't outweigh the trouble." She smiled humorlessly. Stephen knew, both from his old life and his few years with the Rat, that a distressing amount of time was spent with the other temples arranging those political consequences. "No, they can't have meant to assassinate the Archon. His successor is nowhere near so sympathetic to their cause."

"Could they have wished to frighten the Archon?" asked Shane diffidently. "Put him in fear of his life and mortal soul, so that he gives their cause more weight?"

"Possible," said the Bishop. She tapped her fingernail against her teeth. "Very possible. And also possible that they meant to have their own men be seen to stop the assassin, thereby gaining even more of the Archon's favor."

Istvhan whistled. "Risky," he said.

Stephen thought of the poor, stupid young man who had died in his arms. "Very," he said. "There was no chance that child would ever get near the Archon. But they risked a great deal if they sent him, because if someone had prevented him from killing himself, he would have spilled his guts before an interrogator ever laid a finger on him."

"Too many questions," said the Bishop wearily. "I wish I could see those papers that this Marguerite woman took. What do you think of her, Stephen?"

"A woman with her own agenda."

"Trustworthy?"

I am not your enemy, paladin. "I have no idea. I do not think she actively opposes us, but I also do not know that I am a good enough judge of character or politics to make that decision."

The Bishop nodded, accepting this judgment. "I will have someone find the location of the shop for you," she said.

He blinked at her. "Ah...I assumed you would send someone to meet with Marguerite and Mistress Angelica." He felt a pang that he would not be seeing her, but this was a political matter and it needed someone reliable to handle it.

"I will," said Beartongue, leaning back against the cushions. "I'm sending you."

He stared at her, but she'd closed her eyes and was pointedly ignoring him.

"Your holiness, you have diplomats, lawyers, priests..."

"I do," she said. "And a few paladins, too."

"But I am hardly qualified! I swing swords and look imposing. That's what I'm *for.*"

"You also have a passing acquaintance with both these women. That qualifies you as much as anyone else."

"But—"

"Here you go again," rumbled Istvhan. "How remarkably hare-hearted you've become. Do you need me to beat you a few times until you find your courage?"

"You and what army?"

Istvhan grinned. Stephen rubbed his hand over his face. Why did no one understand? He knitted socks and stood guard over things. He wasn't a diplomat. "Truly, Bishop, I'm a poor choice. I was a god-touched soldier. Now I'm not even that. You have people so much more qualified than I am."

"For a formerly god-touched soldier, you've done remarkably well so far. You foiled a plot, comforted the dying, kept out of the hands of the Motherhood, and convinced someone who is most likely a spy for Anuket City to meet with you."

"Dumb luck."

"Then run your luck's length," said Beartongue.

Stephen heard the sound of the carriage wheels change as they pulled off the cobbled street and into the graveled courtyard of the Temple of the Rat, and knew that his fate was sealed. He inclined his head. "Very well, then. With your permission, your Holiness."

"Granted."

CHAPTER 15

Grace woke up a little before noon with her head splitting. She would have just rolled over to go back to bed, but Tab was sitting on her chest making *mrr-rr-r-r-r-ch!* noises. This meant that he wanted either love or food. Probably food.

Grace groaned and rolled out of bed. The civette bounced around her feet while she shoved her arms into a dressing gown. Her head felt like a civil war was occurring in its depths.

I didn't even drink last night. What...oh. Right. Lady Vance.

She grimaced. The memory fugue she'd gone into was probably the cause of her headache. An attack like that was rare, particularly these days, but when one hit, it often wiped her out completely, sometimes for a whole day afterward. It was so bloody unfair, being so exhausted by something she didn't want in the first place. As if her memory had decided to horsewhip her, and then turned around and charged her body for the privilege.

Stupid mind. Stupid Lady Vance. Stupid Phillip.

Stupid me for believing him in the first place.

There were hard-boiled eggs left over in the kitchen from yesterday's lunch. Grace grabbed one and set it down for Tab. The civette grabbed it, chirping happily, and galloped off with it. Eventually she'd find a pile of eggshell, probably in her bed, but she just didn't have the energy to deal with it right now.

Her brain let her contemplate her own breakfast egg for a few minutes, then casually shoved the image of the dead assassin in front of her. She nearly jammed her thumb into the yolk.

Oh. Yes. That. A normal person would probably have remembered that first. Your priorities are all wrong.

She grimly choked down the egg. Well. She'd witnessed a murder. Or a suicide, anyway, over top of a murder. What a thing to get mixed up in.

I'm not mixed up in it. I'm not. I just saw it. I didn't do anything. They can't arrest me for seeing something.

This did not settle the little voice in her head, or the gnawing anxiety farther down that said, *This is it this is what ends it all life has been too easy for too long now it all ends and everything will be taken away from you...*

Tea, she told herself grimly. *Tea will fix this. Or at least it will fix something.*

Grace picked up the tea kettle and went into the workshop. Firing up the stove for a cup of tea was a waste, when the brazier for steam distilling would work just as well, and a whole lot faster. She lit the brazier and set the teakettle over it. Her notebook lay open on the table from where she'd been making notes on the Crown Prince's perfume. She glanced over at it, hoping that she'd still be able to read her own handwriting in a week, when someone coughed behind her.

It was an apologetic cough, the sort that advertises that the owner is standing there and would like to be noticed, but also that they don't wish to put anyone out.

Grace jumped, whipped around, and threw herself back against the table with a yelp.

The paladin was standing in the doorway.

The paladin. Stephen.

It all came back to her so quickly that she reeled as if another attack of memory was coming on.

"I'm sorry!" he said. "I didn't mean to startle you...your friend said to come here and...oh god, you're on fire."

Grace looked down. Her sleeve had trailed through the brazier and was indeed smoking merrily. She slapped it out, grumbling. Fire at least held no terror for her. She'd burnt herself far too many times distilling and smoking and steaming things.

Well, at least he didn't have to save you from burning to death, on top of everything else.

"This was my favorite dressing gown," she muttered. It was also her only dressing gown but he didn't need to know that.

She was aware, yanking it tighter around herself and belting it more securely, that he'd probably seen a bit more than he'd expected. *Great. Wonderful. First you grind on him like a wanton, then you swoon all over him, now you're giving him a show. This is going marvelously. What's next, tripping and falling on his cock on accident?*

Well, it was his own damn fault for breaking in when she wasn't expecting anyone.

Speaking of... "How did you get in?" she demanded.

"The front door was unlocked."

"What? But I always lock it!"

He lifted his hands. "It was wide open. There was a closed sign in the window, but I thought maybe you were expecting someone, and then I worried that somebody might try to steal something if I left, and since your assistant told me to come here..."

Grace narrowed her eyes. "How long have you been here?"

"About four hours."

She stared at him.

"Well, I didn't want to disturb you," he said sheepishly. "I could hear you snoring, so...um...it's not like I could just go into your bedroom."

"No," said Grace wearily. "No, of course not. So you've been sitting out there the whole time?"

"I read your sample book," said Stephen.

Grace made a mental note that Stephen was literate, which not everyone was. Were paladins expected to be?

Well, they have to read prayer books, don't they? Hymnals or something like that? Why am I worried about a paladin's reading materials when I left the front door unlocked last night?

"And then I knitted," he added.

She paused in mid-fret. "Knitted?"

"Socks," he said. "I knit socks. I am a sock knitter. Person. Who knits. Mostly socks."

They stared at each other, then both looked away again immediately.

"I always lock the door," she repeated, mostly to herself. "Always."

"It was a very busy night," said Stephen. "I'm not sure I remembered to take my shoes off when I got home."

"Yes, but..." She bit her lower lip. There was no way to explain to a relative stranger that she always locked it, that locking it meant this was *her* space and not anyone else's and once she turned the key, the world was on the other side and couldn't get at her.

Well, except for Marguerite and Tab, and they didn't count. They were both on her side. At least, Marguerite was, and Tab was as long as she fed him. She wondered if the paladin thought he was on her side too.

Her first response to this thought was a rush of warmth, which was smothered almost immediately by irritation. *A knight in shining armor rides to the rescue of the helpless maiden...again...damn it all to hell.*

Rescue was bad. People who wanted you to be vulnerable and grateful tended to get very angry when you stopped being vulnerable and didn't act grateful enough. Grace had been rescued twice in her life and both times, she'd have been better off keeping her head down and staying put. She grimaced. This was a horribly awkward conversation to have, particularly at this hour, but the sooner it was over, the better. "Look, I don't need you to keep rescuing me," she said.

The paladin looked blank.

"Last night. I know I was...ah...indisposed, but Marguerite could have helped me. I didn't need rescuing. I mean, I'm very *grateful* for your help, it was very kind, but I don't want you to think that I..."

She trailed off. His blank look had, if anything, gotten blanker.

"Um," he said.

"Err," he said.

"Ah," he said.

Finally, addressing the ceiling and not meeting her eyes, he said, "I'm actually here about the papers your friend took from the dead boy. She, um, told me to come here today."

Grace was glad that he was looking at the ceiling, because she could feel the blood in her cheeks and knew she had to have turned beet red. *Of course that's why he's here. What were you thinking? He wasn't here for you. You watched a man die in front of you last night, how egotistical are you that you think a paladin would come here for any other reason than that?*

"Marguerite's not here," she said, turning away to hide her embarrassment. *Fat chance of that. They can probably see you blushing clear to Anuket City.* "I mean, she went out last night and she certainly would have locked up if she'd come back. You could try back later, I suppose."

"Will she be coming back?"

Grace blinked at him. "Well, she lives here."

"Oh. Um. I thought this was where you lived." He went suddenly a bit pink. "Err...that's not to say she *couldn't* live here. With you. Also." He went back to studying the ceiling with sudden intensity.

Oh gods, now he thinks Marguerite and I are lovers. Meanwhile, the only thing I've been sharing a bed with for the last three years is Tab. As if the thought had summoned him, her pet strolled into the workroom and made a beeline for Stephen, making his new-person-to-pet-me chirp.

"What the devil is *that?*" said Stephen, staring.

"Oh, that's just Tab. He's a civette."

"A what?"

"A civette." Grace leaned back against the table, watching the weasel-cat circle Stephen's ankles. "Domestic civet cat. Civet—the perfume—comes from the musk glands of civet cats, but you have to keep them in cages and they don't live very long. It's really quite awful. So somebody got the idea to breed them and make a tame civet cat, which would produce a lot more civet than the wild ones."

Stephen raised his eyebrow as Tab decided to make himself comfortable on the paladin's boot.

"Anyway, my...former partner...got the bright idea that we'd breed civettes ourselves. Swore he had a connection that would get him one and that it would make our fortune. So he spent a great deal of money on Tab." Grace grimaced.

And there is an understatement for the ages. Months without enough money to heat our rooms, working by rush-light because we couldn't afford lamp oil.

"I take it that it didn't go well?" said Stephen gently, leaning down to pet Tab's head.

"No. Tab's a cull. He'd been castrated. No one would sell an intact civette. And he was culled because he hardly produces any civet at all." Grace shook her head. "Phillip was so angry when he found out he'd been cheated. I thought he'd kill Tab in a rage, but I convinced him that even a tiny bit of civet a month would save us money in the long run."

And there is another understatement. Phillip had never beaten her, but there had been a moment, throwing herself over the frightened civette, that she had expected to feel a blow land. But his carefully curated self-image would not allow him to actually strike a woman, so he'd shouted and finally stormed out, and Grace had kept the little animal out of his sight for weeks until his temper had cooled.

"So he does produce a little?"

"Ah..." Grace coughed. "Well..."

Stephen cocked his head, clearly puzzled. Grace sighed. This was not a conversation she really wanted to have with a man that she found attractive, but it wasn't like the morning could get any worse. "Once a month," she said, "I take a clean handkerchief and squeeze his arse with it."

The paladin's eyes went wide and he froze in mid-petting. Tab made a small, grumpy chirp and leaned into the man's hand.

"It's that or they get impacted," she said grimly. *Oh gods. A normal person would have just said "Yes" and left it there. What is wrong with me?* "And then he's miserable and scooting on the floor and there's a stink like you wouldn't believe." *Aaaand I'm still talking about my pet's butt to a man I barely know. Well done, me.*

"Perfume making is clearly a very glamorous occupation," said Stephen. "I had no idea." His voice was grave, but his eyes were dancing. "Do you have a musk deer lurking in the back room as well?"

"No," said Grace. "Nor do I keep a cachalot whale in the bathtub so that I can tickle its throat so it vomits ambergris on command."

"And no tame beavers to provide castoreum?"

"No, although that would save me a great deal of money." She smiled despite herself. "It's just Tab, I'm afraid. He produces less than I need, but I don't use very much civet in my perfumes. And he is a very good mouser as well, which is something."

Stephen nodded. Grace started to say something else, and then the tea kettle whistled, which made her jump all over again, although at least this time she didn't set herself on fire.

"Would you like some tea?" she asked.

"That would be lovely," he said, straightening. "And very kind. I realize I'm intruding terribly, but...well...after last night..." He lifted his hands again in a helpless gesture.

"I know," said Grace. She could feel her cheeks heating again. "Marguerite told you to come. I'm surprised she isn't here, but I'm sure she'll turn up."

Stephen coughed. "Will she? I mean no disrespect, but she did not seem at all at a loss for what to do with a dead body. Or an assassin. Having taken what she wished from the body, I wondered if she might...ah...have sudden pressing business elsewhere?"

This took Grace a moment to parse out, as she found her teapot and poured the hot water into it, along with a handful of tea leaves. "You think she's just going to skip town because somebody tried to kill the Archon in front of her? But she had nothing to do with it!"

"I'm not suggesting that she did."

"Good," said Grace, glaring at him. "Because if you had, you wouldn't get any honey in your tea."

He had the decency to look abashed. Grace stomped into the kitchen, looking for a cup that was clean enough for company. She was annoyed, mostly with herself. They'd been laughing together about civet like everything was normal, and meanwhile he was secretly suspecting her best friend of running off into the night and leaving her to answer questions about an assassination.

Are you quite sure that she hasn't?

Shut up, shut up, shut up!

Marguerite wouldn't betray her. She wouldn't. Grace knew that. Grace *believed* that. Even if her friend was a spy who made her living getting people to trust her, it was...well, it was *different.*

She gave up, washed out a cup, scowled into it, belted her dressing gown even more tightly, and stalked back into the work-room. Stephen hadn't moved, but then, Tab was still on his foot. Grace took pity on him, although she wasn't sure that he deserved it, and scooped the limp civette up.

"I didn't want to disturb him."

"It's fine. Once he's asleep, nothing wakes him up." She set Tab down on a stack of books, where he would undoubtedly wake up in an hour and cause havoc, then poured tea for both of them. "So what happened last night after we left?"

There was a lock of hair that threatened to fall down into Stephen's eyes. He blew out his breath, making it jump. "About what you would expect. I banged on the door until the Archon's guards let me in—which took a lot longer than it should have—and told them there were dead men in the hallway. They hustled the Archon and the Crown Prince out under guard and I got interrogated for two hours about what I'd seen."

"I bet the Crown Prince loved that," said Grace, thinking of the fierce, amused man who had insisted she rub scent on his wrist.

"I don't really know. I didn't see him again." Stephen frowned. "The Bishop didn't mention anything, but I suspect once she knew that I was in custody, she had other things to concern her."

"They didn't suspect you, did they?"

"They would have liked to." Stephen's lips quirked. "It would have been very tidy. But not even the Hanged Motherhood's representative —who was not at all happy to see me—could make himself believe in a paladin assassin knocking on the door and telling them there were bodies in the hall."

"Did you tell them about us?" Grace realized a moment too late that *us* could be taken too many ways and added, "I mean, Marguerite and I being there."

"I said that I'd stepped back into the hall to assist a lady who needed a moment of air when I heard a commotion," he said. "And that she and her companion had presumably returned to the party, and that I had not been introduced to her."

Grace realized that she was still holding two teacups and handed one to Stephen. Their hands touched as he took it, the callused pads of his fingers sliding over the backs of hers, and she realized with a start that he wasn't wearing gloves. The touch felt strangely intimate. Grace felt a blush starting and pulled away.

This is stupid. You just handed him a teacup, that's all. My god, you've climbed the man like a tree and screamed in his ear and fainted on him and made a fool of yourself thinking he wanted to talk to you about something other than the dead man, and now you're blushing over this?

Yes. Apparently she was.

Gods above and below and somewhere in the middle, why *did he have to smell like gingerbread?*

"Look," she said, stepping back, "I've got some work to get done still. I don't know when she'll be back, but you can keep waiting if you want to."

"If I will not disturb you," he said.

"No, it's fine," said Grace automatically, even though it wasn't. She never liked having other people in the workshop, except Marguerite, who didn't ask things like "What are you doing?" and "Is that perfume?" and "Isn't that hot?" Phillip had been worse. He would come in and fiddle with things and move them around and correct her technique. She'd been on her own for nearly a year before her shoulders stopped going up around her ears whenever another person entered the room. But to his credit, Stephen did none of these things. He glanced around, noted the lack of a second stool, then lowered himself to the floor, back to the wall, booted legs stretched out in front. Grace watched out of the corner of her eye as he pulled out his knitting and set to work.

She turned back to the worktable. She really did have things to do this morning, mostly compounding scents. It was delicate work with pipettes and droppers and strips of paper, although all the recipes were fairly basic and she had worked out the details long since. The only sounds in the workshop were the almost inaudible click and slide of the needles and the soft clink of glass. Occasionally she would turn a page in one of her journals, double checking a recipe, or he would lift the teacup and drink and set it back down. Once or twice he started counting under his breath, staring at the sock with intense concentration.

It was strangely peaceful. To share a space with another person who was absorbed in their own work, but still present, still *there*... gods, how long had it been? Phillip certainly never sat still that long, always talking or poking or demanding interaction. Not since her apprenticeship, on the rare days when her master was in a decent mood. Perhaps even before then, when she was at the foundling home, when she would read in companionable silence with another girl. She had only the blurriest memory of those days, mostly the smell of floor wax, but surely there was the smell of books as well.

Of all the things she would have expected of paladins, being easy with silence was not among them.

CHAPTER 16

"Cozy," said Marguerite, strolling into the workshop an hour later.

"I did not hear you come in," said Stephen.

"No, you didn't, did you?"

Grace watched the paladin's lips form a complicated line, as if he was hiding either a smile or a frown and wasn't quite sure which.

"Marguerite is always very quiet," said Grace, amused.

"When I wish to be, yes. Sometimes it's better to make a great deal of noise so that people know you're coming."

Stephen rose to his feet, putting his knitting away and drawing on his gloves. She had forgotten how large he was, and how much smaller the workshop got when he was standing in it. She had to get past him to the door, which involved both of them turning sideways and apologizing. Her nose still nearly brushed his chest.

Gods, there was a lot of chest there. And shoulders.

"I'm glad you're here," she said to Marguerite, trying to hide her reaction. "Can you—er—pour more tea or something while I change?"

"Certainly," said Marguerite, ignoring the fact that there were only two teacups. There was a gleam in her eye that made Grace think that her friend was quite aware of the effect the paladin was having on her. Fortunately, Stephen himself seemed oblivious.

Grace hurried into her room, pulled off the singed dressing gown and dragged on a long tunic and skirt. She glanced at herself in the small metal mirror, realized that she had been talking to Stephen with a smudge of ash across her forehead and grit crusted at the corner of her eye, looked at her hair, looked away, wondered why she cared, and then took the extra two minutes to wash her face and scrape her hair into an approximation of tidiness.

When she returned, Marguerite and Stephen were watching each other the way that her neighbor's cat sometimes watched strange cats in the alley. *Are we going to fight? I don't want to fight, but if you start it, I will finish it.*

Grace's money was on Marguerite to do the finishing, if it came to that. She hoped it didn't. She really hoped it didn't.

Stop. It doesn't matter. He's a paladin, for god's sake. Or at least a knight, now that his god's dead. You're...well, you. If Marguerite tears him in half for the good of Anuket City, that's just life.

"Let's do this in the front room," said Marguerite. "Grace, I love you dearly but if we spend too long in this workshop, you'll get oils and powders on my evidence, assuming I don't lose it in the pile."

"That's fine," said Grace. She felt better having them in the front room anyway. Having the paladin in her workshop when he wasn't also working made her feel exposed, as if he would judge her for the piles of clutter and the places she'd spilled ingredients.

Normal people clean up their workshops occasionally, they don't just pile everything up until the pile falls over and the weasel sleeps on it.

Marguerite fanned the papers out on the table and sat back. "Do you read?" she asked Stephen.

"Well enough."

"Then here is our evidence. We have a signet ring and these papers." She held up the ring. "This is a marker for Anuket City's senate. If you have this ring, you are allowed into the Senate building, and it can be used to place letters under official seal. They are easy to come by and easy to forge, and I suspect I don't need to tell you that they're not the sort of thing an assassin wears to work."

Grace frowned and picked up the ring. It was heavy and had a bright, new look to it. "It didn't fit him either, did it?"

"No."

She weighed the ring in her hand. "How easily could someone come by one, if they wanted?"

"I've got three upstairs," said Marguerite.

Stephen lifted his eyes to Marguerite's face and Grace thought of the cats watching each other again.

She isn't hiding the fact she's a spy from him. Interesting.

Stephen stripped off his leather gauntlets and picked up the papers. His hands were large and scarred with dozens of small cuts across the backs. Grace looked down at her own nimble fingers, at the network of irregular scars from burns and the thick pad of callus on her index finger, where she had never quite learned not to check the temperature of something by touching it.

"Do you work for Anuket City, then?" asked Stephen, looking at Marguerite over the top of the papers.

Marguerite raised her eyebrows. "Subtle, aren't you?"

"My order was never particularly known for its delicacy."

"Let us say that I work for a body of individuals with certain political interests that occasionally align with Anuket City's. Even when Anuket City does not, themselves, appreciate that fact."

"Hmm," said Stephen. Not a negative sound, merely a neutral one. He looked over the papers. "These are certainly incriminating."

"To the point of parody," said Marguerite. "No one gives assassins a contract in writing like that."

He glanced at Grace, and she felt an urge to defend her friend, if not her friend's employers. "I've never hired an assassin, but perfumers are also...um....very secretive." *You think you'll steal my secrets, girl? I'll cut your tongue out—pour hot lead into your nostrils—see how you fare then!*

The memory fugue of the night before was too close. She had to push this memory away before the edges of her vision turned to firelight. The smell of the old man's cologne filled her nostrils: nutmeg, star anise, citrus, heart note of jasmine, cinnamon and heliotrope, base note cedar, ambergris and musk. A smell she could duplicate easily and never would.

"I imagine they are," said Stephen politely. She blinked at him, thinking, *What? What is he talking about?* and dragged the memory of the conversation back.

"Secretive," she said. "Yes. Perfumers steal each other's recipes constantly. But we still have to write things down, because it's impossible to remember everything. So we take steps to disguise what we're writing about."

He inched forward on the chair, clearly interested. He did not smell of ambergris and heliotrope, he smelled of gingerbread and iron. Grace had a strong urge to lean over and sniff him and squelched it.

"Mirror writing," she said. "But people know that one already, so we invent codes. My master referred to jasmine as 'sheep' and civet as 'cattle'. His recipes looked like an invoice for livestock. Even if you got ahold of one, you'd have to figure out all the references before you could use it." She reached out and tapped the papers in his hand. "Why didn't they do the same for this? It's much more important than perfume."

Stephen studied her face so carefully that Grace wanted to squirm in her chair. Finally he nodded, setting the papers down.

"You see?" said Marguerite. "It's much too blatant."

A thought struck Grace. "Is it so blatant that Anuket City might do it to throw people off the scent, though?"

Marguerite shot her a rueful look. "I admit, I was rather hoping you wouldn't think of that."

Stephen snorted and tossed her an approving glance. Grace resented how much that look warmed her, and how blue his eyes looked under the ironic curve of eyebrow.

"It's possible," admitted Marguerite. "It's not smart, but it's possible. But they'd have to hope it fell into the hands of someone like me."

"If the attack had gone a little farther, it would fall into the hands of the Archon's guards."

"And they might be smart enough," admitted Marguerite. "But you run a lot of risks with a trick like that. No good spy relies on people being smart."

"Relying on people being stupid seems equally dangerous," said Stephen dryly.

"You'd think so, wouldn't you?"

"I realize I spend most of my time locked in a workshop," said Grace, "but I think you can generally rely on people to be *inconvenient.*"

"See, there you go," said Marguerite. "You could have a great future as a spy."

"Or a paladin," rumbled Stephen.

Grace made a warding gesture at both of them.

"Gods, is it after noon already? I've got to meet someone," said Marguerite, glancing out the window. She rose to her feet. "I may have more news for you soon, paladin. Assuming you wish to have any more to do with this mess at all."

"I have not the least wish in the world to get mixed up in politics," said Stephen in his deep, solemn voice. "But as I seem to already be mixed up, there is no point in lamenting it. And the company, at least, is congenial."

He glanced at Grace when he said that last. She felt a blush coming on and told herself sternly that she had blushed enough for one day and there would be absolutely no more of that. As usual her skin did not listen to her in the slightest.

Marguerite vanished behind the room divider. Grace heard the door close and the creak of footsteps as she ran up the steps to her own room.

"I should go, too," said Stephen. "I did not expect to be gone so long. The bishop will be wondering if I've run afoul of the heads-man." He rose, looking down at her. His blue eyes had golden flecks in the light from the fire. "What scent did you give the Crown Prince?" he asked abruptly.

She looked up at him, surprised. "Amber and ginger," she said. "And some other things. It's easier to let you smell than to explain."

She turned away and found the jar that she had decanted the scent from. There was still some left in the jar, waiting to be labeled and placed in the library of her creations.

He met her eyes and stripped off the leather gauntlets he'd put back on. Grace told herself that it was completely her imagination that he was doing so very slowly. Then he extended his hand, palm up. She dabbed a spot of oil on her index finger and dragged it down across his wrist. His fingertips trembled almost imperceptibly against her palm.

Perhaps it wasn't her imagination after all.

She stepped back. He lifted his wrist and breathed in, then smiled at her. "I like that."

You inspired it, she didn't say aloud. *You and your maddening smell of gingerbread.* She tried to imagine how the amber perfume would interact with the gingerbread scent, would they clash or complement or... In polite society, one did not lean forward and sniff strange men. She would simply have to live with not knowing. Grace told herself this several times.

The paladin lifted a hand in farewell, still holding the leather glove in his other hand, and let himself out the door. Grace locked it behind him, then leaned against the wall. Her cheeks felt hot.

Why was she so knotted up about the man? It didn't make any sense. She had everything she wanted. She had friends and work and a pet that ate pillows and she made enough money that she didn't have to worry about whether she could replace the pillows Tab ate. Why couldn't she just ignore him?

Why was she so far gone that she'd actually thought he might have come back to talk to her because of who she was, and not because of what she'd seen?

Stupid, she told herself. *Being stupid. You don't want him and even if you do you shouldn't.*

And yet...and yet...

When he had taken off his leather gauntlets, she had looked at his hands. Really looked, not just a quick glance while handing him a teacup. All those narrow white scars across the backs and when she'd taken his hand to put the scent on his wrist, his sword calluses were rough bands against her palm.

What would they feel like across her skin? Was there any pleasure in them?

She snorted at her own thoughts. *What do you know about pleasure?*

Sharing Phillip's bed had involved some discomfort and a fair amount of boredom. He'd come to the conclusion at some point that he was a great lover and that all he had to do was swipe his tongue between a woman's legs to leave her gasping and grateful. Grace's attempts to explain that she didn't actually enjoy that very much had caused him to lay siege to her nightly, leaving her staring at the ceiling wishing he would just hurry up and finish his inexpert slobbering and let her go try to get some work done.

After a few weeks of this, when it became obvious even to Phillip that he wasn't getting anywhere, he called her a frigid cow and stormed out of the room.

It was not the first of their fights, nor the last. Grace had simply chalked it up to there being something deeply wrong with her, as she'd always suspected and Phillip had confirmed. One of the best things about her new life was that she didn't have to worry about her failings in bed.

And yet here she was, thinking about a man's hands. And, if she was being honest, rather more than his hands. She'd found herself with her face pressed into his chest twice now, and she'd be very interested to know what that was like without a layer of leather and mail between them.

All these sword-swingers have muscles on top of muscles...

You're an idiot, she told herself grimly. *You'll just leave another disappointed man in your wake. You should just step away from this whole mess before you break your own heart.*

Anyway, you're making a fool of yourself. He's not interested in you. He's here because of the attempted assassination you witnessed, nothing more. You're basically just a mail drop for Marguerite.

Hell, if Marguerite was in the room, there was no reason that any man would look at her twice. "Which I do not begrudge her!" she told Tab as she entered the workroom. "I'm not interested, and anyway, she is who she is, and it's her job to make men look at her, and she gets a lot more clammy-handed Squires than good-looking paladins who smell like gingerbread."

Tab said, "Mrrr?" and stretched.

"Precisely."

"Mrr."

"I don't even care if he comes back."

"Mrrr-rr-rr?"

"Really, I don't. I mean, he probably will because Marguerite told him to, but that's the only reason he would. I'll probably never see him again once they sort this mess out."

"Mrrr," said Tab, and rolled over and went back to sleep.

She opened the alchemist's tome and stabbed a finger at a random passage.

Let he who has wisdom make note of the signs: the flight of birds, the movement of beasts, the growth of plants, the pattern of fireflies, which often presage a great change in the earth and the hearts of men.

Grace looked over at Tab. The only movement, if it could be called such, was his paws twitching as he dreamed.

"Let's try that again," she said, flipping to another page.

A toxin prepared of the plant called wolfsbane and the root which is like unto wild carrot but having the name water hemlocke will void the bowels and paralyze a man even unto death. Yet this too may be cured, by taking a fowl and placing it against the feet of the afflicted and chanting certain prayers unto the Four-Faced God until the poison is drawn out into the fowl. Then let the same be buried in a deep place of the earth and not fed to dogs, for the flesh is unwholesome...

"I think I liked the movement of beasts better," said Grace. She gave up on the book as a bad job and went to clean up the workshop.

CHAPTER 17

Stephen stared at the ceiling of his room and sniffed at his wrist, at the increasingly faint smell of amber and ginger. And saffron. He couldn't smell the saffron. Had it worn off or was his nose not sensitive enough? For that matter, had the entire perfume worn off? Was he simply imagining that it still lingered?

Ah, yes, this is extremely normal behavior. Lay in bed and smell your arm and think about a woman who's made it clear she's not interested in what you have to offer.

He could still remember the flat, trapped look on her face when she said, "I don't need you to keep rescuing me."

What if I don't want to rescue you? What if I just want to talk to you because you make me laugh and you live in a jumble of vials and papers with a good-natured weasel and do interesting things? Fine, he *had* rescued her. Twice. It was a habit you got into when you were a paladin. It was the job. It wasn't like he meant to keep doing it.

A vision of her in the smoldering dressing gown teased at him. He'd seen the curve of her breast and he hadn't stared, he really hadn't, but once he'd seen that she wasn't on fire...well, it had made an impression. Generously made, probably more than a handful. He'd had an idea from the corset the night before, but would have liked the chance to investigate more closely.

Stop that. You would not.

Well, yes, he would, but it wouldn't be a good idea. It would get... complicated. Lust was too close to passion and passion was much too dangerous when you were basically a berserker fit looking for a place to happen. Not a good idea at all. And it would have been, for example, a *supremely* bad idea to step forward and put his face against her hair to see if it still smelled of cedar, and then to slide his hand down past the neck of her dressing gown and around the curve of her breast.

Terrible idea. Yes. Quite terrible. He examined the idea carefully from all angles, to make sure that he was aware just how terrible it was. His body had definite opinions about the quality of this idea. Stephen had to adjust the blankets.

Then Grace had gone and changed and come back in a shapeless tunic that hid her torso, but unfortunately she'd also put on trousers, and that had dragged his eyes lower. They were faded and frayed and had shiny patches at the knees and along the seat, the sort of thing she probably worked in because they were comfortable, and never mind any poor paladins who happened to be trying not to stare at the way the material hugged the curve of her hips.

Saint have mercy.

Gods, maybe it *had* been too long. Istvhan would thump him over the head and tell him, in poetically crude terms, that he needed to get laid and clear his mind.

It was easier for Istvhan. His brother paladin had...well, call it a lust for life and a certain enthusiastic zeal for the company of the opposite sex. He could go from one liaison to the next without feeling more than general good will for his partner. Stephen, on the other hand...

You overcomplicate things. You always have. You are overcomplicating this.

Very uncomplicated things were happening below his waist. He stared into the dark and grimaced.

Grace Angelica had no interest in him and apparently a distinct dislike of being rescued. He'd been a paladin long enough that he did not expect gratitude. You didn't slaughter bandits or cultists or demon-possessed animals expecting to be thanked. You just did it. And some people did indeed take offense to being saved, as if it were a personal affront that they'd needed it. You got used to that, too. It didn't stop you from killing the next set of bandits. That was the *job*.

Hell, that was half the paladin's rule for the Saint of Steel. *My duty is to serve. I will be sword and shield for the weak against the strong. I will be a symbol for those who require hope. I will bear the burdens for those who cannot bear them.*

There was more of course, about not fighting for wealth or glory, and a great many lesser laws involving dietary restrictions (no raw flesh); duty to one's country, one's family, and one's swordbrothers; the chain of command among priests; and so forth. And the amount of time spent on the exact number and composition of blankets, shirts, and pairs of boots to be granted to each paladin was, to Stephen's mind, a trifle excessive. But the important ones were all at the beginning.

The rule and the battle tide, those were the two things that made the Saint's paladins. Or had, in the years before the god had died. Now...well, the rule was still there. And the tide, but you followed one and hoped like hell not to wake the other. The scent of ginger and saffron wafted past his nostrils again.

It's not like I pulled her out of a burning building. I spent five minutes pretending to swive her in an alley and then took her to get a little air when she was feeling faint. That's not rescue. Any decent person would do the same. Err...well, possibly not the swiving in an alley part. Um.

She'd screamed in his ear with feigned passion. He wondered what she would sound like in the throes of the real thing. Could he make her moan or gasp or cry out his name?

You're not going to find out. Master Perfumer Angelica made it very clear that she is not interested. And why would she be? She's a master craftsman who sells to the nobility. You're just a soldier that a god grabbed hold of, once upon a time. She's an artist. You knit socks.

She is stuck with you until this assassination has been sorted, and then you will politely take yourself out of her life and trouble her no more. And you will go back to your normal life as well, untroubled by assassinations and attractive women accidentally setting themselves on fire. You will serve the Rat until you die and all debts are paid, and then you will rest under the earth and if there is an afterlife, you may find your god in it at last.

It was a straightforward plan. It had held him together for three years. He did not need complications. Not even complications with grey-green eyes and heavy breasts. Definitely not complications that made him laugh...and again, the breasts. *Yes. I do seem to keep coming back to that, don't I?*

He wondered what they would look like, without anything covering them, except perhaps his hands. Stephen sighed. Sleep was clearly not coming tonight. Rather than lie here in the dark, twitchy and aroused, he'd go put in a few hours in the training salle, and see if he couldn't exhaust himself until he slept. At the very least, perhaps it would sweat the scent of Grace's perfume off his skin. And whether that was a good thing or a bad thing, Stephen truly did not know.

CHAPTER 18

"So the assassin was carrying papers from Anuket City calling for the death of the Crown Prince, and had a signet ring from the Senate," said Beartongue.

Stephen nodded. "That's about the size of it."

Morning light streamed through the windows of Beartongue's study, illuminating bands of the desks, which were strewn with papers. It was relentlessly early, and he had been up much too late, brooding. Nevertheless, the Bishop had wanted to meet as soon as her schedule allowed to discuss what information he had gleaned from Marguerite. Stephen hunched over his mug of strong tea, wracking his brain for details.

There were five people in the room—Beartongue, Istvhan, Stephen, and two others. One, Zale, was a slender person with pewter grey hair braided back from their face. Stephen did not know them well, only that they were among the Rat's holy lawyers, the solicitors sacrosanct. The other, a buxom blond woman with a cherub's face and a killer's eyes, he didn't know at all. Beartongue had introduced her simply as, "an associate of the Rat."

"Are you certain those were the same papers taken from the body?" asked Zale.

"I can't be sure," admitted Stephen. "They looked right, but I had no chance to read over them at the time. I am fairly certain it was the same ring."

Beartongue sat back in her chair. "Thoughts?"

"How stupid does the Motherhood think we are?" rumbled Istvhan.

The Bishop snorted. "That is the question, isn't it? They might as well hang a sign around the lad's neck saying 'I am definitely a hired assassin, look at me.'"

"It's the lack of subtlety that offends the senses," said Zale. "Payment in Anuket's coin and perhaps a poison used only by their assassins would have been more than enough. There is no need to ham it up so spectacularly."

"They're not subtle," admitted the Bishop. "But more than that, I think they genuinely believe we cannot be very bright. To their way of thinking, if we were we would serve the Motherhood already." She shrugged.

"What of this Marguerite woman?" asked the blonde.

"Either a spy or a forger," said Stephen. "Likely both. For Anuket City. It is in her best interests to convince us that it is not Anuket behind the attack of course, but..." He frowned. "Does it seem odd to say that I would expect better of her? If she had substituted the papers, they would be less obvious. She seemed insulted by them as well."

"Of course, if she is attempting to frame the Motherhood, it would be in her best interests to act that way."

"She has not mentioned the Motherhood," said Stephen. He frowned again, trying to remember if he had done so, and couldn't remember. "I don't know if she suspects them, but she has not mentioned it to me."

"If you had not seen the youngster in their train, I suppose we wouldn't suspect them either," admitted Beartongue.

"I'd still suspect them," said Istvhan. Beartongue shot him a glance. "I *always* suspect them," he said. "On principle." Zale chuckled.

Stephen took another swallow of tea. Dust motes danced in the light from the windows. The blonde woman's hands were folded on the table in front of her. He wondered how many knives she had on her person right now.

No less than three, I'd wager. And a woman like that carries a garrote as a matter of course. Stephen respected that. There were people who thought that what soldiers did was somehow cleaner than what assassins did, but in his experience, the dead wound up just as dead either way.

"Damn," muttered Beartongue, half to herself. "Damn. I'd like to speak to her myself, but I don't want to spook her. Does she know you're passing information on to me?"

Stephen frowned. Marguerite seemed far too intelligent *not* to realize that, but she also hadn't said anything about it. "I can't imagine she doesn't know," he said cautiously. "Just as I have to assume she's passing information on to her masters, or will when she reports in."

Beartongue nodded.

"And the perfumer?" said the blonde probably-an-assassin.

Stephen felt his jaw tighten. "She has nothing to do with this."

Everyone in the room looked at him. He flushed. "All right, I can't know that. But I doubt she does. She is aware that her friend is a spy, but she herself is...not the type."

Those killer's eyes sliced into him. "Or she is a better actress than you believe."

Stephen thought of Grace groggily setting herself on fire. "I suppose that's possible," he admitted, "but I have my doubts. This information seems as new to her as it is to me. And if she *is* that clever, she is going to be so far ahead of me that I have no hope of catching her out."

Istvhan cracked a laugh at that. When the blonde switched her gaze to him he said, "What? He's honest. To a fault, usually."

"Honest, trustworthy, and unimaginative," said Beartongue. "That last is a compliment, by the way, in this business. There's enough jumping at shadows that someone who just sees what's in front of them is a treasure."

Stephen snorted, but didn't argue. Neither did Istvhan. The blonde inclined her head, as if in tribute to Stephen's lack of imagination. Beartongue rubbed her hand over her face. "Bah. I hate this behind-the-scenes foolishness. My life was easier when I was an archdeacon."

"Before you had to deal with spy networks, you mean?" said Zale.

"Yes, that. And don't sound so smug, or I'll promote you and then it will be your problem."

"Rat forfend!" Zale made a warding gesture with ink-stained fingers. "I prefer to simply try cases, if it's all the same to you."

"Competence is its own punishment. I haven't forgotten your work with the swords." Beartongue put her chin in her hand, turning back to Stephen. "Marguerite said that she would have more information for you in the future?"

"She did, yes."

"Consider that your top priority at the moment. Though I wonder why she is going to such lengths to keep you involved."

Zale coughed. "If I may hazard a guess?"

"Hazard away."

"She may fear that he will investigate on his own if she does not feed him enough information to keep him from doing so." The lawyer-priest gave Stephen an apologetic look. "And—forgive me—but paladins are rarely known for their subtlety of approach."

Even the blonde laughed at that.

"It's a good thought, though," said Istvhan, nodding to Zale. "If he or I go stomping around demanding answers, we're likely to kick over a whole hornet's nest of trouble."

"We may yet need to kick over that hornet's nest," said the Bishop, rising to her feet. "But for now, keep us posted. Cooperate with this woman as best you can, Stephen. The resources of the temple are at your disposal. I trust your judgment."

"I'm not sure you should," admitted Stephen, rising as well.

"Yes, but at least you're aware of it," said Beartongue. She smiled. "Give me one man who is old enough to know his limits over a dozen who don't."

Istvhan accompanied him into the hall. "That went well," he said. Stephen gave him a wry look. "Did it?"

"Our nameless friend in there didn't snap your neck like a twig."

"I suppose by those standards, yes." Stephen shook his head. "Do you know her?"

"Never seen her before in my life. But I don't have to know an individual viper to recognize the breed."

"Interesting company for the Rat to keep."

"They are practical. And ethical, but I suspect that sometimes it is most practical to eliminate someone."

Stephen nodded. He liked Beartongue. He admired her. He even trusted her. He also suspected she was no stranger to rolling the occasional body into a ditch in the name of problem-solving. "Well, and if you're dealing with assassinations, an assassin is certainly the practical one to consult, is she not?"

Istvhan snorted. "Saint's balls, that's exactly what she's doing, isn't she?"

"Certainly seems that way."

His brother paladin shook his head, then paused. "Oh—your healer is looking for you. Needs an escort."

"At this hour?" Stephen winced. He hadn't bathed or eaten, although the tea and the blonde's quiet menace had certainly woken him up. "Dammit. Thank you."

"I'd go, but the trial wraps today. And he requested you specifically."

"No, it's fine." Making sure the healer got where he was going in one piece was more important than breakfast. "At least he's not wandering around the Weaver's Nest by himself." Stephen lengthened his stride and went to go make certain that Brother Francis kept his head.

CHAPTER 19

It rained.

It rained buckets, it rained torrents, it rained deluges and water-falls. It rained for a week straight, while the gutters flooded and the trash floated. The public baths shut down because water from the street was pouring into them and they were fishing dead rats out of the drains. The Elkinslough River, the lifeblood of Archenhold, burst its banks on the fifth day of rain. The vast majority of the city was uphill for just such reasons, but docks and fishing boats and at least one footbridge were torn loose and swept into the Great River, to bob downstream and presumably reach the sea. At least two slums were washed out as well.

Grace stood at the window of her shop, watching drops splatter against the diamond panes, and thought gloomily that she had never seen so much rain. She wondered if the paladins were out there. The servants of the Rat certainly would be, organizing temporary lodging and food lines. She pictured Stephen thigh-deep in muddy water, dragging through wreckage, looking for survivors, and sighed. There was nothing she could do to help. She'd never even had the opportunity to learn to swim. She sent a week's profits to the Rat to help with the clean-up and told herself it was much more useful than getting in everyone else's way.

The rain had other consequences, even away from the river. The ancient walled fortress that formed the original core of the city of Archon's Glory had primitive sewers, and the New City that ringed the walled one had quite good ones. But the outlying quarters had all grown up willy-nilly, and some of them had sewers and some of them didn't. The ones that didn't were under a foot of water. The nightsoil carts couldn't get through and people were dumping chamberpots in the street. Cesspits had overflowed. At least one cemetery had apparently washed out as well, and there were rumors that recently buried bodies were floating around in the street, being used as rafts by rats.

The smell, once the rain stopped, was going to be *extraordinary*.

Grace foresaw several months of making pomanders and scented handkerchiefs in the strongest scents she could brew up. She was already compounding mint and rosemary and sage, trying to find something clean, aromatic, and above all overwhelming.

No one had come to the shop for several hours. It was one of the three days a week that she was open other than by appointment, but it was clear that no one wanted to brave the rain. She should probably just lock the door, and then perhaps go check on her neighbor and see if she needed anything. The old lady liked to yell about sins of the flesh, but she had clung to her home while the area gentrified around her, and Grace felt obligated to visit her every week or so and make sure that she had coal and food.

She was just putting her hand on the sign to turn it when a shadow loomed out of the rain. She took a step back, startled, as the figure opened the door and stepped inside, stamping his feet.

The paladin pushed the hood of his cloak back. Rain clung to his eyelashes, which led Grace to notice how sinfully long they were. Men should not have eyelashes like that, it was just unfair.

"Sorry," he said. "I don't mean to drip on your floor."

"It's fine." Why was her heart pounding?

Never mind that, why is he here? He can't have come to see me...can he?

Stephen swung the steaming cloak from his shoulders and hung it on the coatrack beside the door, where it proceeded to pour water onto the boards. He stared at the puddle in mild dismay. "Ah...do you have a towel or...?"

"Yes, of course." She hurried into the workshop and came back out again. He took the towel and knelt down to deal with the puddle.

"It's fine," said Grace again. "You don't need to worry about it." His shoulders were somehow broader than she remembered. How did she keep forgetting that? "What—um—brings you here?"

He was kneeling practically at her feet. She hadn't been expecting that. Men didn't usually fall at her feet unless they were desperate to buy a new perfume, usually to get out of trouble with their wives.

For all she knew, he *had* a wife. It wasn't like she'd ever asked. Did paladins even get married? Were they allowed to?

Some of them are. I know the Forge God's can. Not sure about the Dreaming God.

He looked up into her face and his eyes were very blue. Then he rose to his feet and she was eye level with his chest, which was entirely too close and absurdly broad.

What is wrong with me this morning?

"Marguerite sent me a message," he said. "To meet her here."

Grace's heart stopped its thumping and sheepishly resumed normal behavior. "Oh. I didn't realize. She isn't here yet. I assume she'll be back." She swallowed and tried again. "I mean, she'll be back. I'm sure. She lives here."

How *dare* she feel disappointed? She hardly knew the man. She had no *right* to feel that way and she didn't *want* to feel that way and—

"I'm glad to see you again," he said. "How is...err...business?" He gestured vaguely to the empty room, and it occurred to Grace that he was feeling just as awkward as she was, or at least was equally bad at conversation.

We talked so easily that first time. Maybe I just need to throw myself on him and scream in his ear until we get over the awkwardness.

"Slow," she said. "The rain's keeping everyone home. Nobody wants perfume, it'll just get washed off in five minutes."

"Makes sense." He shifted his feet. "Ah...I brought you something."

Grace raised her eyebrows. "You did?"

He pulled a small cloth wrapped bundle out of his pack. "It's not much. Um. It's just that I started them here, you see, so I thought..." He pushed the bundle toward her.

She took it, puzzled, then realized what they were. "Socks? Are these socks?"

He nodded.

She felt a small bubble of delight in her chest. "You made these?"

"It's what I do."

They were cream and dusty pink, in alternating zig-zag patterns. They were sturdy rather than elegant, but Grace had far more use for warm socks than for delicate ones.

"These are amazing." She could not remember the last time that someone had made something for her. Had Phillip ever? She couldn't think of any examples.

I suppose technically Tab makes me anal secretions every month, but somehow it's just not as touching.

"How did you learn to make socks?"

"My mother taught me. Our building was full of seamstresses and tailors, we didn't need another one, so she mostly did knitting to sell. People always need socks. And then...well, soldiers *definitely* always need socks."

"I'm impressed. I couldn't make those."

He smiled. "I couldn't make perfumes, so I suppose we're even."

"Well, there's that."

A slightly awkward silence developed. Grace held the socks and wondered whether bringing socks negated coming here because Marguerite had sent for him.

I am definitely thinking too much about this.

He glanced around the small front room, at the tall shelves and the small, neat seating area. "So, um...How does one become a perfumer?"

Small talk, thought Grace. *We're doing small talk now. All right. I suppose I started it, asking about the socks.*

Well, normal people start there, I guess. First small talk, then pantomimed sex acts in an alley, then murder scene. I'm doing this all wrong, as usual.

"One is apprenticed to one," said Grace. "In my case, my master picked me out from the orphanage."

"You were an orphan?" Stephen frowned. "I'm so sorry."

"Almost everyone is, eventually," said Grace. "It's not a big deal." In the orphanage she had been raised in, hardly anyone worried much about their mother and father. Everyone's goal was to get an apprenticeship to a kind master, in a field where they'd be wealthy and respected and eat three meat meals a week.

Nine-year-old Grace's highest ambition had been apprenticeship in the kennels of a great house. She was good with animals but some-what alarmed by horses. Caring for hounds seemed like the best possible life, and if you were lucky, you were treated as well as the hounds were, which in some houses was very well indeed.

Instead, she'd found herself lined up with a half-dozen other youngsters on Hiring Day and a sour-faced old man had stomped up, pulled out a strip of parchment, and thrust it under the nose of the first boy in line. "What do you smell?" he snapped.

"Um. Flowers, sir?" said the first boy.

"What sort of flowers?"

"I d-don't know, sir?"

"Useless," growled the old man, and went to the next child in line. "What do you smell?"

The line of nine-year-olds exchanged looks with each other. Was the old man mad? But the sisters of the Four-Faced God had let him in for Hiring Day, and were nodding and smiling encouragingly.

Grace had no idea what the old man expected, but when she smelled the strip of paper, the scent of roses leapt up at her, followed by something else. "There's two smells," she said, forgetting the *sir* in her excitement. "Aren't there? It's like rose, but something else. Spicy like cinnamon, only not cinnamon. I don't think I've ever smelled it before."

"Huh!" said the old man, pleased. He reached out, grabbed the top of her skull, and turned her head back and forth. "You look sickly," he said at last. "You'll probably die and I'll waste my time training you."

"I'll try not to, sir," said Grace. It did not occur to her until later that she should have lied to try and get out of the apprenticeship. He did not look like a hound master.

"Mmf. Can you keep your mouth shut?"

Grace didn't know how to answer that question. She closed her mouth and looked at him, puzzled.

"Hmmf!"

He stomped away from her to the sisters who ran the home and thrust money into their hands. Even now, Grace had to give him credit, he was not a stingy master. Unkind and bitter and angry at the world, but he did not short the price of her articles of apprenticeship.

"Come on, then," he said, snapping his fingers at her as if she were a dog.

"Please, sir," said Grace, hurrying after him. "What am I to be apprenticed as?"

"A perfumer, dear," said Sister Rhys. She was a large, muscular woman, and when she swept Grace up in a hug, Grace felt briefly that perhaps all would be well. "It's a good, important job. You'll do so well."

The old man cleared his throat. Grace trotted after him, still baffled. She turned back to wave to the other children, her lifelong friends, and then they left the courtyard of the home and she never saw any of them again.

She explained as much of this as she could to Stephen without trying to sound too self-pitying. She remembered having little to complain about. She had clothes and food and a warm place to sleep. Her new master could only work for a few hours a day, so she had a great deal of free time compared to the other apprentices she knew. His arthritis was so bad that he could only beat her occasionally, and it hurt him much more than her when he did. He screamed a great deal, that was all, and threw things when he could manage.

But she'd learned things, too. More than she'd ever expected. A whole world opened up to her, a world of scents, a world where she was actually competent. A world where she could inhale and break a perfume apart into a dozen ingredients in her head. She could do it walking down the street. It made her feel like the possessor of secret knowledge, as if she moved in a hidden world that few other people could sense and fewer could make sense of.

The old man had hired her to be his hands, now that his joints were too swollen to manage the delicate work of handling pipettes and droppers and vials. She learned the hundred myriad processes of perfume making by doing them all over and over while her master hovered over her shoulder barking orders in his cracked, querulous voice. Eventually she became so good at anticipating his needs that he no longer barked orders and seemed to forget that she had an existence beyond him.

It was not until a cough laid him low for weeks and she filled the orders for him that he remembered again and began to suspect her of plotting to take over his business. Instead of screaming at her for clumsiness, he screamed at her for spying, for stealing his secrets, and began to threaten to cut out her tongue or pour hot lead in her nose to keep her from being able to displace him.

She tried to make this threat seem funny and didn't realize until Stephen stared at her in horror that maybe it wasn't as funny as she'd thought.

"Look, it's not like he could have *done* it," she said. "I mean, I would have had to boil the lead for him and pour it up my own nose, and...uh..." She realized that this was not helping her case much. "We were in the artificer's quarter and a lot of other apprentices had it much worse. None of the perfumes ever exploded, and nobody tried to replace my eyes with clockwork even once."

"Did that *happen?*"

"Guild rules said you couldn't experiment on apprentices, but... well..." Grace shrugged. "Yeah, sometimes."

"He still sounds very unkind."

"He wasn't a nice man, no." When Phillip had bought her articles of apprenticeship, the old man had screamed obscenities at her, even while she was steadying the paper so that he could sign his name and sell her away.

This, however, was an even darker road to go down. Grace made an effort to turn the conversation in another direction. "So how does one become a paladin, then?"

Stephen shrugged. "Ah, well. I grew up in Archenhold and when I was old enough to lie about my age, I joined the army."

"The army? Not a sock-maker?"

He laughed. "Sadly, no. The weavers could take their pick of apprentices, and mostly they picked ones that looked easier to feed. I was big for my age and good at hitting things. And the army paid weekly and fed and housed me, so I could pass the money to my mother."

His mother. Having no relatives herself, it rarely occurred to Grace that other people had them. *Yes. A family. Normal people have families. I must remember. What does one say?* "How is your mother now?"

"Dead."

That went well.

"Consumption," he said, possibly moved by her alarmed expression. "She lived long enough to see me chosen by the god."

"And how does *that* happen?" Grace seized on this, which at least should steer them away from family matters. *It won't seem as strange that I have no idea how paladins work.*

"My unit in the army was called out to clear a nest of Wheatshields...oh, hmm. How long have you been in Archenhold?"

"Only about three years."

He nodded. "You might not have heard of them, then. A cult that sprang up about fifteen years ago. They claimed to be followers of the Lady of Grass, but the temple denied that *very* vigorously. Anyway, their theology was...different. Claimed that the Lady wanted humans harvested like wheat, and only when the harvest had been brought in could the seasons turn."

Grace's eyes went wide. "That doesn't sound good."

"It was very bad. They slaughtered villages indiscriminately. They were mostly cleared out by that point, but occasionally you'd get little groups still springing up. Some people just want the apocalypse in their lifetime." He shrugged. "Anyway, my unit was called out, and a group of the Saint's paladins. They—*we*—were...um. Considered the elite."

He looked extremely uncomfortable admitting this. Grace added modesty to the list of Stephen's virtues. "I've heard as much."

"Yes. When the god's blessing took the paladins, it took me, too. I don't know how much you know about that."

Grace shook her head. "Like a berserker fit, I heard."

"Like that, yes. Only the god directed it. Having it come upon me was...unexpected." There was something about his expression that made Grace think that was a profound understatement. "All I knew was that I was in the ranks and then a heartbeat later, something happened in my head and I was in full charge with a group of men I'd only seen in passing."

"I can see why that would be unsettling."

Stephen gave a short, humorless laugh. "That's one way to put it. The army discharged me right then and there, turned me over to the paladins. I barely knew what was happening. I didn't know whether to be more afraid that I was losing my mind or that my mother wouldn't get my back pay."

"And they didn't give you a choice to turn it down?" She felt herself growing indignant on his behalf, imagining a confused young man plucked from the ranks, with holy madness dumped in his lap.

"No?" Stephen looked surprised that she'd even ask. "Well, I suppose I could have, but...ah...once the battle tide takes you, it doesn't really stop taking you. You can't just turn it off." He spread his hands. "Once it woke up, my choices were very limited. Join the order or risk finding myself running berserk with nothing to stop me. The choice was easy, in the end."

Grace shook her head. It seemed like the god could have ordered things better. "Is that how it is for all the paladins?"

"For the Saint of Steel's chosen, yes. I can't speak to any other order. I know the Dreaming God's paladins have to train for years to bind demons. It's easier for us. We just get pointed at the enemy and then the battle tide comes on us." He sighed. "In our heyday, we could tear apart every cultist in a room and not lay a fingertip on their prisoners."

Precision berserkers. No wonder the army called them out. "That seems useful."

"Useful. Yes. We were useful." He shrugged. "Then the god died and we weren't any more. That's all."

His face was calm, his body was relaxed, and his eyes were like raw wounds. Grace looked away. She wondered if he thought he was hiding it. She had a strong urge to go and put her arms around him and that was absolute foolishness, he certainly wouldn't want her pity and who was she to comfort anyone? *Oh god, why did I start down this road, why didn't I talk about the rain instead?*

"Did your mother get the back pay after all?"

Stephen blinked at her, and a little of the wounded look left his eyes. "Yes. She did. The temple takes...took...very good care of our families. When I figured out what it all meant, at the time, I was very glad to have been chosen."

The front door banged. Grace closed her eyes in brief, intense relief, before she had to ask whether he still felt that way, now that the god was dead.

CHAPTER 20

"Good, you're both here," said Marguerite, breezing in. She shook rain off her hat. "I've got the carriage waiting. There's someone I want you to meet."

"Huh?" said Grace.

"Excuse me?" said Stephen.

"Sorry." Marguerite gave her an apologetic smile. "You're coming along because...well, you're mixed up in this. And you, paladin, because sometimes you want a witness that's above reproach." She paused, then said "Also, I don't think you trust any information that comes from me. I mean, I wouldn't if I were you."

Stephen opened his mouth and then closed it again, obviously torn between chivalry and honesty.

"Take some of whatever that thing you sniff is," added Marguerite. "We're going somewhere smelly."

That was all she would say. Stephen looked at Grace, who shrugged helplessly and went to pick up her jar of charbeans and her coat.

All three piled into a carriage. Stephen took up most of one seat by himself and Grace and Marguerite took the other. Rain darkened the windows, so there was nowhere to look but at Stephen. This was...awkward.

Am I looking at him too much? Not enough? Should I look into his eyes or is that strange? Should I not look in his eyes? No, then I look guilty. He already doesn't trust Marguerite.

Why do I care if he trusts me or not? I haven't done anything.

Oh dear.

He smiled at her. In the darkness of the carriage, his eyes were a blue so deep it looked almost black. Grace's stomach turned over and she clutched at the jar on her lap and thought, *Where is Marguerite taking us?*

～

Stephen, meanwhile, was looking at Grace, who had almost vanished into her oversized coat. It made her look very small. He had a strong urge to wrap the coat up tightly around her to keep her safe from the cold and the wet and anything else in the world that might want to cause her harm.

Stop. This is a dangerous road to go down. Stop.

She had seemed genuinely delighted by the socks. He knew it was an awkward gift, completely unromantic, he should probably have brought roses, but after a solid week of rain, there weren't any roses and everybody's feet were getting cold and wet. So he'd brought the socks and she'd actually seemed pleased.

Her smile had shown that crooked tooth. His heart had lurched. Then, like an idiot, he'd gone and asked her about becoming a perfumer.

As light as she'd made of her apprenticeship, it had obviously been dreadful. He wanted to stomp to Anuket City and kick down the old man's door and shake him until his spine rattled.

Then she'd asked him about becoming a paladin, and Saint help him, he'd told her.

He hadn't thought about those first days in years. He'd been a paladin more than half his life. Remembering that wet-behind-the-ears recruit, clutching his pike and hoping he didn't disgrace himself...Saint's blood, he'd been so young.

And then the battle tide had risen around him. A great roaring in his ears, and a golden fire that poured down every nerve. He had looked across the sea of spearpoints and feared them no more than blades of grass. The golden fire spread across the battlefield and he need only walk across it, drawing his sword and letting it fall. The enemy's weapons barely touched him. They were so slow, so weak, and there was a god walking with him.

Dear god, but it had been good.

He realized he was staring at the women across from him without seeing them and quickly looked out the window. The blurred, watery view made it hard to make out landmarks. "Are we going to the Walled City?"

"Correct," said Marguerite cheerfully.

"I am not certain that they would welcome me with open arms at the palace," said Stephen.

"It's fine. We're not going to the palace proper, but to one of the outbuildings."

The carriage pulled up a few moments later, in front of a low stone building built tight against the wall itself. It had a functional, rather drab look about it. No effort had been made to soften the stone with plantings or banners.

Stephen got out first and offered both of the women his hand to descend. Marguerite's smile was ironic under her hat. Grace looked up at him with her clear, grave eyes and took his hand. He suddenly wished that he weren't wearing gloves.

And it is freezing and raining and that is a foolish thing to wish. You are the responsible one, the reliable one. Stop wishing for irresponsible things.

They dashed into the building, following Marguerite. No one challenged them. One bored-looking guard was on duty, but he was not armed, and he only waved a hand lazily at them. "Miss Marguerite?"

"Piper's expecting us."

He nodded and sank back in his chair. From his heavy-eyed expression, Stephen suspected they were interrupting a nap.

They went through a door and down a long flight of stone steps.

The air chilled around them. There was a stone landing and a corridor off it, but Marguerite ignored that and went down yet again.

"We must be quite a long way down by now," said Stephen.

"The old wine cellars," said Marguerite.

"Not the dungeons?" asked Grace.

"No, those are under the administrative buildings."

Stephen watched Grace start to laugh, realize that her friend wasn't joking, and gulp instead.

"They aren't used much," he said. "Most criminals go to the main prison on Waterling Street. It's only the political prisoners and a few special cases they keep in the dungeons."

"Is that supposed to make me feel better?"

"Did it?"

"No."

At the bottom of the stairs was another corridor, and this one Marguerite took. She banged on the last door. "Piper! It's us!"

"Door's open," called a muffled voice.

Marguerite pushed the door open. It was heavy metal and clanged like a prison door. Stephen caught the door and looked through, reaching out a hand automatically to stop Grace from going through before he had checked for danger.

A man in a leather mask looked up at him. He was standing over a dead body and holding a very large knife.

Stephen's hand dropped immediately to his sword hilt. The man in the mask rolled his eyes. "Don't bother, paladin, she's a bit beyond caring right now. Come in."

"This is Doctor Piper," said Marguerite, stepping out of the way. "He does autopsies."

"It's a living," said Piper. "For me, that is. Not for them, obviously. You're the paladin and the perfumer, then?"

Stephen realized that Grace was staring over his arm into the room, her eyes huge. He stepped out of the way and held the door for her. She stepped inside but stayed close to him. He found that he didn't mind.

The room smelled less awful than one would expect, but since he expected it to smell like an open grave, that wasn't saying much. The reek of human decay was in his nostrils, but it was cold enough that it hadn't reached the truly horrific stage.

"You're here about the dead boy," said Piper. "Give me a minute to finish this poor soul and I'll go over it."

"Is he here?" asked Grace. "It's been over a week!"

"No, I did him the first day," said Piper. He set the knife—which Stephen saw now was more of a saw—down and picked up another, smaller one, and prodded inside the dead woman's chest.

Marguerite leaned against the wall, waiting. Grace craned her neck. "How...how did she die?"

The dead woman was very pale, lips purple, hair a ragged halo around her face. Her face was serene, in contrast to the gaping hole in her chest and the man wrist-deep inside it.

Piper cocked an eyebrow at Grace. The mask covered the lower half of his face and was laced together, looking rather like a beak. "Died in childbirth. The family wants to blame the midwife, but I'm afraid they're out of luck. She actually delivered in fairly good order." He gestured vaguely in the direction of the corpse's lower half. Stephen could see a long incision from hip to hip, although thankfully everything was still contained within. He felt slightly ill.

You've killed how many men on the battlefield? Bit foolish to get squeamish now.

Yes, but the god was on me then, and the divine madness, not this cold, bloodless dissection.

"Pretty sure the problem was her lungs," said Piper. "They're a mess. You might want to cover your nose, this usually smells." He reached in with his smaller knife. "Ah! There, you see?"

The scent of putrefaction welled through the room. Marguerite pulled out a handkerchief, grimacing.

Grace's nostrils flared as if she was actually smelling the rot deliberately. Then she went a bit green and turned away, grabbing for the jar she carried.

"Abscess in the lungs," said Piper. "Looks like it burst with the strain of labor. She had consumption. I'm amazed she carried the babe to term." He turned and did something else with the knife. The smell intensified. "Two abscesses. Blessed gods. Hmm, I suppose one burst and filled the lung, and then the strain of coughing opened the other. Never had a chance."

Grace shoved her nose completely into the jar, eyes closed.

It was the most natural thing in the world for Stephen to reach out and put an arm around her shoulders and step closer so that her face was against his shoulder. He had done it any number of times for survivors. The saint put the madness on you and took it off again, and afterward you had people left who weren't part of the fight and didn't need to see the carnage that had overtaken their farm or their village. It was easiest simply to use the paladin's voice, tell them not to look, and help them away from the scene.

And that is the only reason they used us, instead of hiring...oh, clockwork monsters from Anuket City, or golems, say. Assuming they could find a golem maker, in this day and age. Soulless machines kill as efficiently as we did, but they cannot comfort the survivors afterward. Or make reports. Stephen had a fairly cynical idea about which was ultimately more important to a commander.

He tried to keep his grip slack enough that Grace could pull away, but she leaned against him. He could feel her body pressed against his like a burning brand, even through the chainmail.

It would have been so easy to put his other arm around her, fold her into an embrace, and hold her close.

And you are in a room with a man cutting up a dead woman and this is not the time.

"Nearly done," said Piper. He reached down and pulled a blood-stained sheet off the floor and draped it over the body, then set the knife down in a tray. "Give me just a moment." He moved around the room, picking up tools.

Stephen glanced over at Marguerite and saw that she was watching him and Grace with a small, unreadable smile.

Piper finished what he was doing and moved to a basin. He washed his hands with a slab of soap, then wiped them dry. Only then did he reach up to remove his mask. The face revealed looked youthfully handsome, but there were narrow lines around the eyes that told Stephen he was older than he looked. He had dark brown hair, cut short, and he was clean shaven. Stephen didn't blame him. If he had to wedge his face into a leather half-mask for hours a day, he'd probably forgo the beard too.

"All right," he said. "Let's go next door. It'll smell better, and I realize most people don't like to talk over a corpse."

Grace stepped away from him, looking faintly embarrassed. Stephen took a step forward and signed a benediction over the dead woman's body. *Saint of Steel, you...well, I suppose you no longer look over us. In that case, White Rat grant her peace.*

He looked up and saw the other three watching him. He cleared his throat, unwilling to ask forgiveness, but feeling awkward nonetheless.

"...right, then," said Piper. "Follow me, gentlefolk?"

Piper's office was as uncluttered as the morgue. There was a single large desk, bare of anything, and two chairs. Piper grimaced, pulled one of the chairs out from behind the desk, and slid it across the floor to join the other one. He leaned against his desk. "Sorry. I don't get many large groups."

Chivalry not being completely dead, Stephen stood while Grace and Marguerite took the chairs. "So you are the Archon's...ah...?" Stephen began, wondering why Marguerite had insisted they come here.

"Physician to the dead," said Piper. "At least for those souls who don't have their own doctor to do the final graces." He nodded to Marguerite. "She says you're interested in the dead boy from the other day."

Stephen glanced at Marguerite. "He was poisoned, wasn't he? I did not think one would need an autopsy to determine that."

"His fingertips were blue," said Marguerite.

"*And* his toes," added Piper.

Stephen and Grace traded helpless looks. "From the poison?" asked Grace.

"Yes! Exactly!" Marguerite beamed. "But not the one he took!"

They traded looks again. Stephen was a little relieved to see that the perfumer wasn't keeping up any better than he was. "Um...what?"

"The poison he took doesn't turn your toes purple," said Piper. "I'd maybe overlook that, given that people's extremities do odd things when they die, but I was suspicious. So I opened up his stomach and took a look." He folded his arms. "His stomach was a mess. He ate something that *really* did not agree with him."

"He swallowed poison," said Stephen. "We watched him."

"No," said Marguerite, "he ate a poisoned glass pill. I doubt he swallowed very much of it. It sliced up his gums and got into his blood, but it didn't get into his stomach."

Piper nodded to her. "His mouth was a mess and I used gloves to handle him, but the glass was only partway down his throat. But he took something substantially before then. Something that, I suspect, was in the process of killing him. Wrecked his stomach and had already started on the top of the intestine, too." He shook his head. "I suspect he was a dead man long before he ate that glass pill."

"You mean he was poisoned by something else before he took the poison in front of us?" said Grace.

Stephen leaned forward, suddenly alert. "So his employer poisoned him. In case he panicked and *didn't* kill himself."

"*Exactly!*" Marguerite turned in her chair and stabbed a finger at him. "They knew he was going to get caught, and they wanted to make sure he didn't talk."

"He was sweating and sick," said Stephen slowly. "One of the others saw him puking his guts up. We thought it was nerves, but it wasn't. He was dying already." He looked up at Piper. "Who knows this?"

"That," said Piper grimly, "is the other odd bit. The Motherhood sent one of their physicians to...ah...'observe.'" He shoved himself away from the table. "He asked if it could be an ulcer. Or spicy food, if you can believe it. Feh. Spicy food, my ass. They were just bitter that I was the examiner, not one of theirs."

"The Motherhood again," muttered Stephen.

"They do have their pointy little fingers in a lot of pies, don't they?" said Marguerite.

"Do you know what kind of poison it was?" asked Stephen.

Piper shook his head. "I'm not that good," he said. "Sweating, vomiting, blue extremities—but he was also nervous, so the sweating we can maybe explain away. Too many options. And it could have been more than one poison, if somebody decided to hedge their bets. As nasty as things were getting in his guts, I wouldn't be surprised. He had to be having the stomach cramps to end all stomach cramps though." He scowled. "No, I can't tell you what it was, but gods, it's not like I can keep up on all the ways people have of killing each other. But I don't believe for a minute that all that came from nervous vomiting and the poison he took five minutes earlier."

"...huh," said Stephen. "That is...huh."

"It is, isn't it?" said Marguerite.

"What a complicated way to die," murmured Grace.

Piper looked from face to face. "Anything else I can do for you fine people? I have to finish preparing the lady in there for burial."

A thought struck Stephen. "Have you seen any of the severed heads that have turned up around the city?"

"Oh, from the Weaver's Nest Headsman or whatever they're calling him? Saw one."

"And?"

"I could be wrong, but I'm pretty sure the cause of death was decapitation."

Marguerite snorted. Piper spread his hands. "The dead can tell you a great deal, but only if you get to them quickly and have enough to work with. Sorry, paladin. Believe me, if I knew more, I wouldn't keep it to myself. Anything else?"

"No, that should be enough." Marguerite rose. "Thanks, Piper."

In the doorway, Grace turned. Stephen caught the door over her head. "Doctor?"

Piper glanced up. "Yes?"

"Did the baby live?"

"Eh?"

"The woman in the next room. You said she died in childbirth."

"Oh!" Piper smiled. "Yes. A healthy babe, thankfully."

Grace smiled back. If Stephen had not been watching her so closely, he would not have seen her eyes flick to Marguerite's back, would not have followed her gaze and seen how the other woman's shoulders relaxed almost imperceptibly at the doctor's words.

Not asking for herself, then. I see. Stephen stepped to close the door and looked over at Piper. He raised one eyebrow.

The other man's smile dropped away. He shook his head.

"Thank you," said Stephen. He knew that Grace and Marguerite would take it as thanks for the doctor's time, but all his gratitude was for the lie instead.

CHAPTER 21

"Interesting fellow," said Stephen, as they climbed into the carriage. "Interesting story."

"I thought it best you hear for yourself," said Marguerite. "That way you can report to the Bishop firsthand."

He smiled wryly. "Yes, of course. Though you could have just told me."

"I thought Piper would be more convincing in person."

Grace picked at a thread on her tunic. The smell of the dead body lingered in her memory. She'd smelled death before, but never so divorced from other odors. Usually there was blood and mud and sweat and sickness, all mixed up together. The precise smell of death, without any others to taint it, was a strange, sickly revelation.

What would I use to reproduce that?

Nothing. No one wanted to smell like a corpse. *Obviously.*

Normal people do not think about how to reproduce the smell of dead bodies.

She had made the mistake of sniffing the air when Piper opened the dead woman's lungs. It was her old master's habit at work. *Smell everything. Good, bad, it doesn't matter. You need a library of scents to carry around in your head. If you don't know the bad, you won't know what will mask it.*

She wondered how the hell you'd mask that. Heavy smoke, maybe. Something like frankincense. You'd need it so thick that your tongue would go dry.

Stephen had put his arm around her and turned her away. She could still feel the imprint of each finger splayed across her shoulder like an invisible brand.

She was embarrassed to have needed it—*always weak, always needing rescue, god when will you ever learn*—but for a moment, while she leaned against him, he had been large and warm and solid and she had been very aware of the strength of his arm around her and the hardness of the muscle of his chest. Some of that hardness was armor, but not all of it.

"He was indeed convincing," said Stephen. His eyes were on Marguerite. "I...yes, all right. You're right. I would have been more skeptical if you just told me. I believe that Doctor Piper believes what he said."

"And?" said Marguerite.

"And it makes sense," said Stephen. "If you figure a ruthless employer. One who didn't want their assassin talking."

"If you're sending assassins, you're probably already ruthless," said Grace.

He inclined his head. "Yes, fair enough. But there's a difference between sending highly trained professionals, and sending children that you've poisoned for insurance. Two kinds of ruthlessness, I suppose."

"That's why it's not Anuket City," said Marguerite softly.

Stephen's eyes locked on her.

"I *know*," she said. "Assassins they have. Plenty of them. Something like this is too messy. They hire professionals. They've got them to hire."

Stephen grunted. He started to say something else, and the cart struck a patch of rounded cobblestones and began to rattle like breath in a dying woman's chest.

"We'll wait," Marguerite shouted over the noise. "Talk at the shop."

Grace watched Stephen watching Marguerite and felt a pang that she didn't want to admit to feeling. She turned her head and looked out the window instead, at the endless falling rain.

"Give me a few moments," Marguerite said, when they reached the shop at last. "I've been gallivanting around in the rain for hours and I'm soaked through. Let me put on something dry, at least."

"I'll make tea," Grace volunteered.

"I'll...stand here," said Stephen.

"You do it well," Grace assured him.

"Well, I have a great deal of practice."

She smiled at him and his heart did a familiar lurch. *Stop that.*

Marguerite went upstairs. He stood in the doorway of the workshop, at attention for lack of anything else to do, and watched Grace boiling water. Her tea kettle was as battered as a breastplate that had been through the wars.

"Where is your little ferret friend?" he asked finally.

"Probably asleep someplace warm." She poured the water over tea leaves and the scent of bergamot filled the room. It was a pleasant smell, and it harmonized well with some of the other scents in the room. He wondered how she kept them from mingling together, in the apparent chaos of the workshop, or if sometimes her perfumes had a faint hint of tea, or perhaps her tea came out tasting of sandalwood and clove.

"This means something else, you know," said Grace, when the tea had steeped.

"Hmm?" For a moment he could not think what she was talking about. The tea meant something else?

She handed him the cup. The mug felt very small in his gloved hands.

"If he was already poisoned. That means it wouldn't have mattered what you said."

He blinked at her, but the truth slowly worked into his mind, like water soaking through wood. "No. No, it wouldn't have mattered, would it? Nothing I did could have saved him."

He was too old and tired to feel as if a great weight had been lifted. There were too many weights left on him. But a little tension went out of his shoulders at the thought. He had not failed the young assassin. All the failure had been long before he arrived. The best he could do—the best he had done—was make sure that the last voice the boy heard was kind.

Marguerite came back down in dry clothes, wearing Tab like a stole over her shoulders. "I found this trying to get into my room."

"Mrr-r-r."

"Sorry," said Grace. "Did he get in?"

"Nah, just a few more scratches in the door."

"Add it to my rent."

Stephen made a mental note that Marguerite was Grace's landlord, as well as partner and apparently friend.

Somebody banged on the door.

Grace let out a surprisingly vile oath, startling a laugh from Stephen. "We're closed," she said. "Can't they see the sign?"

"I doubt it matters," said Marguerite, peering through the diamond windows. "He's got the livery of the Crown Prince of Charlock."

"I'll tell him to come back later."

"Not the Prince's messenger, you won't. Let him in." She swept the papers off the table and tucked them into her coat.

Grace sighed and unlocked the door. "Can I help you?"

"I've a message from His Magnificence, the Crown Prince," said the man. Marguerite looked smug.

"Oh. Well, you'd better come in then." She opened the door.

The man came in, dripping and bedraggled. He was very handsome, or would be if he wasn't soaked to the skin. He had honey colored hair and his livery fit him like a very soggy glove.

He bowed sweepingly to Grace, as if he was not currently doing a fine imitation of a drowned rat. A heavy gold necklace with an amber crystal swung against his chest as he straightened. "Do I have the honor of addressing the Master Perfumer Angelica?"

"That's me," said Grace. She rubbed her palms down her trousers and offered her hand.

The messenger took it, but instead of shaking, he lifted it to his lips. Stephen had a brief, intense desire to tear his arm off and then perhaps beat him about the head and shoulders with it.

Stop that. Down. You are what's left of a paladin. You do not treat any woman like a stray dog guarding a bone.

Besides, you could have kissed her hand when you first met. You didn't. That's on you.

I was dry humping her in an alley, he reminded himself. *I think we were a little beyond hand kissing at that point, and it hasn't really come up again.*

Grace retrieved her hand, a bemused expression on her face. "I, ah...hello?"

"My name is Ethan DuValier," the messenger said. "I come on behalf of the Crown Prince of Charlock."

He paused dramatically, as if expecting applause or perhaps for Grace to swoon at the idea.

"Uh...okay?" said Grace.

DuValier rallied well, Stephen would give him that. "Yes, His Magnificence has sent me to speak with you on his behalf. He was much struck at your meeting and wishes to engage your services."

"What services is he requesting?"

They had best be her skills as a perfumer, or I will tear his magnificence's arm off and beat him with it, too.

"He is extremely fond of the scent you prepared for him," said Ethan. "He would like to purchase a larger quantity of it, to take back to Charlock when we leave. Say perhaps...ten vials?"

Grace chewed on her lower lip briefly. "I don't have that much made up, I'm afraid, but if the pr—if His Magnificence can wait for three days, I can arrange that."

"Three days is more than sufficient," said Ethan. He smiled warmly. "He will be greatly pleased. And the cost?"

"Seventy-five golden talers," said Marguerite, before Grace could speak.

Stephen did not whistle out loud, but it was a near thing. A golden taler was the highest denomination of coin used in Archenhold. Seventy-five of them could house a family for a year, in a decent neighborhood with sewers and sidewalks. The rent in the too-cramped building he had grown up in was five silver talers a month, and silvers were worth less than half of gold.

Grace's eyes flickered for an instant, but she smiled at DuValier. "A discount for the Crown Prince, I see. Yes, of course."

"We are honored by his patronage," said Marguerite warmly.

Ethan inclined his head, but did not deny it. "He hopes that you will do the honor of presenting it to him personally. I shall come with a carriage in three days, then?"

"Most certainly," said Marguerite, when Grace didn't say anything. She raised an eyebrow at Ethan. "Pardon, Sir DuValier, but either your accent is superb, or you are not from Charlock originally."

He laughed ruefully, and pushed the wet hair out of his eyes. "You've found me out, Miss...?"

"Marguerite. I am the Master Perfumer's assistant."

"Business partner," protested Grace.

"Of course, of course." He glanced up at Stephen. He had an open, friendly expression and warm brown eyes. Stephen disliked him immediately. "And you are?"

"Stephen. I serve in the Temple of the Rat."

"A knight?"

"No. Merely a man-at-arms." Which was not untrue, although it left out a great deal.

"Ah, I see." He turned back to Marguerite. "Yes, Miss Marguerite, I am actually from Anuket City originally. Though it is my good fortune to serve Charlock now."

"You are nearly back home, then," said Marguerite.

Ethan was, apparently, too much of a diplomat to express how little Archon's Glory resembled Anuket City, despite being relatively close together. "Alas, I fear that my service to the crown prince does not allow me to return to Anuket often. But it would be merely nostalgia, in any event. My home is in Charlock now. I traveled there and fell immediately in love."

He smiled warmly at Grace as he said the last words. Stephen resisted the urge to loom over him. He was bigger than DuValier, he didn't need to prove it.

Grace had a distracted expression, and Stephen would swear she was working out perfume details in her head. "Ginger," she muttered, gazing vaguely over DuValier's shoulder. "Have I got enough ginger?"

"Three days, then," said Marguerite firmly.

"Yes, most certainly. I shall leave you to the act of creation. It shall be my great pleasure to see you again, Master Perfumer," said Ethan. He bowed deeply to Grace, with a sweep of his cloak. "My very...*great*...pleasure."

I could ram the cloak down his throat, if the arm doesn't come off easily enough.

"Yes, that's fine," said Grace, sounding even more distracted.

He made a less impressive bow to Marguerite, gave Stephen a perfunctory nod, and swept out the door as if he were the Crown Prince himself and it was not pouring buckets of rain.

It would probably be wrong to hope he drowns on the way back to the embassy.

"Seventy-five golden talers!" said Grace, turning on Marguerite. "My god! Why not ask for a summer home in Charlock while you're at it?"

"You handled that beautifully, though," said Marguerite. "'A discount for the Crown Prince.' I nearly swallowed my teeth."

"I was afraid he'd seen me nearly choke when I heard the number."

"I take it that it doesn't usually cost that much?" said Stephen.

"Gods, no! I don't think I make that in a year!"

"Exclusivity is expensive," said Marguerite, unruffled. "Charlock can pay it and won't even notice. When word gets out as to how much you charge, the nobles will all be dying to get scents from you so that they can impress each other with how much they spent on it."

Grace dragged her hands over her face. "Three years ago, I could barely afford bread," she said, to no one in particular. "I was living on potatoes that were already sprouting and turnips so old they had names."

A rush of fellow feeling rose in Stephen's chest. There was something about poverty that was a little like war. Either you had been there or you hadn't, and it wasn't really possible to explain it to anyone who hadn't. "I've been there," he said, with more warmth than he intended. Grace held his eyes briefly, understanding, and then they both looked away.

"Three years is a long time," said Marguerite.

"Indeed," said Stephen. Three years ago, he'd had a living god... but there was no point in dwelling on it.

"You'll come with me, won't you?" said Grace.

"Yes, of course," said Stephen and Marguerite simultaneously.

Stephen flushed. There was no question who she had been talking to. "I...ah..."

Marguerite gave him a look of amused pity. "You should come too. Makes us look better if we have a...what did you call it? Man-at-arms?"

"What do those even do?" said Grace.

"Well, a man-at-arms would be—"

"A bodyguard that does heavy lifting," said Marguerite.

"—more or less, yes."

"I thought that you were a knight," said Grace.

It shouldn't have stung, but it still did, a little. "Only a simple soldier," he said. "I was infantry before the god called me."

"And they don't knight you in the god's service?"

"Not the Saint," he said. "There are knights called to His service, but I was not one of them." He smiled faintly. "Plus knights are still usually mounted warriors, and I can say with some authority that horses do *not* care for berserkers."

"You act like a knight," muttered Grace, her downturned mouth turning down even farther. Stephen raised his eyebrows. "Oh, you know. Noble. Chivalrous." His chest swelled. "Stubborn." It deflated slightly.

Marguerite grinned. "Come back in three days, then, and you can be our man-at-arms. Assuming your duties allow it."

"The Rat has graciously suggested that I make getting to the bottom of the assassination my top priority. I believe this would fit under that aegis."

"Have they indeed?" murmured Marguerite, giving him a look that clearly had wheels turning behind it.

"You could not have expected that they would be uninterested," said Stephen.

"No, I suppose not." Marguerite stood, as did Grace. Stephen could read the signs when he was being dismissed.

"Three days, then," he said, and stepped out the door, wishing he'd had the nerve to kiss her hand.

"There goes a man who wants you," said Marguerite, as the dark shape of the paladin faded into the rain.

"What?" Grace blinked at her. "No."

"The hell he doesn't."

It was a pleasant thought, but Grace could remember the morning after the assassination attempt all too clearly. How she'd told him she didn't need rescue and he'd had to explain, so awkwardly and earnestly, that he wasn't there for *her*.

Though he *had* given her socks. But, well, socks probably didn't count as a romantic gift, did they? He couldn't know how much she'd appreciate the idea of someone worried that her feet would be cold. "No. He only comes here because you send for him. Because of the... you know...everything."

"I don't think that's the only reason."

Grace sighed. "Then he's probably here because of you, not me."

Of course he is. He didn't take his eyes off her in the carriage. And why would he? Marguerite was brilliant and charming and funny and kind. She had a body that men would fall down to worship, and she carried herself like a pirate queen. Grace begrudged her none of it. She loved Marguerite too. She would much rather have *been* Marguerite than herself, frankly. But what man would look twice at the strange gray mouse, with her cluttered workshop and her weird weasel, when Marguerite was there?

But dammit, sometimes she wished…

"Don't be ridiculous," said Marguerite. "He's decent and honorable and kind and probably says his prayers before bed." She frowned. "Actually, he's a paladin, so that bit goes without saying. What possible use would I have for a man like that? And what use would one have for me?"

Grace found that she had an irrational urge to defend him. Marguerite made him sound so boring. *He knits socks. Surely that must be worth something?* This did not seem like a good argument, so she settled on "He watches you all the time."

"Only because he thinks I'm a spy."

"You practically *told* him you were a spy."

"Yes, well. It's easier to get these things out of the way so that it doesn't come back to bite you later. And the Bishop over at the Temple of the Rat's no slouch, she'd have figured it out even if the paladin didn't."

Grace gave her a skeptical look as she headed back toward the workroom. "Anyway, that doesn't change the fact that he's not here for me."

"He absolutely is. He bristled like a boar when that DuValier fellow was flirting with you. If he's looking at me, it's because he's hoping you won't notice that he's watching *you* out of the corner of his eye."

"You're imagining things," muttered Grace. "And even if you weren't, what would *I* do with a…a man like that?"

Her imagination had some very insistent suggestions. Getting his armor off and seeing how much of that bulk was mail and how much was muscle, for example. *Purely for research purposes, of course.*

Marguerite gave her an amused look, as if she could read some of those thoughts. "Oh, I could think of a few things."

Grace could feel her face getting hot. *Oh for pity's sake! What's wrong with me? I haven't been a blushing virgin since the artificer's apprentice and I deflowered each other at seventeen. And unless he happens to also be a blushing virgin, he'd spend one night with me and go away disappointed anyway.*

Stephen was so damn polite, he wouldn't even tell her it had been awful. He'd probably just discover an intense calling to join a celibate order.

"Not all men are Phillip," said Marguerite gently. "You might consider it."

Grace shook her head. She took a perverse strength from her husband's name. She might be a slow learner, but some things did get beaten into her at last. "No. No, I don't think so. Not even for a man like that."

CHAPTER 22

Three days later, she was sitting in a chair in the front room, waiting for the paladin to arrive.

She told herself that she wasn't looking forward to seeing him. It was just that she needed to be there to unlock the door, since the shop was closed. That was all.

She flipped through her alchemical tome and tried a random page. "What's the future got for me, book?"

...this compound is composed from the noble mineral Sulphur and praised as the black lead of the Wise, being symbolic of the first heavenly sign in which the Sun is exalted, and being in the form of a red oil with a scent of surpassing sweetness...

Grace had her doubts that anything involving sulphur had much in the way of surpassing sweetness. She looked up, just in time to see an armored figure making his way across the street.

She sprang up and unlocked the door before he could knock. Stephen stepped inside.

"You look tired," Grace blurted, and immediately wanted to bite her tongue.

It's true, though. He does look tired. Stephen looked handsome as ever, but the strong planes of his face were softened by weariness, and there were deep shadows under his eyes.

"I am tired," admitted Stephen. He slung his cloak off his shoulders. "There's been a lot of work these last few days. But at least it's stopped raining for now."

"You've been working on the cleanup?" asked Grace.

"We all have." He shook his head. "So many people lost so much, and they didn't have much to begin with. And the flood brought down walls, so...a lot of heavy lifting. And we stood off some looters, although not many. People have been kind."

"Kind is good," said Grace. *That was eloquent. Well done, me.*

"And you?"

"Working." She waved vaguely toward the back room. "It's not a terribly complicated recipe, but the saffron is tricky. Half my workshop is yellow now. And it was a big order."

He nodded. "Was three days a reasonable amount of time?"

"Eh, reasonable enough. I wouldn't mind if I didn't have to hand-deliver it."

"Ah."

"I can't figure out why the Crown Prince wants me there," she muttered, rubbing her palms on her trousers. "Marguerite could hand it over just as easily."

"I believe he finds you interesting," said Stephen, with almost studied neutrality.

"Perfumes aren't that interesting," said Grace. "That is...err...well, *I* think they're interesting, obviously. But a prince? Surely he's got better things to do." The notion that the Crown Prince might find her, personally, interesting was so bizarre that she decided she must have misheard it.

"I think they're interesting," said Stephen.

"You're a *berserker paladin*," said Grace. "I spend a lot of time steaming herbs. Believe me, you're much more interesting than I am."

"You are rather less likely to run amok with steamed herbs, I suspect."

"Run amok?" Grace cocked her head. "Is that a thing you do?"

He stared at her for so long that she felt her cheeks start to heat up. "I'm sorry," said Grace. "Was I not supposed to say that? Damn.

I'm sorry. Maybe everyone else knows. I got here—to Archenhold, I mean—just when your order had the...uh..."

"When the Saint died," said Stephen, almost gently.

"Yes," she said. "I'm sorry. I guess I missed some details. Are you still...uh..."

"Prone to berserker fits? Yes, I'm afraid so."

He was looking at her with an expression that was so clearly expecting something and so obviously braced for the worst that Grace could not think of a damn thing to say. She settled on "Huh."

His dark eyebrows began to climb, rather like they had after she'd set herself on fire the day after the reception.

"I mean, you're not having one now," she said, hurrying to fill the awkwardness.

"No," said Stephen. "You'd know if I was."

Oh dear. I suppose he screams and gnaws on his shield or something. It was difficult to imagine such a violent emotion out of Stephen. He always seemed very calm, if slightly exasperated. "Do you have them often?"

"Not for over a year. It is something I try to avoid."

"Oh! Yes, I can imagine." She struggled to think of something else to say. "I'm sorry for your loss. Of the god, that is. That must have been very hard."

He gazed at her steadily, eyes unreadable. Grace bit her lower lip. "Err...was it hard? I don't know how gods work."

He exhaled. For a moment, Grace thought he might get angry, but he took the question seriously. That was a thing that she was noticing, that he took all her questions seriously and considered them, and felt they were worthy of an answer. She wasn't used to that.

"It is a hard thing to describe," he said at last. "In the moment, it was like being gutted. As if someone had reached into my body and torn out handfuls of flesh and the rest of me had collapsed around the holes."

Grace swallowed. She wanted to reach out to comfort him, but she did not quite dare.

"Since then..." He looked over at the row of little bottles on the sideboard, glittering like cut gems in the lamplight. "Well. Imagine that you had a bottle inside your chest. Glass, like one of these. And there was something inside it...something marvelous..."

He reached out a fingertip and stroked it over the facets of the nearest bottle. "Imagine that it was just there, like your heart or your lungs or your spine. Sometimes you were aware of it, sometimes it had light or heat but mostly it was just present. And once in a great while, you would open the bottle and it would pour out over you, like golden fire."

He was silent for a long moment. Grace almost thought he had said all that he meant to say, until he spoke again. "And then one day, without warning...it shattered."

For an instant, Grace feared that he would suit action to words. But his hands were as gentle as the rest of him, and he stepped back, leaving the bottle intact. He gazed at it, but she did not think he was truly seeing it.

"Like that," he said, his voice dropping low. "All the light and heat gone. A sucking darkness. And you are left with broken glass in your chest, and every time you move, it cuts you to ribbons."

A carriage passed in the street outside. The horse's hooves clattered on the cobbles, then died away into silence.

"I'm sorry," said Grace, almost inaudibly. *Why did I ask? I should not have asked. I should never have said anything.* Gods, of all the lessons she should have learned by now, why hadn't she learned when to shut up?

"I'm sorry, too. Well. We all bound ourselves up as best we could, my brothers and sisters and I. The ones who couldn't, died. The rest of us, I suppose, were too stubborn or stupid or dutiful, so we kept on living."

Everything Grace had said only made matters worse, so she stopped trying to say anything and just put her arms around him instead.

She was trying for an awkward sympathetic hug, since awkward sympathetic language hadn't gotten her very far. Stephen seemed startled. Grace thought for a moment that she'd offended him even worse, but his arms came up around her and he cautiously returned the hug.

His chest was very broad. The hardness was partly chain, but he had no chain on his arms and they were still like warm stone against her back. Her nostrils were suddenly full of the scent of gingerbread.

Heat sprang up between their bodies. She had only meant a single moment of comfort, but she was suddenly aware of her breasts pressed against his chest and that there was only an inch or two separating their hips. Then he moved slightly and that inch vanished as well, and there was only heat running from shoulder to thigh between them.

She had her chin down and her cheek against his shoulder. If she didn't move, she could still pretend that it was only a friendly gesture. *Which it is! Which is all it is!*

It did not feel friendly. It felt simultaneously dangerous and comforting, as if she stood in some safe, sheltered place and she belonged there, and that was incredibly dangerous, that would upset everything, her life was fine as it was and if she didn't pull away, something in her life might change forever.

One of his hands slid down to her waist. She could feel every finger splayed out against her back, as if imprinted there in fire. His arm tightened, pressing her against him, hip to hip, and perhaps it had been too long since she'd felt another body against hers, but a jolt went clear through her and she was suddenly, shockingly aroused. Much more aroused than could be explained by embracing a man in chainmail and gauntlets who wasn't even touching her skin.

Oh god, oh god, what do I do, this can't be right, I didn't mean for it to feel like this...

Her body was clearly very happy to feel like this. Her body wanted to rub up against him and purr. Her body was a goddamn idiot with no more shame than an alley cat.

Why did he have to smell like gingerbread? She could have stepped back and pretended nothing was happening and that it hadn't become something more than she expected, if only he hadn't smelled like goddamned gingerbread!

Grace lifted her chin and looked up at him and his face was right there and much too close, but neither of them pulled away. His eyes were dark with some emotion, but she did not think it was sorrow any longer.

He was not looking at her as if she had taken a friendly hug and made it strange. He was looking at her as if she were a drink of water in a dry land.

She tried to think of something to say and couldn't. She could see the shadow of stubble on his jaw. Her fingers itched to touch it and feel the texture of his skin. Her mouth felt dry.

She licked her lips and his eyes riveted on that gesture, even though she hadn't meant anything by it, she just couldn't talk without croaking but what was she even going to say?

He bent his head toward her and she could feel his breath against her lips.

Footsteps clattered on the stairs from Marguerite's apartment. She and Stephen sprang apart as if they were teenagers and someone's parents had suddenly come home.

"Ah, good you're here." Marguerite looked between them and her eyes narrowed just slightly. Grace told herself that human skin didn't show fingerprints and there was no way that she could know what they'd been doing.

Which was nothing. Which was a hug. People hug. Friends hug. He and I are friends.

Aren't we?

Granted, she hadn't known Stephen that long, but if you couldn't bond over multiple corpses, what *could* you bond over?

"Gods, Grace, you can't wear that."

Grace looked down at herself. She was wearing a clean tunic over one of her better pairs of trousers, the ones that Tab hadn't sharpened his claws on. "I can't?"

"Not to a formal audience, you can't."

"You're not going to spend three hours shoving me into another gown, are you?"

"I will if I have to."

She cast a look of mute appeal to the only other person there. "I think you look lovely as you are," Stephen said gallantly.

Marguerite grabbed her by the collar and began to haul her toward the stairs. "Lovely isn't good enough. You're about to make a year's worth of profits, you're expected to dress for the occasion."

Grace groaned and resigned herself to her fate.

~

Stephen watched Marguerite drag her business partner up the stairs and stifled a sigh of relief. From the hangdog look on Grace's face, this might take awhile, and that was all to the good. He was going to need a few minutes to recover himself from that embrace. Saint's teeth, he'd been within a hair of kissing her and that would have been a superbly bad idea.

It had been pity that moved her to hug him. He knew that. He didn't want anyone's pity, and certainly not hers. And yet when she'd gotten an arm across his chest and leaned in to hug him, despite that, despite the obvious innocence of the gesture, something had ignited in his chest and...well, substantially lower.

The heat between them didn't feel like pity. It felt big and dangerous and important. It felt like it mattered, and that was terrifying, but not nearly so terrifying as the possibility of stopping.

He'd found himself pulling her against him, and she hadn't recoiled, she'd leaned into him, all curves and softness fitting against his body. He had to fight for breath, even as he wished the coat of mail between them to the devil. And the gauntlets, why was he still wearing gauntlets, her hair was falling across his hand and he couldn't feel it through the leather, and what a colossal waste that was.

He'd held her in his arms before and it hadn't been like this. It hadn't been anything like this. Stephen couldn't remember anything that had ever been quite like this.

Oh Saint, it's been too long, it must be that it's been too long, I am starving and anything tastes of a feast...

Then she tilted her head to look up at him and he forgot to breathe entirely. Her wide eyes, with their flecks of green embedded in the gray, held no trace of pity. Astonishment, perhaps. Uncertainty. But also a heat that matched his own. Whatever he was feeling, she felt it too.

Her tongue flicked over her lips and Stephen felt a jolt that went clear through him and ended up directly at his cock. He was a heartbeat from sliding his hand lower and lifting her against him, covering her mouth with his, when he heard that footstep on the stairs.

It was for the best. Saints, it was undoubtedly for the best. Feelings that strong were dangerous. He had survived for three years by not feeling anything but duty, despair, and mild exasperation. He understood those. He could control those.

This did not feel like something he could control.

He pinched the bridge of his nose. *This is the wrong time and definitely the wrong woman. You're already trying to sort an assassination. Settle down.*

Beartongue had been very interested to learn that the assassin had been pre-poisoned. His inclination was still to blame the Motherhood, but as Zale had pointed out, they couldn't blame the Motherhood for *everything*. ("Much as we might want to," the lawyer-priest had said, glumly shoving a lock of pewter hair out of their eyes.)

Tab came out of the back room and began to mrrrp furiously at Stephen. Stephen, not being history's greatest monster, went down on one knee and petted the civette. His fur was coarse and faintly oily, long dark guard hairs tipped with silver over a paler undercoat. Not quite like a ferret, but closer than anything Stephen had encountered.

Tab approved of the petting and stood up so that his paws were on the paladin's shoulder. "Mrrr," he announced.

"You don't say."

God, he'd been so close to kissing Grace. So damn close. He could practically taste her on his tongue. A few seconds longer and it would have been more than mere imagining. He should be glad that they'd been interrupted, or else things would have become a thousand times more tangled than they were.

Besides, what do you have to offer any woman? "I will make sure you always have warm socks," *is not a line to set anyone's heart aglow.*

"Mr-r-r."

"That's your opinion."

"Mrrr!"

CHAPTER 23

When Grace and Marguerite finally came down the stairs again, they found him kneeling on the floor, looking resigned, with Tab draped across him like a lap quilt.

"That can't be comfortable," said Grace.

"I'm a paladin. I've done vigil on my knees many times." He gazed down at the civette. "Generally not with a weasel in my lap, I grant you."

Marguerite opened her mouth and Grace *knew* she was about to make a joke about vigils on one's knees. "Oh, look," she interrupted, "the carriage is here."

Stephen gathered up the sleeping civette and looked around for some place to set him. Grace moved to take the animal and Marguerite stepped between them. "Oh no! I did not spend all that time brushing weasel hair out of velvet for you to get covered again!"

Grace sighed. "On the chair," she said, pointing.

Stephen obeyed, his eyes flicking appreciatively over Grace's clothes. "The time was worth it," he said. "You look entirely suited for a royal audience."

Grace picked self-consciously at her sleeve. The coat of deep blue velvet made her feel as if she was going to attract every scrap of lint in a five-mile radius. But it hugged her figure in places where she wasn't entirely sure that she had a figure, and combined with the belted sash at her waist, made her feel a bit like a pirate.

I bet real pirates don't worry about lint. They worry about other things, like privateers and scurvy.

By the warmth in Stephen's eyes, he wasn't thinking about lint *or* scurvy.

When DuValier came through the door a moment later, he bowed over her hand even more dramatically than he had three days ago. "You are lovely as your wares, Master Perfumer," he said.

Grace had no idea how to respond to comments like this. It was flattering, but it was also clearly meant to be. Honestly, the man reminded her a bit of Phillip.

It's not his fault. They do it differently in Charlock. I'm sure he means nothing by it.

A thought struck her. *Oh dear, does that mean he expects me to compliment him back?* Marguerite hadn't said anything, but maybe it hadn't occurred to her that Grace didn't know. She eyed DuValier's outfit, which was in warm brown tones, with enough gold brocade to dazzle a magpie. What on earth could she say about that?

She fell back on something she did understand. "The fragrance you are wearing is very well-made," she said. "Amber, tobacco, a resinous wood but not sandalwood, which is badly overused." She sniffed. "And a hint of opium, I think. Well put together." Privately she thought that she could have done a trifle better, but it was solid work. Was she supposed to add something else? "It suits you."

DuValier looked briefly taken aback, then beamed. "Your skills are, if anything, far greater than rumor paints them." He ushered them out to the carriage, while Grace was still mulling over the alarming possibility that there were rumors about her.

DuValier handed Marguerite into the carriage, then Grace. He sprang in himself, glanced at Stephen, and gestured toward the back of the vehicle. Stephen, face impassive, moved out of Grace's line of sight. She felt the slight creak of the springs as he settled into the groom's position. Nothing unusual about a groom or a footman or a... what had he called himself? A man-at-arms?...riding at the back of the coach, but it felt strange and oddly demeaning. He wasn't her servant, he was her...her...

What is he, anyway?

Associate? Acquaintance? Unlikely co-conspirator in this strange world of assassins and poisoners? He'd given her socks, surely that meant he was more than an acquaintance. And he'd nearly kissed her —she was almost sure he'd nearly kissed her—and that was worth almost as much as socks.

Friend, she thought. *We will go with* friend.

DuValier kept up a stream of conversation on the way to the Crown Prince's temporary lodgings. It was all light, flattering banter and Grace found it exhausting after about five minutes. Marguerite stepped into the gap, flirting outrageously, while Grace stared out the window and wondered how exactly she would duplicate the scent of expensive carriage with expensive upholstery that was nevertheless just slightly damp and had the tiniest hint of oncoming mildew. *Woods and earths and something warm and slightly dusty to stand in for the velvet...hmm, not sure what to do with the mildew. Perhaps I could use actual mildew. I wonder if anyone's ever tried to isolate that before.*

I wonder if Stephen's cold. It's not raining for once but it can't be warm there. Oh dear.

When the carriage stopped, DuValier got out. He turned as if to help the two women out, but Stephen beat him to it, stepping smoothly past him and offering his gloved hand. Grace smiled at him. *Friend.* And he still smelled like gingerbread.

DuValier looked ever so slightly put out. Stephen's face was like granite. The paladin then compounded the issue by walking a step back and to the left of Grace, in an honor guard position. She looked over her shoulder, feeling his presence there, and his back was sword-straight. He looked positively martial.

Well, he was a soldier before he was a paladin. And I suppose paladins are just divine soldiers. It was still a little unsettling.

She did not seem to be the only one unsettled. DuValier was forced to walk in front of Marguerite and Grace, so that in order to talk to them, he had to keep turning until he was nearly walking backward. He made the best of it, but his eyes kept straying over Grace's shoulder to her watchdog. Marguerite was wearing a serene smile that Grace knew, from long experience, was a stand-in for a grin as broad as the Elkinslough river.

The carriage had pulled into the formal quarters for visiting dignitaries, which resembled a cross between a small palace and a large hotel. It was in the formal style of Archenhold, all stone and arches and tall pillars. Grace was rather fond of how clean the lines were here compared to the style of Anuket City, which never saw a facade it didn't want to ornament or a stone that couldn't be carved into ten animals and an allegorical representation of Prosperity.

"Master Perfumer," said DuValier, as two footmen opened the imposing double doors, "please be welcome in the Crown Prince's home away from home. I regret that I cannot welcome you to the palace in Charlock. Without meaning to disparage in any way the hospitality of Archon's Glory, the surroundings are of course far different and one can never welcome guests as well as one can into one's own home."

"Uh…sure," said Grace. She glanced around the grand entryway, which had very large urns filled with peacock feathers. It smelled of incense and underneath that, of wood polish and bleach. The smell was not unpleasant, particularly given how many buildings stank. "It smells clean."

Marguerite put her hand over her mouth.

DuValier smiled. "You are certainly an original, Master Perfumer Angelica."

"I'm sorry?" said Grace automatically.

"There is nothing to be sorry for. It is refreshing." He glanced over her shoulder again. "Your man-at-arms is welcome to visit the kitchens until you must leave us."

Grace stiffened. Marguerite opened her mouth to speak, but Stephen beat her to it. "Where Miss Angelica goes, I go," he said, in a voice so deep Grace could almost hear it through her boots.

"There is no need to fear that she'll be attacked here," said DuValier, forgetting himself enough to actually address the paladin.

"She might require a jar opened," said Stephen, unruffled. "Or something heavy moved. My duty is clear."

Marguerite needed a minute. Grace, never fond of confrontation, didn't know whether to laugh or squeak with horror. What on earth were they *doing?*

DuValier's mouth opened, then closed. He clearly had not the faintest idea how to respond to such a statement. After a moment, he gathered himself enough to laugh and say, "I suspect that there is no shortage of people who can open any jars that the Master Perfumer might encounter."

Stephen tilted his head so that it was very clear he was looking *down* at the man in golden livery. "I am also very skilled at reaching things on high shelves."

Grace couldn't take it any more. "I'd rather not keep the Crown Prince waiting," she said. Gods, what else would move things along quickly? "And...um...my shoes pinch."

The other three people all looked down at her feet. Grace reddened and fought the urge to shift the feet in question nervously.

"I can fetch a chair," said DuValier hastily.

"I can carry you," said Stephen.

Marguerite's shoulders began to shake with suppressed laughter.

Oh sweet gods and goddesses, are they fighting *over me?*

It was ludicrous. It was absurd. It made no sense. No one fought over a weird little gray mouse like Grace. It didn't happen. But Stephen had nearly kissed her. She was nearly certain that he had. And he'd given her socks, although it was a far cry from giving her socks to fighting with someone. The ballads always made it sound as if having men fight over you was romantic. The reality seemed to be horribly embarrassing and very awkward. Grace didn't know whether she should feel guilty or slap them both.

"You grant your servants an enormous degree of liberty," said DuValier, apparently remembering that it was beneath his dignity to fight with a man-at-arms. He fingered the amber crystal that hung at his throat.

"He's not a servant," said Grace indignantly. "He's...ah..." Oh blast, what did she say?

"Sworn to her service," rumbled Stephen. "By an oath."

"You are?" said DuValier, which was good because otherwise Grace would have said it, and that would have rather spoiled the effect. "I thought you were sworn to the Temple of the Rat."

"I swear a lot."

"*About those shoes,*" said Marguerite hastily. Grace attempted to hobble dramatically. Her shoes weren't actually that bad, but if they kept her standing around in the hall while people argued, she was going to take them off. Possibly in order to hit someone over the head with one. DuValier gave up, turned on his heel, and led them through the building.

Grace had been dreading another formal presentation, but the emissary from Charlock took them up the stairs instead, to a suite of rooms that must have been the Crown Prince's. The architecture here had been softened with dozens of tapestries that were definitely not from Archenhold. They showed scenes of hunting and warfare under a blazing sun. Grace realized that she had no idea what Charlock was like, so far as climate was concerned. "Is Charlock in a desert?" she asked.

DuValier slowed, looking over his shoulder. "Ah, the tapestries. No, we are not a true desert, though parts are certainly very dry. But Charlock encompasses a wide range and the eastern border is very lush. The tapestries are from Baiir. Their weavers are famed throughout the world, and one of their lords commissioned these as a gift to the Crown Prince's grandfather. But of course, they had no real idea what Charlock looked like either, so they produced these. Beautiful, but not entirely accurate." He gave the tapestries an amused glance. "They are part of the furnishings that accompany the royal household when it travels."

Grace tried to imagine how vast a set of furnishings the royal household must have, if a dozen tapestries were simply thrown in as a matter of course. How many wagons must it take? Did the prince bring his own furniture as well? A mattress so that the Royal Lower Back need not suffer the indignity of strange beds?

Another door and a wave of scent rolled out, thick as syrup. Grace picked out notes of amber, vetiver, and yes, sandalwood, but in a minor key compared to the others. The scent was warm and masculine and that would have been fine except that her mind was still stuck on the syrup and went to *masculine syrup* which would be the world's worse euphemism for...well, there was really only one thing it could be a euphemism for. She had a strong urge to laugh hysterically and forced it down.

The Crown Prince was in bed. He was fully dressed, and the bed was on a dais, but there was no getting around the fact that he was reclining against pillows. Oddly, this did not make him look in any way frail. The Archon would have looked small and lost in the expanse of mattress, but the Crown Prince looked like a large, predatory cat. He even had a rather feline expression—the one that said that he was currently lounging and relaxed and that within an eyeblink, he could leap into action and pounce on any small, unsuspecting furry thing in the vicinity.

Grace felt rather like a small unsuspecting furry thing herself.

Several ministers or servants or attendants or...whatever the hell they were, they were much better dressed than Grace, anyway, and probably substantially more important...were standing near the foot of the bed, chatting. They looked up as DuValier entered the room.

DuValier announced them, omitting Stephen, then stepped to one side of the door. Grace and Marguerite moved with him. Stephen stood behind them with the formal bearing of an honor guard. Grace didn't know if he was trying to show up DuValier or if he just had that sort of posture. *Paladins probably all learn how to stand around and look like statues, don't they? Confession, smiting evil, formal audiences, the whole curriculum.*

Marguerite leaned in and murmured "The Crown Prince will tell you to approach in a moment. Walk toward him. A minister will take the box from you and look inside, then you will be allowed to approach. Answer him when he talks, don't start the conversation. It won't take long."

"Right," said Grace. "Right. Okay." Where was the box? She had it, didn't she? She hadn't left it in the carriage? "Um. Where...?"

Stephen handed her the box. Grace flashed him a look of pure gratitude. He nodded infinitesimally.

"Master Perfumer Angelica," said the Crown Prince, in a carrying voice.

She almost said "Yes?" but caught herself. *Right. I have to approach him. I have to walk up to the bed and present the perfume. I have to do this.*

Her hands shook as she gripped the small wooden box. She owned dozens of wooden boxes, suitable for holding perfume vials. There was a craftsman in the Glass Quarter who she probably single-handedly kept employed making them all. She'd always been rather proud of the simplicity of the design, which set off the tiny, faceted bottles, which were made down the road from the boxes by another artisan. She was probably keeping his children fed and clothed as well, given the number of bottles she bought.

Facing the leonine Crown Prince, she suddenly wished that the boxes were more ornate. Set with gold, maybe. For seventy-five gold talers, you bought presentation to go with the perfume, didn't you? Marguerite had been telling her that for years.

She was nearly level with the Crown Prince now and she was absolutely not going to scream or faint or shout "Masculine syrup!" and dissolve into hysterical laughter. She wasn't. She refused.

"Ah, Master Perfumer," said the Crown Prince warmly. "When I return to Charlock, your scent shall be the talk of the kingdom."

Say something. Say something that isn't masculine syrup. *Do it.*

"I am honored that your maj—" *was it majesty or magnificence shit shit masculine shit* "—magnificence enjoys it," she said. And then, wracking her brain for something that was true and reasonably respectful, "I've made many perfumes for people who wanted them because they were fashionable. It is very nice to find someone who understands the fragrance for itself." Nice. Nice was the wrong word. Dammit. "Very gratifying." There, that was better.

He smiled. Her face felt hot. Then suddenly DuValier was leading her away and no one was staring at her and the Crown Prince was talking to someone else, so presumably she had not fainted or vomited or screamed "Masculine syrup!" at a foreign head of state.

She had no idea what happened next. Did they have to stand around the room waiting? Did something else happen? Was she going to get paid? Presumably the Crown Prince didn't just hand you money, someone else did it.

Stephen took her arm. She leaned against him, grateful for the solidity. He was a paladin. He did honor guard things. He must know what the polite thing to do next was.

Apparently they got to leave the room. DuValier opened the door and bowed them through it, looking past Stephen as if he did not exist. The neighbor's cat did that sometimes, when there was a strange dog in the alley. The dog was too large to fight, so the cat chose to believe it was not real and gazed through it, bored.

"How are your feet?" he asked.

Grace blinked at him, then remembered. "Oh! Fine. Pinchy. I should...um. Go home. Take the shoes off. Yes."

"Yes, of course. The carriage will be waiting." He reached out and took her hands. Given that her arm was threaded through Stephen's, and DuValier was currently ignoring the paladin, this took a certain amount of finesse, and Grace was actually rather impressed at how well he managed it. "I fear that the court will be returning to Charlock in the next few days. However, I hope that when next I return to your city, you will allow me to call upon you?"

"Yes, of course," said Grace, only half paying attention. "You know where the shop is." Had they gotten money? She would have to ask Marguerite.

DuValier handed both women up into the carriage with great ceremony and attempted to slam the door. Stephen had hold of it already and it only moved about three inches. The envoy looked briefly puzzled, then stepped back as if it had been his own idea, bowed in the general direction of the carriage, and turned away.

Stephen jumped up into the carriage and dropped onto the seat opposite them. The driver slapped the reins and they pulled away from the embassy.

"Thank the gods that's over," said Grace, sinking into the cushions with a groan. "Marguerite, did we get paid?"

"Oh yes." Marguerite dropped an ornate leather pouch into her lap. "A functionary handed it to me. Princes don't get their hands dirty with filthy lucre, and presumably Master Perfumers aren't supposed to either."

"This one does," said Grace, counting up the coins. "Particularly when there's this much of it. Gods, I'll be able to pay taxes in advance for once. And pay off my tab at the glassblowers."

"You could even get higher-class packaging made," said Marguerite.

"Let's not go nuts."

Her friend snorted and rolled her eyes, but abandoned this line of thought to look over at Stephen. "Do I want to know what that display back there was all about?"

"I don't trust him," said Stephen, looking more inscrutable than usual.

"He's a political envoy, of course you shouldn't trust him. But it's not like we were in any danger of handing him a housekey."

"Mmm."

CHAPTER 24

Stephen did feel somewhat ashamed of his conduct, although only somewhat. He had been rather less than gracious. It was just that men like DuValier frequently needed to be reminded that the woman they were attempting to charm had extremely charmless protectors.

Grace didn't ask for your protection.

Well, she'd gotten it anyway.

She certainly didn't ask to be treated like a bone that two dogs were fighting over.

He gritted his teeth and said, "I apologize if I made you uncomfortable."

Grace, who was staring out the window, said, "Huh? What?"

"At the embassy. I apologize if my conduct made you uncomfortable."

"Oh. It did, yes." She leaned over and patted his arm. "It's all right. I was nervous too. I kept thinking I was going to say something wildly inappropriate or start giggling hysterically at the Prince."

"You'd hardly be the first," said Marguerite.

It was on the tip of Stephen's tongue to say that nervous had not exactly been what he was feeling, but he decided to let it go. He was still recovering from the near-kiss earlier, he didn't need to deal with any more fraught emotions today.

"Well, at least the rain's let up," said Grace, watching the city go by the windows. "I was running out of oakmoss."

"Oakmoss?" said Stephen.

She cocked an eyebrow up at him. "It's a moss. Grows on trees."

"Oak trees, perhaps?"

"You're quick."

"I have my moments. Does it not grow in the rain?"

"Oh, it grows fine, I just can't go out to collect it without getting drenched." She gestured vaguely north. "There's an oak wood across the Elkinslough, in the commons, where I harvest most of it. I'll probably pick up half my body weight in mud, but at least I can get some. I'll go tomorrow if it holds."

"You walk?" said Stephen, surprised.

"I'm hardly going to rent a carriage like this to take me out there and then sit there while I traipse around for an hour. And it's not like I own a horse. So, yes, I walk."

"I'll come with you," he said at once.

Grace folded her arms. "I don't remember inviting you," she said. She still seemed a bit amused, but Stephen could sense the annoyance lurking just under the surface. Marguerite gave him a cautionary you-are-moving-on-thin-ice look.

"Sorry. Let me try that again." He raked a hand through his hair. "Please allow me to accompany you."

"Why? It's not that interesting. I walk around and pull moss off trees. It's like mushrooming, only even more boring and you don't get to eat it afterwards."

"Am I really the only person concerned about the severed head situation in this city?" said Stephen. "Really?"

"I'm sure the people who had their heads cut off were very concerned," said Marguerite.

"At least briefly," added Grace.

Stephen gazed at the ceiling and wondered if the Rat would heed a prayer for strength. Grace took pity on him. "All right, I admit, I'd forgotten the head thing. Are they any closer to catching him?"

"No. Captain Mallory, the man in charge, is a decent man, but they're giving him nothing to work with, because it's in a poor quarter and...well." He shook his head.

"Have they found any more? Maybe he stopped."

"I'm going to go out on a limb and say that once you're in a place where you chop people's heads off for the fun of it, you probably don't come back from there," said Stephen. "But no, they haven't. Although with the rain lately, that doesn't mean he stopped. Any victims could have been washed out and we'd never find them."

"It's mostly in Weaver's Nest though, isn't it?" asked Grace.

"Not any more," said Stephen gloomily. "Weaver's Nest is half underwater right now, so nobody knows where he's gone. If he's moved on, we won't know until we start finding more heads." *And she wants to go somewhere miles from the city where no one can even hear her screaming...* "If it's a richer area, they'll complain that Mallory hasn't solved it yet and put someone else on it, probably a political appointee, and it'll take twice as long. The Rat's sent criers to every neighborhood telling people not to go out alone, but not everyone can listen."

"Still no sign of the bodies?" said Marguerite.

"No." Stephen had a theory, but he didn't want to say it. Some things were best not uttered aloud.

"I wonder if he's eating them," said Marguerite, immediately uttering it aloud. Stephen put his hand over his eyes. So much for protecting anyone's delicate sensibilities. *Really, I should have known better.*

"All of them?" Grace looked skeptical. "That's a lot to get through. And you can't eat the bones."

"Fine, maybe he's chopping them up and selling them as meat. That's why he has to get rid of the heads, so they aren't obviously human."

"And the hands and the feet," said Grace. "Hmm. Where did those end up, do you think?"

"In the water with the head, maybe," said Marguerite. "But they'd decay a lot quicker, wouldn't they?"

"Fish could eat them," said Grace.

"Ghouls," said Stephen. "I am surrounded by ghouls."

"There's no fish in the Elkinslough," argued Marguerite. "Not live ones, anyway. That river's full of shit and dye run-off and god knows what else."

"There's catfish."

"There are not."

"I have personally seen catfish," Stephen volunteered. "They don't look healthy, but they're there."

"Fine," said Marguerite. "So these unhealthy catfish are eating the severed hands. There, you see? Perfect crime."

There was a lengthy pause while everyone considered this.

"What were we talking about again?"

"*Please* let me come with you to get the moss," said Stephen. "So you don't wind up as a pile of severed hands inside a diseased catfish."

"Well, when you put it like *that...*" Grace gave him that crooked grin that hurt his heart. "All right. Be here at the shop after breakfast."

The sun was still out the next day, although it didn't look happy about it. There was a thick layer of cloud and the light had that bright, indirect quality that threw everything into sharp focus, particularly the mud coating the hill, the stones, and the trees to well over head-height.

"So much mud," said Grace, shaking her head. "Have you ever seen mud like this?"

Stephen looked over the hillside, remembering a village in the rainy season, where the mud was so thick that horses couldn't get into it. One of the local clans had split over who was to be the new lord, and the losing side had been thrown out and had taken over the village and put anyone suspected of being loyal to the winner to the sword. The clans hated to have outsiders involved, but they were horse lords, used to mounted combat, and could not wait until the mud dried to ride their steeds into the valley. They needed someone to get in while there was still someone left to save.

The battle tide had carried him forward. Shane had been there too, and Galen and Wren. Blood had pooled in the pocked surface of the mud when they were done. They had barely been able to walk afterward, their thigh muscles cramped from the effort of wading through the knee-deep mud, of lifting feet with twenty pounds of wet muck stuck to each shoe.

In the end, they saved nine people out of thirty. The look in the lord's eyes when he saw how pitifully few had survived, the horror and gratitude mixed up together, stayed with Stephen long after the muscles unknotted and he was able to walk normally again.

"Stephen?"

"No, never," he lied. "Are you sure you want to keep going?"

"If I don't do it today, I'll just have to do it later on, and then it'll probably be raining as well as muddy." Grace shook her head. "I doubt it's going to stay clear for more than a day or two."

Stephen sighed. She was likely right. He floundered out into the mud, hearing it suck at his boots. "Stay there, I'll try to find the best route." He gazed at the sodden mess of the hillside and added "Or the least awful route, anyway."

They were both mud splattered by the time they got to the top. Grace had worn her most battered tunic and trousers, so she looked better than he did. Stephen was not looking forward to getting the mud out of his armor.

At least the Saint's chosen don't wear much armor on the bottom half. If I had to get this mess out of full chain, I'd give up and turn it into a flowerpot.

Grace, being shorter, had sunk deeper into the mud. He held out his arm, which was purely a chivalrous gesture and should not have made every sense in his body focus on the six square inches of his arm that she was touching. Not even when she leaned against him and her breast brushed against his elbow. He was wearing leather vambraces. He couldn't actually feel that touch. It was completely his overheated imagination that it seared him all the way to the bone.

"Are you sure there's moss here?"

"Well..." She eyed the trees, which were now only covered in mud to shoulder height. "I mean, there was. And there probably still is, it's just...under..." She poked at the mud, which was starting to dry and crack. "But I can't very well go around cleaning off trees in hopes I find something."

She put her hands on her hips and peered upward into the branches. "We're looking for a little plant, about yea big, pale gray-green. The leaves look like dozens of antlers. I mean it's a moss, not really a plant, so I guess they're not leaves exactly but you get the point."

Stephen shaded his eyes against the white glare of the sky and peered from branch to branch.

"Ah..." Grace cleared her throat. "That's a maple, not an oak. You want to look in one of the ones with the bark like this."

"Sorry," he said. "I'm a city boy by nature. Most of the time I spent in the woods was going from one place to another. I didn't look at a lot of trees. Or...well, I looked at them, but I didn't pay much attention, except to whether someone was hiding behind them or not."

"Different skills," said Grace generously. "If it helps, I didn't leave Anuket City until I was twelve. Then my master dragged me out to find some of the more common things because he didn't like the way his supplier was preparing the oils." She smiled crookedly. "He had to be carried out in a litter because he couldn't walk so far on his own, so it was the two bearers and me in the middle of a piece of parkland, and they didn't know what to think. Nobody ever hires them to wander around in the woods, looking for herbs."

"And now?" he asked. "Do you come out here often?"

Grace frowned up at the crisscrossing branches. "I used to. Not here, but out of Anuket. To get away from my...partner."

"Marguerite?"

"No. Before then. Another perfumer, he..." She waved her hand. "We didn't get along well," she said, with a note of finality.

Stephen watched as she wrapped her arms around her torso,

almost unconsciously making herself smaller. He made a mental note to find this former partner and loom over him very insistently.

"Were you unhappy?" asked Stephen.

Grace clearly had to think about it. "I suppose so. Yes, I must have been, but...it's so hard to say. I was so relieved, you see." She gnawed on her lower lip. "To be out of my apprenticeship and able to sell my own perfumes. I hadn't known how I was going to do that. And relief feels like happiness, if you don't know the difference. I don't know that I'd have been able to tell you that, at the time. It took distance, and I was still so close to it then."

"We're all very close to our lives," said Stephen. "Most of the time, anyway. And then?"

"And then I wasn't," she admitted. "Relief wasn't enough any more. But I'd been there so long, you know, that it took...well, a long time."

"It's all right," he said, seeing her flush at a memory. Yes, he was definitely going to loom over that partner, and perhaps gently express the thought that human joints were such fragile things. "There's no shame in that."

"Isn't there?" asked Grace. "It seems like if I was wiser or cleverer or...or more experienced, or something..."

"No." He was using the voice, he could hear himself doing it, but he believed it and he wanted her to believe it as well. "You can't blame yourself for not knowing what you were never allowed to know."

"I'm happy now, I think," she said. She clearly meant it lightly, but then the truth spilled out anyway. "Or I would be, if there weren't all these assassinations and bodies and documents and whatnot. Sometimes I still am, and it startles me, because I don't feel like I have a right to be happy when all this is going on."

"You always have a right to be happy," he said.

Her face lit up. She was looking in his direction and for a moment, Stephen thought that look was for him. His chest tightened much harder than it had before and he took a step toward her, almost involuntarily.

"Look!" she said, pointing.

It was over his shoulder. The feeling fled. He turned and found that she was pointing at a branch well above his head.

"Is that it?" he asked, squinting. It looked like a clump of hair on a twig.

"That's it! Now I just have to get up there." She approached the tree, frowning. It had a Y-split in the trunk, and he could just imagine her trying to climb up onto it, despite the slick coating of mud.

Saint's teeth, if I wasn't here she'd do it and probably break her neck. Does no one on earth think of safety? Ever?

"I have a better idea," he said. She turned toward him. Stephen bent down, wrapped his arms around her hips, and lifted her up to reach the oakmoss.

"Waaaa!" She clutched at his shoulders, torn between laughing and horror.

"Can you reach now?" he asked.

"I think so." She leaned forward and he staggered back a step to keep her in position.

Within about five seconds, Stephen knew that he had made a severe miscalculation. His jaw was pressed against the soft curve of her belly and one of her breasts was actually resting on top of his head. *Saint's bloody tongue, what was I thinking?* He groaned.

"Are you all right? Am I too heavy?"

"You're fine," he said. The weight was not the issue. At all. It was her hips against his chest, the fact that he was drowning in softness... dear god. He tried to hold still and think of something else. Anything else. Nothing came to mind.

Actually quite a lot came to mind, but it was mostly images of finding a convenient tree trunk, lifting her up a few inches higher, and burying his face between her thighs. Tasting her until she was soaked and gasping and then lowering her onto his waiting cock— sweet gods alive and dead, *why* had he picked her up? He hadn't been thinking, and now he was thinking quite a lot and about all the wrong things.

It would be a terrible idea, he told himself. *Sex in the woods is lousy.*

You get pine needles in places. And right now it's all mud and mosquitoes. Terrible, horrible idea.

His body did not agree. His body had definite opinions about the matter.

Stop. You are the responsible one. You are not going to make love to a woman on a mud-infested hillside. That is not responsible. She will get bug bites. So will you.

Grace leaned forward even farther and he could feel her muscles tensing as she reached for the highest bit of moss. Her breast pressed against his scalp. "Nearly there," she said cheerfully. He heard the sound of the knife scraping on the bark. It was a sound that would cool nearly anyone's ardor, and he embraced it gratefully. *Knives. Yes. She'll stab you. You'll deserve it. If you were as honorable as a paladin should be, you'd probably stab yourself for her.*

"Done!" she sang out. "Let me sheath this knife so I don't stab you...sorry, did you just say something?"

"...nothing."

Stephen set her down, or tried. In practice, this meant that she slid down the front of him, body pressed against his, one hand on his biceps and the other holding the knife and a bag of thready green moss.

"We did it!" she said, beaming up at him with shared triumph.

It was too much. His god had been of steel but he was only flesh and bone. "We did," he said, and lowered his mouth to hers.

CHAPTER 25

Her lips were like ice against his, and for a moment all he could think of was that she was cold, of course she was cold, it was a cool day and they'd been standing around in cold mud and he had not realized. He wanted to wrap his body around hers and breathe warmth into her.

He pulled one of his gloves off and lifted his hand to her cheek. It was cold under his palm, but the heat that sprang up between them threatened to burn him where he stood.

He'd pictured this since yesterday. He would go slowly, carefully, as delicate as a moth's wings. Sudden passion would only scare her.

It would sure as hell scare *him*.

Gently. Carefully. Let her pull away, if this isn't what she wants.

Grace's mouth opened under his and all his good intentions went straight to hell.

She tasted of salt and sage and her mouth was as hot as her lips were cold. He pulled her tight against him and her hands slid up his back, pressing her body even closer. The space between them seemed intolerably large, even if it was only a few layers of clothing and— well, admittedly a chain hauberk, that wasn't nothing, even if he was vaguely astonished that it didn't turn to ash and fall away the longer they kissed.

He tangled his bare hand in her hair, feeling the strands curling around his fingers. His lips left hers and he trailed kisses over her jaw, down her throat, feeling the cold skin warm under his touch. She made a small, pleased sound in the back of her throat, almost a whimper, and he thought he might lose control right then and there.

Control.

What little he had was already slipping, burned away by the heat between them, by the sounds she made as he set his lips against her pulse and felt it beating fast, by the sensation of her body rubbing against his.

Dangerous, whispered his mind. *This is dangerous.*

The tide rising in his blood was red, not black, but it was too much alike, too close. He could lose himself too easily in the heat of her body. This was a tide that could wash away his past and his duty and everything else that held him back and kept him sane. If kissing her was doing this much to him, how much farther would it go?

He didn't know. He wanted very much to find out, to let passion burn away the hollow, lonely places for a moment, to be with her and for a few minutes to not be broken.

She was melting against him, her hand curling against the back of his neck to draw him closer. *More,* he thought, mental voice hazy with lust. *More.* He could give her more. He could give her everything, could stoke the fire between them until it consumed them both.

She gasped, and even though it was from pleasure—he was nearly certain it was pleasure—the sound, and the thought for an instant that he might be hurting her, shocked him free of the tide.

Stephen lifted his head and stepped back.

"I'm sorry," he said, releasing her. "That shouldn't have happened."

Her eyes had been heavy-lidded, her mouth lifted in a smile. He watched realization slash across her face as if he'd slapped her. He felt like the lowest worm in creation.

Shit. You didn't want to hurt her and this is what you get. Saint's bloody tongue. Her face relaxed into chilly immobility, but the hurt in her eyes felt like a knife in his ribs. He honestly would have rather she stabbed him.

"Grace, I'm sorry, that wasn't what I meant to—"

"I see."

"Dammit, Grace, I didn't mean..." He reached out for her, then stopped. She skittered away from his touch as if he were diseased.

She held up a hand. "It's fine. You're not interested. I am not interested either. No one is interested."

"It's *not* that I'm not interested, it's..." What could he say? *I would take you right here, right now, if I could, but I'm afraid I might run mad and kill us both?* This wasn't the sort of thing that put a woman you'd kissed at ease.

"Then what is—no. No, you know, don't tell me." She turned away and began stalking down the hillside. "*I* am not interested. That's all that matters."

She was not a terribly good liar. Her swollen lips and mussed hair didn't help.

"It's just...I'm a *paladin*," he said, chasing after her. "One of the Saint of Steel's."

"Is your order sworn to celibacy, then?" Each word sounded as if it had been carved out of ice.

"No, of course not, but..." He raked his hands through his hair. "I'm sorry. I shouldn't have done that. I shouldn't have done any of this. I know, the last few days, I...I might have let you think there could be something between us, but..."

"I wasn't the one who insisted you come here," said Grace.

Which was true and shut him up. *Probably that's a good thing. If Istvhan were here, he'd put me in a headlock and tell me to not say another word.*

"Anyway, you've got a lot of nerve," she said, squelching and sliding down the hill. He wanted to offer her his arm again, and didn't dare. "I don't recall suggesting there *be* anything between us. You may have rescued me a time or two, but that doesn't mean I'm going to fall at your feet. My life is very good and I love it and I *don't* wish to see it disrupted."

. . .

And that would have been a very good line, thought Grace, *if I hadn't fallen on my ass immediately afterward. The gods are not being kind today.*

She clawed her way back to her feet, feeling her left boot fill with mud, feeling the cold wet mud chase out any lingering vestiges of the warm sensations she'd felt when Stephen was kissing her.

It had been good. Damn him to hell, it had been *so* good. As good as the first real kiss she'd shared with the artificer's apprentice, the one where the sheer novelty of someone *wanting* to kiss her had fired up her nerves and every new sensation felt like a revelation. Kissing hadn't felt like that for a long time. And his arms around her had felt so solid and so protective. She'd felt safe. She *never* felt safe, but for just a moment...

Evidently it hadn't been nearly as impressive for him.

She tried to think of all the ways she could have done better—moved her lips more or done something fancy with her tongue. Rubbed against him harder. Apparently whatever she'd been doing hadn't been enough, because she'd been five seconds and a good excuse from shucking her clothes off right there and then he'd set her down and apologized.

Phillip had been right, she thought morosely. She was just terrible in bed and there was nothing else to be said about it. Apparently she was even terrible at kissing. And it was entirely like a paladin to apologize to you for how bad you were at something. And the bastard still smelled like gingerbread.

He tried to help her up. She just looked at him. Somehow he didn't crumble to dust.

If he did, even the damn dust would smell like gingerbread.

She wanted to cry and scream and throw things, but damned if she was going to do it in front of him. Crying in front of Phillip had been bad enough, but Stephen would actually pity her, would probably try to comfort her, and she couldn't take that. She had her pride. She had precious little else, but damned if she was going to let him play the rescuer one more time.

"I don't need your help," she said, once she was back on her feet.

"I have looked out for myself for years, and I am very good at it. You don't need to trouble yourself on my account."

"Would it be so bad to have someone else watching out for you?"

"It hasn't gone so well for me in the past," snapped Grace. Gods, what did he want from her? *First he kisses me, then he shoves me away, then he tells me I need someone to look out for me...why can't he make up his damn mind?*

Her lips still felt bruised from the kiss, and the frustrated throb between her legs was gone but not forgotten. And the fact that she had felt, for a moment, as if someone else was watching out for her only made her furious. *Goddamn paladins.*

"You're not worried about your safety?"

"I walked here from Anuket City with the clothes on my back and a civette. In winter. I'll manage."

Stephen inhaled sharply. "I...see."

She doubted that he did. She'd gone on foot in a storm, and what should have taken three days and a ferry crossing had taken five. It had been a mild storm by Archenhold winter standards, but it was still a minor miracle that she hadn't lost several toes.

"That's a hard walk in winter," he said.

"I was most worried about Tab," she admitted. "I had him in my shirt and I kept checking to see if he was dead. Every time, I thought *this is it, he's finally gone.*"

She didn't know why she was telling him this. She was still angry at him, and she still sure as hell didn't want his pity. Maybe it was just her fate to have earnest, awkward conversations with this man.

Normal people flirt. I think. Apparently we just exchange terrible life stories.

Stephen did not look flirtatious. His jaw was so clenched that she was surprised she couldn't hear his teeth grinding. The lips that had moved so tenderly over hers were set in a hard, implacable line.

"You shouldn't have had to do that," he said.

"No, I shouldn't have. But life is what it is, and I wasn't going to wait around for another asshole to make up his mind over whether or not he wanted me."

She took a bitter pleasure in how white he went at that. She turned away, skidding and sliding, wanting nothing more than to be home where she could be alone and the tears could come out without shaming her.

"It's not that," he said. "It's....I belong—I *belonged*—to the Saint of Steel. I can't trust myself. I can't *be* trusted. It's dangerous. *I'm* dangerous."

"The gods forbid I trust a paladin," she said hollowly. Stupid bastard. Besides, she did have someone she trusted already. Marguerite watched her back. Marguerite had never failed her. Unlike *some* people who smelled like gingerbread.

She wrinkled her nose, trying to get the smell of him out of her nostrils, and caught a whiff of something else.

"Do you smell that?" asked Grace, suddenly alert.

Stephen looked startled at the abrupt change of subject, but sniffed. "Smell what?"

"I don't know. Smells like...something burnt. Acrid. Only not." Grace looked around the waterlogged woods, vaguely expecting to see smoke.

"Can't be burning, not in this. You couldn't get wood to light if your life depended on it."

She shook her head. The smell was more complex than simple woodsmoke. It had a heavy, tongue-coating quality, a smell of sour milk and charred bone. And yet she could pick up another note on top. Something sweet, almost a floral, which made no sense at all. Rot? No, rot was a different sweet note. She couldn't place this one. "I have no idea what this is."

He nodded. Frustrated, Grace realized that he didn't get the import of that. "I don't think you understand. *I don't know this smell.*"

Stephen cocked his head. "Should you?"

"It'd be like you seeing an animal and not knowing what it was. It's not a thing that happens often. Different kinds, different colors, different variations, but not completely different animals. Does that make sense?"

"It does," he admitted. "Can you—ah—follow the smell? Figure out where it's coming from?"

At least he's taking me seriously, thought Grace. She scowled. It would be easier to stay annoyed if he hadn't been so respectful of her talents. "I don't know. I'm not a slewhound. Let's find out."

She tromped back and forth for nearly twenty minutes, trying to get closer to the smell. They plowed through water-logged laurels and low, scrubby half-dead madrone. Eventually they were nearly on top of it—or at least, she thought they were—and she was still no closer to understanding it.

"Some kind of plant decaying?" asked Stephen.

She wiped her nose on her sleeve. "Maybe?"

They stood there in silence for a minute, while Grace's nose ran and she began to feel increasingly foolish about the whole situation. *Here I am, dragging him halfway to perdition to try and find a random weird smell...*

He didn't seem bothered. He was polite and solid and gave no indication of impatience. She had an urge to kick him in his over-muscled shins for being so damned decent about the whole thing.

"Well," she said finally, wiping her nose again, "I guess it's a mystery."

She turned to go and promptly put her foot down on a severed head.

CHAPTER 26

"Ohmyfuckingshitfuckshitgaaaaaaah!"

Grace shrieked and recoiled so sharply that she nearly fell. Stephen lunged to catch her, full of horrified visions of stepping on sharp nails, spears, spikes soaked in the foul water of the flooded Elkinslough. "Are you all right? Are you hurt? Did you—"

Then he saw it too.

The head was on its side, cheek sunk in the mud, and it was *fresh.* The eyes were wide open and there weren't even flies on it yet. The blood on the ragged stump of neck glistened wetly. A man's head, not particularly old, with a day's growth of beard. His features were slack and his pupils huge, but if the head was more than an hour old, Stephen would eat his sword.

Grace clung to him, her anger forgotten, hands locked around his tabard, eyes locked on the dead man's face. The print of her boot was marked in mud on the cheekbone.

"Oh my god," she said. "Oh my god. *I stepped on his face.*"

"It's all right," he said automatically, putting his arm around her. "It's all right."

"It is not all right!" she snapped. "I stepped on his face! *That is not all right!*"

She wasn't wrong. Stephen abandoned this line of thought. He also abandoned the completely unworthy desire to track down the absent Brother Francis and yell: *Look,* now *will you take the severed head thing seriously?*

Instead he said, "No, it's not. But we need to get out of here." All he could think was to get Grace away, in case the killer was still nearby. His hand dropped to his sword hilt and he scanned the trees, looking for movement, but saw no one.

"Shouldn't we...should we bury...I..." Grace clamped a hand over her mouth. "What do normal people do when they find a head?" she mumbled through her fingers.

"They tell the city guard. Which we will. But we're getting out of here before the killer comes back."

This had clearly not occurred to her. Her greenish pallor turned to white. She stepped away from him and looked around wildly.

"Come on," he said. "To the river. Go, go!"

They went. Her nose kept working like a slewhound's. "There was something on that head," she muttered. "Or near it. That smell."

"The killer? Or the method of killing?"

"I don't know! Does cutting someone's head off smell like that?"

"Not in my experience," said Stephen. He'd cut exactly three people's heads off in his life. It happened less than people thought. They tended to fall down before you'd got the sword all the way through, and unless the angle was exactly right, you chopped into their collarbone instead.

Grace swung around to stare at him. "*Your* experience?"

"They were all very bad people," he said. He could see the foot-bridge ahead of them, but he kept his hand on his sword.

The bridge was in terrible shape, caked with mud, but still sturdy. They'd crossed it on the way to the hill and they crossed it again now. Grace was practically running ahead of him.

The river felt like a wall between them and the killer, even though Stephen knew that was foolish. The odds were very good that the killer was now on the same side they were.

During the day, he thought grimly. *Not in the city. Is he getting bolder? Did he dump the head here and the body in the river?*

They weren't terribly far from Weaver's Nest here. Had this been a logical expansion of the killer's range as people moved out of the slum? There had been a few makeshift structures in the woods where people might have been camping after being flooded out. They needed to be warned...unless one of those belonged to the killer.

The city guard can check this much more effectively than I can. This is a job for armed men in pairs at least. I have to get Grace to safety first. Then I can come back, or send some Rat priests. The city guard were not particularly bad men in Archen's Glory, but they were men with badges and Stephen, like most paladins, was skeptical of martial men who answered to no divine power. He didn't plan to set the guard to rousting homeless people without someone to make sure they didn't get too enthusiastic in their questioning.

"Turn here," he said. "There's a raised boardwalk now. We spent most of the week putting it up so that people could get out of the wet." Grace nodded.

She was shivering. The mud had caked most of the way up her back. He wanted to wipe it off, and if he tried she was going to take his hand off at the wrist and he'd deserve it. He pulled his cloak off instead and dropped it around her shoulders.

"I don't need—"

"Grace," he said tiredly, "let's pretend for a little bit that nothing happened except for the severed head. Please. I can only handle one horrible mess at a time, and at least this one isn't my fault."

She gave him a sidelong glare, then grunted what he chose to believe was agreement.

His boot heels rang on the boardwalk. It was cobbled together of scrap wood and wouldn't last more than a season without reinforcement, but it was doing its job. Grace's footfalls were softer, though she had stretched her stride until she was nearly running. His cloak was very large on her and she pulled it up over one arm, wrapped tight around her shoulders.

There was a temporary guard post set up near the flooded area to prevent looting. Stephen made for it, trying to balance his need to hurry with the fact that Grace had just had a nasty shock and also her legs were a lot shorter than his.

He wanted to apologize again, for the whole sorry mess, for the day, for everything he'd done wrong and everything he hadn't done right, but he didn't quite dare. *And what good would it do? Make me feel better, make her feel like she had to forgive me...no. Keep your mouth shut.*

It's about time you did.

There was a woman at the front of the guardpost. Stephen knew her from the past week of work and knew she would probably take him seriously. He stepped up and said "We're going to need people. We just found another head."

He did his best to shield Grace from too much interrogation in the hour that followed. It was a great deal of sitting and waiting and then telling the same story to yet another person, who went and got someone else, who also needed to hear the story, and so on and so forth. It would have worn down even a hardened trooper used to the chain of command—it *did* wear him down, in fact—but he had to imagine it was worse for Grace, who was not used to being surrounded by gruff, armored men who wanted to hear the same story a dozen times over, was definitely not used to stepping on random body parts, and who had also had a really dreadful afternoon.

Fortunately, there was a fire in the guard post, which helped. They sat beside it. Stephen still stood whenever the next person to report to came in. Grace stopped bothering.

"Not much longer now," he said, after the third or fourth person had come by to hear the story.

Her eyes flicked to him. "Truly, or are you trying to keep my spirits up?"

"Truly," he said. "That last was the district watch commander. Once more, probably, to whoever he puts in charge of tracking, and then you'll be done."

Grace inclined her head, staring into the flame. Her back was sword-straight, her chin lifted. She looked proud and so vulnerable that it broke his heart. He wanted to throw himself at her feet and beg to protect her from the rest of the world. Except that he was the one who had hurt her the worst today, and the best thing he could do was choke down his own pride and find someone else to help her.

He went to the woman at the front and made yet another request.

"How are you holding up?" asked Stephen, in that gentle voice that made her want to either climb him like a tree or hit him with a brick, depending on her current mood. She was currently in hit-with-a-brick and expected to stay there for some time.

"I shouldn't be so cold," muttered Grace. Despite the fire, she felt half-frozen. She still had Stephen's cloak wrapped around her and it wasn't enough. "Why am I still so cold?"

"You've had a shock," said Stephen. "People get cold after that. I don't know why."

She burrowed into the warm folds, inhaling the smell of gingerbread, hating it for smelling like him, relishing it because it smelled so much better than standing water and rot and that horrible, lingering burnt smell.

She hated him for being so calm and so understanding and hated herself for being weak and cold. On one level, Grace knew that she'd stepped on a *goddamn severed head* and you were allowed to be miserable and panicky afterward, and on the other, Stephen looked as if he could step on severed heads every morning, greet them politely, and get on with his day.

Goddamn paladins.

Normal people are allowed to be upset by something like this.

Normal people don't step on severed heads.

She couldn't believe that she'd been joking about it yesterday. Had it only been yesterday? And then there one was, the remains of a living, breathing person, ice cold and turning like a rock under her foot.

Everyone had been very nice. The guards had asked her for her statement and she was able to tell them, with great precision, where the head was. She knew the area well, even in the mud. Stephen had done most of the talking, but in that, he'd deferred to her absolutely. Even when the man from the guard had looked at Stephen for confirmation of her story, he'd simply said, "She knows much better than I do."

What she *really* wanted, in her heart of hearts, was to throw herself into Stephen's arms and have a good cry at the horror and have him hold her, not because he wanted her or because he was strong and she was weak but simply because she was miserable and exhausted and wanted a goddamn hug. But she still had her pride. She hadn't broken down in front of Lady Vance. She hadn't stopped walking in the snow, even when her feet were frozen and she was sure that Tab was dead. Pride had been her only trustworthy companion for so long that she wasn't going to let it go.

So she straightened her back again and simply asked, "When will I be allowed to leave?"

"In a few moments," said Stephen. "You will be escorted home."

"I don't need—"

He lifted a hand wearily. "Not me. Someone else. I realize that I would not be your first choice right now."

Goddammit, he was even going to be considerate about *that.*

The man who arrived to see her home had golden hair and a handsome, chiseled face. He wore the cloak of the Saint of Steel and carried a sword. He introduced himself as Shane. He also smelled like gingerbread, and Grace did not know how much more she could stand.

Stephen saluted Shane. Shane saluted Stephen. Grace tamped down a scream.

Stephen looked at her as if he wanted very much to say something, but she turned away. There were things that he could say that would fix it, but nothing that he *would* say. And she was not inclined to forgive.

It had been such a good kiss. Why did he have to ruin it?

Shane did not make conversation. That was fine. She did not want conversation. She had no small talk left in her and if she had to have one more awkward, earnest conversation today, she was going to start chopping heads off herself.

They were most of the way back to her home, the paladin walking in polite silence beside her, when she finally snapped and rounded on him. *"Why* do you all smell like gingerbread?!"

Shane blinked at her. His eyes were blue, but a much lighter shade than Stephen's. He actually took a step back in the face of her apparent rage. "I beg your pardon, miss?"

"Gingerbread!" she snarled, knowing that she sounded completely out of her head. "You! Stephen! Why do you paladins all smell like gingerbread?"

A sudden smile crossed his face, so bright and fleeting that she almost thought she'd imagined it, and then he was immediately solemn again. *"Oh.* The cinnamon and ginger. It's a muscle rub that our brother Istvhan makes. He says that it's an old family recipe. It works very well, but it does smell rather strong. The ginger is heating, you see, and there's some kind of pepper in it as well. It's better than camphor, which some soldiers use."

A muscle rub. Of course. Why hadn't she thought of that?

"It's not all paladins," said Shane, almost apologetically. "Just Istvhan's friends."

"Well, he does good work," said Grace savagely, as if she was accusing the absent Istvhan of a mortal sin.

Shane blinked a few times then said timidly, "Yes?"

Normal people do not...oh, hell with it.

She thought about asking Shane why Stephen had suddenly panicked and told her he couldn't be trusted. Then she thought about how exactly that would sound—*Please explain why your brother-in-arms suddenly decided he wasn't interested in me after the best kiss of my life*—and ground her teeth so hard that her jaw throbbed.

"Are you all right, miss?"

"Fine," she growled.

Unlike certain other paladins she could name, Shane had the sense to stop talking.

She had never been so glad to see her street and her shopfront and the cat in her neighbor's window. She felt as if an age of the earth had passed since the morning.

"Is there someone waiting for you?" asked Shane gently. "Or who can come and stay with you tonight?"

It was Grace's turn to blink. "God, I hope not." The last thing she wanted was to have to talk to yet another person right now.

The paladin coughed. "It's just that…ah…after you've had a shock, it can be helpful…"

He trailed off. Grace could only guess that her expression was not conducive to discussion. "Ah, forget I said anything. Is this your house?"

"This is it," said Grace. "Thanks for…" She waved a hand, too completely out of words to even bother finishing the sentence, and closed the door in the paladin's face.

CHAPTER 27

Stephen's day had started at dawn and dragged on until it was too dark to continue searching the hillside. They did not turn up any more heads, nor the body formerly attached to the one they had.

"It's all commons land on that side of the Elkinslough," said Mallory, the member of the city guard who had been put in charge of the head situation. "People shouldn't be camped there, theoretically, but we're turning a blind eye until the flooding's subsided. But we don't know if the bastard's stalking them out there or just using it to dump bodies until...well, until his usual hunting ground's dried out." He scratched at his balding scalp and cursed quietly to himself. "And if you go downstream not even a quarter mile, there's a good ten or twelve neighborhoods right there, and bridges right into them."

Stephen had run into Mallory a few times and respected him enough to think that the man was angry about anyone being killed, not just the fact that the killer might now be moving into wealthier neighborhoods, but he also knew that the heat was going to be turned up on the man to stop it now that people with actual power were feeling threatened.

"It doesn't make any damn sense," said Mallory wearily, leaning back against the wall. "They found another head this morning. Probably only a few hours before yours."

"Did they!" Stephen hadn't known that and the other guards had been admirably tight-lipped. "Near here?"

"No," said Mallory. "That's the problem. It was the opposite direction. Just on the far side of the Scarlet Quarter."

"...shit," said Stephen, with feeling. "He's doing two a day now?"

"Or there's a copycat. The gods know that the broadsheets are screaming about the Red Headsman every damn day, it wouldn't surprise me. And we're still no closer. We've gotten descriptions of suspicious people from all over, and none of them look remotely alike."

Stephen sighed. "Demon?" he asked. "Jumping bodies?"

"Mmm." Mallory shrugged. "I suppose it could be. Didn't look much like demon possession to me, but at this point, I'll grasp at any straw."

"One of the Dreaming God's paladins might be able to help."

"Eh, worth a try." Mallory glanced at him and seemed to recall that he wasn't talking to one of his own men. He pushed himself away from the wall. "Thank you for your help, paladin. We'll send word around to the Bishop, maybe the Rat can help us get word out to the people staying in the commons."

"Thank you," said Stephen. He bowed to Mallory and made his way, slowly, to the Temple and home.

Shane was in the hallway when he arrived. "You got her home safely?" asked Stephen.

"Yes."

"And...?"

The blond paladin looked at him, shook his head, and turned away. "And I don't know what you did to that woman, and I'm not entirely sure I shouldn't call you out for it."

"You probably should," said Stephen, to Shane's retreating back. The other man shook his head again, but didn't answer.

Stephen sighed and made his way first to the baths and then to his own room and his virtuously empty bed.

Despite physical exhaustion, sleep eluded him. He lay in bed, staring at the ceiling, replaying a scene over and over in his mind:

Grace's face, smiling, a little flushed, looking up at him with heavy lidded eyes, and then the flash of baffled hurt, and the sudden retreat into a mask of brittle indifference.

He could not stop seeing it. He had managed to drive it out briefly, in the flurry of activity, but even tromping through the mud with the guard, whenever they paused, whenever his mind wandered for even an instant, he was seeing those wounded gray-green eyes. The memory laid him open like a lash, cutting deeper each time.

It's for the best. You should not have gone even as far as you did. The sooner you stopped it the better. Letting it happen at all, that was your fault, and yes, you should be ashamed.

Passion...hurt...indifference.

His fault.

Stephen sighed, swung his feet off the bed, and went to hammer on Istvhan's door.

Istvhan was shirtless and sleepy-looking. Had it been an emergency, Stephen would have used the knock for quick waking and Istvhan would have been armed, armored, and ready for battle in under a minute. As it was, he leaned against the doorframe, yawning. "What's going on?"

Stephen sighed and took refuge in ritual. "Shrive me, brother, for my heart is heavy."

"Saint's balls," said Istvhan, no longer looking sleepy. "At this hour? Did you murder someone?" He held the door open so that Stephen could enter.

Istvhan's room held different personal touches than Stephen's: a rug to soften the floor, a small painting of a bird, a few books on a shelf. Stephen's room mostly held baskets of wool and half-completed socks. Otherwise, it was the same. Stephen reached for the chair that he knew would be there and pulled it so that his back was to Istvhan. Any paladin could take another's confession, but among the Saint of Steel's chosen it was most often done back-to-back. That way if you were on a battlefield together you could guard each other while you spilled your sins before the enemy rolled over you.

"All right," said Istvhan. He heard the creak as the other man sat down on the bed. "Unburden your heart, brother. The Saint hears..." He coughed. "Well, *I* hear you anyway."

Stephen told him.

"You got me out of bed for *that?*"

"I couldn't sleep."

"So rub one out like a normal person."

"*Istvhan.*"

The other man groaned, hooked his foot under the leg of the chair, and hauled it around so that Stephen faced him. "It's lust, you idiot. It's normal. We're allowed to feel it—yes, even *you.* I'm not going to grant you absolution for wanting to jump this woman's bones." He held up a hand. "And neither are any of the others, so don't go knocking on their doors either."

Stephen put his head in his hands.

"So you took her out looking for moss and got turned on. It's really not a sin, brother."

"I kissed her."

"Still not a sin, unless you think she didn't want to be kissed."

"No." Stephen had to admit that Grace had seemed quite pleased to be kissed, at least at first. "No, that part went well."

"Then not a sin."

"Then we had an argument."

"Still not a sin."

"I said some very stupid things."

"Unsurprising, but not a sin."

"Then she stepped on a severed head."

"Wait, *what?*"

Stephen told him. Istvhan blinked a few times. "I gotta sit down."

"You're already sitting."

"I need to sit down...more." He looked vaguely around the room, got up, then sat down again. Judging by his expression, it didn't help. "Why didn't you *start* with the severed head?"

"I don't feel guilty about the head. It's not like I'm the one who severed it."

"Yes, but..." Istvhan pinched the bridge of his nose. "You might have mentioned it!"

"I had Shane take Grace home while I reported to Mallory. Then I took the guards back, they picked it up, end of story."

"You did have quite a day, didn't you?"

"You could say that."

"And despite the severed head situation, you're still wracked with guilt."

"The severed head did not have a lot to do with the rest."

"No, but it would be a great excuse to go back and comfort the lady." Istvhan wiggled his eyebrows in a manner that left very little to the imagination.

"I can't," said Stephen. "You know I can't."

"I know nothing of the sort. I don't see what the problem is."

"The problem?! The Saint is *dead!* There's this giant hollow... thing...in my chest. I'm broken. *You're* broken. We're all of us broken."

Istvhan shrugged. "Lots of people get broken in life, Stephen. We're not special."

"Very few people had their *god* ripped out of their *souls.*"

"I'll give you that. Still. If we limited loving to just the sane, undamaged people, the next generation would have about three people in it and presumably humanity would die out shortly afterward."

Stephen grunted.

"Look, we've suffered. No argument. What does that have to do with you lusting after this perfumer?"

Stephen raised both eyebrows. "Our order *died.* Our head priest burned his own temple down. You, personally, were in a coma for four days."

Istvhan dismissed this with a wave of one large hand. "And? You think we're so damn special because of it? Our misery was so much bigger than other people's misery that we can never function again?"

"That's not it!" snapped Stephen. "That's not—it's not—look, she can't rely on me, all right? And being reliable is all I'm good for, and if I can't even do that, what business do I have with any woman?"

"Have you considered just having a fling? Hell, have you considered just getting your cock wet and taking the damn edge off?"

Stephen had an immediate urge to deck his brother-in-arms for saying such a crude thing about Grace, but squelched it because it would only prove Istvhan right.

"What if I snap? What if I'm dangerous?"

"What I can't figure out is how you didn't get over this as a teenager like the rest of us did!"

Stephen glared at him. Istvhan, immune to glares, folded his arms.

"I wasn't a screaming berserker as a teenager."

"You're not one now either," said Istvhan. "I mean, you don't scream. You make this sort of growling noise when you go. Now, Galen, he wails like the unquiet dead, but—"

"*Istvhan.*"

"Look, if you can't laugh about the homicidal fits that make you a menace to society, what's even the point?"

Stephen groaned. "All right, all right. Suppose I did keep going, what happens then? What if the tide rises while I'm...while we're...ah...?"

"A fair thought," said Istvhan. "Except that the privies are still standing."

"What does that have to do with anything?"

"Well, if we were in danger of slipping into uncontrolled berserker fits out of lust, I expect that at least one of us would have done it by now. It's been three years, don't tell me you haven't taken matters into your own hands."

Stephen flushed. He had, of course, and yes, it had been in the privies, too. "Well..."

"Shit, I've caught Galen there three times. In the last month."

Stephen tried desperately to get the conversation back under control. "I don't know why you care," he growled. "You're sleeping alone at night, same as the rest of us."

Istvhan coughed.

Stephen turned and stared at him.

"The bishop," said Istvhan, almost apologetically, "is a marvelous woman. And of course she could not have a liaison with anyone in the hierarchy, for obvious reasons, but as we stand outside the hierarchy..."

"Saint's teeth," said Stephen. "You're nailing *Beartongue?*"

"Well, it might be more accurate to say she's nailing me," admitted Istvhan. "She's a decade older than I am and between you, me, and the gods, I'm having a hard time keeping up. I'm honestly thinking about taking one of these assignments to the far north, just so I can get some rest."

Stephen blinked at him a few times, a slow grin spreading across his face. "You *dog.*"

"It's not serious," said Istvhan. "Well, not for her, and I know better than to get my hopes up. Still. It can be done, man, that's all I'm saying. We may be broken men, but we're still men." He paused, then inclined his head. "And women, as the case may be, although never tell Wren I ever implied anything about her having needs of any sort."

"My lips are sealed," promised Stephen. Wren, of all their brothers and sisters, was the one most determined to prove that she was made of iron and stone. He rubbed his hands together. "All right. Perhaps that's not the concern, so much. But aren't you afraid you'll get jealous?"

"What, of some other man with Beartongue? I'd throw my arms around him and call him my savior. Perhaps we could arrange a duty roster. A woman in her forties with a lot of aggressions to work out is a terrifying glory."

Stephen folded his arms. "The emissary from the Crown Prince keeps flirting with Grace. I wanted to tear his head off and drink blood from the stump."

He said this very calmly and Istvhan took it the same way. "I won't say it's the best thing, but plenty of men feel that way about the women they're attracted to."

"Plenty of men can't go into a battle rage with no way to call them back." He swallowed. "Remember Hallowbind."

"Hallowbind wasn't us," the other man said. "Well...not you and I, anyway." Several of their fellows had been at Hallowbind, but no one *ever* talked about it, and they weren't about to start now.

"It could have been."

"Yes, it very well could have been. But only because the god died. None of us have run mad since then, have we?"

Stephen looked away. "No. Not completely. But the tide's risen for all of us since then."

"And we damn well snapped out of it, too."

"If by 'snapped out of it' you mean you choked me until I saw stars, yes. I supposed we snapped out of it."

Istvhan shrugged. "It worked, didn't it?"

"I keep thinking of golems," said Stephen, when the silence had sat for too long.

"Golems?" Istvhan's eyebrows drew together. "The men they used to make out of clay?"

"Those, yes."

"Were they even real? I've only heard stories."

"Same here. But the stories are all the same. They never stopped a task. You'd set the golem to dig a well and it would dig to the center of the earth."

Istvhan waited.

"We were only ever killing machines," Stephen said. "But at least there was a way to turn us off. Now..." He raised his hands helplessly. "Now we just keep going, like the golems did. Easier not to start at all."

"You're talking about making love, not digging a well. Believe me, brother, you've got to stop sometime. Otherwise there's chafing."

Stephen rolled his eyes. "That's not what I'm talking about, and you know it. What if I did let myself fall in love and something happened to her? Saint's blood, Istvhan, she could get mugged in an alley and I might panic and take down half the temple before one of you managed to hit me over the head."

"Yes. So? Is your plan to cut yourself off from feeling strongly about any woman, ever, for the rest of your days?"

Stephen shrugged. "I didn't say it was a *good* plan."

"It's suicide under glass is what it is. Might as well have asked for the knife three years ago."

"Maybe. But at least I'll do some good before I die, and pay the Rat for the care He's shown us."

Istvhan rose, shaking his head. "It's no way to live," he said. "And I love you, brother, and I want better for you than that." He stood looking down at Stephen. "Go find someone else to shrive you, Stephen. I won't grant you absolution for wanting more."

CHAPTER 28

Grace's night was also restless, initially for the same reasons and then for wildly different ones.

After Shane dropped her off, she made tea. Marguerite came down and she said, "Please, not now," and Marguerite said, "Okay," and went away again. Tab twined around her ankles and she stared into the tea and thought about kisses and failing and that glorious, heart-stopping moment when his mouth had closed over hers and then the equally heart-stopping moment when he told her it was a mistake.

"I knew better," she told Tab.

"Mr-r-r."

"My life is fine."

"Mrr," said Tab, who clearly believed that since she had a civette, her life was as wonderful as anyone could wish for.

How dare he kiss her? How dare he sit in her workshop and knit? How dare he be comfortable to be around?

She flipped open her alchemical text. *For all Matter is at base only Duste, but the Seeker who knows the way may assemble all things again from Duste, metal and reagent, star and stone, even unto Life Itself...*

She didn't realize she was crying until a tear splashed onto the page.

Civettes were not known for their empathy. Tab hooked his claws into her trousers and climbed up, demanding petting, unconcerned that his human was making strange face noises. Humans always made strange face noises; a weasel learned to deal with it. Grace buried her face in his side, smelling the slightly gamey scent of his fur, breathing in great gasping sobs for all the things that could have been and weren't, even though she knew better than to wish for them.

Tab rapidly got tired of being squeezed, and squirmed free. Grace took her tea and followed the civette into the bedroom. It had been a long, brutal day and she wanted it over with.

Even that, it seemed, was going to escape her. In the small hours of the night, she woke because of a sound she couldn't identify. Her first thought was that Tab had knocked something over, and she almost went back to sleep, but then a board creaked. She knew that board. It was the one to the left of her usual spot at the worktable, and it only creaked when a person leaned their weight on it.

There was someone in the workshop.

She came instantly, shudderingly awake.

I have to barricade the door. Where is Tab? If he's out there—if he gets hurt—

"Tab!" she whispered as loudly as she dared, which wasn't very. "Tab, where are you?"

A long, long silence. Sweat sprang up on her palms. Her scalp felt damp.

Then: "Mrr-rr-ch-ch-chk?"

He was in the bedroom. *Oh gods and saints, thank you.*

There was no lock on the door from her bedroom to the workshop. Why would there be? Her workshop was as much her private domain as her bedroom. Hell, more private. The worst someone would see in her bedroom was dirty laundry. In the workshop, they would see recipes, techniques, equipment...things that *mattered*.

The board creaked again.

I've got to warn Marguerite. How do I do that? I'd have to go through the workshop to get to her, and he's right there.

No, I've got to stay in here. Maybe I can bang out a message on the ceiling.

Do I pretend to be asleep?

Memory—Phillip's voice saying *Grace, sweet, are you awake? Grace, wake up, I've got someone for you to meet...*

Her lips curled sourly. She'd pretended to be asleep through a number of indignities, and the only good it had ever done her was another set of memories to jump up and grab her by the throat when she didn't need it.

No, she had to make sure no one was getting in here and that was all there was to it.

She slid out of bed as silently as she could, easing both feet down. What did she have that could bar the door? Her chair under the doorknob, that was the only thing she could move.

She would have sworn that she knew her bedroom intimately, even in the dark, but suddenly she could barely remember where anything was. Against the wall, yes, but where? She felt around with shaking hands, trailing her fingers over the night table, the dresser, searching.

More sounds came from the next room as the intruder lifted something, set it down again. Was he looking for something? Money? Something easily sold?

Her hands closed over folds of cloth. Yesterday's clothes, tossed onto the chair. She pulled them off, let them drop silently to the floor, and picked up the chair.

The legs scraped softly against the wall. The noises in the other room stopped.

Grace abandoned stealth for speed, spun around, took three steps and crammed the chair as tightly under the doorknob as she could, kicking the back legs so that they wedged firmly against the floorboards.

Footsteps crossed the workshop again, running this time. Grace threw her shoulder against the door, preparing to hold the door with her body if she had to.

Instead she heard another crash, the jangle of bells as the front door was yanked open and then the footsteps receded into the night.

Silence.

"Was anything stolen?" asked Marguerite.

"My notebooks," said Grace. She felt numb. The magnitude of the loss was so immense that she couldn't get her head around it. In a few moments, she would wake up and this would have been a dream, and the stack of sloppy, tea-stained books, with pages leaking out the sides, would still be on the table.

Marguerite sucked air between her teeth. She, at least, understood what that meant. "Did they get all of them?"

"Five out of six." Grace shook her head slowly, turning the remains of the last notebook over in her hands. It was the oldest one, and probably the only reason that the thief hadn't taken it was because the binding had given out. Pages had been dumped all over the workshop floor, one with a boot print square in the center.

She had gathered them all up and eventually she would put them back in the right order. But it was such a tiny scrap of knowledge to have preserved, back when she barely knew what she was doing. Grace stared down at the pages in front of her, her small, tight scrawl of handwriting, writing questions that she'd answered a dozen times over in later notebooks.

This is it. This is where it all goes wrong and everything gets taken away. You knew it was only a matter of time.

"Why would they do this?" she said softly. "Why would anybody steal my notes? They're nearly impossible to read anyway."

"Another perfumer, perhaps," said Marguerite. "You made a splash at the reception and gave the Crown Prince something he liked enough to order more. A rival might have wanted to steal the recipe, and sent someone who didn't know what they were looking for, so they took them all."

"But I'm no one," said Grace. "Hardly anyone knows I exist."

"You are very mistaken there," said Marguerite. "You are a rising star. Many of the best people wear your scents."

"What? I sell what—two or three vials a week? I'd lose money on this space if you didn't take the rent in perfumes."

"That's exclusivity."

"Yes, but..." Grace laughed hollowly. "It doesn't matter now. I'll have to recreate half the scents from memory. I've got no notes left. Years of experiments learning what doesn't work, all gone. If they wanted to ruin me, they did a very good job."

She dropped into a chair. She couldn't seem to get enough air.

I can handle this. I've been here before. I was here when I arrived in Archon's Glory...and when Phillip bought my apprenticeship.

That was the wrong thing to think. Her vision swam and she remembered the smell of cheap paper and watery oak gall ink, the very cheapest tallow candles, as she wrote as much as she could remember, knowing that she was forgetting so much, so many tiny fractional amounts, how many drops, how many parts per hundred, the head note, the heart note, Phillip never saying he blamed her but his disappointment becoming more evident with each passing day as she could not reproduce the scents that had drawn him to the old man's shop to begin with.

She put her face in her hands.

"Grace!" said Marguerite. "Grace, it's all right, we'll find them, we'll get them back."

He never said he blamed me. He married me the day after he bought out the apprenticeship and I was so eager to prove to him that it hadn't been a mistake, that he hadn't been wrong, that I was the genius he said I was.

She dug her nails into her palms. Tallow and sex and the wool blankets, still faintly damp. That was the smell of that first tiny room they stayed in. There was no way to keep the damp out. Her earliest journal, the one spread in loose pages across the floor, had wavy, swollen edges from that room still.

The smell flooded her nostrils again, making her faintly ill. Maybe it was memory, or maybe it still clung to those pages. Phillip telling her what a great lover he was, promising her passion and pleasure and love and fortune once they had those scents in hand.

I was an investment in the future. Like Tab. And we both worked out about the same, didn't we? A pair of culls who ran away together. We made it, but only for a little while. I couldn't even get him to declare my apprenticeship over. Now it's all going away again.

"Grace!" Marguerite sounded frantic now. A moment later, the familiar rich, acrid scent of charbeans reached her nostrils, chasing away the scent of tallow and damp wool and sex. Grace breathed deeply, letting her lungs fill.

She was not back there. She had far more resources this time. Even if it was over, even if everything came crashing down, even if the books were only the first thing to collapse, she was not lost. She had lost everything too many times not to have taken precautions.

They're still there, aren't they? Panic sank sweat-slick claws into her throat. What if they weren't?

"I have to go," she said, standing up. "I have to go—check something—" and darted to her room, throwing on clothes and ignoring Marguerite's questions.

It was easier once she was outside, on the sidewalk. She was walking and she had a clear goal. There was nothing she could do while she was walking except walk. Her brain gibbered at her, but Grace was in a little clear space where she could ignore it, and the smell of poverty and tallow and sex that kept trying to fill her nostrils.

The graveyard on the edge of the Glass Quarter was small and shabby and overgrown. Very rich people had been buried there once, but their descendants could not afford to pay the army of groundskeepers the space required. The chapel walls still stood, but the stained glass had been taken down and sold and there were only wooden shutters in their place. Swallows nested in the eaves. There was one elderly caretaker, who kept the graves clear, while the edges of the yard softened with weeds and the roof of the chapel turned to verdigris and moss.

Grace was well known there. The caretaker straightened when she walked in and waved to her. Grace waved back. She liked him. He didn't mind her harvesting plants from the edges for perfumes —"Fewer weeds for me to pull, lass."—and she made sure that he had a vial of his wife's favorite scent every year for her name day.

In the far back corner, there was a run-down mausoleum overgrown with dog roses and goldenrod. The family had died out long ago and the door hung open. There were no bones inside now, only dusty shelves with fragments of old cloth. The marble building had sunk badly on one side and water pooled in the bottom, so no one was likely to want to take it over.

Under the pretense of harvesting roses, Grace wiggled through last year's canes and stretched a hand up inside the mausoleum. Tucked up against the ceiling, out of the way, was a small slot that would have held a statue of the Four-Faced God.

Her fingers touched oilcloth, and the knot in her chest loosened slightly.

Still here. I'm not completely helpless. It's still here.

She didn't take the package out. She already knew the contents: two changes of clothes and a pouch full of coins. A month's expenses, two if she was careful. Enough to get her and Tab somewhere safe and start again.

There were three other stashes across the city. One was tucked in her neighbor's abandoned dovecote. One was in another graveyard. The last was near where she'd gathered the oakmoss, in a dead tree. She didn't quite trust that one, the tree was too obviously hollow and someone might find it, but a stash outside of the city was essential. You never knew when you might have to cut and run.

Normal people probably didn't worry about that. Normal people had nice, normal lives. Grace only had her own life, and it had taught her that you took precautions because life changed too often at other people's whims and sooner or later, everything would be taken away.

"Right," she said. "Right. Okay. Not completely lost yet."

You haven't lost everything. There's still Marguerite. She won't let you down.

As she had done too many times already, she straightened her shoulders and went to go pick up the pieces.

CHAPTER 29

Stephen woke up stiff and sore and his first thought was that he was a miserable bastard of a man who'd hurt a woman who deserved a whole lot better.

It wasn't until he'd gotten up and downed some tea that he realized his first thought on waking hadn't been about not getting out of bed forever.

It seems that I am being dragged back into the feeling world whether I want to be or not. I only wish guilt had not been the hook to drag me with.

It was about to get worse. He was on his way to sword practice when a familiar voice hailed him. Stephen turned and felt his sense of guilt twinge even harder.

Jorge still had the kind of face that made maidens sigh and former maidens get a bit weak in the knees. The scar through his right eyebrow made him look rakish and dangerous. Another quarter inch and it would have cost him the eye. Stephen knew because he was the one who had put it there.

And even if I had managed the strike, he would probably look devastating in an eyepatch as well. That was the problem with the Dreaming God's paladins. They looked good in anything. Granted, the Saint of Steel's chosen were nearly unkillable so Stephen couldn't complain too much. For one thing, Jorge had been the one who bashed him over the head when the madness had taken him, three years earlier, and Stephen had lived and hadn't even had any long-term damage.

On the other hand, it would have been nice to have the kind of face that made people pay close attention. Certain perfume makers, for example.

The sight of the scar still made him wince, though. It had been too damn close.

Jorge had never held it against him, but of course he wouldn't. Paladins turned forgiveness into a competitive sport, given the chance.

"Are you keeping well?"

"Well enough. No...incidents." His eyes rose involuntarily to the scar on the other man's face.

"You are not to blame," said Jorge firmly, gripping his forearm. "You were in a situation no man could endure and you fought the madness as best you could. You have nothing to feel guilty for."

Jorge's voice was deep and calm and sincere, a voice that anyone would trust. Stephen had no doubt of his conviction. Almost, he believed him. Almost.

"Don't use the voice on *me*," he grumbled. "You think I don't know what you're doing?"

Jorge started, then grinned ruefully at him. "Sorry. Force of habit. But it's true."

"My god is dead," said Stephen. "Leave me my guilt at least, or the only way they'll be able to tell I'm a paladin is by the armor."

Jorge laughed and slung his arm around Stephen's shoulders. "You seem cheerful."

"Everyone is saying that," said Stephen. "I don't know why. I'm up to my ass in failed murder plots and the Motherhood would probably like me thrown in prison on suspicion of something or other."

"Pfff, they want everyone thrown into prison. Don't get a swelled head over it."

"Also I tripped over a severed head yesterday."

"Oh, it was your head!"

Stephen knew what he meant, but gave him a look anyway.

"You know what I mean. That's why I'm here. Apparently you gave them some idea, so they sent me over to lay hands on the head."

Stephen blinked slowly at the Dreaming God's paladin, digesting this. "...I see."

"They wanted to know if there was anything demonic going on."

"Do demons often chop their own heads off?"

Jorge's smile faded. "It wouldn't even be the fifth strangest thing I've seen demons do. But anyway, no, I didn't feel any taint left behind. You can't always tell of course, and if a demon was subtle enough and the host took it willingly, I wouldn't be able to feel a damn thing. But I don't think it's demons."

"Plain ordinary human malice?"

"I didn't say that." Jorge gnawed on his lower lip. "I don't know. Something's off about it. But then again, I was standing under the palace holding onto a severed head, so the whole situation was pretty off."

"That's one way to put it."

"Anyway, the higher-ups sent me here to tell Beartongue."

Stephen nodded. "I'm not surprised. The Temple's getting worried the killer moved with the flood. Bad enough when he was working in one area, but if he's expanded his range, we can't even warn people what areas to take precautions in." He ran his hand through his hair.

"Yep," said Jorge. "Well, the Bishop's waiting for me. Take care of yourself, eh?"

"I'll do my best," said Stephen. "Somebody has to." He glanced down. "Are they keeping you in decent socks?"

"The finest socks a temple can buy."

"Then get on with you."

He waved to the other paladin and went to the salle. He had barely reached the doorway when he realized that someone else was in there, and that they were on edge.

It was Marcus. One of the younger paladins, assuming that any of them could be called young any more, was thumping a cudgel savagely against the pells. After the...incident...with Galen and

Stephen, the paladins did not practice against each other. There were too many risks. They were undoubtedly suffering for it, in fighting form, but given the alternatives...

Stephen watched him for a moment, noting the dark sweat staining his shirt and the trembling that the blows could not quite hide. He leaned against the wall next to him. "Do you want to talk about it?"

Marcus slammed the cudgel down again. Stephen waited.

"I had a wife once," said Marcus. "Before. Did you know that?"

Stephen shook his head.

"She's probably married the blacksmith by now, has ten kids."

Stephen had his doubts that one could have ten kids in three years, but decided it wasn't the time.

"It kills me," said Marcus. "I hope she did. I hope she forgot me. Everyone thinks I'm dead after Hallowbind. It was easier to stay dead. But it kills me."

"Not knowing?" asked Stephen.

Marcus nodded, then shook his head, then did both at once and had stop until the dizziness passed. "I don't know. It might be worse if I knew. If she did marry the blacksmith, and he made her happy, I don't know whether I'd want to kill him or to fall to my knees in gratitude. Because I couldn't. And I'd hate him and be so grateful. It... kills...me." He punctuated each word with a strike of the cudgel.

"You love her?"

"More than anything," said Marcus. "I shouldn't have let her go. But maybe I did the right thing. I don't know. I can't know."

Stephen held up his hands, unthreatening, and approached. Marcus eyed him, still trembling, but there was no sign of the tide.

When he was close enough, Stephen wrapped his arms around his brother's shoulders and held him tightly.

Slowly, slowly, Marcus's muscles loosened. He slumped against Stephen and drew in a deep, ragged breath, then another one.

They had all lost so much, but they still had one another. It was so little compared to a wife and a god, but it was all they had.

"Better?" asked Stephen finally, stepping back.

Marcus nodded. There was no shame in his face, nor should there have been. Stephen knew that he had done the same for Galen, not a month past. They took it in turns, being the strong one.

I did the right thing with Grace. He slapped Marcus on the back. "Go. I'll clean up." *We have to be strong for each other. I can't leave them.*

The thought came to him, unbidden, that she had never asked him to leave his brothers, nor even suggested it. *I have my own life.* That perhaps their lives could have interwoven without one consuming the other.

No. Stop second guessing. You are where you need to be.

It is not fair to ask a woman to fill the hole left by a god.

Marcus sighed and reached for the cudgel. Stephen stopped him. "I'll put it away," he said. "Go do what you need to do."

Marcus left for the baths, and Stephen put away the equipment he'd left behind. Trying not to think about how he would feel if Grace found someone else. *I don't know whether I'd want to kill him or to fall to my knees in gratitude.*

That seemed to sum it up.

He left the salle, reaching out two fingers as he passed, and extinguishing the candle that burned in front of the god who was dead.

Grace got up in the morning and went to work. She would have preferred to lay in bed with a sheet over her head, but she had orders to fill and no one else was going to fill them. The gold talers from the Crown Prince would hopefully tide her over long enough to recreate some of her recipes, but the existing orders still needed to go out.

Fortunately, most of the orders were easy ones that were well-lodged in muscle memory. It took her twice as long to prepare them because she kept stopping to write down what she was doing, but she only tripped up a few times, usually when she started thinking too much about what she was doing.

Seven drops of sandalwood...oh blast. Is it seven?

And of course once you started thinking about it too much, it all became meaningless inside your head, like staring at a word until you no longer knew how to spell it or if it was even a real word after all. Seven drops? Was seven even a number? What the hell was a drop? Was sandalwood even real?

Grace found herself desperately missing the alchemical tome. At this point, she would usually flip it open and find a passage at random. The book was so pretentiously meaningless that everything else looked more real and solid by comparison. It settled her nerves amazingly.

The gods only knew where the book was now. In a pawnshop, maybe. Perhaps she'd find it in a few years, gathering dust somewhere, and greet it like an old friend.

She sat back from the work, sighing, and the bell rang over the door.

Oh gods. She'd flipped the sign to open without thinking, but the shop shouldn't be open. What if someone wanted a fancy formula that she didn't have memorized? Grace wiped her hands down her thighs, hoping that Marguerite was in and would field it.

"Master Perfumer? Hello?"

Grace recognized DuValier's voice and her first thought was panic that he might be here to demand a refund. *No, no, he can't, I won't have enough to live on, oh no...*

"Master Perfumer Angelica?"

What if he wants more, that would be bad too, maybe not as bad, but I can't remember how much saffron goes in the Crown Prince's perfume, I'll need time to recreate it, I can't...

She gritted her teeth and stepped back from the table. There was no sense panicking. She was already panicking, but she knew it was foolish. She had to see what he wanted.

"Master DuValier," she said, coming to the door. *Is it Master? Envoy? Crap, I can't remember.* "May I help you?"

He reached out a hand. Grace extended hers reflexively and he bowed over her hand. "I certainly hope so."

"There isn't something wrong with the Prince's order, is there?" *Please say no, please say no.*

"No, no, not at all." DuValier smiled at her. "I am not here on business."

The phrase seemed meaningless to Grace, except that it had not included the dreaded word *refund*. "Oh?" she said, hoping that he would say something she could latch some meaning on to.

"Yes. I fear that we were to leave the city today, but the Crown Prince is feeling indisposed. A cold, no doubt, from the recent damp."

"It has been very damp," agreed Grace. She tried to imagine the leonine Crown Prince with a cold and couldn't do it, but presumably golden warriors got the sniffles like everyone else.

"It is vexing for him," said DuValier. "He has already been delayed because of the floods, and now that the roads are cleared, to take ill..." He shrugged. "But the delay has left me at loose ends, as I had discharged all my duties in the city already."

"Okay?" said Grace. What on earth was the man doing here? Had he come to visit just to tell her about his schedule and the Crown Prince's cold?

"I thought of you," said DuValier. "And I have enjoyed the time in your company, and thought I would ask if you were free for the after-noon meal?"

Of all the outcomes of the conversation, Grace had not imagined DuValier asking her to lunch. "Uh," she said. Her initial instinct was to refuse. He'd been very rude to Stephen and...no, dammit, she was *glad* he'd been rude to Stephen, Stephen was an *ass*. A metal-plated ass who had no right to kiss people that well and then be unaffected by it.

There was no harm in having lunch with DuValier. He was pleasant and even if he flirted too much, he was probably lonely. All his friends must be in Charlock, if he was looking for companionship with a business acquaintance he'd met twice. She'd just go have a pastry or something with him and be pleasant.

It might even mean that if the Crown Prince wanted perfume in the future, Duvalier would put a good word in for her. There were worse fates. Hell, if everything did go bad and she had to leave the city and set up shop somewhere else, there were worse places than Charlock.

She smiled determinedly at him. "Sure. Let me go find a cloak. There's a place around the corner that bakes cheese pies that are always worth the trip."

CHAPTER 30

Marguerite breezed in that afternoon and said, "Any luck with the journals?"

Grace shook her head. "I've only just gotten back myself. DuValier wanted to take me to lunch."

Marguerite paused in the doorway of the workshop, eyebrows rising. "Did he, now?"

"Was that odd?" Grace sat back from her notes. "Dammit, I knew it was odd."

"Not particularly," said Marguerite. "You're an attractive single woman. He obviously had noticed."

Grace snorted. "If you say so."

"You are," said Marguerite. "And anyway, if you won't agree with that, at least agree that you're a talented perfumer."

"I am a damn good perfumer," said Grace. In this, at least, she was on solid ground.

"In Charlock, that counts for quite a lot. You smell nice and maybe he likes your type."

"I'm pretty sure he's just one of those people who flirts a lot. He flirted with you, too."

"Yes, but he didn't take *me* to lunch." Marguerite perched on a stool, found Tab snoozing in the glassware, and ran her hand over the civette's back. "So?"

"So what?"

"So what did you talk about?"

Grace moved a few drops of oil from one vial to another, sniffed, and sealed the cork up with satisfaction. What had they talked about? She tried to remember. "Uh. Anuket City, mostly. Where he was from. Where I was from. That sort of thing." She honestly couldn't remember it all. She'd spent a lot of it wondering if she was talking too much or not enough or if she had to say something or if a polite grunt would suffice.

The thought came to her unbidden that it had been far easier to talk to Stephen. She hadn't worried so much about whether she was doing it right. They had just...talked. Sometimes about terrible, embarrassing things, but the words had come out regardless.

Stop that, she told herself. *It doesn't matter. Clearly you weren't saying the right things, anyway.*

Marguerite, who had a grasp on human nature like some people had a grasp on a knife hilt said, "Where's your watchdog today?"

Grace's lip curled.

"Ah." Marguerite sat back. "The gathering expedition did not go well, I take it."

"I stepped on a severed head," said Grace.

"*What?!*"

The saga of the head and the guard took so long to relate that Grace was beginning to hope that Marguerite had been distracted. She should have known better. The spy fixed her with a gimlet eye and said, "And Stephen?"

Grace muttered something into the notes she was trying to recreate.

"Grace..."

"He kissed me."

"And?"

"And then he said it was a mistake and he couldn't be trusted and that there couldn't be anything between us."

"He *what?!*"

Grace didn't know if she should be gratified or worried that her friend sounded at least as indignant about that as she had about the severed head.

"How was the kiss, anyway?" asked Marguerite, when she had finished condemning Stephen to the lowest of the seven hells. Grace hadn't known that there was more than one hell, but apparently Marguerite had access to more of them than she did.

Grace groaned and put her head in her hands.

"That bad?" And then, when Grace didn't respond, "Oh no. That good?"

"It was amazing," said Grace bitterly. "Toe-curling. *Hair*-curling, not that mine needs any more of it."

"Shit."

"I'd have let him fuck me right there, if it hadn't been three feet of mud."

"The mud does put a damper on things."

"Yeah." She rubbed her face, then realized she'd left a smear of ink on her cheekbone and fumbled for a cloth. "Goddamn paladins."

"Well," said Marguerite. Then she paused for perhaps half a minute, while staring at Tab without apparently seeing him. Tab rolled over to give his most inviting belly-rub wiggle, but Marguerite didn't seem to notice. "Well. At least you know he felt it too."

"I do?"

"Men don't panic and give you a speech about how there can't be anything between you if there isn't something between you," said Marguerite. "Unless you blurt out that you're in love with them, and that's different."

"I definitely did not blurt that, and I am not in love with him," said Grace.

"Are you sure?"

Grace opened her mouth, shut it again, and glared at the page. "...mostly."

"I mean, I wouldn't blame you if you were. Shoulders for days and toe-curling kisses? What's not to love?"

"What happened to, 'what would I do with a man like that'?"

"That's me, not you. And you note he's not curling any of *my* body parts."

Grace groaned again. "So you've got all the answers. What do I do?"

"At the moment? Nothing. He screwed up, he can make it right. Or not." Marguerite shrugged. "Anyway, the murders aren't solved yet, so it's not like he won't be back at some point. Or he won't be, in which case you're better off without him."

"I wish I had your confidence," said Grace.

"He's a paladin," said Marguerite. "They only have a couple of emotions and the primary one is guilt. You'll see."

For three days, Stephen alternated between resolve and guilt so thick that he could practically taste it. He could not pursue Grace. He knew that. It wasn't fair to her. It wasn't fair to his brothers. He had done the right thing.

He had also done it in the most ham-handed manner possible. He'd initiated the kiss and then pushed her away. If he'd just controlled himself, none of it would have happened.

Why hadn't he controlled himself?

The question nagged at him morning and evening. He walked a much subdued Brother Francis through the tent camp in the Elkinslough woods. He helped a party of gnoles dig a culvert for their flooded warren. He traded jibes with Istvhan and nearly broke his foot on a submerged block of stone. And every time his thoughts strayed for even a moment, he saw Grace, and the stab of hurt across her face that he had put there.

Stephen stopped trying to knit socks. It left his mind too free. He found himself blankly staring into a ring of needles and yarn while guilt lashed him, and thought, *I have to fix this.*

This was easier said than done.

What the hell was he going to say? *"I have to apologize to you and beg you to forgive me because I can't knit any more and it's making me crazy. Or at least crazier."*

This did not seem promising. Stephen might not be an expert on the human heart, but he did not see that going over well.

"I'm so very sorry that I hurt you, I want you but I feel guilty about it because my brothers need me."

No, that didn't make any damn sense, did it? What did wanting Grace have to do with the other paladins needing him? It had been a kiss, not an offer to move out of the Temple and then relocate to the far side of nowhere. She'd think, quite rightly, that the one had nothing to do with the other.

He stared at the sock, which had not grown by so much as a row in the last three days.

Maybe the one *didn't* have anything to do with the other.

Istvhan would tell him that he was using it as an excuse. Istvhan did not know everything, but he had his moments now and again. Stephen set the sock aside. He was going to have to face up to the fact that he'd made a mess of things and go and apologize. Which was itself fraught because he knew his apology might not help and that meant that he was apologizing for himself, not for her. It wasn't her job to absolve him of the fact that he'd been an ass. If all he wanted was absolution, he should probably be asking Istvhan to take his confession again.

But dammit, she had to know that she hadn't been wrong. He'd led her down a road he had no right to go down, and it was entirely his fault and none of hers. That she *was* attractive and he was just too damn broken, that was all.

It was a long walk to the Glover's Quarter, during which he prepared and discarded three different speeches, and eventually settled on, "I'm sorry, I was an ass," and seeing where things went from there.

When he finally arrived, the door was ajar. That was odd. Stephen tapped on the frame, then pushed it open. He took two steps inside and Marguerite lunged out of the back room. "You're here!" she said.

"Uh...yes?"

For a moment the spy looked as if she were about to throw herself on Stephen's chest. He braced himself, but she stopped short in front of him.

"How did you find out so—no, no, of course. Rat. Rat has eyes everywhere. Right." She clutched her forehead. "Right. You're here. Thank the gods. What are we going to do?"

"About what?" asked Stephen, feeling as if he'd missed some vital part of the conversation.

"About Grace!" She blinked at him, then slowly the animation faded from her face. "That's not why you're here."

"I came to tell Grace about the severed head...err...situation..." He was starting to feel genuinely alarmed. Marguerite had been unflappable in the face of a boy dying of poison and a body being cut up, but her face had gone pale and she kept wringing her hands. "What's happened?"

"It's Grace," she said. "She's been arrested."

~

Well, thought Grace. *This is a thing that happened.*

Normal people did not get arrested. Probably.

When the men showed up to take her away, she'd opened the door. She thought they were there about the break-in. It had been a very confusing few minutes for everyone.

Everyone had been—oh, not nice, exactly, but professional. Almost everyone, anyway. There had been two men from the royal guard and they were very professional and told her that she was under arrest and she stared at them blankly and said, "Um...what?"

"For poisoning," said the third man, who was wearing the indigo robes of the Motherhood. He was less professional.

"Poisoning?"

"That is the charge, ma'am," said one of the royal guard. "You'll need to come with us, please."

"Poisoning who?"

"The Crown Prince of Charlock," said the Motherhood man, in what he probably thought were dramatic, sepulchral tones.

"He's been poisoned?" asked Grace, somewhat ruining his delivery.

"Apparently so, ma'am," said the guard, giving the Motherhood man a dark look. "That's why we're here."

"But who poisoned him?" And then, when the guards looked stoic and embarrassed and the Motherhood man started to turn purple. "Wait, you're arresting *me* for poisoning *him?*"

"Yes, ma'am."

"But he seemed nice," she said.

The guard opened his mouth as if to say something, then closed it again. "If you could just come with us, ma'am."

"Oh dear." She wiped her hands on her apron. "I hope we can sort this out quickly."

"You have the right to legal counsel," said the guard, which did not answer the question.

"Can I have a few minutes?" she asked, thinking vaguely that she was in the middle of heating the oakmoss and it was right at the critical bit and if she could just get it done, then when she'd cleared this whole mess up, it wouldn't be completely ruined.

"To finish your witchcraft? I think not."

"I'm afraid not, ma'am," said the guard, with a quelling look at the priest.

"Oh," said Grace. Dread began to creep through her chest, long grey tendrils wrapping around her heart. *This is it. This is where it all goes bad. This is what going bad looks like.* "Oh, I see. All right."

She turned off the heat. The oakmoss would be ruined anyway. She'd have to get more.

All that trouble and I got kissed and rejected for nothing. And stepped on a head.

She turned back and discovered that there were five more people in the room. "Wait, where did you all come from?" *Are they really sending eight people to arrest me? What do they think I'm going to do, throw perfume in their faces?*

She began to think that perhaps this wasn't a mistake after all, and that she might not be able to clear it up with a simple explanation.

The new arrivals began to move around the rooms, picking things up and looking at them, taking them out of their assigned places and setting them back down somewhere else.

"Please don't do that," said Grace, feeling the dread growing. "Please, I won't be able to find anything again."

They ignored her. The guard took her upper arm and said, very gently, "It's time to go, ma'am."

"But they're making a mess! I know where everything is, and if they move it..."

She trailed off, as one of the men opened the door to her bedroom. "Wait, what are you doing?"

He cried out in surprise as Tab shot out of the bedroom and into the workshop. "What the hell is *that?*"

"That's Tab, he's a civette, please don't startle him, he's a sweet boy but he bites if he's nervous, but he doesn't mean it!" Panic began to override the dread. What if something happened to Tab? What if he bit one of them and they killed him?

"Your familiar?" asked the Motherhood man.

"My what?"

"Familiar spirit! To aid in witchcraft!"

"I'm not a witch? Um, he eats my pillows sometimes, I don't know how much help that would be?"

One of the men grabbed for him. Tab scooted away, clearly unsettled by all the new arrivals. A babble of voices rose up behind him.

"Catch him!"

"Don't let him get away!"

"That thing is evidence!"

"Get it!"

"Wait, stop, you'll scare him—!"

The front door jangled as yet another person came through. Tab saw the opening to freedom and bolted.

"Tab!"

Grace wrenched free of the guard and gave chase, but she was too late. The civette vanished into the alley. She was on the steps, calling his name, when the guard caught up with her again.

"Ma'am, please don't do that again."

"But he's going to get lost or trampled or something!" She stared up at the man's impassive face, trying to make him understand. "He's not supposed to go outside. He's not *good* at it."

"I'm sure he'll turn up again," said the man. "Now come with me. I'm afraid we don't have time for this."

"But—"

"No buts, ma'am. Please come with me."

Grace rode over in a carriage, which was much less padded than the one that the Crown Prince had sent for her. *I have spent more time in carriages in the last few weeks than I have in my entire life beforehand.* It also smelled better, probably because of the lack of fabric to mildew. The guards smelled mostly of lanolin and hints of clove for their armor, with a touch of sweat, although one of them was wearing some kind of hair oil that had a cheap-tobacco-and-orange scent and was doing him no favors at all.

The Motherhood man smelled like frankincense gone slightly sour on the edge. Frankincense didn't normally go sour like that, so it was probably body odor seeping through. Grace leaned back against the wall of the carriage, wondering if there was a polite way to ask him if he was wearing a fragrance that happened to have notes of sour sweat. *Probably not.*

They did not go to the palace. They went instead to a large building in the shadow of the wall of the Old City. There were bas reliefs carved along the roofline and a line of shrubs planted along the front, but there were also bars on the windows. Grace dug her fingers into her tunic and felt panic rising hot and heavy in her throat.

"Is this the guard station?" she asked. Her voice came out as a squeak.

She probably imagined the flicker of pity in the guard's eyes. "This is where you'll be held until the trial, ma'am."

"The trial? But don't I talk to someone first? I need to clear this up. This is all a misunderstanding."

"There is no misunderstanding, *poisoner*," growled the Motherhood man.

"But—" Grace didn't understand any of this. "Nobody's even asked me if I did it!"

"I'm sure if you're innocent, you've got nothing to worry about," said the guard. He didn't say it as if he believed it, or as if he expected Grace to believe it. She got the impression that it was like saying, "Bless you," if someone sneezed, a thing you said by rote to move the conversation along and get past the awkward moment.

"But—"

He gave her a weary look and Grace closed her mouth, embarrassed. She was apparently being arrested wrong, on top of everything else.

They went into the building. It reminded Grace of the Crown Prince's embassy, the same smell of bleach and wood polish. *No vases full of peacock feathers, though. And no incense.* They went up two flights of stairs to a hallway, and then another guard stood up from his chair and the royal guards signed a sheet of paper and went away, and the new guard and the Motherhood man walked her down the hallway. There were a number of featureless doors. The guard unlocked one on the outside wall and gestured inside.

"You'll be staying here, miss," he said.

"I will?"

"Yes."

She stepped inside. There was a table and a chair and a bed and a small privacy screen. The window had a wooden shutter over it.

"But—" she said, and the lock clicked shut behind her.

CHAPTER 31

Stephen did not go berserk.

It was a near thing. The tide, which was always lapping around his metaphorical ankles, rose at least to his waist. Only the knowledge that the only thing that would help was calm, clear, methodical action kept him grounded.

"Who took her?" he barked at Marguerite, then realized what he was doing and took a step back. *Attention!* he snapped to himself, hearing the voice of his old drill sergeant in his head. The man was ten years in the ground and Stephen would probably hear his voice until the day he died. His body responded. Paladins were not military, but he'd been a soldier long before he was a paladin. *Parade...Rest.* Hands behind his back, feet a studied distance apart. Yes. All right. Calm, clear, methodical action.

Strangely, Marguerite seemed to understand what he was doing, and waited until he had settled into the formal parade rest. "Palace guards," she said.

He nodded sharply.

"They had a Motherhood man with them."

Stephen felt his hands curling into fists against the small of his back and moved back to formal attention. "Did you see where she was taken?"

"The old officer barracks. The one they've converted."

Stephen forced himself to breathe normally, in rhythm. *Mis-ter Brass did-n't pay his tax...* After a moment he said, "That could be worse." At least in the old barracks, it was being treated as a governmental matter. Had Grace been taken to the Hanged Mother's temple, he would have had to stage a one-man assault on the building, and while there was a depressingly good chance that he would succeed, the resulting carnage would have been somewhat detrimental to the image of the broken paladins.

"It could be a great deal better, too," said Marguerite. "I tailed them as far as the building, and I've got people trying to work out what's happening, but it'll take me a few hours. Meanwhile..." She spread her hands, and for the first time, Stephen noticed the disaster in the room. "The workshop is even worse," she said. "I've been trying to clean up. They turned the place over searching for something."

"What were they looking for?"

"That's one of the things I don't know yet. I don't even know what she's been charged with."

Stephen gritted his teeth. "You think it's related to the assassin?"

"Pretty long coincidence if it's not. And there was a break-in a few days ago, where a bunch of her journals were stolen, and I'm starting to think that wasn't a coincidence either."

Stephen's conscience did not so much needle him as knife him in the kidneys. A few days ago? They might have had some warning. And she hadn't told him about the break-in because he'd been an ass who shoved her away on the hillside, and if he hadn't come here to apologize, she could have been whisked away by the royal guard and he'd never have known what happened. Hell, if Marguerite hadn't been here...

"Where were you?" he asked, then winced at the accusatory tone. "I don't mean like that, just..."

"I know." Her full lips twisted in a smile that most red-blooded men (and a few red-blooded women) would have found intensely attractive. Stephen could only think of Grace and her downturned lips, with their permanently thoughtful expression. Saint have mercy. "I've got someone watching the house at all times."

"You what?"

"One, I'm a woman in a line of work that's...oh, not dangerous, exactly, but certainly prone to occasional upset. Two, we're two women living alone with a good-natured weasel for a guard. A watcher only makes sense."

"And they didn't see the burglar?"

"They saw him but didn't get a look at his face. They're just a watcher, not a guard."

A thought seized him. "Where's the weasel?"

Marguerite shook her head. "The front door was wide open when I got here. I suspect he bolted."

Shit. Grace would be heartbroken.

"I'm hoping he'll come back. In the meantime..." She sighed, raking her hand through her thick black hair. "I'll finish the cleanup while I wait for reports."

"You don't have someone to clean it up for you?"

She looked at him as if he had just said something very strange. "This is Grace's home," she said. "Strangers got into it. You can't just have strangers fix it again. They wouldn't know where things went or how she liked them set up."

And so a spy was cleaning up the workshop. A spy that, Stephen was beginning to suspect, was a very high-level operative indeed.

"I'll let you know as soon as I know anything," she said.

"Please do," said Stephen. "But I think, this time, I can make things move more quickly."

"Oh?"

"I believe," said Stephen, "that it is time for the Bishop to meet Miss Angelica."

Grace had made three circuits of the room and found absolutely nothing useful on any of them.

The table was bolted to the floor. The wooden shutters on the window had slats to allow airflow, but they weren't just closed, they were a single solid piece of wood with a bit of decorative carving to make it look like a pair of normal shutters.

I suppose that's polite of them, to make it look like I'm just spending the evening in an inn. Not prison-like. I'm just not allowed to leave.

She wondered if the Motherhood was not so sure of their case, or if the Archon was just very civilized about how prisoners were treated. Or perhaps it was only prisoners suspected of crimes against the crown. Presumably if they thought she was a pickpocket, she'd be in an ordinary jail cell with all the other riffraff. Maybe there was something to be said for being accused of a high-level assassination attempt.

On the other hand, if they thought I was a pickpocket, they'd probably either fine me or give me a couple lashes and let me go.

Grace was not eager to find out what lashing was like, but people didn't die of it all that often, did they?

The room, like the rest of the building, smelled of bleach and wood polish. The mattress was clean and free of vermin and the sheets smelled like laundry soap. It was entirely her imagination that it also smelled of despair.

This is it this is how it all goes this is how they take everything away from you in the end this is what that feels like...

Her mind went back to Tab, bolting out the front door. God, what would happen to him? He caught mice fine, but he wasn't good at survival. Would someone find him and try to sell him as a pet?

Please, gods, let it be as a pet and not as a fur stole.

She wrung her hands together, then went to the wooden shutter and sniffed at the space between the slats. It had rained again, so the air was washed briefly clean of human stenches, and now smelled mostly of rain and Elkinslough mud, with a faint edge of petrichor, probably from the shrubs planted in front of the building.

She closed her eyes. Petrichor, the smell of rain on dry earth, was one of the smells she loved the most. If she could have made a perfume that smelled like that, she would have worn it every day.

The door opened behind her. Grace jerked back and tried not to look as if she had been sticking her nose out the window sniffing. Normal people did not stick their noses out of slats in the window and huff air.

"You can't get out that way," said the Motherhood man.

"I wasn't trying to get out," said Grace. "I was trying to breathe."

He scowled at her. The guard behind him cleared his throat, and he stepped forward. Grace abandoned the window and resigned herself to sourness and frankincense.

"Sign this," said the Motherhood man, shoving a sheet of parchment across the table at her. "It'll speed things along."

Grace blinked at him, then down at the paper, and began to read. *I, Grace Angelica, hereby confess to the attempted murder of the Crown Prince of Charlock by means of foul poison...*

"I'm not signing this!"

A look of chagrin flashed across his face. Grace wondered if he didn't know that she could read, or if he had simply expected her to sign the paper because he told her to.

"If you sign this, everything will go a great deal more quickly," he said. "We can get on with things."

"But it isn't true!" She wondered what *get on with things* meant. The trial? The conviction?

God help her, an execution?

"Things will be much easier for you if you cooperate."

"That's enough," said the royal guard. "You ask them to sign, you don't threaten them. This isn't the boonies. We're civilized here."

Grace had a brief urge to cheer for civilization.

The Motherhood man snatched the unsigned confession off the table and stalked to the door.

"Dinner will be at eight, Miss Angelica," said the guard, as if they were staying at a high-quality inn. "If you have need of anything, please knock on the door and someone will attend you." He paused, then added gently, "I suggest you do not abuse that privilege."

"I won't," said Grace, and heard a squeak in her voice. The air in the room seemed suddenly close and hot, the candles producing a stifling amount of heat.

The door closed behind him. The lock clicked. Grace went back to the shuttered window and put her face to the slats, trying again to breathe.

CHAPTER 32

It did not occur to Stephen until the carriage ride over that he was imposing greatly upon the Bishop. She oversaw a temple with nearly a hundred assorted priests, lawyers, and associated staff. She was arguably one of the most important people in all of Archenhold, let alone in Archon's Glory. And she had nevertheless dropped everything for one broken paladin when he begged for her assistance.

She sat calmly in the carriage across from him, her hands folded neatly in her lap. One of her personal secretaries sat beside her, scribbling notes, but Beartongue did not speak, merely gazed out the window. He was certain that her mind was working like one of the automatons from Anuket City.

"Thank you," he said abruptly. "Thank you for all of this. I know I am asking a lot."

She lifted her eyes to his face and smiled, and he knew a little of what Istvhan felt. *A woman like that is a terrifying glory.* It occurred to him that of all the people he had met, on the battlefield and off it, Bishop Beartongue was the closest to true greatness.

"Stephen," she said gently. "Your people have stayed with us for three years now, and in all that time, none of you have ever asked for anything, except perhaps to be allowed to push yourselves even harder. I know that the quartermaster had to practically force you to accept a stipend, never mind a wage, and that the housekeepers have to report when you have torn a sheet or broken a chair, because it would not occur to any of you to do it. And I know that every single one of you would die in the Temple's service, without question or complaint."

Stephen looked down at his gloved hands. "Well," he said. "We'd complain. Probably."

She snorted. "And now you come to me and beg me to represent your friend, which is already within the Rat's mandate, and which will tweak the Motherhood's whiskers, which is a personal joy of mine. And you look as if you are asking to borrow an army or my firstborn or something equally terrible."

"You're very busy," he said.

"I am." She nodded to him. "But the day I turn down a cry for help because I am busy is the day the Rat turns His face away from me. And I would deserve it."

Stephen put his fist over his heart and bowed his head like a soldier to his monarch, or a paladin to his god.

They reached the building. Beartongue alighted and nodded to the secretary. "Go find whoever is in charge," she ordered. "I want copies of every warrant and details of every charge."

"Yes, Your Holiness."

They swept into the building. The secretary peeled off. The bishop stalked up the stairs and Stephen flanked her.

"Prisoners are held up here," she murmured to him. And then, more loudly, "I have come to see Mistress Angelica. Please direct me to where she is held."

The two guards in the Archon's livery saw the vestments of the Temple of the White Rat and immediately stepped to the side to let Beartongue pass. One nodded. "Right this way, your holi—"

"Hold!" snapped another man, stepping into the hall.

"Oh, it's you, Jordan," said Beartongue, unimpressed. "Burn any good books lately?"

His nostrils flared but he did not rise to the bait. "By what right do you wish to see the poisoner?"

Stephen bristled. *They're neck deep in it, of course.* Marguerite had said as much, but the sight of the indigo robes was working on him like red on a bull. He wanted to charge the man and perhaps trample him.

"The right of legal counsel," said Beartongue.

The Motherhood man wore dark colors with slashed sleeves. *Higher rank than the usual guards,* thought Stephen, *and used to having someone to back him up. He doesn't have a sword but he expects someone to be standing behind him who does. Older. I could take him I expect but a man like that always has a trick up his sleeve.*

The Archon's guard looked from Beartongue to the Motherhood man and back again.

"Poisoners do not need lawyers," said the Motherhood man. "They fall within our mandate."

"All citizens are entitled to protection under the law," said the bishop. "That falls within *our* mandate. Would you like to take this matter to the Archon? I am willing to go now."

His eyes narrowed. Then he muttered a curse and stepped aside, but not very far. The Bishop would have to squeeze past him.

"Allow me," murmured Stephen, and stepped in front of her. He walked forward. The Motherhood man could either get out of the way or take a mailed shoulder to the chest. He chose to get out of the way.

"Watch your temper, Jordan," murmured Beartongue as they passed. "You don't want another round of dyspepsia like last time."

"Your *concern* is *noted*," said Jordan, biting off each word.

"We had to call a healer to the court, as I recall. It was quite disruptive to the proceedings."

"The Motherhood still won the case," said Jordan.

"Did you?" Beartongue smiled over her shoulder. "I'm glad. Everyone should win occasionally."

"Um," said the guard, who clearly wanted to stop the Bishop from passing the correct door, but also did not want to interrupt the sniping between the two priests. "Um. Sir?" He cast a pleading look in Stephen's direction.

"I believe we have arrived," said Stephen.

The guard unlocked the door and stepped back. Stephen went first, ostensibly to guard against attackers. In reality, he would have probably trampled the bishop trying to get through the door.

And there was Grace.

She was just turning from the shuttered window when he saw her, and the fear on her face tore him up like an enemy blade. Then she saw him.

Stephen did not know if he had ever seen such relief in another person's face, and his mind flashed back to Grace saying, "Relief feels like happiness, if you don't know the difference."

"You found me," she said. She lunged across the room and almost —almost—into his arms. He lifted his hands to catch her.

"Of course," he said. *Of course I found you. I'll always come for you if you need me. Always.* A promise he couldn't make, not aloud, not at all. He was too broken, too unstable. The day she needed him might be the day the tide rose. But a reckless part of him wanted to gather her up in his arms and make the promise anyway, just to ease the fear in her eyes.

She halted a step away from him, suddenly wary, her eyes lifting uncertainly to his face. He flinched, knowing what came next—the remembered hurt, the icy brittleness. He could not bear to see that again, so he took the coward's way out and turned away, letting his arms drop. "Grace, may I introduce Bishop Beartongue, of the Temple of the Rat."

Grace bowed in the Anuket City fashion, palms against her thighs. "Your...uh..."

"Holiness," said the Bishop. "But in this case, I believe you can simply call me Bishop. Or Beartongue, if you prefer." She looked around the room. "Well, the accommodations are not the worst I've seen. Are they feeding you?"

"Yes," said Grace. "It's...uh...not terrible. I wasn't very hungry. Your...Bishop."

"Being arrested does tend to ruin the appetite," said Beartongue.

"Now, then." She sat down at the table. "Tell me everything that happened from the time the guard arrived."

Stephen knew that it was his place as guard to stand behind the Bishop, so he did, but it meant that he was watching Grace's face. Her eyes kept straying up to him and he did not know what to do. Smile encouragingly? Look away? The usual thousand-yard-stare of guards and soldiers seemed wildly out of place.

When Grace got to the confession that the Motherhood man had asked her to sign, though, his fingers tightened on the back of Beartongue's chair so hard that the wood creaked. The bishop scowled fiercely. "Vultures," she growled. "*Unethical* vultures."

"What would have happened if I'd signed?" asked Grace.

"It would certainly have made our job harder," said Beartongue. She nodded to Grace. "You were right not to sign." She tapped her nail on the table pensively. "Well, at least we know what they're trying to charge you with, anyway. So it was good for that much."

"What happens to me now?" asked Grace. "Do I get to go home?"

The Bishop sighed. "No," she said. "I'm sorry. We are still working out the exact details, but I'm afraid it seems unlikely." She glanced around the room. "Will this serve you for now? Do you have anything that you need us to ask for, while we plan your defense? Foods you can or cannot eat, or holy books that you might pray?"

"No," said Grace. "No, I'm fairly boring. Uh..." She paused, her eyes flicking to Stephen. "Could I have charbeans? The smells...they make the smells go away."

"I believe that can be arranged," said the Bishop. "You will likely be here for at least a week. Is there someone who can watch over your shop? If you need assistance making arrangements, this is what the Rat does. Please don't hesitate to tell us."

"Marguerite should take care of the shop," said Grace. "But Tab..." She looked up at Stephen, not at the Bishop. "You have to find Tab. Please. He ran out the door, he'll be in the street...he'll get trampled or someone will catch him or...*please.*"

Stephen had seen her nearly faint, watch a suicide, watch an autopsy, step on a severed head, and discuss her arrest, and Grace had never cried. But when she asked him to find Tab, there was a tremble to her lips and a thickness to her voice that made him want to weep himself.

He would have promised anything at that moment. He would have climbed mountains or murdered kings. Fortunately, this was much simpler. "Of course," he said. "I'll find him. He can't have gone far."

"I'm going to step outside," said Beartongue, master of subtlety. Stephen could feel the bishop's eyes boring holes in the back of his neck, then the door creaked and closed.

Grace looked up at him. He looked down at her. The silence stretched out and became unbearable.

"I'm—"

"It's good to—"

"Sorry."

"See you."

They both stopped. They coughed. They stared at different corners of the room.

Finally, Stephen said "So I was a bit of an ass."

"A bit, yeah."

"For that, I'm very sorry. Can I do something to make it up to you?"

"Well, you could get me out of here."

"Working on that." He shoved a hand through his hair. "But I'd try to do that anyway. Are you sure there isn't anything else? Vigil on my knees, perhaps?"

"I don't think I need anything vigilled. Is that even a word?"

"No, but we can make it one."

Grace gave him that crooked smile, marred only by a suspicious shine to her eyes. "But you found me. How did you know?"

"Marguerite had someone watching the shop and they told her. I came by to apologize and then..." He lifted his hands and let them drop. "I went to the Rat. I would have come sooner, but I didn't think they'd let me in by myself."

"I'm glad you're here now."

"So am I," he said, and then, because he could hear Beartongue and Istvhan shouting at him inside his head, he took two steps forward and held out his arms.

And if she just stares at me like I'm history's greatest fool, it will be no more than I deserve.

Grace looked at him for a long moment while his heart sank and then she stepped forward into his embrace.

He closed his arms around her and felt a jolt through him. Not lust, but a sensation like a tumbler in a lock or a bone jarred back into the socket. This was *right*. This was where he was supposed to be, at this exact moment. All his certainty that he had been doing the right thing by stepping away from her was burned instantly away.

In service to the Saint, he had always known where he was supposed to be. On the battlefield, when the golden fire took you, you knew that of all the places in heaven and earth, this was the singular place where you were meant to stand. Since the god had died, he had not felt that certainty. It was one of many things that he had assumed was lost, that he would never feel again.

With Grace's head tucked under his chin and his arms around her, he realized that this, at least, was a certainty that humans could give each other.

They stood for a long time. Stephen did not dare kiss her. It was too soon and too much. But their lungs found a rhythm together and his heartbeat slowed and he found himself stroking her back, fingers moving over each vertebrae as if counting rosary beads.

It was all too soon when she sighed and stepped back. "The Bishop will be waiting for you."

Stephen rather suspected that the Bishop would be entirely understanding if he showed up an hour late, stinking of sex, with love bites on his neck. Possibly even congratulatory. But this did not seem like a diplomatic thing to mention, so he didn't. "Yes," he said. "I should go. I'll find Tab."

The hope in her eyes frightened him and warmed him both, all the long ride home.

CHAPTER 33

Once back at the Temple of the Rat, the Bishop summoned her staff and dealt them back out again like a deck of cards. "Percy, go and roust Zale. Mur, I'll need three copies of those charges. Stephen, find Istvhan, inform him that you have been relieved of your current duties, and join me in my office."

Stephen saluted, and was marginally surprised when the others didn't.

Five minutes later they were assembled in the bishop's office.

"Zale," said the Bishop, "you'll be Miss Angelica's defense."

Zale looked startled. "Uh...with all due respect your holiness, I'm a property lawyer."

Stephen groaned internally.

"Yes," said the Bishop, unruffled. "And my two best lawyers who handle this sort of case are currently both in Aquila-on-Marsh."

Zale cursed softly and said something under their breath that sounded like, "Sin-eaters."

"You're what I've got," said the Bishop. "You've been trained to handle this, even if it was some time ago. And you stall remarkably well."

Zale's narrow face pulled sideways as they scowled. "There's that, I suppose."

"And the presiding judge is Consul Gucciard and you know he's always had a soft spot for you."

Zale sighed. "Fine, fine. You win. I am probably the best for the job." They encountered Stephen's curious look and said, "It's nothing prurient. I turned up some bottles of a rare vintage in an estate I was working on and contacted Gucciard. I knew he'd give a fair price to my client, and he was grateful to have the first chance at them."

"At this point," said Stephen, "I would not care if you had a torrid affair with him and thought that you could wrap him around your finger. In fact, I would prefer that."

Zale snorted. "Sorry to disappoint."

"I don't suppose you'd consider...?"

"He is not my type and I am not at all his. I fear it's going to be plain old legal wrangling." Zale lifted their eyebrows. "Speaking of which, I may require your services as a character witness for the accused."

"Of course. Anything."

Zale nodded. "I'll go over there now, if you'd like to accompany me."

"Unfortunately I must decline," said Stephen. He looked out into the rain-soaked street and felt his heart sink. Still, paladin, faithful until death, etc. "I am afraid that I have a date with a weasel."

Grace was bored. She was terrified and worried and fretful, but mostly she was extraordinarily bored. She had examined every piece of furniture in the room in minute detail, including the undersides. There was nothing under the bed and nothing under the chair, but someone had thoughtfully scratched a penis into the underside of the table.

She slept fitfully at night, then stayed in bed as long as possible. She had absolutely nothing to do but sit in the room and try to breathe out the window, so sleep made the hours pass. When sleep failed, she did what humans have done since time immemorial while lying alone in bed, bored out of their skulls, and slid a hand between her legs.

Unfortunately there was only one man that she was thinking about. She hadn't wanted to think about him for days, but he kept clanking into her fantasies anyway.

"Dammit, Stephen," she muttered. She'd worked so hard not to think about him for the past week, and suddenly he was back, holding her in his arms and smelling like gingerbread. She'd been angry and yes, he'd apologized, but more importantly, he'd *found* her. He was so strong and she was so tired and it would be so easy simply to give over to that strength and let him rescue her one more time.

Stop thinking about rescue. Rescue is not sexy. Think about the smell of gingerbread and the way he kissed you on the hillside.

This wasn't hard. She'd felt that kiss to the roots of her hair. She just had to imagine those gloved hands sliding lower, the roughness of leather against her skin...

Someone knocked on the door and she nearly jumped out of her skin.

Sixteen hours alone in the room and the minute I start touching myself and thinking of paladins, somebody's banging down the door. Typical.

It can't be the Motherhood, they don't knock. Suppose they'd have gotten an eyeful if they did.

"Give me a minute!" she called, throwing on her clothes from the day before and hurriedly washing her hands in the basin. She looked at her hair in the tiny polished steel mirror and gave up any hope of fixing it. *Oh well, if they wanted me to look pretty, they shouldn't have arrested me.*

"Come in," she called.

The person who came through the door was slim, silver-haired, carrying a stack of papers. "Good morning," they said. "My name is Zale. I am a solicitor-sacrosanct from the Temple of the Rat. I've been sent to represent you."

"Oh," said Grace. "Oh, uh. Okay. Thank you."

The lawyer-priest smiled. "May I use your table?"

"Yes, of course." She stood looking down at the papers they were spreading across the table. Were they going to ask her sign another confession? No, this was the Rat, they represented the downtrodden. Stephen trusted them.

"Has anyone told you what's going to happen next?"

Grace shook her head. "No. Err..." *They'd have to do something before they execute me, don't they? They won't just take me to the headsman? Someone has to say "Guilty!" first, right?*

She attempted to convey this to Zale, who put their head in their hands. "Well, in theory," they said. "In practice...I won't say that some people don't simply get dragged to the headsman. Or the hangman, depending on the place."

Marguerite will do something. She won't let them just kill me.

"However," said Zale, "the Temple of the Rat has taken an interest in your case, and will be assisting you." They smiled warmly. "Although I confess, this could have been much better timed, and you may curse my assistance before long. Murder and poisoning is not my forte."

"It's really not mine, either," said Grace.

"Because I have to ask," said Zale, "and please don't take offense, but did you happen to poison the Crown Prince?"

"No!"

"It's just that it changes the defense somewhat if you did, you understand. I'm certain you would have had a very good reason, but I wouldn't waste my time trying to prove you didn't, and we'd go to trying to prove that you had no choice and that, as my friend Sarkis would say, 'He needed killing.'"

"I didn't poison him," said Grace. "I've never poisoned anyone. I know people think perfumers and poisoners are practically the same thing, but I don't know any poisons. I've burned myself a lot and made myself woozy a few times, but that's as much damage as I've ever done to anyone, even me. I can't even put out rat pellets for fear Tab will get it. Err...Tab's my civette."

One of Zale's slender eyebrows rose higher. "I see that this is going to be a particularly interesting case," they said. "Or perhaps you are simply a particularly unusual client. What is a civette, and why does it eat rat pellets?"

Grace put her head in her hands. "All right. So once upon a time, someone decided to breed a domestic civet cat..."

"Fascinating," said Zale, when she was done. "Alas, not particularly relevant to the case, but fascinating nonetheless." The lawyer tilted their head, looking like a grave, silver-crested bird. "I suppose we must speak of less happy matters now. Do you understand the trial system?"

Grace shook her head. "I don't know anything," she said. She could hear a note of despair in her voice and tried to rein it in. "Until Stephen showed up, I didn't even know if anyone knew where I'd gone, or what happened, or if anyone was going to defend me."

"*I* will defend you," said Zale firmly. "I fear that I am not the best possible person for this, but I am the best possible person available at this time, which is much the same thing." They spread their hands. "I am a solicitor sacrosanct of the Temple, even if my expertise lies primarily in property disputes. My murder cases were mostly years ago, but the laws have not changed that much."

Somehow, hearing the lawyer admit their failings made Grace feel more confident. And they smelled like wintergreen and ink and clean laundry and that helped even more.

"So," said Zale. "The trial. Have you ever seen one?"

"Um. I saw someone hanged once?"

"Ah...no. That's the execution. That's after the trial has gone very badly. Well, for the accused, anyway, I don't know about this particular case. We are going to try to avoid any of the hanging bits. May I?" They gestured to the table.

"Yes, of course." Grace dropped into a chair across from them, as graceless as a sack of potatoes. Zale settled themselves as neatly as a bird perching.

"Trials are alarming. There is no question of it. But I will sit with you and the Motherhood is not allowed to do anything but yell at you."

"I hate it when people yell at me," said Grace faintly.

Zale sighed. "Ah...well. I am afraid there's no help for that. They will yell and I will yell back and occasionally it will descend into a great deal of shouting, and whoever shouts the most convincingly wins." They smiled. "I am afraid that we are, compared to something like the Anuket High Courts, a bit uncivilized. We all talk at once and there is a great deal of yelling and frequently it goes on until the judge yells at us both and demands that only one person talk at a time."

"But you'll do the talking?"

"I will talk until my tongue falls out, if I must."

"And tomorrow is the trial?"

"Two days from now. The Motherhood asked for a slight delay, and we agreed. There will be at least three days, I expect—one for the prosecution to lay out their charges and evidence, one where we all call character witnesses, and then a ruling." Zale shoved the errant lock of hair back from their eyes.

"Why would they ask for a delay?" asked Grace. She was torn between the desire to get out of the cell and the fear that every day was a day wrested from the headsman.

"I suspect they are hoping for the Crown Prince to die," said Zale.

Grace blinked.

"Oh, not in so many words. But an actual dead body carries a great deal of weight. If they can delay until he expires..." Zale shrugged. "That's a guess, you understand. It's possible that there's something else. But the delay works in our favor as well. The Rat will do everything they can to get to the bottom of this."

"Why?" asked Grace. "It's not that I'm not grateful," she added, when Zale's eyebrows shot up. "But you don't even know me, and you're going to all this trouble...I mean, I tithed some to the flood relief, but I don't understand why you're helping."

Zale relaxed, their mouth curving up at the corners. "Ah. Well. It is the Rat's duty to defend those who have no legal defense. We are, in effect, everyone's lawyer. But you are not wrong in thinking that you are being granted an extraordinary breadth of aid. We would still try to help, certainly, but we are spread as thin as anyone trying to do good in the world." They gathered up the papers on the table, tapping the edges into neat, precise lines. "But the Motherhood wants to prove you guilty of crimes against Archenhold, and if they succeed, they prove their worth to the Archon. The Archon is likely to favor them more, if he thinks they are rousting genuine threats. I doubt I need to explain why we would prefer not to have the Motherhood holding any more power than they already do?"

Grace shuddered. "No. Not at all."

"Well, there you are. And something strange is clearly afoot, with all these poisons and a poisoner on the loose. The Bishop wants to get to the bottom of things. And finally..." They spread their hands and smiled, half-rueful, half-kind.

"Finally?"

"Paladin Stephen likes you," said Zale. "And anyone that keeps our paladins happy, instead of moping and clanking and suffering nobly around the temple, is worth fighting for."

CHAPTER 34

Stephen stood in the drizzling rain, staring at the water gurgling in the gutters, and thought, *If I was a civette, where would I hide?*

Unfortunately, the answer seemed to be, "Anywhere I wanted to."

A weasel was a long, thin, narrow shape, perfect for fitting into very small holes, and when you looked at ground level from the perspective of a weasel, the world was made of holes. Drainpipes, rain gutters, cracks in the brickwork, a stack of pallets, the neighbor's ruined dovecote...

This would be much easier if I had about fifty men. We could establish a perimeter. No civette comes in or out.

Lacking the manpower, he had to settle for poking into every crevice that looked weasel-sized. At least one passer-by looked at him very suspiciously, then hurried off. He wondered if he looked like a burglar or like someone concerned about the drains.

Speaking of drains...Stephen crouched down and peered into the drainpipe from the roof. He didn't see anything, but he stuck his ungloved hand in anyway, feeling for fur.

Nothing. He grimaced, face pressed against the wet brick, as he wedged his hand further up the pipe. His nostrils filled with the scent of...well, of wet brick. Was there a name for the smell of wet bricks? Grace probably knew. Did she make it into perfume? Did anyone ever want to smell like that? It seemed unlikely, but then, a great many people apparently wanted to smell like a weasel's nethers, so there was no accounting for taste.

There was something intensely unsettling about sticking your arm in a hole. Even if it was just a drainpipe, some small nagging bit of Stephen's brain was waiting for jaws to close over him. It was the sort of story that little boys in the slums told each other, looking into the storm drains. "I dare you to stick your arm in there." "Billy's cousin did and something bit his arm off!" "Nuh-uh." "Uh-huh." And then there would be shoving.

He extracted his arm, unbitten but also devoid of civette.

Should he check the dovecote? Probably, yes. It looked like there might be a dry place inside. If he was a civette, lost in a strange place, he would certainly want to be dry.

He looked around. This was technically breaking and entering, even if he wasn't going to take anything. What on earth would he say if Grace's neighbors caught him? "Don't mind me, ma'am, I'm a paladin. Just checking your dovecote for rogue perfume weasels, now that your neighbor's been arrested on suspicion of poisoning a visiting head of state."

It would probably be best if he did not actually have to explain this.

The dovecote was falling down and clearly had not housed doves in quite a long time. Stephen lifted off the back door, which was propped against the doorway. The inside was indeed dry, and contained straw that might be older than Stephen himself.

He knelt down and crawled inside on his hands and knees, poking in likely corners. Nothing...nothing...something? He felt oilcloth under his fingers. It was warmer than the surrounding air, unexpectedly so. He gingerly reached both hands into the corner and found a sizable bundle, wrapped tightly in cloth. When he lifted it out, something clinked.

It looked to be an oilcloth sack full of clothes and, judging by the sound, a stash of coins. And square in the middle of it, in a hollowed out nest, was a round ball of civette.

~

Grace was not expecting a tentative knock in the middle of the night. Her heart stuttered. The Motherhood? Her lawyer? Stephen?

Marguerite? Oh god, she hoped it was Marguerite. It seemed strange that her friend hadn't come to visit her, not even once. If Stephen hadn't said that she had been at the workshop, Grace would have feared that the spy had been captured as well.

Maybe she's lying low so that the Motherhood doesn't pick her up as an accomplice. She's probably working like a dog to find some way to get me out of this, but she doesn't dare come here until it's time for the trial.

"Hello?" she asked tentatively.

"Hello? Are you there?"

The voice was familiar, but not one she was expecting. "DuValier?"

He pushed open the door. "Master Perfumer...Miss Angelica?"

The envoy looked tired. There were dark circles under his eyes and his clothes looked less immaculate than usual. The toes of his boots were scuffed and the amber crystal bounced against a plain shirt, devoid of embroidery.

"Err," said Grace. She thought that she had abandoned hope, but it flared unexpectedly. "Oh my goodness, DuValier! You're here! You can tell them—the Motherhood people—you can explain I didn't poison the Crown Prince. You can fix this!"

"Miss Angelica," said DuValier sadly. "I regret I cannot."

"But you know I didn't poison him!"

"I know that," said DuValier. "I know. I believe you. But I cannot say who did, and the Motherhood says that if I do not know who did, then I cannot know who did not. They are determined that you are responsible." He spread his hands. "I tried to argue, but..."

Grace sat down heavily. Her hopes had hardly risen enough to be dashed, but she felt a stab of sorrow anyway. "Oh."

"I will do my best to help," said DuValier. "But I fear that I've come because I need your help."

She lifted her eyebrows. "I'm not exactly in a position to help anyone, as you can see."

"It's your expertise I need," said DuValier. "If we can only determine how the Crown Prince was poisoned, or with what, perhaps both of you can be saved."

Grace stared at him, puzzled. "I don't know anything about poisons."

"But you know perfumes. And if we work through this, step by step...Please? I know we haven't known each other long." He took Grace's hand and pressed it between his palms. "But I am at wit's end and there are so many perfumes and it could be any of them."

Grace shook her head helplessly. "I don't know! I don't even know if you can kill people with a perfume! People *think* you can, but...I mean, they say you can make poisoned gloves, but I can't imagine that'd actually work."

"One would think, but one hears of subtle poisons, and gloves would be a good method."

"I suppose." Grace gnawed on her lower lip and reclaimed her hand. "You have to use very strong scents to overcome the tanning smell, so if it smelled, no one would notice. But I don't know anything that can kill you just by touching it." She met his gaze and shook her head. "Truly, I don't."

DuValier sighed and ran his hand through his golden hair, looking less courtly and more forlorn. "I am grasping at straws," he admitted. "But my liege is dying and he is—he is my friend."

His voice did not quite break, but there was a fracture in the timbre that cut Grace to the quick. She touched his shoulder. "I'll help if I can," she said. "Help me think of poisons, and we'll see if I can think of any way to get them into a perfume."

They spent nearly an hour at it, and at the end, Grace didn't feel like she'd helped at all. They kept coming back to gloves, but all the poisons that either Grace or Ethan—"Call me Ethan, I beg of you. Formality is for a less urgent time,"—could think seemed doomed to fail.

"You'd blister," she said. "All of these, surely your skin would blister so you'd take the gloves off. It would be awful, but I'd think you'd know it was the gloves. Has the Crown Prince's skin blistered?"

Ethan shook his head. "He is very weak," he said. "Weak and he sweats and keeps no food down. His fingertips are blue. It is...it is very hard to see a man of his strength brought down so quickly."

"Blue..." murmured Grace. "Blue. The assassin—the attempted assassin—he had blue fingertips. And he was sweating and vomiting." She looked up at the Crown Prince's friend. "Could it be the same thing?"

"The one who the paladins caught? I thought it was something he had taken to avoid capture. One of the glass pills."

"Yes, but no. Or also. Uh..." Grace hurriedly sketched out the situation with the double poisoning. "It could be the same thing. If it's the same, then...oh dear..." She tried to remember what Doctor Piper had said, but he hadn't named any, had he? There had simply been too many. "You should talk to him. He might be able to help more. And he's a doctor."

"Piper?" DuValier leapt to his feet. "I will go at once." He caught her hand once more and held it to his chest. "Miss Angelica—Grace —thank you."

"I don't know that I've done anything," protested Grace.

He dismissed her protest as he strode to the door. "On the contrary, I don't think you know how much help you've been. I'll seek out this Piper at once. Thank you."

The door shut behind him. Grace sighed and slumped back in her chair, feeling helpless to stop anything. *It's as if the world is careening out of control, and we are all trying to pull on the reins or stop the wheels, but we are so small and the world is so heavy.*

She had done her best. There was nothing more that she could do. But curled up in bed that night, she prayed to whatever god listened to small perfumers that the Crown Prince would recover from his illness, and not merely because she hoped to live to see another day.

CHAPTER 35

Stephen knocked at the door early in the morning. When Grace said, "Enter," he unlatched it and went in. She'd obviously been picking at her food. It looked nearly untouched, and the toast had been shredded into bits. He couldn't blame her. Being on trial for poisoning would kill anyone's appetite. Fortunately, there was at least one thing he could fix.

"Tab is safe," he said.

She leapt to her feet. "You found him?"

"He was hiding in the dovecote behind your neighbor's house, sleeping in a sack full of clothes."

"Oh!" Her whole body sagged in relief. "Those are mine. It must have smelled like me."

Now that was interesting, Stephen thought. There had been money in the sack as well. He recognized someone stashing materials for a quick getaway. "He's back at the Temple now, and the cook is stuffing him so full of tidbits that he's going to look like a sausage."

She put her hands over her eyes and when she took them down again, Stephen was horrified to see her cheeks were wet. "Grace..."

"I know," she said, turning away. She dashed the tears with the heel of her hand. "I know. But he's all I've got, you see."

If he had thought, he would have lost his nerve. All the reasons and the fears would have risen up to stop him. But he did not think. He saw only that she was crying, and he cupped his hand around her face and wiped his gloved thumb across her cheek. Her skin, even flushed, was absurdly pale against the dark brown leather.

She gave a small, watery chuckle. "It's all right," she said, as if she were the one who should be reassuring *him*. "I'm all right. You found him."

"He's not all you've got," he said, desperate to chase the tears away. "You have friends who love you and a great skill and a career..."

She took a step back, holding up her hands as if to ward off a curse. "No," she said. "No, don't. I know you're trying to help, but don't. I can't." She searched his face, as if looking for understanding. "If you have things, you lose them. They all get taken away. You always lose everything eventually."

"Everything?" he asked.

She nodded. "I was an orphan. Then my master bought me away, and I lost what little I had. I served for nine years before I realized he was never going to fulfill the articles and name me a tradesman. So Phillip—my partner—bought the articles of apprenticeship from him, and I lost everything again. I couldn't even take my notes. I had to recreate everything from the ground up. It took nearly a decade. And then...well." She turned away. "When I came here, I had nothing again. I had to steal food for Tab. I had no way to convince the guild that I'd finished my apprenticeship. I didn't even try. But I built it up again. And here we are, and they're going to take everything away again." She flicked her fingers out in an odd, fatalistic gesture.

He wanted to say, *I could be yours.*

He wanted to say, *You won't lose me.*

That was the realization that was sinking slowly through his body. He was hers for the taking. All his resistance had been swept away, as surely as the Elkinslough had swept parts of the city away, and left only wreckage behind.

"I don't know how many more times I can start over," she said.

"I've already lost everything," he said. "There's nothing left to take away." He put his fingers under her chin and tilted her face up towards his.

Grace's eyes were magnified by unshed tears, her lips just parted. He wanted very much to kiss her.

One kiss, he thought. *Surely one more kiss can do no harm.*

He knew it was a lie even as he thought it. One kiss could break a man. And the second lie, he knew, was that he would stop at only one.

He did it anyway. He could no more have resisted than he could have chosen not to follow the god when the golden fire came upon him, so many years ago. He gathered her up in his arms and lowered his lips to hers.

It was good. It was so damn good. She clung to him as if he were the only solid thing in the universe, warmth and heat and softness pressed close against him. He tangled his fingers in her hair, pulling her even closer, drunk and dazed on sensation.

She made a tiny sound in the back of her throat and he answered with a growl of his own, lifting her against him. Saint's teeth, he needed this. He needed her. He needed...something.

And what does she need?

The thought nagged at him, even as he slid his hands down her sides, feeling the dip at her waist and the flare of her hips under his palms.

She's locked in a room that's one step up from a prison cell and you're the one who's supposed to protect her. Who will protect her from you? She needs your help, maybe she's afraid to reject you. How would you know?

Grace did not kiss him like she was afraid. She kissed him like a woman with nothing left to lose. But he could not know and he could not risk comfort turning to cruelty. Slowly, reluctantly, he broke off the embrace, kissed her tenderly at the corner of her lip, then stepped back.

"Are you going to apologize now?" she asked wearily.

He had to smile, even thought it hurt a little. But the pain was well-deserved, and they both knew it. "Only if you tell me I need to."

"No," she said, gazing up at him. There were no tears in her eyes now. "No, I don't think you do."

He pulled off his glove and cradled her cheek, letting his thumb drift across her lower lip. She turned her head a little, and then her tongue flicked out and touched the pad of his thumb and he stopped thinking noble thoughts of any sort and started wondering if the narrow bed in the corner was big enough for two people.

The sound of the door opening was like a crack of thunder. They sprang apart. Zale bustled in, arms full of papers. "Oh good!" the lawyer-priest said. "You're here already, Stephen."

"Errr," said Stephen. "Yes. I, ah..." Grace had a small smile and was carefully avoiding his gaze. "Arrived. Early."

"We'll all go down to the courtroom together, then," said Zale.

"You'll be in court with me?" asked Grace.

Stephen nodded. "I will not leave your side," he promised. "The Motherhood will attempt to intimidate you. I am there to prevent it."

Among other reasons.

She smiled up at him.

"This will be the shortest day," said Zale, as they led the way out into the hall. "The Motherhood will present the charges, and I will explain that I plan to refute them. Then they will present their physical evidence."

"Then do we present ours?" asked Grace.

"In theory, but we haven't got any." Zale shrugged. "It's extremely hard to provide physical proof that you *didn't* poison someone, particularly when we don't even know what the poison used was. Most of our defense comes down to character witnesses, and that's tomorrow. So today will be short."

"Who are our character witnesses?" asked Grace.

"Paladin Stephen and your friend Marguerite. And I have a written statement from your neighbor."

Grace bit her lip. "Is...is it a good statement?"

"She says that you are a good girl who respects your elders and knows how to pet a cat."

"From her, that's remarkable praise."

"I gathered, yes."

They passed by the guard post. Grace paused at the top of the stairs, looking around, then let out a long sigh of relief. "The rest of the world is still here," she said. "I was starting to wonder."

"The courtroom is in an attached building," said Zale, "but we can go out through the courtyard if you like. If you begin to feel dizzy or bothered by the open space, please tell me at once."

"It's only been a few days," said Grace, bemused.

Zale shrugged. "I'd expect it more if you had been locked up for longer, but things take people differently."

They crossed the courtyard. It was drizzling and gray and there were no breaks in the sky. Grace felt as if she'd traded one ceiling for another one, albeit higher and soggier. Still, the air had the brief cleanness of rain. She inhaled deeply, smelling rain and wet brick and the green tang of the trees that were grimly eking out a living against the stones.

Stephen walked behind the two of them as they crossed the court-yard, back in his position as man-at-arms. Grace did not know whether to be grateful for his presence, or guilty that she had dragged him into this entire mess.

"I'm sorry," she said. "I know you both have duties...I don't mean to be so much trouble."

"To represent the accused is my duty," said Zale simply. "You are no less worthy than any other person."

Grace exhaled. "I feel very foolish for having been arrested at all," she admitted. "If I could just have explained better..."

"That is very normal," said Zale. "And also very incorrect. There was nothing you could have done. When the powers that be have decided that you are guilty of something, it does not matter if you tell the truth. In fact, it offends them. When you are proved innocent, the Motherhood will likely be angry that you let them believe you were guilty at all."

"That makes no sense," said Grace.

"Not to reasonable people," said Zale, opening a door in the wall and gesturing for her to enter. "Fortunately, that's why there are lawyers."

CHAPTER 36

Judge Gucciard was a bull of a man who looked as if he could take off his black robe and stand in for one of the bailiffs if need be. His neck was thick and his hair was cut to military shortness. Grace steeled herself to pass in front of him, but to her surprise, he gave her a sympathetic look and nodded familiarly to Zale. She dared to hope that he would not automatically assume that she was guilty, as so many judges were rumored to do.

Her hopes were raised yet again when he started by saying, "I don't like this. You're asking me to try a woman for attempted murder when we don't even have testimony from the victim that there *was* an attempt."

The Motherhood lawyer was named Jordan. He had not been the man who tried to get her to sign the confession, but he had appeared once or twice, mostly glaring and standing behind guards. He looked as if he had swallowed something that had not agreed with him, continued not to agree with him, and anticipated not agreeing with him all the way to the end. He waited until Gucciard had finished speaking and said, "The Crown Prince is very ill and cannot attend. His emissary will testify to that effect." He nodded over to one side of the room, where DuValier sat at a long wooden bench.

Grace felt a pang of relief. Surely DuValier would explain that she could not be responsible. Perhaps this would be cleared up sooner than anticipated, and it would all be a very unpleasant memory.

"Hmm," said Gucciard.

"I am certain that you understand that it is important to be seen to be dealing with this matter swiftly, your honor," said Jordan.

Gucciard looked as if he, too, had swallowed something that didn't agree with him, but he reached out and grabbed a sphere of rock crystal on the table and banged it down. "Very well. Trial is now in session. What have you got?"

She leaned over to Zale. "What did that mean, important to be seen to be dealing with this?"

Zale did not take their eyes from Jordan, but murmured, "Politics. Charlock is very unhappy. We must be seen to be acting to find those responsible."

Grace nodded. *Perhaps this is just a smokescreen while they find the real culprits, then.* It was a comforting thought, though she was immediately suspicious of comforting thoughts.

Certainly the Motherhood lawyer did not act as if this were a smokescreen. He spoke like a preacher, denouncing poisoners as "the vipers in the bosom of a just society" and pointed a trembling finger at Grace. "I shall show your honor, beyond a shadow of reasonable doubt, that this woman is of a piece with those coiling serpents, making her nest within the walls of this city that she may more easily pour poison into the blood of the innocent!"

Grace had a strong urge to look behind her and see who Jordan was talking about. No one had ever called her a coiling serpent before. *I can't possibly coil. I can't even sit cross-legged for very long without my rear end falling asleep. And you don't put perfume into blood. That would be very strange.*

"Yes, yes," said Judge Gucciard wearily. "I'm sure you will. Defense?"

"I'm sure they won't," said Zale, "since my client's never poisoned anyone."

"Is that your opening statement?"

"Would you like a longer one?"

"Sweet Lady of Grass, no." Gucciard cracked a smile. Grace started to think that she could have done far worse for a lawyer than Zale, even if they claimed to primarily work with property disputes.

"All right," said the judge, turning back to the Motherhood side of the room. "I suppose you have evidence of all this?"

"If it pleases your honor, we present our written evidence first. Books of poison, from the very home of the accused." With a conjurer's flourish, he held up a leatherbound book. "Five such."

It took a moment for Grace to recognize the cover, not because it was unfamiliar but because she could not believe that it was here, in this room.

"Those are my journals!" said Grace. "My recipe books!" She rose to her feet in outrage, and Zale pulled her back into her chair with a thump. "Someone stole them from my workshop a few days ago!"

"But you do not deny that they are yours," said the Motherhood man, looking down his nose.

"No, of course not! Where did you get them?" And then, a sudden horrible certainty churning in her gut, "Gods above and below, you stole them from my workshop!"

"Collecting evidence is hardly stealing. Particularly not books of poison. It is our mandate to root out such."

"Those aren't poison! They're perfume!"

"Oh really?" He opened the top book and began to read. "...*To construct a poison such that both Rats and Men shall fall dead without cure, begin with the boiling of antimony in a crucible of gold and add to this the Urine of a Dog and five leaves of the plant called Monk's Hood—*"

"That's not one of my journals," she said angrily. "It's a weird book of alchemy. I've never made any of the recipes in there. I don't own a gold crucible and I don't spend a lot of time getting urine from dogs."

"But you don't deny that this book was in your possession?"

Zale put their hand on her sleeve. Grace snapped her mouth shut.

The judge leaned forward. "Miss Angelica, I find I am interested in the answer to this question."

She looked at Zale. Zale sighed and nodded to her.

"It was," she said. "It was a gift from my old master. I keep it around because…" *Don't say you use it for divination, the Motherhood would have a field day with that.* "…sometimes it's good for a laugh, how wrong he was about perfumes."

The explanation sounded absurd, even to herself.

The Motherhood man smiled and handed the book up to the judge, who looked it over, frowning. *I should have said it was a sentimental attachment because of my old master. Dammit.* Grace couldn't really blame herself for not thinking of that on the spot, given that most of her sentiments about her old master were along the lines of "at least he didn't pour hot lead up my nose." Still.

"Speaking of your old master…" murmured the Motherhood man. "You were apprenticed to Master Garvan in Anuket City, were you not?"

Zale nodded to Grace again. "I was."

"And yet we find that your articles of apprenticeship are registered to another person, is that correct?"

"They were sold," said Grace. Her stomach, already churning, felt as if it was about to boil over. *Don't mention Phillip. Nobody needs to know about him. It's not important.*

"A person who never registered you as a master with the guild. Did you complete your training with him?"

"I did."

"Then why are you not registered as a master?"

"He was a very absent-minded man," said Grace.

Judge Gucciard made a faint sound, either of amusement or disbelief, she couldn't be certain.

"There is no Perfumer's Guild active in either Anuket City or Archenhold," said Jordan, "as I am certain Your Honor is aware."

"I wasn't," said the judge, "but I suppose now you're going to tell me more about it than I care to know."

"They are instead registered with the Tanner's Guild," the Motherhood man continued.

"The tanners?" Gucciard shot Grace a puzzled look.

"In the early days of the art, our primary trade was in masking the scents of the leather trade," said Grace. "No one wants to wear gloves that smell of ammonia."

"Ah."

"Gloves," murmured the Motherhood man. "Yes. One hears stories of poisoned gloves."

"One also hears stories of oracular goats and headless ghosts walking the halls of the palace," said Zale testily. "Would you like to claim my client is responsible for those as well?"

One of the bailiffs chuckled. Gucciard narrowed his eyes. "The method used to deliver the poison remains unknown," said Jordan. "I simply wished to point out that Mistress Angelica is not a recognized master in her guild, despite claiming the title here."

Zale put their fingertips on her arm, presumably to still any outburst. Grace sank back. *I didn't claim it. I didn't mean to. Marguerite told me no one cared and they* didn't, *not until now.*

"Is there a reason you did not register as a master?" asked Gucciard.

"The master who bought my apprenticeship made it..." *what to say what to say don't say that he was your husband don't say he held it over you shit shit shit* "...more trouble than it was worth. I had meant to find a master here who might vouch for my skills, if I produced a masterwork." Grace stared at the table.

"But you did not," said Jordan. "Did you?"

"It has been difficult," said Grace. *We're all secretive to the point of paranoia. No one wants to give their name to someone who will set up in competition. I'd have to go back to Anuket City and I haven't had anything like the money.* "I have been working toward it. It is not an easy thing to do."

"Is there a point to all this?" asked Zale. "We're trying to determine if my client poisoned a man, not if her guild paperwork is in order."

Jordan sniffed. "It is noteworthy that no *legitimate* master is overseeing what she does. And that she lied about her qualifications in order to present a...substance...to the Crown Prince."

Grace gritted her teeth. Where was Marguerite? Marguerite could explain all that, talk circles around this awful man, laugh off the guild qualifications as a misunderstanding, or at least take responsibility for them. Where was she?

She was not here. Apparently that was all that mattered.

"If it pleases your honor, Emissary DuValier will now speak to the Crown Prince's condition," said Jordan.

"It's about time," said Gucciard.

DuValier stepped up into the witness box. He gave Grace a small smile as he passed and her frayed nerves loosened a little. He knew her. They were, if not friends, at least friendly acquaintances. He'd explain that this was all a misunderstanding.

"The Crown Prince is near death," said DuValier. "It is unlikely he will recover. His physician tells me that his symptoms are consistent with poisoning. He is feverish, weak, and his fingertips are violet. He can keep down neither water nor food. I am afraid that he will not last the night."

"I'm sorry to hear it," said the judge. "When did this start?"

"A few days ago," said DuValier. "Though I am told that some poisons will show no signs until they reach a tipping point, beyond which there is no return. His physician has sweated and purged him to try to drag out the poison, but..." He spread his hands.

"You say this started a few days ago," said the Motherhood man.

"Yes."

"Can you be more specific?"

"Certainly." DuValier gave a pained smile. "It began the day after Mistress Angelica delivered her order of the Prince's perfume."

"And you believe that she could be responsible?" asked the Motherhood man.

Grace waited expectantly.

"It is the only link that I can find," said DuValier. "We changed his sheets, his food, his clothing. Her perfume was the only constant. I believe that there is no other conclusion, except that Mistress Angelica poisoned my liege."

...what?

Wait, what?

"And what led you to this conclusion?" asked Jordan.

"She is very knowledgeable of poisons. Even last night, when I went to beg her for information that might save the prince's life, she spoke of all the poisons that she knew, the methods that they might be administered—"

"That's not true!" Grace cried.

The Motherhood man was on her like a terrier on a rat. "Did you not speak with him last night?"

"Yes, but—"

"And you spoke of poisons?"

"Yes, but not—" The Motherhood man tried to speak over her, so Grace raised her voice to be heard. "Not like that! He asked me if I could think of anything that might be responsible and I told him I didn't know much but I tried to think of anything that could help!"

"Everyone settle down," said Gucciard, slamming the crystal globe against the bench. "One at a time. Miss Angelica, you say that you did speak to him?"

"Yes, but..." She glanced at DuValier and finished, numbly, "it wasn't anything like that. I thought he was asking for help, and I didn't know much, but I tried..."

"You. DuValier." Gucciard pointed.

"She seemed very knowledgeable to *me*. We spoke of poisoned gloves and other poisonings that she had known."

Grace wanted to scream but it did not seem wise to antagonize the judge. Or perhaps it didn't matter any more. Perhaps she was as good as sentenced already. DuValier's words seemed to come from very far away. This could not be happening. This was definitely not happening. She would wake up and this would be a dream and she would not be losing everything.

Lost lost losing lost everything gets taken away everything...

She could feel the memory fugue coming on. *Oh god, not now.* Scraps of words drifted by her: "...motive...the prince...obsessed... meetings..." but none of them made any sense.

Ginger and spice filled her nostrils as Stephen put his hand on her shoulder. She could not hear his voice, but she could feel him speaking. The words didn't matter. What mattered was the scent of gingerbread and steel.

She took a deep breath, filling her lungs, and the world swam back into focus. She was not alone here. One very broken paladin was with her. She was not entirely lost. Not yet.

It appeared that DuValier had finished speaking. Zale stood and said, simply, "This isn't a case. We are trying this woman based on nothing but testimony from a man who is not a doctor, who lacks the imagination or the training to determine how the poisoning occurred, and so jumped to conclusions and then had a conversation in an attempt to entrap my client. I could go find the man who cleans the floors of the guest embassy and claim he was poisoning the floor wax. I don't know what precisely goes into cleaning the floors, but I'm fairly sure they use lye and if I phrased things right, I could spin you a tale about how the man used toxic substances to clean the floors and now the prince is sick. It would have just as much substance as this story, and just as much proof to back it up."

"Prove that she did not, then," said Jordan.

"Prove that *you* did not," snapped Zale. "Given that one need not be present for a poisoning, it's awfully difficult to prove, isn't it?"

"If you two are quite done sniping at each other," said Gucciard wearily, "I believe I have had enough for one day. Court will re-adjourn tomorrow morning."

He stood. Everyone rose as he left. DuValier looked in Grace's direction with a pitying expression, and Grace felt raw rage fray at the edges of her vision.

Is this how berserkers feel?

Well, if it was, it seemed that Grace would make a very poor one. Zale put a hand on her arm and she felt an immediate urge to apologize. The lawyer and Stephen led her out and she allowed herself to be led.

"This could be going better," admitted Zale, as they returned to Grace's cell. "Gucciard is a reasonable man, but there is a great deal of pressure from Charlock, and thus pressure from the Archon on him. He may simply decide that there is evidence that you *are* a poisoner, even if you are not the one who poisoned the Crown Prince." They flipped loose strands of silver hair from their eyes. "And as he is also a practical man, ultimately, I cannot be as confident as I would like that he will not throw you to the wolves to appease the Archon."

Grace nodded, not because she agreed or understood, but because you nodded when people spoke in that tone. Her mind ran in little gibbering circles. She could not believe that DuValier had turned on her. It made no sense. *A poisoner a poisoner a poisoner...*

"What about the other poisoning?" asked Stephen. "Can that be used to throw this into doubt?"

Zale sighed. "Possibly, but then we have to deal with the fact that Grace was present when the man died of poison. Which is circumstantial evidence, but the Motherhood will make a great deal out of it. I'll drag it up if it looks like we have no other options, but it could just as easily backfire on us."

"What can we do now?" asked Stephen.

"Find evidence that Grace isn't a poisoner," said Zale dryly. "However one does *that*. I suppose sworn testimony from a god might do it."

"Fresh out of gods," croaked Grace. She swallowed. Her throat felt dry. "I can't believe that they stole the books from my workshop."

"Fighting dirty," said Zale. "But evidence is evidence, unfortunately. And there are no laws about how one obtains it, except that they can't beat it out of you."

"At least they didn't do that," said Grace. Stephen made a low rumbling noise and put his arm around her shoulders. Grace turned her face toward the side of his chest and tried to take comfort, but all she could think of was that she was going to be executed without even a chance to get the chainmail off him and see how much of the hardness was metal and how much was muscle.

Yes, very helpful. You're probably going to be burned at the stake and you still want to get in the man's pants. Priorities have never been your strong suit, have they?

"They stole the books from the workshop," said Stephen thoughtfully. Grace could feel the vibration of his voice against her cheek.

"Could there be something else in the workshop that might exonerate her?"

"It's worth a try," said Zale. "We might as well grasp at straws now rather than later."

"Then I will check," said Stephen. He bent his head and brushed his lips across Grace's forehead, then hurried to the door.

CHAPTER 37

Stephen walked. The dark streets were slick with rain and the lamps left long puddles of light across the cobbles. It had settled to a heavy mist now, slicking his skin like sweat and dripping off the ends of his hair.

The workshop had been useless. How could you prove someone wasn't a poisoner? It wasn't like proving an alibi. If Stephen found the jar of perfume she'd rubbed on his wrist, that would only prove that that particular batch wasn't poisoned. No one was denying that it was perfume. The batch given to the Crown Prince had been destroyed, according to that slimy little envoy, so they couldn't even test that. Stephen would have offered up his own flesh if it would have helped.

He raked his hands through his damp hair. The gloves caught in the tangles and yanked strands loose, but he didn't care.

What the hell am I going to do?

He had no answer. He kept walking. He did not know where he was going, only that if he walked long enough, surely the answer would come to him, some kind of answer, *any* kind of answer. His boots clicked on the pavement.

Mister Brass didn't pay his tax...headsman gave him forty whacks...

Two people were turning down an alley as he passed by it. One was young and drunk and Stephen couldn't make out anything beyond that. The second one turned their head, very briefly, and Stephen caught a glimpse of their face.

Even through the haze of rage and despair, something jarred him. Something wasn't right. The person's face was smooth and unlined as porcelain. For a moment, he thought they must be wearing a mask, but they blinked and their lips parted slightly as they turned away.

Makeup? There were some types of makeup that might produce that strange, poreless clarity. White lead and fat was the one everyone had heard of, but hardly anyone used it any more, the way the lead ate away the skin was too well known. Stephen remembered seeing a few great ladies in his youth that still wore it, but they were long dead, and he had only been a young boy who could get away with staring at his supposed betters on the street.

He absolutely could not get involved with someone else's problems. He couldn't. He had to save Grace.

He nevertheless seemed to be turning down the next alley and moving as stealthily as possible to the cross street.

The youngster was drunk. You're just checking to make sure that nothing shady is going on.

For a moment he was afraid that he had missed them. The buildings here turned and twisted and the road turned and twisted with them. It wasn't as bad a neighborhood as Weaver's Nest, not by a long shot, but it was very old and things had been thrown together haphazardly over the years. He almost overshot when he heard the sound of a drunken stagger scraping against a wall—a surprisingly distinctive sound, in his experience, and realized that he'd found the cross-alley.

Unfortunately, there was a large wooden gate in the way, with a chain holding the halves closed. Someone had probably gotten tired of the alley being used as a cut-through to avoid the busy street corner. Stephen eyed it speculatively. Could he get over the top? Maybe, but not quietly.

There was a gap at the hinges on one side. Stephen peered through it. He could see a slice of alley and then his quarry came into view.

"Back herrrre?" slurred the younger one.

The smooth-faced man said nothing, but put a hand on the younger one's shoulder.

You're about to watch a trick turned in a back alley. This is certainly helping your court case.

"Give me...a min...min...ute..."

The smooth-faced man brought his other hand on the youngster's other shoulder, and then, before Stephen could move or even react, that too-smooth jaw yawned open impossibly wide and closed over the back of the other man's neck.

It happened so fast that Stephen did not even have time to cry out. At first he wasn't even sure what had happened—surely it couldn't have been what it looked like? The man's mouth couldn't have opened so jawlessly wide, it was a trick of the light or...

The youngster dropped. The smooth-faced man went with him, lowering him to the ground. Stephen heard a series of wet crunching noises that sounded, the Saint have mercy, exactly like someone eating a carrot.

He's dead. No one's neck makes that sound who's still alive. Shit, shit, I was too late, I was too late, but how could I have moved fast enough for that?

He could feel the black tide starting to rise, promising him that he could snap the chain, tear the gate off its hinges, grab the murderer, whatever he was, whatever *it* was, no human could bite through someone's spine like that...

Almost he gave into the tide. It would have been so easy, so well-deserved. He could fix nothing else but surely he could fix this.

The smooth-faced man rose to his knees. He pulled a pack off his back and reached in and removed something pale and round, holding it between his hands.

A strange, acrid scent filled Stephen's nostrils. It was bitter and made his jaw ache and worse, it was *familiar.* He'd smelled it just a few days ago, standing in the sun in a mud-filled meadow, while Grace's nostrils worked like a hunting dog's and she tried to find the source.

The man hadn't been biting the drunk young man's neck.

He'd been biting his head off.

I found him, thought Stephen. The thought was so bizarre that it had neither triumph or fear attached to it. It sat in isolation in his mind. *I found the one leaving the severed heads.*

The smooth-faced man turned the object in his hands and it gazed blindly past Stephen.

It was—not a mask. Something like a mask. A clay model of a head, perhaps. It looked like porcelain, like the smooth-faced man himself. It was hairless and the neck ended in a thin, tapered spike.

As Stephen watched, horror warring with equally horrified curiosity, the smooth-faced man pulled the headless corpse upright and pushed the clay head into the stump.

What the hell?

There was a great deal of blood. Decapitations, in Stephen's experience, were messy. The man wiped it off with his sleeve, showing no more emotion than if he were wiping away water, bent his neck and covered the clay head's mouth with his own. He breathed into the mouth, several times.

Is he kissing it? What kind of sick—

The head inhaled and opened its eyes.

Stephen's gorge rose. He fought it back. This was magic, the bad kind of magic, the kind that no one could be expected to understand. Whether the smooth-faced man was a wonderworker or a demon or something else entirely, he didn't know. He only knew that it had to end.

He leapt for the top of the gate.

It was not so easy to pull himself over a wall as it had been when he was twenty. He pushed himself up until his hips were level with the top, in time to see two figures gliding away down the alley. One was walking hesitantly, as if drunk, and the taller one was holding it upright.

Stephen landed, feet skidding on the wet stone. Blood and rain mixed at his feet. He sprinted after the pair, kicking something out of the way—*it's the head, you know it's the head no don't think about it no don't look at it*—trying to keep his feet.

When he reached the mouth of the alley, they were gone.

Stephen staggered into the compound of the Temple of the Rat, rain slicking his hair to his forehead, throat ragged from having run too far, too fast. He had to get word to the City Guard but the temple had been closer, and he was no longer able to run across an entire city without stopping for breath. The drizzle had turned into a deluge and steam poured off his cloak as he stood gasping for air in the cloister walk.

As luck would have it, the first person he saw was Zale.

"Stephen?" said the lawyer-priest, their eyes going wide. They were wearing a heavy over-robe that showed signs of having been thrown hastily over a dressing gown and carrying a steaming teapot and a mug. "Are you all right?"

"I found what's leaving the heads," gasped Stephen. "I need the Bishop."

Zale raised their eyebrows. "*What? Not who?*"

Trust a lawyer to seize on that. Stephen nodded. "What. It's not human. I don't know what it is. Bad magic. Gotta see the Bishop. Send a message to the guard." He burst into a coughing fit. "Sorry. Ran...ran all the way..."

Zale looked down, then shoved the mug into his hand. "It's tea. I was going to be up late working on Mistress Angelica's defense, but... well. Drink this. I'll get the Bishop."

Stephen collapsed gratefully on the bench, holding the mug in his fingers. Grace. He hadn't been able to find anything that would help Grace. He had to get the guard after the smooth-faced men, then he could go back to helping Grace.

Something teased at his brain, but he couldn't bring it into focus.

The tea wasn't bad. It didn't taste like hay. He wondered if Zale's rank as a solicitor-sacrosanct meant that they got the good tea.

He had nearly finished the mug when the Bishop arrived. Despite the hour, she looked as if she had been awake and working. Her secretary padded after her, looking significantly worse for wear. "I've sent a runner for Mallory. Can you lead them back to the alley?"

"Yes, of course."

She gave him a bemused look. "Paladin Stephen, forgive my crudity, but you look like hammered shit. Are you certain?"

He dredged a smile up from somewhere. "It's what we do," he said.

"Look like hammered shit?"

"Keep going. Even when we look this way."

She shook her head. "I'll expect a full report, but in the morning. Once you've done what you can...well, I suppose it's useless to ask you to get some sleep, but do what you can."

"Go through it again," said Mallory. "I'm not accusing you of lying, but I'll be honest, if you weren't a paladin and if I didn't have a head right in front of me, I'd think you were drunk."

"Oh Saint, if only," muttered Stephen.

Mallory snorted, then glanced around. His rank and file were fanned out, checking the nearby streets and asking the locals if anyone had seen the two men enter the alley other than Stephen. Two more men were hunched over the head, one human, one gnole, gazing at it in rapt concentration. Satisfied, he pulled a flask out of his jacket and handed it to Stephen.

The liquor burned on the way down. Straight rotgut whiskey, nothing fancy. Stephen grimaced, grateful for the warmth and less grateful for the taste. He handed the flask back. At least the burn briefly drove away the rank stench of the alley. In fact—

"The smell," he said abruptly. The thing that had been bothering him earlier snapped into sudden focus. *Don't you smell it? It's not burning, but it's like burning...* "The smell. There's a smell on the heads. I think it's..." He swallowed. "I think it's the thing's saliva, when it bites the head off. Or something like that. I smelled it before. Why don't I smell it now?"

The guard captain glanced at the two men. They shook their heads, looking remarkably similar despite the fact that one was four feet tall and had striped fur. "Too much rain," said the gnole constable. "Smell gets washed away." He wiped at his nose. "Humans can't smell. Right now, a gnole can't smell either."

Stephen groaned. Of course, the rain would have washed away anything. There wasn't even blood left in the alley, and the sort of rain that could wash away a decapitation certainly wouldn't leave a smell. "If we can get something that still has that smell, we could get a slewhound on it, couldn't we? And maybe track down the...whatever they are?"

The captain nodded. "Should be able to. But not in this." He gestured, his cloak flapping like oilcloth wings.

"Can we get a sample off the head we found earlier?" asked Stephen. "It still stank."

The captain groaned. "I'm sure it did," he said wearily. "Except we preserved the damn thing in paraffin in case anyone would be able to identify it."

Stephen swore.

"Should have saved it for a gnole," muttered the gnole. His partner sighed, as if this was a fight they'd had already.

"What does it smell like?" asked Mallory.

"Heavy. Acrid. Burnt. It was thick and...dammit." He found his vocabulary failing him. *Grace would know better words. She could probably name all the notes, maybe even whip up a batch in her worksh—*

He froze, thinking of Grace, her downturned mouth screwed up in a scowl of concentration, her nostrils working, as she tried to identify the strange scent.

Could she?

Or if she can't identify it, can she duplicate it?

It couldn't hurt to try.

"I have an idea," he said.

CHAPTER 38

"Absolutely not," said Jordan, the Motherhood representative. "You want us to give a poisoner access to her workshop? Why not simply put a murderer in the armory while you're at it?"

"You can put someone to watch her," said Stephen. "To make sure she's not doing anything dangerous."

The Motherhood man looked down his nose. "And how would any of *us* know what a poisoner looks like at work?"

Stephen ground his teeth. The man from the city guard with him looked from one to the other, frowning.

"Listen," said Stephen, clinging to his patience with both hands. "This is important. There is some kind of monster—thing—out there biting off people's heads. This could help."

"And you expect me to believe that the person we happen to be holding on suspicion of poisoning is the only one who can stop them?" Jordan snorted. "And you, who have been guarding her this entire time, are the person who spotted this? How *convenient.*"

"Oh come on! Do you think I'd lie about a thing like this?"

The guard cleared his throat. "Paladin Stephen was able to lead us to the scene of the crime," he said, almost apologetically. "There was indeed another victim there."

"I'm sure there was," said Jordan, his eyes sliding down Stephen's body to the sword at his side, then back up to his face. "Severed heads are so difficult to manufacture, of course."

"I don't like your implication, priest," grated Stephen.

"I'm sure you don't."

He was no Beartongue to match words with the man. Stephen turned on his heel and stalked away, feeling the chance to save lives sliding away from him. "We'll talk to Grace," he said to the guard. "She might still be able to help."

"Of course I remember the smell," said Grace. "Duplicate it?" She frowned, worrying at her lower lip with her teeth. "Maybe. I could get close, I think, though I'd have to do some very bad things to some very good ingredients. The burnt hair smell would be the hardest, because hair just burns up and is gone. I might be able to substitute antler, though. If I burnt antler slivers and condensed the smoke... hmm. Possibly."

"Could you tell someone else how to do it?"

She looked up at him and he could see the blue smudges under each eye. He hated to ask her to do anything, let alone this, but there was no condemnation in her eyes, only apology. "I don't think so," she said. "I mean, I could tell them where to start, I guess, but I'd have to smell it at each stage to know how close it was. It would take days. I'm guessing you don't have much time if this monster is on the loose."

"No," said the guardsman. He reached out and patted her arm. He was a genial old man with a round, cherubic face, who reminded Stephen of Brother Francis the healer. "No, we're running a bit short of that at the moment. But if you can write down a description for us, maybe, we'll take it around and read it to the boys so that if they smell something like it, they'll know they might be close?"

"Of course," said Grace. "Anything."

He produced a sheet of foolscap and a pen, already sharpened. Grace sat down at the small table, uncorked the ink, and began to write. She had cramped but exact handwriting, and Stephen could guess why.

Paper is expensive stuff. You need a lot of it to make notes, when you're a perfumer, but it still isn't cheap.

He glanced over her shoulder and stifled a sigh. She was making a perfumer's notes, which undoubtedly explained the smell with great precision and which would probably do the layperson no good at all. "Primary note – burnt antler or horn, notes of black cherry, river mud, blood meal, would likely fix well in civet base."

Well, he'd asked. And it was a start. You probably couldn't hand a slewhound a burning antler and ask them to go after that, though. But gnoles had a better sense of smell than humans, and perhaps the gnole constable could do something.

It was more than they had now, at any rate.

She finished writing, scowled at the page, and blew gently on the ink to dry it. "If you bring me samples, I could compare them?" she offered.

"I'll see what we can do," said the guardsman.

Stephen did not dare kiss her as he wished in front of the guardsman, and certainly not the sour-faced Motherhood priest. But a thought came to him, tinged with irony. "Thank you, Mistress Angelica," he said, flicking his eyes toward the priest. He bowed over her hand and lifted it to his lips.

She laughed. It was a short, choking sound, less humor, more an acknowledgement of how absurd the situation had become. But it was still a laugh and still a kiss, and at the moment it was the best that they could get.

Morning came too early, or not early enough. Stephen wondered if Grace saw the dawn as one day closer to freedom or one day closer to execution. His stomach clenched.

She looked calm, sitting behind the table. Too calm. Her face had the carefully blank look that he recognized from far too many captives waiting to learn their fate. He'd rescued people who looked like that. Presumably he'd failed to rescue people who looked like that as well.

"If it please your honor," said the Motherhood man, "an additional witness has arrived. May we present him?"

Zale straightened in their chair, eyes suddenly sharp.

"Go ahead," said Gucciard wearily. "I don't suppose it's the Crown Prince?"

Jordan licked his lips, clearly weighing his words. "I am told that the Prince is near death's door, your honor."

"I'm told the same thing," said Gucciard. "I'd feel better if I could see that for myself, but dying monarchs don't feel the need to entertain mere judges. Carry on, but make it good."

"Our witness is the husband of the accused," said the Motherhood man. "Phillip Artemisian, of Anuket City."

Husband?

Stephen's first thought was that there was some mistake. He looked over at Grace and her lawyer. Zale's eyebrows had shot up. Grace herself was so pale that she looked as if she might faint.

"Hullo," said Phillip. He was a slim, wiry man, with sandy hair, and he was, Saint have mercy, rather relentlessly handsome. He gave Grace a small wave. "Been awhile, hasn't it?"

Husband?

Grace's lips moved, but no sound came out. Stephen began to think that it wasn't a mistake after all.

Judge Gucciard tapped the bench. "Miss Angelica? Is this man indeed your husband?"

Grace croaked something, swallowed, and said, "He was."

"Was?"

"I thought...I thought..."

"Did you think he was dead?" asked the Motherhood man.

Grace shook her head. Zale held up a hand, leaned in and murmured a question. Stephen strained his ears and heard Grace say, "I thought he would have divorced me. I ran away. I didn't think..." Zale nodded and attempted to find a palatable way to present this to the judge.

Stephen's eyes were locked on Grace's face.

Half of him was screaming that he had been kissing another

man's wife, and the other half was urging him to stand up, stalk over to the miserable little shit, and wring his pretty neck like a chicken.

Where have you been? How dare you leave her to face this alone? Why did she have to walk to Archenhold in the snow without you? What have you been doing?

And then, looking at Grace's bone-white face, he knew the answer.

She'd walked here to get away from him.

What had she said, that day on the hillside? *I got tired of waiting for some asshole to decide if he wanted me or not.*

This man? Really?

"Your profession?" said the Motherhood man.

"Oh, I'm a perfumer," said Phillip. "That's how we met. We were in business together. Except that, uh…" He seemed to remember something, and swallowed. "She was always into other things, you know. Herbs. Spices."

"Spices?" said the Motherhood man sharply.

"Err, not spices. The other thing."

"Poisons?"

"Right, that's it."

"They cannot possibly believe this man's testimony," said Zale, just loud enough to be heard. "This is absurd."

"Is there a problem, Solicitor Zale?" asked the judge.

Zale stared at the judge, then gestured to Grace's husband and waved their hands in the air, a gesture that managed to be both meaningless and supremely eloquent. The judge hid a smile behind his hand.

"Your opinion of the character of the accused?"

"Oh, well." Phillip rubbed the back of his neck. "She was a good girl, but so odd. Normal people don't act that way, you know. And so jealous. Always thought I was cheating on her with the other ladies, don't you know."

"Because you were," said Grace, sounding less furious and more simply astounded. "Lady Vance. Lady Morgan. That one girl you brought home to try and get me in bed with. I moved into the workshop because you kept bringing women home!"

The Motherhood man cleared his throat loudly, possibly to try to cover this outburst.

"Well, there, you see," said Phillip. He gestured at her. "Always jealous. Convinced." He leaned forward and said, in the judge's direction, "You see how it is. I bought out her articles of apprenticeship, you know. Felt sorry for her." He gave Gucciard a sly man-to-man look. "You know how it is. The lady cries and you'll do anything. Ended up married to her."

Grace went, if anything, even whiter. Her scarred fingers dug into the tabletop so hard that he expected to see blood oozing under the nails.

"But then it was just one thing after another…" Phillip rolled his eyes.

"What did you do, when she became jealous?" asked the Motherhood man.

"Oh, hell. What can you do? I told her there was nothing to it, but she never listened."

"Did she become angry?" asked the Motherhood man.

"Grace? Spitting mad."

Stephen watched the icy brittleness closing over her face.

"Well, there you see?" Phillip gestured to her. "She goes cold when she's mad. Normal people yell and get it over with, but not her."

"Cold enough to attempt to poison you?"

Phillip paused. "Well…" he said reluctantly. "I don't think she ever did *that*."

"But she did leave you."

"Oh, yes. Ran out on me with a valuable animal and took half my recipes with her."

"That is a *lie*," hissed Grace between her teeth. "A filthy lie. Those were *my* recipes. You only bought my apprenticeship in order to use them."

"But you don't deny you left him and took the recipes?" snapped the Motherhood man, lifting his head like a warhorse sighting the enemy.

Grace said nothing. Zale was too experienced to wince, but Stephen watched them write the word *shit* three times on the paper in front of them, in an elegant copperplate hand.

The indigo-clad man's lips curved. "In your opinion, Master Perfumer Phillip, would you say she was capable of murder?"

Phillip looked at her, then away. "Well, I wouldn't have thought it at the time," he said, "but when I heard about the trial, I can't say I was surprised. Soon as I heard, I said to myself, *You had a narrow escape, my man.* She always was a cold one." He gave Gucciard that sly look again. "In every way, if you know what I mean."

The mask of ice cracked. Stephen could see raw anguish underneath. Grace bit her lower lip so hard that a thin line of blood sprang up, shockingly red against her skin.

The tide roared in Stephen's ears.

He did not realize that he was walking forward. He could not conceive of why the Motherhood man was looking at him with that expression on his face, or why Phillip's mouth was hanging so foolishly open. Why would they look at him like that? And why were they standing so close?

He would have liked very much to close his hands over Phillip's throat, but he was not quite so far gone as that. Instead he placed both hands on the railing of the little witness box. The wood let out a groan of strain.

From a very great distance away, he could hear Gucciard shouting for order, and demanding the bailiffs restrain that man. Did someone need restraining? Undoubtedly. Stephen would help the bailiffs as soon as he had finished expressing his displeasure to Phillip. He was a paladin. Paladins were helpful that way.

"Uh," said Phillip. "Um. Uh. I. Uh. Hello. I didn't mean. Um."

The wooden railing snapped in half.

As if the lawyer were standing directly beside him, Stephen heard Zale say, with real regret, "Well, that's torn it."

The noises seemed to suddenly get a great deal closer. Stephen took a deep breath, then another, fighting back the tide. He had come very close. Much too close. Saint's bloody teeth, what had he been thinking?

You were thinking that he hurt her. You were thinking that he was a worthless failure of a man and needed to be hurt as badly as she was. You were...

...jealous.

"Order!" shouted Gucciard, slamming the quartz globe against the bench. "Order, dammit! I will have order! Bailiffs!"

"I...um...hello. You're...uh...um."

"Order!"

Hands closed over Stephen's upper arms. "Come quietly," the owner of one set of hands said. "We don't want to cause a scene."

"I believe," said Stephen, as the tide began to ebb, "that I have already caused a scene."

"You certainly have," said Judge Gucciard acidly. "Bailiffs, this man is in contempt of court. I want him out of here."

Stephen bowed his head. He could have shaken the bailiffs off with great ease, but he did not. Zale had put their head down on the desk in clear dismay, but his eyes were all for Grace, whose expression had turned to horror.

Always the reliable one. Not so reliable now, are you?

The shame of it engulfed him. He barely registered being led out the door, the walk from the courtroom, the wide eyes of the functionaries watching him being taken away.

He had failed Grace. He had failed his fellow paladins and the Temple of the Rat. He had given in to the tide, and he had done it in public, where there would be no hiding it. The Motherhood would have the word spread across the city, probably before he'd been locked away.

Being locked away might be what was best for everyone.

They held him in the foyer of the building for what felt like a long time, until a barred wagon came. They were taking no chances. He allowed his hands to be shackled and did not resist.

There were eyes on him from various corners of the courtyard. He felt them gawking and could imagine what they were thinking.

A mad paladin. One of the Saint's. Everyone has been waiting for them to snap. It was only a matter of time.

Shouldn't let them walk around like normal people anyway.

A menace.

Everyone's been waiting.

The grind of wheels on the cobbles rattled his teeth in his jaw, but could not shake the thoughts.

Lock them up.

Lock them all up.

When the god had died, Stephen and Shane had nearly killed two paladins of the Dreaming God. If Istvhan had not collapsed, it would have been three against two and they most certainly would have succeeded. But Jorge and his brother in arms had—oh, not covered it up, not exactly, but never made an issue of it. They were used to demons. This, to their mind, had been similar.

At Hallowbind, the Saint's paladins had gone mad with no one to stop them. There had been six paladins and two local men with them. They knew that there were two of them because they found two left hands. They hadn't found a great deal else. By the grace of the Rat, they were to meet a Rat priest, who had come upon the unconscious paladins and what little was left of their victims, and somehow...someway...the word had not gotten out.

And now Stephen, in one blighted moment, had destroyed that tiny grace, that the world did not quite know what shadow the broken paladins lived under.

They knew now.

CHAPTER 39

The wagon stopped. He was pulled out roughly, chains clanking at his wrists.

"What the hell is this?"

"A knight, by the look of it."

Not a knight. Only a soldier. Only a failed paladin. He said nothing.

"Well, la-di-dah. Put him in the cell with Stinker."

Stephen told himself not to resist. *Don't give them an excuse. They already think you're a mad dog, if you try to bite, they'll try to kill you, and you'll end up taking this place apart.*

It would have been so easy. The two guards were big men, but they were used to rousting drunks. They thought they were better than soldiers because they fought dirty, but they had never seen a berserker. They thought that he would go into a panicked rage perhaps, but they had no idea of the truth.

I could kill everyone in this room and my heart wouldn't even speed up.

It wouldn't even have been hard. He could have gotten the two holding him before the black tide had even fully settled. His hands were cuffed in front of him, but iron wouldn't hold against the tide. At most, he might leave the chain intact long enough to wrap it around the neck of the one on the left. The one on the right flinched a little more than his comrade, and Stephen wanted him gone first. You could never tell with the nervous ones. An elbow to the face to stun him, and then Stephen would put the back of his head into the wall. It would only take one blow to leave the man leaking blood and brain across the stones.

And then there would be red darkness and the calm at the heart of the whirlwind and who knows where it will end? I've already shamed my brothers enough. And what will become of Grace?

So he did none of these things. He allowed the two guards to lead him down the hallway, while other prisoners growled and spat and cursed and mocked.

They put him in a cell near the end. He held out his chained hands through the bars, and the flinching guard grumbled but the other one unlocked him.

The cell was not large. There was another man in the corner, or else someone had left a pile of soggy rags in the corner, one of the two. He could definitely see why they called the man "Stinker." The smell was foul enough to cut through the stench of blood and piss and unwashed flesh that permeated the cell block.

The guards walked away. Stephen ignored the other prisoners for the moment, scanning the boundaries of the cell. Metal bars, set in mortar. A door held by chain and a padlock, not the internal lock. That puzzled him for a moment until he looked at the rust on the bars and checked the walls for water marks. There it was, a clear line about eight inches off the ground. *Ah. Not underwater during the flooding, but definitely some damage.* Some of the prisons, being in cheap, low rent areas, had flooded completely, and few had escaped completely dry. The lock mechanisms would have been the first thing to weld into a useless mass of rust.

There was a narrow trench at the back of the cell that served as a drain. Presumably the prisoners would not be trusted with chamber pots. There was also a bucket of water, although it looked about as sanitary as a chamber pot, and, of course, Stephen's fellow prisoner.

The pile of rags moved. A fresh wave of stench rolled through the cell. Stephen put his arm over his face, grimacing. No one who smelled like that could be healthy. Hell, he was surprised anyone who smelled like that was still *alive*. There was something terrible going on there, perhaps gangrene. The man stank of death.

Prisoners in the next cell gagged and moved away from the bars.

"You all right?" he asked gruffly, keeping his mouth covered.

The prisoner said nothing. Stephen leaned against the bars, seeking clearer air.

This is how it ends. I'll rot in this cell until they drag me out. Maybe it's better this way. Here, there's nothing I can do to shame the Saint any longer.

If there's any grace left to me, though, please give me a cleaner death than this man.

"Hey, you there. Are you all right? Is there anything I can do?"

The prisoner turned his face toward Stephen, and he had his answer. He fell back a single step.

Oh.

The smooth-faced man looked up at Stephen and smiled.

"Ah," said Stephen. Even to himself, he sounded very calm. "I see."

The smooth man rose to his feet. Another wave of rot filled the cell. The other prisoners shouted, wordless complaints and demands that someone do something about the smell. Stephen registered retching sounds and cursing, but he never took his eyes from the smooth man. *Of course he stinks. That body is a few days old now, isn't it? I wonder if they simply ride around on the corpses until they fall apart, or if they take them somewhere else. For all I know, they might dig their own graves and lie down in them.*

"Do you talk?" said Stephen. "Whatever you are?"

The smooth man did not reply. His mouth stretched open, much too wide.

Stephen nodded to himself.

For a moment he thought of just letting it come for him. It was no more than he deserved. But the thought of his body getting up and walking around, of the damage that he might inflict, even after death...no.

The smooth man reached out with hands gone soft and swollen with rot.

He had been fighting against it for three years now. With occasional slips, he had held up well. But in the end, he always knew he'd fall from grace at last.

One of the very last paladins of the Saint of Steel turned and embraced the tide.

~

Grace was having a nightmare.

She suspected that it was real life, but it was easier to think of it as a nightmare. Surely this could not really be happening. Her husband could not have found her. Stephen could not have tried to attack him and been dragged away. At any moment she would look down and find out that she was not wearing any pants and then perhaps her teeth would start to fall out and she would wake in bed with Tab on her chest and everything would be a dream.

But she did not wake up. The door closed behind the bailiffs and the paladin and she stared at Phillip and he stared back at her, rubbing his throat, and still she did not wake up.

Gucciard banged the crystal against the table. "Well, gentlefolk, I think we need a recess after that."

"Thank the Rat," said Zale, and put their arm around Grace's shoulder.

"Grace—" croaked Phillip, his voice sounding thick and hoarse, not at all its usual smooth tones. It was easy to ignore that voice. She let Zale steer her out of the room and into the little chamber off to the side and she slumped down in the corner while the lawyer rubbed her hands and told her that everything would be all right.

"It won't," she said, sounding not much better than Phillip.

"Yes, it will," said Zale. "I've been in worse messes than this. I've been tied up in a back bedroom by a man who wanted to murder me and marry my client. I got out of that and we'll get out of this too."

"What will happen to Stephen?"

"He'll get thrown in a cell. Disrupting the peace, probably. The Rat will get him out. It's what we do."

Grace closed her eyes. The violence had horrified her, not because she hadn't wanted to see Phillip beaten within an inch of his life, but because she *had.* For a minute she'd wanted to cheer and then she realized what was happening and wanted to leap up and stop Stephen before he did something irrevocable.

But he'd stopped. He'd stopped himself. And his face, when he realized what he'd been doing, had been a mask of horror to equal Phillip's. He had gone with the bailiffs as quietly as a lamb.

"Marguerite will come," she muttered. "She'll set this right. She'll explain it all." She took a deep breath and shoved herself up the wall until she could stand on her feet. "She'll fix it."

"She has promised to be here this afternoon," said Zale. "Though I don't want you to be discouraged if her testimony does not cause the judge to waver. There are many ways that we can draw this out and demand a retrial."

Grace shook her head. "She'll fix it," she said. "You'll see. That's what she does. She fixes things like this."

Don't make me a liar, Marguerite. I'm counting on you. Please. Zale gave her a skeptical glance, but Grace pretended not to see it.

Stephen was never certain if he was not conscious for parts of the tide or if he simply didn't remember them afterward. There were always gaps in his memory later, stretches that were only a whirling darkness.

For example, he seemed to be standing in the cell, holding the smooth man's head by the tapered stump, with very little memory of how he had removed it. Had he simply grabbed and pulled? It seemed like the most logical method, really.

"Holy shit," someone said in the next cell, "he pulled that guy's head off!"

Well, that answered that.

The head twitched in his hands. The mouth champed on empty air, biting at nothing. Stephen decided that even in the grip of the tide, he did not like that very much, so he bashed it against the iron bars.

It made a hollow popping sound and broke apart into shards. It looked like ceramic. The mouth stopped moving, but he smashed it again, just in case, and tossed it toward the back of the cell.

The door was held shut with a lock. The lock was solid enough to resist most assaults. Stephen took the bars of the door in one hand and a bar of the cell in the other, set his foot against the wall, and heaved.

Metal screamed and yielded as easily as flesh.

"Holy fuck..." someone breathed behind him.

"Hey, mister, do this one next!"

"Hey—"

Stephen walked down the line of prisoners, hearing shouts and then cheering and then his heart was too loud in his ears and the tide rose up again.

Grace looked around the courtroom. Marguerite wasn't there.

She waited while the Motherhood men filed in, the bailiffs, the judge. Marguerite did not join them.

At least Phillip also wasn't there, which was a tiny shred of comfort. She stared at her hands and thought fixedly about Marguerite, not Phillip. She felt like a small child in bed, knowing that a monster was out there, but as long as she did not give any sign that she knew the monster existed, it could not get her.

The monster had already claimed one of her protectors. She could not afford to acknowledge it. She would go into another fugue and fall down weeping in the courtroom and she would look pitiful and guilty and mad.

Marguerite will come. Marguerite will save me.

Except that she didn't.

Zale stalled as best they could. Even through the increasing haze of despair, Grace admired that. There was no way to disguise the fact that one of her character witnesses was now in jail and the other was curiously absent, but the priest tried. They asked for recesses. They talked about the lack of evidence. They asked Grace about perfumes and deliveries for poison, and highlighted the fact that she didn't think it was even possible to kill a man that way. They pointed out that no one had seen the Crown Prince and they were relying on accounts of his illness from a man who had personally testified against Grace.

But the water clock's drops kept falling. And at last, with what Grace thought was a pitying look, the judge adjourned the case until tomorrow.

She barely heard the words. Zale spoke to her, and she nodded as if she understood, but she understood only one fact.

Marguerite hadn't come.

CHAPTER 40

Zale stayed with her for over an hour. She was vaguely aware of it, and some part of her knew that she would remember their kindness later, and then some other, larger part whispered: *There is no later. Marguerite didn't come to save you. No one is going to rescue you.*

It's what you wanted. Never to be rescued again.

"They're going to execute me, aren't they?" she said. She tried to keep her voice calm, but it shook anyway.

The lawyer-priest took her hand and gripped it firmly. "They are going to try," they said. "The Temple of the Rat will not allow the Motherhood to proceed so quickly. We will fight for a new trial and perhaps demand better evidence of the Crown Prince's illness." They paused, and then said, somewhat reluctantly, "Although, if he dies, I am afraid you will be tried as a murderer rather than merely an attempted murderer, and things will become...more difficult."

"How?"

"How will it become more difficult? Well, at that point, we are dealing with an act of war. Charlock will demand someone be held accountable and here you are. The Archon will demand something swift and public."

Grace swallowed. The priest's fingers were slim and strong and seemed to be the only thing holding her here, in this room. If they let go, she thought she might become weightless and drift up through the ceiling, or perhaps simply die and save the Motherhood the trouble. "No," she said. "How will they execute me?"

Zale went very still.

It's bad. It's very bad. It must be.

They turned to face her, and put their other hand over the top of hers. "Poisoners and witches belong to the Hanged Motherhood," they said. "You would be burned alive."

"...oh."

She'd known it would be bad. But it had all seemed distant and impossible. It would not come to that, surely. Everything would be taken away, but not like this.

Burned alive. Pain searing up her legs and smoke choking her lungs, on and on and on, not a distant impossibility but a thing that was going to happen and take an eternity while it happened.

Zale grimaced. "This is the coldest kind of comfort," they said. "Rat willing, it will not come to that. But we will not let you suffer. We will slip you a drug of some sort, so that you are not aware of what happens to you."

"Poison for a poisoner," said Grace hollowly.

Zale squeezed her hand. "I will do everything in my power," they promised, "to keep you from that."

"I know," said Grace. Even through the horror, she felt guilty. This poor priest had thrown their lot in with hers, for no reason except that Stephen had asked them to. And now they had an unwinnable case with not a single soul to speak on her behalf, and Stephen had been dragged away in chains.

My fault. All my fault.

She found herself patting Zale's hand. "It's all right," she said. "I know you're doing the best anyone can do. Please don't feel guilty."

Zale stared at her, then shook their head slowly. "There is absolutely no chance," they said, "that you poisoned the Crown Prince. I've met plausible murderers in my day, but..." They stood up, sighing, and shoved the rogue lock of hair from their face. "I'm going to go back to the temple and see what I can do to spoke the wheels of this trial. The Motherhood dragged it all out so they could get their witness in. Surely they can grant me another day or two. Perhaps long enough to find your friend."

Grace shook her head slowly. Marguerite had not come to help her. The one person she had trusted above all others. "I wouldn't count on it," she said softly. "I don't think she's going to be found."

Zale bowed their head. The door closed behind them with a soft, final click.

Hours passed, while Grace sat on the bed, gazing at nothing. Night fell. Her captor brought food. She stared at it, her stomach roiling. Eventually she drank the water on the tray, but the thought of eating was nauseating. She stared at the candle on the tray, watching it burn down, wax sliding down the sides. The smell of cheap tallow filled her nostrils, but for once, she did not think of Phillip.

Burned alive burned alive burnedburnedburnedburned

Something knocked on the window.

Grace jerked back in her chair, nearly sending it over. *What? I'm on the second floor! What the hell could knock at my window?*

Is it a bird? No, it's after dark—a bat?

Another thud against the shuttered window. It wasn't a knock so much as something bashing against it. If it was a bat, it was the size of Tab.

I can't even open them to see what it is. Although if it's that big, I don't know if I want to.

The wooden shutters exploded inward. Grace threw herself out of the chair and scrambled backward. Had the Motherhood decided not to wait? Was she going to be murdered right now, right here?

A dark shape crouched below the windowsill. Slowly it rose, shedding splinters and bits of broken wood. It had blood on its face, blood on its hands, eyes like dark holes, ringed with bruises.

Grace slowly rose to her feet as well. She took a step forward, then another. She knew what she was seeing, but she could not quite believe it. But there it was, underneath the smell of blood and sweat and a horribly familiar burnt smell...the faintest whiff of gingerbread.

"Stephen?"

Stephen didn't remember going through the window, which was too bad because of course it was the first thing that Grace asked about.

"How did you *do* that?" she said, staring at the destroyed shutter. "We're two stories up!"

Stephen staggered, slumping against the wall. "Don't know. Not sure."

"What?!"

"Berserk," he said vaguely. The tide was starting to recede. He hurt. He hurt a lot. He had snapped the padlock on the cell door, which was a thing he could do, but there was a bruise forming across his fingers where he'd gripped the bars and pulled. He wished he had some of Istvhan's muscle rub with him.

"You climbed up the wall?!"

"Maybe?" Things had gotten a little blurry. It was so hard to hold a conversation afterward. He couldn't remember words or what order they went in sometimes. He made an effort to focus. "No. Think I dropped down from the roof."

"That's not any better!"

"I could go out and climb up?"

Grace did not look as if this was any better. He felt vaguely ill-used. He was trying to meet her halfway, what more did she want?

"But how did you do that?!"

Stephen shrugged. He had grabbed something and pulled. If it came down on his head, he got out of the way. If it did not, he pulled himself up by it. It wasn't hard. Dear god, he hurt.

The door banged open and a guard rushed in. "What's the commo—"

He stopped. He saw the broken window. He saw Stephen. He reached for his sword.

Stephen bore the man no ill will, so he picked him up and

dropped him out the window as delicately as possible. Unfortunately this involved the tide rising again, and then there were a few minutes of red darkness and when he came to again, he was standing in the room at the end of the hallway with the remains of the guard desk in splinters at his feet and Grace clutching his elbow and saying, "That's it! It's dead! *And it's furniture!*"

Now that was odd. He didn't normally attack desks when he was berserk. Why would he have done such a thing?

Two more guards rushed up the stairs, weapons drawn. Ah. That was the reason. The desk had beautiful hardwood spindle legs. He tore them free. The guards were so slow. Everyone was slow. The front one's sword was going to come down right there, right where he thought Stephen's shoulder would be, so all Stephen had to do was move out of the way and put the leg of the desk in the way and then swing the other leg up across the side of the man's head. The man fell down. It was going to take him years to hit the ground, so Stephen stepped around him and repeated with the second guard, except that he hadn't gotten his sword up, so Stephen just poked him in the chest with the chair leg and watched him roll down the stairs for the next decade.

Things went a bit gray again. He distinctly heard a groan and then Grace saying, "Please don't get up, or my friend will have to hit you again." They must have answered in a way that did not require him to hit them. That was good? Maybe?

Grace's hand was on his elbow. He knew it was her, she smelled like sage and even in the depths of the tide, he would never have lifted a hand against her. That was comforting, which was strange, because berserkers were rarely comforted, nobody worried about comfort when you were smashing up the furniture and roaring like a wounded bull.

"The window," said Grace, with the patient air of one who is repeating herself.

"Eh? What?" Stephen tried to focus. They were on the landing. Had they walked there? They must have. There was a large window with wooden shutters. At the bottom of the stairs, the guard had discovered that he had a broken leg and seemed to be very upset about it.

"Can you open this window?" Grace said again.

The words necessary to explain that yes, he could, seemed so insurmountable that Stephen just kicked the shutters out instead.

It was only about a half-story down. He could have managed that even in his right mind. He jumped, landed, turned.

Grace stood framed in the window. Stephen beckoned. He'd catch her. Did he have to explain he'd catch her? Saint's balls, more words.

The world slipped sideways again. When he could focus, he was walking through an alley with Grace beside him, steering him with a hand on his arm. Apparently she had jumped down after all.

"A plan," she was saying. "We need a plan."

"Okay," said Stephen.

They turned again. Were they trying to lose pursuers? He looked back over his shoulder, but saw nothing. It seemed rather late in the evening. Had it been dark before? Yes, surely it must have. It had been dark when...when he...

"What's your plan?" said Grace.

Wait, he was supposed to have a plan? Damnation. He tried to drag himself further to normal functioning. As soon as he did, everything started to hurt. Istvhan always said that was why berserkers were considered cursed in the old days, not blessed. It had nothing to do with the fact that you murdered people. Murdering people was a hobby back then, even a vocation. No, it was that you were superhuman and unkillable right up until it wore off, and then all the muscles that had been working far beyond mere human capacity wanted to let you know just how badly they had been abused in your service.

"Plan," he said.

"Are you sure you're all right?"

"No." Stephen recognized that branch of the conversation as a trap. If he went there, he would have to think of even more words, and then she would just come back to the plan part anyway, except that he would be out of words. "Plan. A plan. Leave the city."

"What happens if someone tries to stop us?" said Grace.

"Kill 'em."

He thought this was a perfectly reasonable plan and did not know why she screwed her face up like that. "Where will we go?"

"Uh..."

He had to pause for a minute and put his head against the cool, damp brick of the wall.

"You don't look good," said Grace.

"No."

She patted his shoulder as if he was a dog. He didn't mind. He liked dogs. Dogs did what you asked, or at least what they thought you were asking, and just wanted a job to do and a nice warm place to lie down afterwards. That seemed like a good life. The infantry had been a bit like that, except they hadn't always gotten the nice warm place afterwards.

"How about I make the plan?" she said.

"Would you?" Gratitude suffused him. He was a berserker. The only plan he was good at was hitting the enemy until they fell apart or he did.

"Let's go this way."

"Okay."

CHAPTER 41

Steering a no-longer berserk paladin was like steering a good-natured but potentially belligerent drunk. Stephen was obedient enough, but he ran into things, and then sometimes he tried to fight them. Grace had to disentangle him from a pitched battle with a rain barrel and convince him to drink the water instead.

He seemed a little less groggy once he'd gotten some water in him. She wondered how long it had been since he ate or drank anything. A berserker fit couldn't possibly last a whole day, could it?

Unless it's more like delirium. He seems to be sliding in and out. If I can just get him somewhere safe to sleep it off...

Grace knew on some level that she should be worried that he would turn on her, but she couldn't muster any real concern. For one thing, she had just broken out of her holding cell, which undoubtedly meant that she was admitting guilt, as far as the judge and the Motherhood were concerned. Death by berserk paladin had to be preferable to being burned at the stake. For another thing, it was *Stephen.* Gods have mercy, she trusted him. Her body trusted him. Even when he was attacking the rain barrel, there was nothing in her spine or her skin or her nerves that told her she was in danger. And as soon as she grabbed his arms, he went baffled and docile again.

"Come on," she said. She had to get him somewhere safe. The

shop was obviously out—it was the first place the guards would check. The Temple of the Rat would be safe, but she couldn't quite trust that Zale wouldn't turn around and hand them back in to the authorities. They were a lawyer, and this was definitely not legal. So Grace had been steering Stephen toward the graveyard by the Glass Quarter, and the little boarded up chapel there was dry. It was probably the best that they were going to get.

Besides, he's a paladin. The gods are supposed to look favorably on them. Some of the gods. Not the Hanged Mother, obviously. But it's a chapel to the Four-Faced God, and They won't mind us using Their chapel. I hope.

She wished that she could go ahead and scout out the path, but she was afraid to leave Stephen. He might take it in his head to fight a building. In his current state, he might even win. So she held her breath and waited for long minutes at each cross street, looking for guards or flashes of indigo.

It might have been luck, or the grace of the Rat, that they saw no one who would take notice of them. This area had faded into genteel poverty long ago, as evidenced by the state of the graveyard. It was not rough enough to require more guards, but it was also a place where people kept firmly to themselves. She'd always found that useful when hunting for plants. It hadn't occurred to her that it might be useful while running from the law, too.

Badger stripes flashed at her from the mouth of the opposite alley as a gnole turned to look at them, then looked away again immediately. Grace hurried down the street, avoiding the pools of light left by streetlamps. The lamplighters had come and gone long since, but if he tried to fight a streetlamp, someone was bound to notice.

But he did not try, and Grace's heart leapt with relief when she saw the worn metal gates of the graveyard.

Stephen looked up wearily. "Graveyard," he muttered. "Am I dead?"

"Not yet."

"Always...next time." He laughed softly, his chin dropping to his chest as if he were about to fall asleep.

The gates hadn't opened in years, but the little caretaker's door around the side was less visible anyway. The door was locked, but there was a key under the flowerpot. Grace knew this because the caretaker had shown her once. "Master key," he said. "It'll open the gate if I'm not here and you get locked inside." She felt a pang of guilt for taking advantage of the old man's hospitality, but desperate times called for desperate measures.

She led the paladin through the graves. He seemed inappropriately amused by the headstones, but did not try to fight them. "Light a candle?" he said.

"We can't light a candle," said Grace. "Someone will see it."

"The dead'll see," he agreed.

"Later. We're going to the church."

"Vigil?"

"No. The choir loft is still intact and the wood's not rotted out. If we can get up there, it's an enclosed space, it'll be warm enough."

"...'kay" said Stephen. He had been slurring his words since before they reached the graveyard. Whatever strength the berserker fit had given him, it was long gone. Grace just hoped that she could get him someplace horizontal before he collapsed completely.

The door opened with only a soft sound of oiled hinges. The caretaker did his work well. Grace sighed with relief.

"Eh?"

"It's all right. We're nearly there."

"...'kay."

Getting Stephen up the ladder to the choir loft was an experience that she was not going to soon forget. She kept worrying he'd forget what he was doing and try to fight the ladder. But about halfway up he seemed to grasp what he was doing, and went up the rungs with a speed that Grace could only envy.

The choir loft was bare wood, but even that was warmer than stone. The windows were shuttered, but cracks of reddish light shone through—the dull ambient light of the city at night. She wondered what time it was. Much closer to dawn than midnight, she guessed.

She pulled his cloak off his shoulders and spread it on the boards. "Lay down."

"...'kay."

She wasn't even halfway down the ladder when he began to snore.

It only took her a few moments to retrieve her stash from the mausoleum. She didn't worry that Stephen had slipped away in her absence. She could hear him snoring when she entered the church. *Gods, do I have to worry that the sound will give us away?*

She went back up the ladder and dropped the oilcloth cloak over him. "Roll over," she said. "On your side."

"Mmmgh?"

"Roll over." She shoved his shoulder. He obediently rolled sideways and the snores settled down to deep, even breaths. She wished she'd been able to get his armor off, but frankly, after the day he'd had, a stiff back was probably the least of his concerns.

Grace sat in the dark listening to him breathe and thought, *I can go now.*

She'd rescued him. She'd gotten him to a safe place before he collapsed. She'd shoved water down his throat. They were even now, weren't they?

I could leave. Run for the next city, whatever it might be. Change my name. Tab's in good hands. Marguerite doesn't care about me. I don't even have to worry about taking my books because they've all been impounded anyway. This is my chance.

She'd have a much better shot at getting out of the city unobserved by herself. Little grey mice were much less noticeable than large men in armor. All she had to do was pull the cloak off him and strap on her pack, and she could be out of the city by daybreak.

It was the wisest thing to do. She'd lost everything, just as she always knew she would. What they didn't tell you, once you'd lost it all, was the crazy relief that erupted in your heart. *Relief feels like happiness, if you don't know the difference.* The axe had fallen, the worst had come. Nothing more could touch her. Grace had nothing left to lose except her life.

Stephen shifted under the cloak and muttered something in his sleep.

Nothing left to lose...except a broken man who had given up what little he had left to save her.

The red-orange light of the city was colder than firelight. It lay unkindly across the planes of his face. He looked old and worn and weary.

I could go.

I should go.

Grace unlaced her boots and pulled them off.

This isn't wise.

You're only doing this because he kissed you. You're letting lust do the talking.

She pulled the oilcloth cloak back.

Get out while you have the chance. He's dangerous. He told you himself that he couldn't be trusted.

She lay down next to him and pulled the cloak over them both. The wooden boards were hard, but he radiated heat like a furnace.

You can still get away.

She closed her eyes and sleep dragged her down immediately.

Grace lay on a wooden floor and heard someone call her name.

"Grace...Grace, wake up."

It was Phillip. She opened her eyes, puzzled. She was on the floor of the workshop, a blanket pulled over her. Why was she sleeping in here? Was something wrong with an order?

"Grace, sweet, there's someone I want you to meet..." And then a giggle. A very feminine giggle.

Memory swung down on her like the headsman's axe. He had gone out. Probably to meet one of his lovers. He'd stopped even bothering to deny it any more, and she stopped even bothering to ask. There was no point any longer. She'd worked herself to the point of exhaustion, because if she was thinking about essential oils she wasn't thinking about what he might be doing.

Except now, apparently, he had brought one home.

"Come on, Grace, come out." There was a wheedling note in his voice that he always used when he was trying to seduce her.

Grace closed her eyes again and pressed her cheek against the smooth wooden boards, trying to blot out the voice, and then the sounds that followed. When she did not come out of the workshop, Phillip must have decided that one woman was enough. Perhaps he thought that he would make her jealous, or perhaps he wasn't thinking of her at all.

Eventually the noises stopped.

She was no longer jealous. She was so tired of him. She did not care if he had his hand under half the skirts in Anuket City. She just wanted it all to be over. The only thing she cared about was not showing weakness any longer. As long as those other women did not think she cared, then...then she won. Or at least she didn't lose completely.

It did not feel like winning. It felt like bleak loneliness, like she and Tab were walled off from the entire world. If they died tomorrow, would anyone even notice?

I have to leave, she thought. *I have to get away. This is never going to get any better.*

Oh god, I am so very tired.

Tears slid down her face onto the wooden boards. She tried to muffle her sobs in her arm. She did not want Phillip to hear and think he'd won.

"Grace."

He was too close. He was right behind her. How had he gotten in? She inhaled sharply, and her lungs filled with the scent of dust and damp and...gingerbread?

"Grace, love, wake up. I think you're dreaming. Please."

She opened her eyes. The light through the cracks in the shutter was daylight now, and the arm around her waist belonged to—

"Stephen?"

"Yes."

He lay on his side, chest against her back, his arm under her head to pillow it. She could hear his voice through her bones as much as her ears.

"Are you awake now?"

"I think so," she said. The memory fugue had gotten tangled up with the dream, brought on by the feeling of wooden boards under her, but the scent of gingerbread and churchyard drove them out again. They were good scents. She stretched. "Are you...ah...?"

"Berserk?" He chuckled ruefully against the back of her neck. "Not any longer. I'd probably hurt less if I was."

"You tried to fight a *rain barrel.*"

"I'm sure I had a good reason."

She snorted. Her hip was stiff from the hardness of the boards, and she knew that she should probably move, but he was warm and solid and if she moved, he might move his arm. She was much gladder of that arm around her than she was comfortable admitting. So she didn't move, and neither did he.

"You stayed," he said.

"I almost didn't," she admitted. "It would be easier to escape on my own."

"If they catch us, we'll be in a lot of trouble."

"They'll burn me at the stake," she said. "What about you?"

She felt his shrug against her back. "I'm sure it'll be unpleasant. I'm more worried about the others. This is just proof we can't be trusted."

"The other paladins?" Grace thought of poor, worried Shane who had walked her home.

"Yes."

"I'm sorry."

"So am I. Why did you stay?"

Don't blurt out that you're in love with him. Marguerite might have abandoned her, but that was probably still good advice. Grace sighed, turning in his arms. "Because it turned out, I still had something left to lose."

He raised his eyebrows, puzzled, and she gave up and kissed him.

CHAPTER 42

It was not terribly easy to kiss someone while lying nose to nose with them on a wooden floor, but Stephen fixed that by rolling over and propping himself upon his elbow so that he leaned over her. His mouth opened on hers and it seemed that the heat between them had not died down at all. If anything, it was worse. It felt as if someone were squeezing Grace's insides in an enormous vise and if she did not find a way to relieve the pressure, she was going to die of it.

There was only one way that the night was ever going to end, but it was still a physical shock when he lay his hand across her breast. She gasped and then he broke loose and cursed softly and grabbed the finger of his glove in his teeth, yanking it loose.

"Are you sure you're strong enough for this?" she asked. The dawn light illuminated a long scrape above his eyebrow and deepened the shadows under his eyes.

"If I were dying, I would still be strong enough for this." He stroked the hair out of her eyes and pressed his lips against her forehead.

She wanted to leave it there, but she couldn't. They might very well die—they probably would, in fact—and Stephen deserved better than to die feeling dissatisfied. "I should warn you," she said. "I'm not...I'm not much good at this."

He took this statement with the same grave consideration that he took everything, even as his hands kept moving in her tangled hair. "Why do you say that?"

Grace swallowed. She did not want to say Phillip's name. If it hung in the air between them, she didn't know if she could keep going. "He...uh...told me. I wasn't..."

Stephen kissed her.

It was fierce and passionate and left very little room for conscious thought. His previous kisses had been tender, or tried to be, at least. This one wasn't. This felt like a claim being staked. The heat of his mouth warmed a cold place inside her, and she pressed closer against him, smelling gingerbread and metal and sweat.

When he had kissed her rather more thoroughly than Grace had ever been kissed in her life, he set his hands on her shoulders, pulled back, and said "He isn't here. I am."

It was hard to undress each other in the dimness. Eventually they gave up and dealt with their own respective clothing. It took Stephen rather longer, and she heard the chink of chain and a good deal of quiet muttering. It made her laugh.

"It's not usual that the gentleman's clothes are more complex than the lady's," she said.

"The gentleman isn't usually carrying an anvil's worth of metal around on his back."

She waited under the cloak, not sure if she was feeling anticipation or terror or both. Her stomach did not have butterflies so much as full-grown civettes cavorting through her innards.

He stretched out beside her, sliding his hands under the cloak. There was...certainly a lot of him. Grace laid her palm flat against his chest, wondering what she was supposed to say, or if she needed to say anything at all.

For a moment desire overwhelmed her and then, as he folded his arms around her, the fears came rushing back. This part was always so exhausting. Was she moaning enough? Making the right sort of noises so that he would feel smug in his skills at pleasing a woman? Gods. She and Stephen had had so many awkward conversations already, could they have one more where she said, "I don't care about all this groping and moaning, I don't even care if I come, I just want you inside me so I don't feel so alone?"

She closed her eyes and leaned into him, only to find him leaning away. "You've gone very stiff," he said. "Are you certain you want this?"

"Yes," she said. "I want you. I just don't want to disappoint you."

"You won't."

She sighed. "You say that."

He lifted his hands, which had been hovering tantalizingly close to her breasts. "We don't have to do this."

"No!" She fought the urge to grab his hand and pull it back down, then decided that was a stupid urge to fight and did it anyway. His skin was very warm and he inhaled sharply as her breast filled his palm. She covered his hand with her own. "I worry that it's not enough. Whatever I'm doing. That you'll think I'm not enjoying it. Then I start thinking too much about what I'm doing and..." She shrugged, knowing he'd feel it.

"I see." Stephen sounded slightly distracted, although because of the breast in his hand or an attempt to parse this conversation, Grace couldn't be sure. "This has been a problem, hasn't it?"

She was glad that the darkness hid her blush, and then he laid the back of his hand across her cheek and she realized he could feel the heat. "Yes," she mumbled. Trying not to think of Phillip and his demands and the way that any physical pleasure had eventually been lost in performing to soothe his ego.

He kissed her forehead. "We are in an abandoned church, on the floor, and if there is not a price on both our heads, there will be soon. I spent a good bit of yesterday berserk. Frankly, I am more concerned that I will last all of ten seconds and then fall asleep on top of you."

Grace's laugh was half relief, but it was still a laugh.

He laid a finger across her lips. "Why don't we just agree that this is...ah...a trial run and neither of us may be at our best? And if we survive, we'll work the rest out later."

It couldn't be that easy. Could it?

He breathed against the side of her neck and she shivered.

Perhaps it could.

"Deal?" he said.

"Deal," she whispered.

His hands stroked over her body. He did not squeeze her breasts or pinch at her nipples, he simply touched, as if he were memorizing the shape of her. Grace closed her eyes, feeling a strange kind of relief. She did not have to pretend to respond when he did this. She just needed to occupy this dark space and feel and not worry that he'd be insulted.

Her gasp was unfeigned when Stephen's fingertips stroked across her wrist and down into her palm. His fingers were hard with calluses, but the touch was so light that she shivered. She bit her lip.

He learned from that. The next long stroke of his fingers over her ribs and down her hip was as delicate as silk. Grace dropped her head back and gave herself up to feeling.

He had remarkably clever hands. How clever, she hadn't realized, until he slid his fingers down between her thighs and touched her in ways that neither Phillip or the artificer's apprentice had ever managed.

"Good *god*," she said out loud.

He burst out laughing. It broke the tension. "So that's good, then?"

"Yes. Oh yes."

"Good."

He was so big. She thought that she was used to that, but now that she was actually underneath him, it struck her all over again. Flat muscle under her palms and a sense of weight over her. Contained strength. She felt as small as Tab.

She caught at his shoulders as he began to slide downward. "Not that," she said. "Please I...I don't really enjoy that." *Oh god, not more wet slobbering around, it was all going so well...* She braced herself for his reaction. Most men thought they were doing you a favor when they did that. It wasn't in Stephen's nature to get huffy when rejected, but paladins tended toward martyrdom by nature. *Listen to yourself. Oh, I'm so disappointing, no, don't touch me there, no wonder men think you're shit in bed. If his cock went as limp as an earthworm in a puddle, you'd have no one but yourself to blame.*

"All right," he said. He didn't sound either angry or particularly martyred. He slid his fingers slowly across her tender flesh and she nearly came up off the floor. "But this is still good?"

"Yes," she said hoarsely. "Yes, that's—that's fine."

Something pushed against her hip. Something large and very firm. Apparently her fears of earthwormhood were unfounded.

"Good," he said, and kissed her.

Stephen was going to kill Phillip. He had already made a mental note that the man needed killing, but now he was going to make it a priority, assuming he survived the next day or two. What in the Saint's blessed name had the man *done*?

Well, it was obvious what he had done. He'd taken a beautiful, responsive woman like Grace and taught her that the price of pleasure was a performance to puff up his pride. Given that Grace was, to put it kindly, an absolutely piss-poor liar, it must have made the marriage bed a nerve-wracking experience.

Suddenly that first encounter in the alley clicked into place. She'd cried out like a wanton and moved like a virgin. The Saint give him strength.

And she *was* responsive. That was the hell of it. You simply had to pay attention. Her breath hitched and caught whenever he touched her. She shivered and trembled when he dragged his fingertips across her skin. Her nipples were hard as...well, as hard as he was, and that was saying something. And when he finally slid his fingers down between her legs, she was so wet that he nearly spilled in his breeches like an untried boy.

He couldn't wait for very long. Thank the Saint they'd agreed that this was only a trial run, because he didn't think he had much time left. He slid inside her, only halfway, and stopped. He couldn't seem to get enough air and every fiber of his being was screaming to drive forward and take her, take her now, and once he started he knew he would not be able to stop.

"Grace," he said hoarsely. He shifted his weight to one arm, found her hand, and slid it down between their bodies. "Come for me, love. Please."

He felt her hesitate. Well, of course. This wasn't the sort of thing a man obsessed with his own skills would ask their lover to do. But there was a better than even chance they were both going to die tomorrow, and damned if he was going to let her go to the gallows or the pyre without a memory of pleasure.

"Are you sure?" she asked.

"Saint's blood, yes."

Her touch was quicker and surer than his. He could feel her body pulsing around him as she brought herself to the edge, and then she began to push against him, taking him deeper, her breath coming in short gasps as she moved.

Saint's blood. The feel of her pleasuring herself on his body was shredding a lifetime of tight control. He gritted his teeth so hard that his jaw ached.

When she cried out and clutched at him, he nearly sobbed with relief. Her body clenched around him like a fist and that was all he needed and more than he'd ever imagined. He drove into her, no longer tender but hard and fast, his entire world narrowing down to the heat of her body. Every thrust wrung a cry from her and almost he would have worried but she was meeting him with every stroke, fingers digging into his hips, and he knew that he was not alone.

It took an eternity, or no time at all. He collapsed over her, trying to take his weight on his forearms so he didn't crush her, while his whole body shuddered. At some point, she had wrapped her legs around him. He barely remembered it. Hell, at the moment he could barely remember his own name.

"Well," he said hoarsely, when he could think again. "Well. For a trial run, that wasn't bad."

"No," she said, and laughed softly, sounding surprised at herself. "No, it wasn't, was it?"

He rolled to one side, settling her against him, her head on his chest, his arm around her. "I'm going to fall asleep," he said. "I know it's the worst sort of manners. But I am completely done."

"It's all right," she said, and yawned to prove the point. "I'm not going to last long myself."

"That's all right, then," said Stephen, and fell asleep almost at once.

CHAPTER 43

He woke hours later, hungry and thirsty and sore in unexpected places. The light had changed again. Had he really slept the whole day away? Grace was still in his arms, though. That part had not been a dream or a fantasy.

And most likely I should be beating myself up for taking her when the tide was barely receded, but... He found that he regretted nothing, except for the lack of blankets and mattresses and possibly the part where they were probably both going to get burned at the stake.

All right, I regret a lot of things. Just not that.

Grace yawned and stretched against him. He felt her breasts slide across his chest and thought, *Well, perhaps a little more soreness won't kill me.*

At that moment, Istvhan poked his head over the edge of the ladder and said, "Am I interrupting anything?"

Grace woke with a yelp. Stephen, who would have trusted Istvhan with his last breath and last drop of blood, nevertheless grabbed for his sword and then remembered he didn't have one on him. He cradled Grace against his chest and glared over her head.

"What's going on?" she asked, slightly muffled. "Did they find us?"

"Stand down," said Istvhan. "We're not under attack just yet. And put some clothes on. I'm a friend," he added, probably for Grace's benefit. "I'd offer to shake your hand, but...ah..."

"How the devil did you find us?" asked Stephen.

Istvhan sighed. "They've got slewhounds over every inch of the bloody city. Your doing, as I understand it. That thing you killed in the prison had the smell still on it and now everyone's on the hunt for the head biter things. And since your scent was mixed up with it, a dog eventually led them here. Fortunately for you, I happened to be in that group, and I said I'd check the chapel."

"Are they outside right now?" Stephen stiffened.

"No, you daft fool, I walked in, heard what was going on, recognized who was doing the yelling, and turned around to tell them the place was empty except for a couple of fools getting laid. We all had a good laugh and kept going."

Grace turned the color of fresh beets. "I see," said Stephen.

"Then I rousted the rest of the order and here we are." Istvhan folded his arms. "And a hell of a mess you've gotten yourself into, might I add."

"They were going to execute her."

"Yes, well, now they're going to execute all of us," said Istvhan.

"What?!" Grace clutched at the blanket. "What do you mean?"

"Well, when they come for you, there's going to be seven paladins in the way," said Istvhan.

"The Bishop will be furious," said Stephen.

"The Bishop will understand. And if she doesn't, well, I wanted to head up north and catch up on my sleep anyway."

"Are they all outside?" asked Grace.

"Two of us are inside!" called Galen from down below.

"Oh dear god," said Grace.

"As I said, you might want to get dressed. Or not, it's up to you. I warn you though, we're very noble and all but we do ogle."

"Turn your back," grumbled Stephen.

"I'm on a *ladder*."

"Then close your eyes."

Istvhan rested his elbow on the edge of the choir loft and put his hand over his eyes. Grace scrambled for her clothes.

"Sorry," said Stephen. "Istvhan's sense of humor is...well..."

"Functional?" suggested Istvhan. "Unlike the rest of you people."

"Yes, where *is* Shane?" asked Stephen.

Istvhan's teeth flashed in the gloom. "Also outside."

Grace, hastily dressed, advanced on Istvhan. *"You!"*

The paladin looked over his shoulder, as if someone might really be lurking on the ladder behind him. "Err...me?"

She crouched down until she was nearly nose to nose with Istvhan. "You make the muscle rub that smells like gingerbread!"

"Oh, *that.*"

"It smells amazing," Grace said, sounding rather angry about it.

"The one with turmeric is better," said Istvhan, "but it also dyes you bright yellow and no one wants to use it."

"I would love to smell it sometime."

Stephen felt a tiny pang of jealousy but squelched it. Perhaps Istvhan would be willing to teach him something about scents. Enough to be able to ask intelligent questions, anyway.

He followed Grace down the ladder to discover three more paladins had appeared inside the church, like some kind of armored conjuring trick. "Someone's coming," said Wren laconically.

"I hope it's not the caretaker," said Grace. She frowned. "Or I hope it is, so that I can apologize. I didn't mean to break into his church."

There was a clatter of hooves on cobbles in the distance, and a creak of metal. Stephen tensed, then heard a familiar voice saying "So this is where you've all gotten off to."

"Okay, who told the Bishop?"

Everyone looked at Istvhan, who looked hurt. "I did *not.*"

Bishop Beartongue shoved her way through the front door, trailed by her secretary. "No, he didn't," she said. "You lot are so bad at secrecy that it would make a spy weep. You stood in the damn courtyard talking about where you were going, and then you all ran off. I had three reports before the gate slammed shut behind you. Next time, leave in clumps and talk about it in your rooms, and you might get a whole hour lead time."

She put her hands on her hips. "Paladin Stephen, I can't help but notice that you're not in a jail cell."

"Um," said Stephen. "Yes. I can explain."

"Don't bother, the corpse was explanation enough."

"Corpse?" said Grace. "You killed someone?"

"It wasn't human!" protested Stephen. Basic honesty compelled him to add "At least, um...I don't remember killing anyone else... yesterday, anyway."

"We are going to have one hell of a debriefing if we survive the night," said the Bishop. "Miss Angelica, good to see you. Glad you're well."

"I'm sorry I broke out of jail," said Grace. "It wasn't my idea."

"No, it's fine," said the Bishop. "I mean, it's not fine, but it's honestly the least of my worries right now." She sighed. "I suspect we haven't got long until the people who were undoubtedly following my carriage report back to their superiors where I was dropped, which means that the guards should be along presently."

"I'll give myself up," said Stephen.

"They will have to go through us to get you," growled Istvhan. The other paladins were all inside now, bunching up around Stephen and Grace. "We will not sacrifice a brother merely to smooth over relations with Charlock."

"Charlock?"

"That whining emissary of the prince believes that you are both poisoners and wants you executed without further delay. Or, he says, Charlock will become extremely angry. And the Motherhood is backing him."

"Which is reason enough for the Rat to intervene," said the Bishop. "No executions without a ruling, and not without a chance for appeal. We are not at war and it would be mere vigilantism. Isn't that right, Captain?"

She pitched her voice up on the last sentence, but Stephen had already heard the scrape of boots on the steps of the church.

"Your holiness," said the guard captain. He started to salute, then paused halfway through, apparently unable to decide who he was saluting. "I see you've...ah...located the fugitives."

Stephen admired the man's attempt at diplomacy. He couldn't very well arrest the Bishop without causing an incident that would be far more trouble than it was worth. Not Captain Mallory, unfortunately—Stephen didn't know this man. He could see two guardsmen behind the captain, and at least one more outside. They had crossbows. He stifled a sigh. He had been shot by a crossbow before. It was not a memory he cherished.

"Paladin Stephen," said the captain, "you are under arrest. And Miss Angelica, I am afraid that you must be returned to custody as well."

"Over my dead body," said Istvhan.

"And mine."

"Mine as well."

The captain winced. "Your dedication to each other is admirable, but let us not be foolish. No one wants bloodshed."

The Bishop opened her mouth, then paused, cocking her head. Carriage wheels rattled on the cobblestones, and then came running footsteps.

"Captain!" shouted a regrettably familiar voice. "Captain, have you found the criminals?"

It seemed that the Motherhood had arrived.

"Shoot them!" shouted the Motherhood man, bouncing up and down. "Shoot them all!"

The guard captain looked at the paladins. He looked at the Bishop, who had her hands on her hips. "I am not going to order my men to shoot at warriors who are just standing there and not doing anything," he said.

"They're criminals!"

"Then bring me a writ of execution for them. Because that's what this would be."

"It would be a bloodbath," said Istvhan, not quite under his breath. "But mostly not our blood."

"There will not be a bloodbath!" hissed the Bishop. "I absolutely forbid a bloodbath at this hour!"

"We could wait until morning?"

"No one is having a bloodbath at any hour!"

There was a thunder of wheels on the cobblestones. "Oh," said the Bishop. "Someone else. Yay."

Grace gave up and sat down. Her feet were tired. Stephen stood over her like a guard dog. It was oddly soothing. She leaned against his leg and he reached a hand down and tangled his fingers in her hair.

The carriage was gold. Despite the darkness, the coachman's livery gleamed with brocade. "Oh sweet Rat," muttered the Bishop. "It's the Crown Prince's coach."

"It can't possibly be the prince," said Istvhan. "Isn't he supposed to be dying?"

"I don't know why it can't be the prince. Everyone else seems to be here. A dying foreign ruler would just about fit in."

The door opened and DuValier sprang out. Stephen growled, low in his throat, and stood up straighter. "Istvhan, loan me your sword. I need to kill this man."

"No one give him a sword," ordered the Bishop.

"I am feeling distinctly conflicted here," said Istvhan.

One of the paladins, a woman with a curiously blank expression, unhooked a long dagger from her belt and handed it to Stephen.

"Thank you."

"Technically that wasn't a sword," said the Bishop. "I applaud your threading of the needle there. Dammit." The paladin smiled so fleetingly that Grace barely caught it.

DuValier looked into the chapel and threaded his way through the milling guards. "You!" he said to the guard captain. "The Crown Prince is dead and this woman is his murderer. I demand that you arrest her at once!"

"Do you have a writ of execution?" asked the guard captain.

DuValier paused for only half a heartbeat. "No. It is not execution, it is justice. I demand you take her into custody!"

"Come and try," said Stephen.

A strange, prickling energy seemed to spring up around the paladins. Grace did not know if it was real or if she was imagining things, but her skin felt suddenly raw and exposed. The seven men and women standing between her and DuValier were suddenly no longer seven individuals but a single unit, linked by an unseen bond. She could almost see the air vibrating between them.

"Oh *no*," said Beartongue, almost to herself. "Oh no, no. Rat, stop them."

Istvhan laid his hand on the hilt of his sword. Stephen laid his hand on his dagger. Every other paladin did the same, simultaneously, an eerily synchronized behavior that made the hairs on the back of her neck stand up.

The guard captain took a step back. The men with crossbows, who had been pointing them mostly at the ground, swung them up and looked to him uncertainly.

It's the berserker thing, thought Grace, *it must be, they're doing it. Only it's not just Stephen half out of his mind and fighting water barrels, it's all of them. Oh god. Stephen listened to me, but none of the rest of them know me, they won't listen, I can't stop this, everything is going to explode and people will die and I don't know how to stop it—*

She took a step forward. "Everyone, stop!" she cried. Her voice sounded thin and weak, like a nightmare where she couldn't shout loudly enough to call for help. "Stop, *please!* I'm not worth this! I'll go back with them!"

No one seemed to be listening, except the bishop. Beartongue shot her a brief, sympathetic glance and took her arm, tucking it through her own elbow. "Goddamn paladins," she muttered. "All right. Let's you and I walk in front. Ours won't go through us...I don't think...and the guards hopefully won't shoot us."

This was easier said than done. Trying to move Istvhan and Stephen was like trying to move a wall. They didn't move. They stared straight ahead. Grace could hear teeth grinding.

Holy Rat and every other god, is this what they're like when they're about to go berserk?

She was starting to realize that Stephen had not been anything like fully berserk last night. He'd been exhausted and dragged out and slipping in and out, sure, but this was something much, much worse. The hairs on the back of her neck stood up.

Beartongue gave up with an exasperated noise and pulled her around the side of the line of paladins. The woman on the end moved to get in front of them again and Beartongue growled, "Stand *down*," so fiercely that she sounded like an actual bear. The woman stood down.

"Captain," she called, striding in front of the line of paladins and facing the guard captain. "We are in a very precarious situation here, and I think you do not wish to make it any worse." Grace, still beside her, nodded furiously.

"What do you suggest?" asked the captain, his eyes flicking down the line of silent paladins and the charged air between them.

"If your men would kindly lower their crossbows?"

"Please don't let them die for me," whispered Grace. "Please. I'll give myself up. Just stop this happening."

"Working on it," said Beartongue, eyes locked on the captain.

It came to Grace that she had no fear of the men and women behind her. She probably should. She'd seen the mayhem that Stephen was capable of, even weak and dragging. The seven paladins could undoubtedly cut a swath of destruction to rival a siege engine.

And if they are all like Stephen, they are as brittle as glass and it would destroy them utterly, even if they survived.

The captain squared his shoulders.

"Arrest this woman!" hissed DuValier.

Beartongue had pinned the captain's gaze. Grace watched her flick her eyes to DuValier, then back to the captain, rolling them expressively.

It reminded her of Zale talking to the judge at the trial. She could almost feel the power dynamic shifting. *We, the two of us, are the adults here, and can you believe what we have to deal with?*

"Sir Emissary, you have no authority here," said the captain, in a clipped voice. "You do not give orders."

"The prince will hear of this!"

"You said that the prince was dead," said Beartongue.

"The next prince!"

"Oh, is he here too?" asked the captain wearily.

Another coach pulled up. Beartongue threw her hands in the air and stomped around in a small, furious circle. "Another one?" she said. "Really?" The guard captain made a small noise of despair.

A man stepped out of the coach and stalked toward the chapel. He was tall, broad-shouldered, and wearing gold-ornamented armor that managed to be both functional and elegant. The two men that flanked him were armed to the teeth, in ways that even a paladin might find excessive.

The man was dressed in warm colors, but the expression on his face was as cold as winter. His boot heels rang on the wooden floor like the crack of the headsman's axe. His gaze swept over the guards with their crossbows and paladins with their drawn swords. Grace recognized his face immediately. She had once spread perfumed oil on his wrist.

"It would seem," said the Crown Prince of Charlock, "that I am only just in time."

CHAPTER 44

"You're not dead!" said Grace.

Her voice shattered against the deafening silence like a dropped glass. She felt her face start to heat up—*gods above and below, armed men on every side with crossbows pointed at you and you* still *find a way to do something embarrassing*—but the Crown Prince snorted and then everyone started talking at once, very rapidly.

"If you're not dead—"

"Your magnificence, you have impeccable timing—"

"—then who is—"

"What is going—"

"This changes nothing—"

"Istvhan, if you please?" said Beartongue, exasperated.

The very large paladin cleared his throat, inhaled, and roared, *"Silence!"*

Everyone quieted immediately. The Crown Prince put up an eyebrow.

"As you can see," he said, "I am very much alive."

Bishop Beartongue pursed her lips. "For a man so recently on his deathbed, you seem quite healthy."

The Crown Prince made a soft scoffing sound. "I knew I was being poisoned the first day. It seemed wiser to let my assassin believe that they were succeeding. I put it out that I was not feeling well and did not allow anyone except my personal guard to approach. I drank only spring water and ate only fruit I peeled myself."

"But the symptoms..." said Grace, bewildered. "Your envoy—DuValier—he came and told me all the symptoms and asked for my help to figure out how you were being poisoned."

"Did he?" The Crown Prince's eyes swept the crowd. "How very interesting."

DuValier, who had been inching towards the doors, bolted.

Two paladins—Grace didn't know their names, a bearded man with haunted eyes and a rather absurdly handsome redhead—stepped in front of him. DuValier pulled a knife. The redhead did something with his hands and suddenly DuValier no longer had a knife and was on his knees, clutching his wrist.

The Crown Prince flicked his fingers. The two paladins picked the envoy up by the arms and carried him forward.

"I...ah..." DuValier looked around wildly. "Guards, this man is an impostor! Arrest him!" The guards did not move.

"Now what symptoms would those have been, hmm?"

DuValier hung between the paladins in sullen silence. Grace cleared her throat. "Fever, vomiting, blue fingertips..."

"How very interesting." The Crown Prince tilted his head. "Tell me, faithful servant, how would you have known these symptoms when I did not stay poisoned long enough to develop them?"

DuValier's eyes flicked from side to side, seeking an opening that was not there.

"Who do you work for?" said the Crown Prince. "My brother?"

The envoy opened his mouth, then ducked his head and grabbed the chain around his neck in his teeth. He bit at the amber crystal and almost had it in his mouth when the Crown Prince grabbed the chain and jerked it, hard.

The clasp broke. The crystal fell to the ground and shattered. A little liquid seeped out onto the floor.

DuValier's face, already white, went gray.

"No," said the Crown Prince. "No, you will not have the swift way out, faithful servant. I think you will return with me to Charlock and we will learn many interesting things together." He nodded to the two heavily armed guards with him.

The two paladins looked at Beartongue.

"This is a matter for Charlock," said Beartongue. "We have no jurisdiction." Her eyes lingered on the Crown Prince's face. "Though I hope you will not stoop to torture."

"Torture?" The Crown Prince flicked his fingers. One of the guards spat on the ground obediently. "We are a *civilized* nation."

"I...I request sanctuary," said DuValier. "Sanctuary...this is a church!" The paladins handed him over to the Crown Prince's guard. "You cannot deny me!"

"You are correct," said Beartongue. "I cannot deny you. When your case goes to trial in Charlock, the Temple of the Rat will provide you with a lawyer." She nodded to the Crown Prince. "Your Magnificence, please keep us informed as to the timing of the trial."

"Naturally," said the Crown Prince. "And now, I believe it is time to leave this city, before someone else takes it in their head to poison me. Or it rains again." He glanced upward as if personally offended by the sky.

They turned. The city guards shuffled out of the way. The Motherhood man had gone very quiet, his hands tucked into the sleeves of his robe.

Grace couldn't let it go. She stepped forward, away from Stephen.

"Your Magnificence?"

He turned his head. "Master Perfumer Angelica," he said, as courteously as if he were receiving a guest at the dais. "I hope that you are not going to ask me for leniency for him?"

"No! Oh, no. But how did you know where to come?" asked Grace, baffled. "Here, of all places?"

"Ah." His smile was genuine this time. "Your partner. The short woman with the hat. I am afraid I did not catch her name. She came into my rooms—for which I will have words with my guards—and informed me of what was occurring here."

Marguerite.

A cold place inside Grace's bones seemed to warm. *Marguerite.*

Her friend had not abandoned her after all.

She bowed very low to the Crown Prince and he turned and strode from the church. The sound of DuValier's boots dragging against the floor as the Prince's guards carried him after seemed very loud.

Beartongue's shoulders sagged with relief as soon as they were gone.

"Captain," she said. "I think we've done enough here. Let us let these nice people go home."

"These *nice people* are still fugitives," said the Motherhood man, although not with a great deal of confidence. "Your *paladin* attacked several guards."

"And killed none of them," said Beartongue. Grace heard Stephen make a small sound of relief. "Furthermore, they were wanted for a crime that turns out to not have occurred at all."

Stephen cleared his throat. "Grace is innocent," he said. "I kidnapped her from her cell and attacked the guards. If anyone is to be blamed—"

"It wasn't like that!" said Grace. She caught Beartongue's eye and the two of them exchanged a meaningful look. She did not know the other woman well, but she suspected that Beartongue was very close to throwing her hands in the air, yelling, "Paladins!" and stomping away. If she did, Grace would be right behind her.

Instead, Beartongue turned to the guard captain. "I will take them to the Temple of the Rat and keep them there, under guard, until we sort out the legalities," she said. "Will that be satisfactory?"

"That sounds like a very fine solution, your holiness," said the guard captain with obvious relief.

"I do not find it satisfactory," snapped the Motherhood man. "The Motherhood—"

"The Motherhood's mandate extends to poisoners," said Beartongue. "This woman is not a poisoner. It is not your place to prosecute assault on city guards. If such is to be prosecuted, the Rat will see that justice is done."

The indigo-clad man snapped his mouth shut, turned on his heel and stalked out of the church.

"Right," said Beartongue wearily. "Let's go home, shall we?"

Stephen and Grace walked side-by-side, and Stephen would be hard-pressed to say who was drawing more comfort from it. Their strides were the wrong length to match, but he was moving slowly anyway. He was leaning on her more than he should, he knew, but he was bone-deep tired and Grace, apparently, was stronger than she looked.

They made about three blocks and then Beartongue managed to hail a carriage and shoved both of them, herself, and Galen into it. "Not me?" asked Istvhan plaintively.

"Get the next one. You take up a bench by yourself." Istvhan clutched his chest in mock sorrow, then slammed the door, grinning. The driver slapped the reins and they rumbled through the streets.

Galen was red-haired, handsome, and hilarious. He was also prone to night-terrors that left his screams echoing through the temple halls. You couldn't touch him when was having terrors, you just sat by the bed and talked to him and hoped some of it was getting through. In a twisted way, Stephen was sometimes grateful that Galen's terrors manifested that way. Far more of the paladins spent sleepless nights, Stephen included, and at least if you were sitting with Galen, you were doing something useful and not just staring at the ceiling replaying your own failures over and over again. And there was something about sitting there, using the trustworthy voice, over and over again, that convinced you as much as anyone else.

He'd gotten better. They'd all gotten better, over the last few years. *Except me. Except...was it only yesterday that I gave in?*

No matter how things fell out, he had attacked guards doing their duty and branded the Saint of Steel's chosen as a menace. He closed his eyes, exhausted at even the thought of what to do about that.

"We'll be at the temple soon," said Beartongue.

Grace's hand crept into his. She squeezed. He squeezed back automatically. Comfort was important. Even if he had none left, he could still comfort someone else. It was no different than sitting with Galen, in the end.

The carriage rattled to a halt and they all stepped out. Even the brief immobility had made Stephen's back and knees stiffen. He was used to his muscles complaining after a berserker fit, but either he'd forgotten the extent of it or he'd aged more than he realized in the handful of years since the last one.

Probably the latter. He felt old. And yet Grace was beside him, looking up at him, and despite himself, his heart lifted a little.

Perhaps not quite so old as all that.

"My rooms are this way," he began, and then stopped. It had only just occurred to him that she might not wish to share his bed again, that perhaps the heat of the moment and the fear of death had led Grace to a place that she would not wish to revisit. "I...ah..."

A servant bustled up. "There's hot water in the baths," she said. "If you follow me, Miss Angelica?"

"I...oh...um..." She cast Stephen a worried look over her shoulder. "I...ah..."

"It's all right," said Stephen. "A hot bath sounds very good. I'll probably take one myself."

"Right. Uh."

"I'll see you very soon," he said. And then, because he couldn't leave it like that, he bent down and kissed her forehead, hoping that she'd read whatever she needed into that gesture.

And Saint or Rat or any god who is favorably inclined, I hope what she needs is the same thing as what I need. And if it isn't...

Well, he hadn't lied. He had already lost everything. If he hadn't broken yet, one more thing wouldn't break him.

He squared his shoulders and turned his back while Grace walked away.

CHAPTER 45

"Stephen? Stephen, are you awake?"

Stephen opened one eye, saw Shane standing over him, and said, "Gnnnrggzzz."

"Captain Mallory wants to see you. It's about the heads. He says you don't have to come, but you might want to see this before they destroy it."

Very few things could have gotten Stephen out of bed, the way he was feeling, but that was one of them. He crawled out of bed, rubbing futilely at his neck, which hurt slightly more than every other part of his body. "Shit. Okay. Give me ten minutes."

"There's a runner waiting. You don't have long."

"Then give me five minutes."

He dragged on clothes. There was a tap on the door and Galen poked his head inside, dark red hair gleaming like a banked fire in the dim room. "I've got willow tea," he said.

"Bless you. My lands and wealth are yours."

"So...that's a couple baskets of yarn, right?"

"And a half-knit sweater."

"You can keep it. Here's the tea. Word is you were in the tide for awhile yesterday."

"Yeah." He slugged down the tea, which was too hot and too bitter and also the only thing that might help. "Couple hours. Not far in, but you know…"

Galen nodded. There was no judgment in his eyes, just concern. "Yeah, figured you'd feel like shit."

Stephen drained the last of the tea and stepped outside. It was early yet. After dawn, but only barely. The air had a chill to it.

Mallory's runner didn't look old enough to shave, and saluted with an enthusiasm that made Stephen age several hundred years on the spot. He fell into step beside the youngster. "Where to?"

"A warehouse off Long Dog Road, sir."

"Mmm." Near Weaver's Nest, but not close enough to the water to be drowned out. Stockyards on the far side, though, so Weaver's Nest was arguably the largest concentration of victims nearby. *Well… human victims.* Stephen briefly pictured one of the smooth men's heads on a cow's shoulders and didn't know whether to laugh or shudder.

It was full daylight by the time they arrived. Mallory stood outside the warehouse's side door with a half-dozen constables. He looked even more grim and emotionless than usual, which was saying something.

"You wanted to see me, Captain?"

"Thought you might want to see this," said the captain, gesturing inside the building. "We've had priests and the clever boys who take things apart look at it. Now I want it all smashed, just in case. Since you fought one of them, and put us on the right track, thought you might want to see it, too."

Stephen frowned, not sure if Mallory meant *see it* or *see it smashed.* He followed the captain inside the warehouse, puzzled.

It was a small warehouse as these things went, but even so, large parts of it were empty. There was a jumble of papers and blankets in a far corner, which could have been a squatter's nest or crude sleeping quarters. Slum weavers flew back and forth on the rafters, through a broken window high on one wall.

Stephen wiped at his nose. The thick, acrid smell was stronger here than it had been since he fought the smooth man in the cell. But he didn't smell any decay, just the heavy burnt smell and dust.

Taking up about a third of the floor was a pottery. There was a table covered in white dust, a beehive-shaped kiln, and dozens of freestanding shelves holding mugs and plates in neat rows.

"Come around the back," said Mallory, gesturing.

Stephen stepped around the shelves and froze as if he'd run into a wall.

The shelves in the corner were exactly the same as the others, but instead of mugs, they held clay heads, placed upside down so that the delicate points rose up into the air.

"Are they alive?" he asked.

"Not as far as we can tell. We don't know how they work." Mallory grimaced. "We sent the slewhounds out and nabbed three of your smooth men, but it was actually a gnole that led us to this place. Caught the smell as the guards took one apart and said there was a building that smelled just like it down here."

Stephen stared at the row of clay. *What would happen if you put one in a dead body? Would it come to life, or is there more to it than that?*

"Do they know what they are?" he asked finally.

Mallory shook his head. "No one's seen anything like this. A rogue wonderworker? Some trick of ancient magic? Your guess is as good as mine."

"I was thinking of golems the other day," Stephen said. "All the stories about what happens when you don't tell them to stop."

"That's one of the things we thought of," said Mallory. "But a golem head? No one's ever heard of such a thing."

The gnole officer that Stephen remembered from the alley came up behind them. "A gnole hasn't," he agreed. "But a gnole thinks this is..." He screwed his muzzle up, clearly searching for the correct word. "*Efficient*, yeah?" He looked back and forth between the two humans. "Eh?"

Mallory frowned. "Efficient?"

"Maybe a gnole's words are wrong." The striped guard frowned.

"But a gnole's cousin works at a pottery, yeah? Big clay, big pots. Not easy. Big clay gets in a kiln, maybe clay explodes, yeah?"

Mallory and Stephen both nodded. Firing clay could be tricky, and sometimes the clay exploded in the kiln. There were limits to how big a pot you could make before it cracked or collapsed under its own weight.

"Well." The gnole waved his paws. "A golem is being big, yeah? Very big. Not easy. These..." he gestured to the clay heads "...*easy*. Small. Small kiln, small head."

"And if one gets damaged, you can just pull the head out and put it in another body," said Stephen slowly. "A whole army. Just add corpses."

"Thanks," said Mallory. "I didn't need to sleep at night or anything." He looked over at the gnole. "Efficient was the word. You were right." The gnole looked professionally pleased.

Stephen retreated from the shelves. He didn't want to turn his back on those lifeless heads. Even bodiless, if their eyes opened, or their mouths...no, he didn't want to think about it.

"Was there anyone here?" he asked.

"No. Cleared out ahead of us. We don't know if he was another smooth man or not." Mallory jerked his head in the direction of the squat kiln. "Bricks are still warm, though. Those big ovens hold heat for days, but he's not long gone."

"So he's still out there," said Stephen.

"Looks that way." Mallory glanced over two silent men, both the size of Istvhan, who were waiting in the shadows. "You boys ready?"

"Say the word, captain."

"Then get to it. I want those things destroyed."

Mallory had been right, Stephen thought, as the first of the men hefted a sledgehammer. He *definitely* wanted to see it smashed.

CHAPTER 46

"*There* you are," said the Bishop, as Stephen was ushered into her office. "You were supposed to be under house arrest."

"Oh." Stephen coughed. "I forgot." And when she gazed at him silently, "No, really, I did. Captain Mallory sent for me, and I didn't even think..."

Seated in front of the desk, Grace twisted to look up at him. She was surprised at how much she had missed him in just the last few hours. When he walked through the door, part of her brain said, *Yes, he's here, everything is normal now, we can relax,* which was frankly rather terrifying.

Beartongue sighed. "Well, even the Motherhood can't blame you for answering a summons from the guard. Though I suspect they'd try." She waved a handful of papers at him. "Sit down. We've still got a few things to go through."

"Yes, of course," said Stephen. The memory of his behavior in the courtroom, almost occluded by the night's events, came rushing back. "I've disgraced the order. There is no excuse for what I have done. You must lock me away. I would not have tried to escape, if it had not been for one of the smooth men there."

Beartongue put her chin on her fist and studied him impassively. "What have you done, exactly?"

"I gave in to the tide," he said. "In public. In a court of law. I cannot be trusted."

"Yes, it was carnage," said Beartongue dryly. "The way you beat the judge to death with his own gavel was terrible. Bailiffs hanging off the chandeliers. Zale said there was a river of blood ankle-deep."

Stephen blinked.

"*Orrrrr* you lost your temper and did something stupid and then realized it was stupid and surrendered to the bailiffs immediately, without resisting arrest." She leaned back in her chair. "Really, Paladin Stephen, if that was your idea of a berserker fit, I'm surprised the Saint of Steel's chosen were ever called in for anything more dangerous than a garden party."

"....uh."

She waved her hand. "Yes, yes, you're a paladin, wallowing in guilt over how you are the very worst person ever is part of the job. I've already had Galen in here this morning apologizing for using too much force on that DuValier fellow and Marcus taking all the blame for your actions because apparently you had a conversation about his ex-wife that he thinks put the idea in your head in the first place."

Grace started laughing helplessly. Beartongue gave her an amused glance. "Oh, sure, you can think it's funny. You're not the one they're confessing to. There's a reason the Rat doesn't call paladins, although I admit they have their uses."

Stephen tried to wrap his head around the situation. "So...you don't want to lock me up?"

"Fortunately for you, both the Motherhood and the guard are sufficiently embarrassed by the whole affair that they have mostly decided to ignore it. Your ill-conceived jailbreak has been somewhat confused by the fact that Miss Angelica was being held for a non-existent crime. No one is terribly *pleased* with you having beaten up..." she checked her notes "...seven guards, but the Temple will be offering a generous payment and in one case, a pension."

"But the damage—"

"Paladin Stephen, if I am to believe reports, you were berserk for an entire day, yet somehow the entire injury that you did, in a city full of people, was breaking a man's leg. Who was attacking you."

"But the guards at the jail?" Stephen shook his head. "I don't remember what I did to them."

"Then let me enlighten you. You choked one, who will be eating soup for a week but is otherwise unharmed, and the other one ran away. He's the pension. Apparently now he's been branded a coward and can't command discipline among the prisoners." She waved her hands. "I am sorry to inform you of this, my dear paladin, but your berserker fit did slightly less damage than the average bar fight. I am aware that you were apparently killing machines under certain circumstances, but I fear those circumstances have not been met."

"...oh," said Stephen, in a very small voice.

"The primary damage appears to have been a statue of a warrior outside the jail. We have numerous reports of a man matching your description violently attacking the statue and eventually toppling it. It was an expensive statue and the grandson of the sculptor is very upset."

Stephen sank deeper into his chair.

"You have been released to the Temple for discipline, you are forbidden from carrying arms in the presence of the Archon for a year and a day, Judge Gucciard wants a personal apology, and I am supposed to dock your pay to cover the statue, but since I don't actually pay you, we'll just let that bit pass." She waved a hand. "Consider yourself disciplined. No dessert for a week. Etc."

Stephen bowed his head.

"Really, I'd appreciate it if you at least checked with me before you go haring off and taking all your fellow paladins with you. Although apparently that's technically Istvhan's fault, so no dessert for him, either."

"Yes, your holiness."

Beartongue sighed. "Stephen, really. Have I ever been less than reasonable in the time you've known me? Do you really think that if you came in and said that it was an emergency and you were breaking Grace out of prison that I *wouldn't* hand you a crowbar and a rope?"

"No, your holiness."

"Damn straight." She turned to Grace. "As for you, Miss Angelica, I have no control over your dessert situation. However, I fear that in order to exonerate Paladin Stephen of the charge of kidnapping, I was forced to claim that you were the mastermind of the jailbreak."

"I was," said Grace hurriedly. "I absolutely was!"

"But—" Stephen began.

The Bishop made shushing gestures at him. "Hush, you. It's easier if you don't leap on this particular sword. Miss Angelica, all charges have been dropped except for that one, and I believe that I have brokered a useful solution. If you are willing to recreate the smell of the clay men for us, as soon as possible, then the guard has agreed not to pursue charges for that against you or your accomplice here."

Grace blinked. "That's all?"

"That's all."

"I won't go to jail?"

"It is the belief of the Rat that your talents will serve the community far better in this way." She coughed. "Zale was all for charging the Motherhood with false imprisonment and wringing money out of that particular stone, but Zale is in a mood and I have persuaded them that this is a better solution for their client. You can, of course, refuse and go that route, but it will drag this all out interminably."

"Gods, no!" Grace shuddered at the thought.

"Then you can go home," said the Bishop.

"Really?"

"Really."

Grace expected to feel relief or shock or joy. Mostly, though, she just felt confused. After everything, she could just...go home? Like nothing had happened? Was that possible? There had been assassins and poison and DuValier and the Crown Prince.

"Right..." she said. "Right. Uh...but Bishop Beartongue, your holiness...what *happened?*"

"Eh?" said the Bishop.

Grace waved her hands helplessly. "With the Crown Prince and everything. What was going on? Is it over?"

Beartongue groaned and dug the heel of her hand into her forehead. "What happened, Miss Angelica, is that we were all caught up in someone else's game. We've been catching the edge of a power struggle in Charlock and thinking that it must have something to do with us."

Stephen raised both eyebrows. "The Crown Prince mentioned his brother last night."

"His brother, next in line to the throne—or anyway, he was until this all happened. Now I suppose the question is whether he can claim deniability or not. To make a horribly complicated story as short as possible, someone, most likely the Prince's brother, hired DuValier to assassinate the Prince." She waved her hands. "We still don't have all the pieces to the puzzle, but I believe that they felt an assassination here in Archon's Glory would make investigation much more difficult for the authorities in Charlock. The Prince's brother could consolidate power at home and even if it did eventually get traced back to him, he'd be able to bury it. Possibly he could even arrange for a war with us to really muddy the waters."

Stephen's lips went white. Grace put her hand on his arm.

"But if they wanted to kill him, why send an assassin who wasn't any good at it?" asked Grace.

"Aha!" The Bishop pointed a finger at her. "An excellent question. That was what tripped us up. We kept thinking it had to be something to do with the Archon or the Motherhood. But it really had nothing to do with us at all. A failed attempt needed to be made on the Prince's life so that the successful attempt could be blamed on the same people. It was all about controlling the eventual investigation so as to exonerate the Prince's brother. 'The Prince has been assassinated by unknown people' is a far different investigation than 'Assassins targeted the Prince and succeeded on the second attempt.'"

"And then we foiled the first attempt on accident," said Stephen.

"Exactly." She slumped back in her chair. "Frankly, I'd be surprised if that was the only attempt. Deliberately failing to assassinate someone is far more tricky than you'd think, given how many people manage it by accident. But again, we don't have all the pieces to the puzzle, so that's only a guess. At any rate, DuValier presumably ran out of pseudo-assassins and had to scramble to find a new scapegoat. The Crown Prince's interest in Miss Angelica's perfumes was the opening he needed. A woman with no family ties and a somewhat—forgive me—cloudy past was a godsend for him. All he had to do was frame you and then put a word in the Motherhood's ear."

"Doctor Piper!" Sudden guilt twisted Grace's gut. "I told DuValier about him—I completely forgot—is he okay?"

"Piper's fine." Beartongue nodded once, thoughtfully. "There's another puzzle piece, then. Someone broke into his office and tried to steal some of his notes. He drove them off with a bonesaw." Her lips twisted as if she were eating something sour. "And as profoundly as it pains me to admit it, the Motherhood was genuinely acting in what it thought was the best interests of Archenhold. By making you seem like a single disturbed soul, acting alone, they hoped to prevent war with Charlock. That's why they tried to discredit your character so profoundly. Little birds in the court tell me that DuValier was pushing for an argument of misguided patriotism, but the Motherhood refused."

"I am still not inclined to be charitable," growled Stephen.

"You don't need to be. But if it makes you feel any better, the Motherhood gentleman demanding that you all be shot by the guard has been demoted and sent elsewhere for his...ah...'excess of zeal.'" She grinned. "You should have seen Jordan's face. Thought he was going to keel over right there."

"So it's over?" said Grace. "People aren't going to come after me?"

"I can't swear to anything. I've been two steps behind this whole time." She sighed. "I swear, I'm getting old. I should retire, but then it'd be someone else's problem, and I don't dislike anyone enough to do that to them. That said, I don't think there's any reason for anyone to come after you." Her eyes flicked to Stephen. "You could consider keeping a bodyguard around for a bit, of course. If it would make you feel better."

Grace felt her cheeks warm. "I should go. Marguerite's probably wondering what happened to me."

"Ah," said Beartongue. She cleared her throat. "That is another matter I wanted to discuss with you."

"Is Marguerite okay? She didn't get in trouble for breaking into the Crown Prince's bedroom, did she?"

The Bishop pursed her lips. "As near as I can tell, *Marguerite* is unlikely to get in trouble for anything."

Grace grinned. "She can usually talk herself out of anything."

"No," said the Bishop. "I mean that she's been dead for six years."

"Come again?" said Grace.

Beartongue tapped her fingers on her desk. "The spy for Anuket City known as Marguerite Florian died six years ago. The body was identified by three witnesses. She was in Anuket City at the time."

"*What?*"

"I don't believe that you're saying that Grace has a ghost as a land-lord," said Stephen. "Are you?"

"A ghost, no," said Beartongue. "An impostor, yes."

Grace shook her head, unable to process this. "She's not an impostor. She's my friend."

"That, I suspect, is true," said the Bishop. "But your friend is not Marguerite Florian." She leaned back in her chair, steepling her fingers. "There is another spy from Anuket who matches the same general physical description. They lost contact with her four years ago, and she is presumed to be dead or working for another power."

It was too much, too fast. Grace could not quite get her head around any of it. Marguerite, an impostor? Did it matter? Why did it feel like betrayal? *It's not. She changed her name and left her job, that's all. You did the same thing. It had nothing to do with you.*

She forced a laugh. "How bizarre. Well, I'll ask her, although she presumably has her reasons."

"I suspect that it may prove more difficult than you think," said the Bishop gently. "But I've kept you too long. I'm sure you want to go home, not stand around and listen to me speculate." She made a shooing motion. "Paladin Stephen, take this nice woman home."

CHAPTER 47

The workshop was very quiet. Grace opened the door with her heart in her mouth.

It was clean. She'd been sick with dread, imagining what it would look like after the Motherhood men had searched it, but everything had been tidied and put to rights. She wouldn't be able to find anything for a week, but at least it wasn't a jumble of broken glassware and spilled herbs.

Stephen stood in the doorway. "Marguerite cleaned it for you," he said. "When I came here initially, she was trying to clean it all up and put it back the way you'd want it."

Grace nodded. Her journals stood in a large stack on the counter. The alchemy tome was on top, no worse for wear for its time with the Motherhood. "They didn't burn them after all," she said.

"Not so long as they were evidence," said Stephen.

"Did the Rat get them back?"

"I don't know."

Grace had her doubts. She reached for the alchemy book and opened it, meaning to look for another passage at random. Instead, the book fell open about a third of the way through, to a thick sheaf of papers.

"My god," said Grace softly, picking them up. "My god."

"What is it?"

"The deed to the building." She had had too many shocks today. She simply stared at it, a neat legal document, everything in order, her neighbor's signature as witness, Marguerite's looping scrawl at the bottom. A numb feeling was spreading through her chest. "Although I'm not sure how a woman who is six years dead signs a building over to me."

The last page was not a document. It was a note, folded in half. She opened it.

I'm sorry to run like this. You've probably got questions, but there's a few too many people sniffing after me. I did my best to sort everything out before I left. I'm sorry I couldn't say goodbye in person. Pet Tab for me.

I'll see you around.

Marguerite

Grace handed the note silently to Stephen. He read it and looked up at her. "Should we check upstairs?" Grace nodded.

Marguerite's apartment upstairs was swept bare. The only thing that lingered was a scent so faint that only a perfumer could have caught it.

"She's gone," said Grace. The numb feeling in her chest seemed to be expanding outward in every direction.

"I'm sorry," said Stephen. He put his arm around her shoulders and Grace leaned against him. The heat of his side chased away a little of the numbness. He was here. He was solid. Did she dare think that there was someone else she might rely on?

"Do you want me to leave?" he asked quietly.

She looked up, startled.

He smiled, although it did not quite reach his eyes. "What two people do when they have been running for their lives may be quite different than what they'd choose to do otherwise. If you'd prefer that I go..."

"No!" Grace clutched at his tabard and felt immediately embarrassed. "No...not unless you want to. I mean. Ah..."

He lowered his head and kissed her, which stopped the words before they could get out of control.

Thank god, thought Grace. *Thank god. I didn't screw that up.* And then she stopped thinking at all, because her body had not forgotten and the heat between them was still there. If anything, it had flared even hotter.

It did not take long for them to find their way to the bedroom.

The bed, which had always seemed a fine size for Grace, appeared to get a great deal smaller when Stephen sat on it.

I should probably be grateful we even made it to the bedroom. We could have gone right there on the floor, and I'd end up with splinters in my backside and not even care.

"Another trial run?" she said hoarsely, as Stephen shed his armor.

"Yes. Absolutely."

"Oh thank god," she said, and dragged him down beside her.

Stephen had no objection to another trial run. In fact, if the trials kept being this good, the real thing might well kill him.

He had a better idea what Grace liked this time and he did it, delicately at first, then harder and faster. The pulse in her throat beat against his lips and he tasted sweat across her skin.

"Yes," she whispered, almost inaudibly, "yes, please—more—"

Well, he was the reliable, responsible one. He certainly was not going to let her down now.

His back twinged a warning—he'd been abusing his body quite brutally the last few days—but he ignored it. Some things were worth the pain.

She cried out under him. His name or a god's, he couldn't tell. Both, perhaps. She clutched at him, all shyness forgotten, dragging his hips to hers, and he obeyed. He was not the sort of man to tease or torment his lover. Everything Stephen had was hers for the taking, and for once he did not ask himself if it was enough.

Perhaps it was not quite as intense as the night in the chapel, but the bed was certainly a good deal more comfortable and there was a lot to be said about not being in terror for your life. The side of his neck prickled with her breath as she gasped against him. This time he was sure that it was his name. For a moment he lost the rhythm entirely, but his body knew what it was doing even if he did not.

"Grace," he said hoarsely. *"Grace."*

She was the only thing in the world and he was with her and for a little while, it was enough.

Afterward, they lay side by side, not speaking. Grace listened to his breathing slow. She turned her head against his chest and thought perhaps she should say something, but she didn't know what.

I should say something. Something so he knows that I care and I don't want this to end. Um.

She tried out several phrases inside her head and they all sounded very stupid. Stephen wrapped his arm around her and he was also not speaking and she wondered if he, too, was trying to find something to say.

Marguerite would tell me not to say—

"I'm hopelessly in love with you," Grace blurted.

—that. Definitely don't say that. Well done, me.

He was silent. Grace felt her hard-won peace shatter into smaller and smaller fragments, the longer that silence stretched on.

"It's all right," she started to say, when the alternative was to scream.

"I'm scared," he said.

Grace closed her mouth. Of all the things that she had expected him to say, this wasn't it.

"I love you," Stephen said. "Probably more than is safe, for someone like me."

Grace missed the next few words because her relief was so profound that she thought she might need to use the chamberpot.

"I am so much less than I was," Stephen said, sitting up. "The man I was before...*he* would have deserved you. Now..." He lifted his hands helplessly.

"I never met that other man," said Grace. "*You're* the one I want." She scowled up at him. "And anyway, I'm not exactly a prize myself."

"You are a prize beyond price."

"No, I'm not. I'm prickly and I don't like people touching my things and I still don't know if I can sleep in a bed with another person when I'm not half dead." She folded her arms. "And sometimes I smell things and my brain shuts down and I nearly faint."

"Sometimes I go berserk and begin killing people," said Stephen dryly.

"Yes, well." Grace looked away. "You haven't yet. Even when you were getting attacked by guards, you didn't kill any of them."

"I might have."

"I might have run amok and stabbed people with a broken perfume bottle, but I didn't."

He reached out and trailed a fingertip down the length of her arm. Her skin prickled with awareness.

"Despite what the bishop said, I must be dangerous," he said. "I nearly killed one of my brothers once."

"You only attacked people who were a threat to you," she said. "Maybe you thought he was a threat to you."

Something flickered across his eyes. She couldn't tell what. "What if a day comes when I can't be trusted?"

"Then we'll deal with it then. Now should we get up?" she asked, abandoning the line of conversation before it could get even more horribly awkward. *Not that we're not good at those by now.*

"Do you need to work?"

"Probably. At some point." She nestled against him. The sheer size and solidity of his body astonished her, even now. It was certainly too early in the day to go to sleep. Perhaps a nap would not be amiss, though.

The bell over the door jangled. Grace cursed. Stephen sighed and sat back. "I suppose you should deal with that."

"I can't have left the door unlocked..." Grace began, and then she heard footsteps and cursed again.

She threw her tunic over her head and stepped into her trousers. "We're not open," she called, pushing the door to the workshop open. "I'm sorry if—"

"Aw now, don't be like that, sweetheart."

Grace froze.

The warmth in her heart and her belly turned to ice. Her stomach clenched.

Phillip.

CHAPTER 48

"I'm sure you were expecting me," her wayward husband said. He smiled at her, a smile that had once made her melt and then had made her suspicious and which she now wanted to hit with a brick. "Felt we ended things on a bit of a sour note, eh?"

She stared at him. Her blood roared in her ears, but it was not the memory fugue. This was happening. This was really happening right now, in front of her.

"Don't be mad, sweetheart," he said. "What was I supposed to think, when those Motherhood fellows showed up and told me you were a poisoner? They made it sound open and shut, they really did. Tried to tell them that you didn't seem like the type, but you know how they twist a man's words around."

Grace felt her lips curling back from her teeth. "Get out," she whispered.

"Don't be like that," he said again. "Said I was sorry, didn't I?"

"No," she said. "No, you didn't." She had never been the sort of woman who threw things, but if she'd had something heavy near to hand, she would have hurled it at him. "How dare you. How dare you come *here*?"

This is my place. I made this place. This is all mine. I built it without you.

Phillip was looking her shop over with a proprietary air. She felt as if his eyes must be leaving tracks over the woodwork, as if she would have to scrub it down to get rid of the taint of his gaze.

"Ah, don't be like that," he said again. "Good place, here. Good business, is it?"

"It is *my* business," she said.

"No one giving you trouble about the apprenticeship, then?" Such a casual sentence. Such a world of threat in it, and if she tried to call it out, Phillip would look hurt and say, "Don't be paranoid, sweetheart, I didn't mean it like *that.*"

"There's no trouble," she grated. "On the acceptance of a master-work by the guild, I am free and clear."

"Been making masterworks, have you?" His tone was dismissive.

"That's for the guild to decide."

"I could make it easier for you. I've still got them, you know, just need a reason to—"

"I don't want anything from you." God, this was too much talking. "Leave. Get out."

Footsteps behind her. *Stephen. Yes.*

Phillip's eyes went wide. He took a step back and Grace pressed the advantage, walking forward. She did not want Phillip to fear Stephen, she wanted him to fear *her*, but by god, if the paladin knocked him off balance, she would take it.

The footsteps halted. She darted a glance over her shoulder and saw Stephen leaning against the wall by the door, arms folded. *Backup. In case I need him.* Her nerves steadied. Not just because she had backup, but because he wasn't moving in. This was her place, and he trusted her to handle herself, and to let him know if she needed his help.

She looked at Phillip with calmer eyes. It had been years, but she still knew him intimately well, knew all the tells. No stubble, but the dark circles under his eyes, the mustache drooping and unwaxed, the curl of hair against his collar where it had been too long between trims. She did not know last year's fashions from this year's, but his clothes did not quite fit him, as if they had been imperfectly tailored or he had lost weight.

"You're broke," she said, astonished at how calm she sounded. "You've driven the business into the ground, haven't you? That's why you agreed to come with the Motherhood. You were hoping to get out of Anuket City before the creditors came looking."

Phillip's eyes flickered to Stephen again. "It's not like that, sweetheart..." he began, but his heart didn't seem to be in it.

"Get out."

She walked forward. She didn't know what would happen. Would he back up? Would she have to stop before she ran into him?

He backed up. He reached the door and put a hand on the knob, and Grace knew that she had won.

"Get out," she said again. "Don't come here again. I'll send divorce papers to the shop."

Phillip looked at her—really looked at her—for the first time since she'd seen him in the docket. A trace of the smile she'd once loved crossed his face. "Don't bother," he said. "I lost the shop a year ago."

He opened the door and went out and didn't look back, and Grace never saw him again.

She sagged backward and had to catch herself on the back of one of the chairs. Her heart was pounding so hard that she could see the flicker of her pulse in her vision.

"Don't worry," said Stephen, not moving from his post by the wall. "If you still want a divorce, he testified against you in court. That's legal grounds."

"Thank you," she said. "Thank you for not rescuing me." She took a deep breath. "I needed to do that myself."

Stephen gazed at her, his eyes shadowed with something she could not recognize. "I never doubted you could," he said. "You were magnificent."

She smiled up at him. Relief bubbled in her chest. It felt like joy, if you didn't know the difference, but sometimes even if you did.

"Also, my back has gone out," he admitted.

Grace's hands flew to her mouth. "Oh my god! Are you all right?"

"I can't move," he admitted. "I would have laid down on the floor, but that would have rather derailed your confrontation. And I don't think I can get back up again."

"Oh god! Get an arm over my shoulders, let's get you to the bedroom."

It was not significantly more difficult than steering him when he was coming down from the berserker fit, except that he hadn't seemed to feel pain before. Judging by the whiteness of his lips, he was feeling it now.

"Give me just a minute," he said, falling heavily onto the bed. "It'll pass. Just a bad spasm. I think." He grinned weakly at her. "I may have abused those muscles rather a lot in the last few days."

"You shouldn't have—*we* shouldn't have—"

"Worth it. A thousand times worth it. Though I fear it may be a day or two before I can...ah...rise to the occasion again."

Grace put her face in her hands, not sure if she should giggle or scream. "What do I do? Do I get a healer?"

"No, no. A few stretches and things will loosen up." He pulled his knee to his chest and grimaced. "I'm sorry."

"You don't have to be sorry!"

"Yes, but..." He laughed softly. "This is not exactly the way I hoped to spend time in your bed."

Grace rolled her eyes.

"Also, while you needed no help in dealing with Phillip, if he'd been a problem, I'm afraid I could have, at best, fallen heavily on him."

A rueful giggle escaped her. She leaned her forehead against the doorframe "Oh god! It might almost have been worth it."

Stephen's laugh turned into a hiss. "Ahh...there." He sat up gingerly. "That is a little better. It will get me home, at least."

"Are you sure I shouldn't send for the healer?"

"Not for this. I promise that I will sit in a hot bath and allow them to prod me and yell at me afterward." He shook his head. "It is what comes of being a berserker. Your body goes on and on and on, past any normal man's...and then everything you've done to it lands on you at once. The spasms pass, at any rate. Until they don't."

He took a deep breath and stood. Grace waited nervously to catch him, but he did seem to be better, at least temporarily.

"Well," he said. "This has been a very long day, and it is not getting any shorter. I don't suppose...ah...you would wish to see me again tomorrow?"

"I'd like that," said Grace, and meant it.

After the door had closed, and she had locked it firmly, she stood in her workshop. It felt oddly empty. There was no Marguerite, nor any chance of her return. Even Tab was still at the Temple.

And yet...and yet...

It's mine. My place. It hasn't been taken away.

She sat down on the chair in the silence and breathed the air, the mix of scents, spilled oil and burnt wood. Hers. Her own. Nothing she needed to think about or worry about, no one to ask anything and require a response.

She took another deep breath and felt her shoulders loosen, just a little. *I wanted my normal life back. And it's here. Not quite the same, maybe, but...here.*

She lit the burner and set to work.

Stephen came back the next day, carrying Tab, who strongly protested such liberties being taken with his person. As soon as the civette saw where he was, he launched himself from the carrier, darted between Grace's feet, and went under the table to sulk.

"I don't even get a hello?" she said, amused.

"*Hello,*" said Stephen, in a rather more suggestive voice than she'd ever heard him use. He tilted her chin up and kissed her.

It was still good. Dammit, it was still really, really good.

"I didn't mean *you*, but I'm not complaining," she said, once she could breathe again. "But how is your back?"

"Sore. It has been pummeled by the finest healers with the hardest hands that the Temple can offer. I am told that I cannot engage in any strenuous activity and I am not to get in any fights for at least a month."

"Well, hopefully that won't be too hard," Grace said.

"The fights, no. The strenuous activity..." He ran his thumb across the inside of her wrist, and Grace felt herself flush.

Gods, what is wrong with me? I've bedded him twice already and I'm still blushing like I'm fourteen again.

He grew solemn again, looking into her eyes, and stepped back. "Ah...Grace..."

She knew what was coming next. Well, what was one more awkward conversation, really? *The gods know, our entire relationship seems to be based on them.* "What happens now?" she asked.

Stephen shifted his feet. Chain clinked softly as he moved. He did not pretend that she was talking about the next five minutes, or about Tab or his back or anything but the two of them.

"I could not leave my brothers," he said. "They need me." He stared down at his hands. "We need each other."

"And I can't leave my shop," said Grace. "This is what I do." She was also staring at her hands, thinking about how relieved she had been to be alone last night...but also how peaceful it had been, that first day, when he sat knitting in her workshop. Could it work? Could two people who generally worked alone in silence manage to work in silence together? "We do live in the same city," she said cautiously.

"We do." He cleared his throat. "It is not a long walk, from the Temple. I suspect I could do it several times a week, at least. If my back doesn't go out."

They both looked up at the same time and met each other's eyes.

"Could your brothers spare you that much time?"

"I expect they could manage. Could you take so much time away from your work?"

"A surprising amount of my work is letting things simmer for hours at a time."

A smile slowly broke across his face. "Well, then. If you do not mind the company while you work...?"

He reached into his pack and pulled out a ball of finely spun yarn, with needles already stuck into it. "I don't suppose you might need another pair of socks?"

EPILOGUE

"Thank you," said the Bishop. "For testifying on my paladin's behalf."

Doctor Piper rolled his eyes. "It was underhanded of them to even try that one. You can't charge a man with murder for tearing the head off a three-day-old corpse, even if that corpse is walking around at the time."

"Nevertheless, the Rat is in your debt."

"I am so deeply in the Rat's debt that the scales will never balance."

"He does not keep a ledger, you know."

"No, but I do." Piper's lips twisted in something less than a smile.

The Bishop shook her head, but did not press the matter. "Take me to your prisoner, then."

"Prisoner," muttered Piper. "I don't think that's the right word. I'm not sure what would be. 'Subject' maybe."

"Either way."

Piper led her from his office and down the hall. "Did they find the source?" he asked over his shoulder.

"Yes and no," said the Bishop. The smooth stone hall underneath the palace was dim and quiet, the light always the same regardless of the time of day. She wondered if Piper even paid attention to day and night any more. "The slewhounds traced the scent to a pottery. They found a dozen heads on shelves, and the kiln was still warm, but whoever worked there was long gone."

Piper nodded. "Follow me," he said.

There was only one cell beneath the palace, and it had the look of being added as an afterthought. The bars were bolted to the stone, not cemented in. But the single occupant did not look as if he had been testing the bars.

Beartongue stared at the smooth man slumped in the corner. The scent of decay hung thickly in the air. Doctor Piper handed her a scented handkerchief and she held it to her nose. "Do you know what he is yet?" she asked.

The porcelain-like mask stirred slightly, watching her, but made no other move.

"I've got no idea," said Piper. "The body's rotting away, but I don't know if the head would survive on another corpse or if they're strictly one use only."

Beartongue turned her head slightly to meet the doctor's eyes.

"No," said Piper. "I put another dead body in there, a fresh one that nobody was going to want back, and he ignored it. I'm not doing it myself. I realize that I'm not much of a healer, as people think of them, but there's some things that are too far even for me."

The bishop nodded. "Have you learned anything?"

"Nothing," said Piper, disgust evident in his voice. "Nothing I didn't know an hour after seeing the one your paladin killed. They die if you smash the heads, and then you've got a broken clay head and a dead body. I'm no closer to knowing if this is some dreadful new monster or a rogue wonderworker or..." He trailed off helplessly.

"It would be one hell of a thing for a wonderworker to do," said the Bishop. "How would you even learn you could do that?"

Piper shrugged. "Have you heard the theory that everyone is a wonderworker, it's simply that most of us are never in the situation to learn what talents we may have?"

"I can't say I have, no."

"Have you ever given an order to a hermit crab?"

"What?" Even under the inhuman gaze of the smooth man, Beartongue broke into an incredulous smile. "A hermit crab? No."

"Then how do you know you aren't a wonderworker with the power to control hermit crabs?"

"I see your point. But there's a far cry between giving orders to hermit crabs, and making clay heads that you jam into a corpse's neck."

"For you or me, perhaps."

Beartongue resumed studying the smooth man. His lips parted slightly as he breathed, but that was all. "Damn," she said softly. "I was hoping for more."

"You and me both. Any luck elsewhere?"

The Bishop turned away. "As much as can be expected. Thanks to Miss Angelica's skills, vials of the scent are going out to the Temple of the Rat in every city in a hundred-mile radius. They won't be able to hide for long."

"That's g—" Piper started to say, and then he froze.

The smooth man was making a sound at last. It wasn't much of one, just a soft, nasal whistling, mouth open, as the head wobbled on the decaying shoulders, but it went on and on, long past the time that any human would have run out of breath.

The smooth man was laughing.

Beartongue stepped back from the bars, her face resolute. Her sigh of annoyance was unfeigned. "Well. We're going to have to deal with this, aren't we?"

"It seems likely."

"See this one is burned," she said. "It'll give the Motherhood something useful to do for once." She gave the smooth man one last look, then turned and walked away.

ACKNOWLEDGMENTS

I honestly expected to write a totally different book. I did. I was all set to write the sequel to *Swordheart,* which I promise is still in the works, and then, on a very long drive to a castle in Ohio—yes, there is a castle in Ohio, no, it is not relevant to this anecdote—I listened to a podcast that did an episode on the history of perfume. I was spellbound by ambergris, castoreum and the spice trade, the links to alchemy and poisons, and I thought "Man, that would be a great profession for a heroine. She could get accused of being a poisoner and have to get loose. She'd need a good lawyer. And a love interest."

I had the book about half plotted by the time we got to Point Pleasant. As I am terrified of Mothman, this drove the book idea out of my head for a bit, but then I got enough signal and presence of mind to order books on the history of cosmetics and perfume-making. By the time I got home from a weekend at the castle, I had the majority of the book in my head and I just started throwing words at the page.

I had it in my mind that I was going to write a fluffy romance. I am a great fan of fluffy romance. I am told that there are generally fewer severed heads and rotting corpse golems in fluffy romance, so possibly this book didn't quite get there, but I'm certain I can write something fluffy eventually. Probably.

Fluffy or not, I hope that you enjoyed a return to the world of the Temple of the White Rat. I love those people. As for the broken paladins...well, the tale of the Saints of Steel is not over yet. In between that promised sequel to *Swordheart,* I am hammering out Istvhan's story, and sooner or later, both will come out and probably neither will be fluffy, but there will definitely be love and romance and possibly upsetting magic.

Thanks go as always to my faithful editor K.B. Spangler, she of the coping butter, to copyeditor and livestock consultant Shepherd, to my valiant proofreaders Cassie and Jes. And, most importantly, to my husband Kevin, who is really not every single one of my heroes, I swear, but is patient and long-suffering and responsible and makes sure that both the chickens and I get fed.

T. Kingfisher
    North Carolina
    Jan 2020

ABOUT THE AUTHOR

T. Kingfisher is the vaguely absurd pen-name of Ursula Vernon, an author from North Carolina. In another life, she writes children's books and weird comics. She has been nominated for the World Fantasy and the Eisner, and has won the Hugo, Sequoyah, Nebula, Alfie, WSFA, Cóyotl and Ursa Major awards, as well as a half-dozen Junior Library Guild selections.

This is the name she uses when writing things for grown-ups. Her work includes horror, epic fantasy, fairy-tale retellings and odd little stories about elves and goblins.

When she is not writing, she is probably out in the garden, trying to make eye contact with butterflies.

 twitter.com/ursulav

ALSO BY T. KINGFISHER

As T. Kingfisher

Swordheart

Clockwork Boys

The Wonder Engine

Minor Mage

Nine Goblins

Toad Words & Other Stories

The Seventh Bride

The Raven & The Reindeer

Bryony & Roses

Jackalope Wives & Other Stories

Summer in Orcus

From Saga:

The Twisted Ones

As Ursula Vernon

From Sofawolf Press:

Black Dogs Duology

House of Diamond

Mountain of Iron

Digger

It Made Sense At The Time

For kids:

Dragonbreath Series

Hamster Princess Series

Castle Hangnail

Printed in the USA
CPSIA information can be obtained
at www.ICGtesting.com
LVHW021929221223
766927LV00068B/25/J